Overnight Sensation

Other books by COLLEEN CURRAN

Fiction

Something Drastic

Plays

Cake-Walk

Sacred Hearts

Triple Play:
Amelia Earheart Was Not A Spy
A Sort of Holiday
El Clavadista

Senetta Boynton Visits the Orient

Sibyl and Sylvia

Local Talent

Whale Watch

Maple Lodge

The Pillbox Hat

OVERNIGHT
Sensation

COLLEEN CURRAN

GOOSE LANE

Edited by Laurel Boone.
Author photo by Peggy Curran.
Book design by Julie Scriver.
Printed in Canada by Transcontinental.
10 9 8 7 6 5 4 3 2 1

Canadian Cataloguing in Publication Data

Curran, Colleen, 1954-
Overnight sensation

ISBN 0-86492-292-2

I. Title.

PS8555.U67094 2000   C813'.54   C00-900149-2
PR9199.3.C79094 2000

Published with the financial support of the Canada Council for the Arts, the Government of Canada through the Book Publishing Industry Development Program, and the New Brunswick Department of Economic Development, Tourism and Culture.

Goose Lane Editions
469 King Street
Fredericton, New Brunswick
CANADA E3B 1E5

For Pat Curran,
a great sports writer and a Hall of Fame father

Acknowledgements

Before this book was *Overnight Sensation*, it was *Something Else*, and the two people I must thank first and foremost, who have known it since then, are my sister, Peggy Curran, and Laurel Boone, my editor at Goose Lane Editions. Peggy and Laurel, if I were Bette Midler, I'd sing a song about what you've done for me, but I know how Peggy feels about *Beaches*, so I'll just say a great big "thank you" here.

Then I must thank the Canada Council for the Arts for giving me a grant that enabled me to write this book. Thank you for believing in my work.

I wouldn't have known about many things in *Overnight Sensation* had it not been for the following people, who invited me to Moondances and sent me chain letters and got me close to Tanguay Prison. They let me in on what it's like to be backstage at a talk show, they went to the Lizzie Borden Conference with me, they had experiences with dog training, and much, much more. And some of these people are the reason I wrote a sequel to *Something Drastic* because they asked me what happened next. One of them even said, "More, please!" in print. How could I refuse my friends and relatives? So in no particular order, not even alphabetical, I thank them for everything they did to help me make this *Overnight Sensation*: Katie Curran, Sheila Sullivan Brown, Louise Abbott, Sile McGovern, Kathy Michael McGlynn, Sandra McVey, John Rutledge, Leslie Manion, David Lopushinsky, David J. Miller, Reinhold Mahler, Mary Beth Walsh, Jan Peterson, Susan Altimas, Patricia Bissonnette, Dan Delaney, Jane Hackett, Tim Taylor, Patricia Poirier, Corey Castle, Jacques Basko, Maeve Binchy, Catherine Sofer, Janice Kennedy, Susan McCracken, Claire Crawford Guinn, Donald J. Guinn, John Wilson, Joan Foster of the CLSC, the Roaches of Rochester, Penny Mancuso, Ella Bateson, the members of the Triumvirate Theatre Company, Liz Gordon, Norma Jean Horner, Janet Amos, Allen MacInnis, the Funsters, and everyone who read and liked *Something Drastic*. Merci, cheris!

If you eat all your vegetables, dessert will follow.
—*fortune cookie message received by*
Lenore Rutland, January, 1992

I honestly believed every word of what I sang
or spoke. I survived because I had an attitude.
Everything in life comes down to attitude.
— *Doris Day*

1

If I could have one learning experience in my lifetime without living through it, it would be John Ferguson. I still can't believe I wrote all those letters to him, all last year, even when I had to know way deep down that he wasn't reading them, and he wasn't coming back.

I guess I could write to the postmaster in Hellman, Florida, and ask for the return of all the letters I sent to the PO Box forwarding address Fergie left me if they're still sitting there, waiting. But I suppose they got sent off to some sendee-never-picked-them-up office. The US Postal Service probably trashed them, a whole year of my life put through the shredder. I don't need them. I can remember the good things that came out of my year-long learning experience, so I don't have to see those letters again anyway. And not seeing them will save me from seeing all the awful please-come-back, why-did-you-leave-me, was-it-my-fault stuff I wrote to Fergie when he took off like that. And left me with a broken heart and way too many bills! But John "Fergie" Ferguson's gone for good now. I can live a Fergie-free life.

If I look at everything I've got going for me in this New Year, I have way more assets than debits. I am in the Red. Or is it the Black? I think Red is the wrong colour to be in, even though it should be the good one, red is a colour of celebration, and to be "in the Reds" means you've got the best seats at the Forum. But what colour is on the ARRÊT STOP signs? Red could be saying HEY, WHOAA! YOU'RE BROKE. ARRÊT! STOP SPENDING, YOU GOT NOTHING LEFT, YOU OWE MONEY ALL OVER TOWN. Whatever colour I'm in, I know I'm way better off now than last year at this time.

Madame Ducharme called from Tanguay. She misses the dogs and wants me to bring them for a Visiting Day. Maybe if I bring her dogs to the prison, they'll let her keep them. As mascots. If Reine Ducharme was Elizabeth Taylor as a Serial Killer, they'd let her keep her yappy little dogs in the cell with her. Of course, it would be a much more lavish and swanky cell than the one Madame Ducharme says she's got. This list of things she wants me to bring her, I don't know! Reine says the guards are fine with the whole list. But . . . her expresso machine? Maybe she's promised to make them all café au lait. I can't believe they'd let you have that in prison with you. Maybe it's her way to be popular, get to know the other girls better. But she's in there for poisoning people, I don't think they'll let her mix drinks. Maybe she wants it to trade?

Or she has some other use for it, maybe it's like a pressure cooker and has the potential to explode? Or act as a distraction while they make a prison break? Everything makes more sense than that Madame Ducharme just wants decent coffee. I'll find out when I get there. I can't see them letting me through with the knitting needles. I wouldn't let me past with them if I was a prison guard. And all her balls of wool? They're probably to make everybody mittens and tuques or an afghan for her cell. It's probably all really innocent, it's a pastime, but to me they all seem like utensils for escape. I'd make some kind of ladder out of the wool, or a lasso. Or — I wouldn't, but maybe somebody desperate would — a noose.

I wonder what Madame does all day. I've never asked Reine what kind of work projects the women in there do. I read once that you get paid something like $2.50 a day as a salary, and you can use that to buy yourself things or have it as a nest egg when you get out and start your new life in your halfway house.

I wonder what they make at Tanguay — license plates? Novelty ones would be interesting, but in Québec they'd probably only let us have novelty plates, en français. Reine's would say TI'CHOUX for the dogs. Other provinces can have fun with their licences. Ontario even. If I was in the pen, that's the kind I'd want to work on, if I had to.

Of course you could get obsessed by the person who ordered ELVIS 4VR or ROCKER or SEXY or GO4IT. You might want to look him up when you got out. You show up on the guy's street and stand across the road staring at his car till he comes out of his house and yells at you, "What are you looking at?" You say, really cool, "That. I made it." And for a second he thinks you're from the plant in Windsor or Detroit, you were on the line that assembled his car. He asks you, and you say, "No, sir. I was in prison. I hammered out your licence plate, BIG MAN. Har-har."

Why did I think up something like that? Am I getting weird, becoming a fixating person? Just because I have to visit my next-door neighbour in prison? That's not an everyday occurrence. Especially when you're the one who put her there. I know it was her crimes that put her there, but it was her confessing to me that got the evidence. It's amazing that we're still friends. It's even more amazing that I'm stuck with her dogs!

I can hardly believe this. I just got a call from Fiona Phee's "people," one of her producers, Fiona thinks I'd be a great guest on her show! With the theme "Neighbours of Neighbours Who Kill." Only I guess as Americans they spell it Neighbors of Neighbors Who Kill. (Why do we keep all the U's in our words when they don't? Is it because of the Queen? And us and Great Britain?)

They want me to be on *Fiona!* because of Madame Ducharme, who makes me the Neighbor of a Neighbor Who Killed. The production assistant, Amity (what a strange name — the same as the town in *Jaws*) said they read all about Madame's murdering Half a Dozen Jurors, it was in all their papers. Fiona Phee read it herself personally and said, "This, this Rutland woman, she has to be on my show. She has to!"

They came up with the theme of the show because of me.

Amity says *Fiona!* is "right on the pulse of America, every time, all the time, so we tape this next week."

NEXT WEEK!

So I have to rearrange my life, get time off at Festin, you name it.

The *Fiona!* people go ahead and assume you'll jump at the chance to be on their talk show, seen by MILLIONS AND MILLIONS OF PEOPLE. And who wouldn't?

January 11, 1992

Dear Lenore,

I know we've discussed your going on *Fiona!* and I realize that you're quite excited about this, but I can't say I'm not concerned.

I watched her on the tape you'd made of her show on Barbie Fetishists. Fiona Phee is VILE. She's vicious, insincere, manipulative, sensationalistic, she carves up her guests. She had that man who makes evening gowns for his Barbie in tears. She has no respect for anyone, she's an egomaniac. Her show is a forum for her to spout HER views on everything — clichés and clumsy bon mots.

I'm being somewhat judgemental, I realize. Today is the very first time I have ever watched her show, but I did do some research first. I made some calls. Prior to having her own chat show, Fiona Phee was a constant chat-show-circuit guest. She called herself a Social Critic. Her most famous statement was that, while some people are in the asylum, "a lot of people are on the grounds, if you get what I mean." If I get what she means, Fiona Phee thinks that practically everybody is crazy.

You are not crazy, Lenore. But many of the people on her show are. They are bona fide nut jobs, as Daniel would say. And the guests who aren't certifiably "on the grounds" are washed-up has-beens or in drug rehab.

This Fiona Phee is a scary woman. In the words of Geena Davis, "Be afraid, be very, very afraid."

XXXX Heidi

Dear Heidi,

Thank you for writing, even though you live upstairs! I like not having an answering machine if it means I get letters. I appreciate the research you did for me. You even watched her show! We can discuss it some more when I finally see you. (This new schedule you're on!) About what you're worried about: Fiona's not mean to all her guests. And the celebrities she has on aren't all washed up. People just thought they were, or that they were dead, but then they showed up on *The Love Boat*. I am going to see Madame Ducharme tomorrow, I have to bring Brioche et Montcalm! I will ask her then if she minds me telling all of America about her Crime. If she does, I'm off the hook with *Fiona!* I'm sure they have a long, long waiting list of other Neighbo(u)rs who could fill in for me.

Lenore

My third visit to Tanguay, and I'm still not over thinking how easily it could have been me in there. I could have been incarcerated for Fergie's crimes. He'd still be away wherever he is, and I'd be Doing Time for him. Because I was his girlfriend, and he was living in my house when he was disappearing cars and growing marijuana in my back yard. Yeah, sure, I didn't know, but they still might have put me in for being an aider and abetter. I didn't kill six people I was on Jury Duty with, like Reine Ducharme did, but still! You see all these convicted woman-felons in there on visiting day, and it makes you think how lucky you are that your parents brought you up with the Fear of God and the Law.

Another thing about Tanguay Prison, it's pretty far up, you drive and you drive, all along the Métropolitain, and even then it's not enough, there's still further to go! This time I was doing it with two barking dogs.

And then when you finally get there, it doesn't look like a prison, more like a big, ugly pre-fab school or a Club Price. It's right on Henri-Bourassa Boulevard, next to the Régie des Automobiles, with people getting their drivers' licenses. Little cars with Driving School signs pulling out every few seconds, filled with people taking their tests. Right next to a place filled with women being penalized for being dangerous or really unlucky in love. Living close to so many cars with keys still in them, maybe even with their motors running, is kind of handy, prison-breakout-wise. As long as you broke out in twos and one of you could pretend to be the student and the other one the examiner.

In the movies, whenever people go to visit someone in prison, it's somewhere way out of town, with nothing else around, and the place is surrounded by high fences with men with guns in towers. If there's a breakout, they always have to run through a swamp, and a great big woods, pursued by bloodhounds.

Not at Tanguay. You're not only next to the driving school, you're practically on a Métro line. (You'd have to take a bus to get to the station but they're pretty frequent.) The men's prison is off in the distance and really looks like one, with a dome and everything.

I'm so glad Reine's imprisoned close to home. Imagine if they put her in Kingston, and I had to drive all that way on the 401 with those yappy dogs.

Of course there was lots of crying and barking for the Madame and child reunion. Reine feels that Brioche looks thinner, she's been pining for her maman.

The dogs and I were Reine's second, third and fourth visitors this week. (I hope she regards me as the second visitor and not Brioche or Montcalm.) Her first was a journalist who wants to do an exclusive interview with her for *Saturday Night*. Reine's never heard of it. Well, no, she's French. She's not an anglo who gets it free with *The Gazette* for living in Westmount. I told her it's a very intelligentsia up-market magazine, featuring the people they think are in Vogue. It always has Mordecai Richler or someone from his family writing in it. Or on the cover. Them or one of the Bronfmans. I told Reine I usually give my copy to Elspeth, who doesn't live in the land of the free magazine, but I will give my next free one to her.

I'm surprised the journalist didn't give her a copy. His name is Randall Kingfisher (yes, like the bird). He's from Toronto. Reine says he speaks French really well and throws in joual, to be sympathique or something. She's not fooled, he's "Un anglophone de Toronto," but she's still going to let him interview her.

She's thrilled I'm going to be on *Fiona!* even though she's never seen it. She asked if les chiens would go on with me. I lied! I said the journey there and back would be too traumatic for such a short stay. (As if I want to drag them along when I get to be on TV!) I promised we'd get a tape of *Fiona!* for her. Reine said when I get the actual date and time I've got to tell her, they'll make a party and all watch it in the lounge. The guards will let her because they know she's "La Vedette de Tanguay."

I don't know how I feel about that. She's my neighbour, and I have her dogs, and she's sort of a friend, but she killed six people, SIX. Even if she thought it was for the worthy cause of balancing the scales of injustice, she was wrong. And she's no vedette, but I guess me going on *Fiona!* is going to make her an even bigger vedette than she already thinks she is.

As for les petits chiens, boy, do I wish they'd grant her extended canine visits. Or let her keep them there permanently, let her be like the Birdman of Alcatraz. She could be La Dame des Chiens, the world expert on lap dogs. Monique Mercure could play her in the film. And if they did it as a movie in the States, she could be played by Genevieve Bujold. Or Meryl Streep, she hasn't done a Québécois accent yet.

So I have Reine's blessing, sort of. I can do *Fiona!* Nothing can stop me except me, and I don't think I will.

Fiona!

January 10, 1992

Dear **Lenore Rutland**,

Thanks a lot for accepting our invitation to be a guest on **FIONA!** We're sure America will benefit from hearing what you have to share with them as one of our **Neighbors of Neighbors Who Kill**.

Your Business Class ticket will be waiting for you at the American Airlines ticket counter at Aéroport Dorval.

A limo and driver will be there to meet you upon your arrival at Greater Rochester International Airport.

We can't wait to meet you! Happy Trails.

Amity Smith
Production Coordinator

The BREWSTER Hotel
in the heart of Rochester

Thursday, January 16th, 1992

Dear Heidi,

You'll get this after I'm home, but this is the first time in my life I get to write a letter on hotel stationery. So I'm doing it. And whatever I don't use, I'm taking home.

Less than a week ago I didn't know about any of this, and now I'm here! My room is really beautiful, it matches the fancy white bathrobe I'm now wearing that comes (and stays) with the room. If I want to buy it, it costs $125 US plus applicable taxes. No thank you.

I had a great time here today. I'm glad they make you get here the day before the show. The limo guy was there holding up my name in the Greater Rochester airport. I thought it might say Guest on *Fiona!* under it, but no. And the limo had everything you could want, but how many of the fifty cable TV stations can you watch, and how badly do you need a Scotch and soda from their car bar at ten o'clock in the morning? When you're twelve minutes on the Innerloop from your hotel?

My driver, Jamal, was really friendly. He said yesterday he picked up Billy Mumy, Angela Cartwright and June Lockhart for the *Lost in Space* reunion. *Fiona!* specializes in reuniting still-living members of past TV series. Jamal said June and Billy and Angela all came in on the same plane,

and it was as if they were the Space Family Robinsons
again, Mother and kids. I asked him if Angela had any
stories about *Make Room for Daddy* or *The Sound of Music*
or about her sister Veronica who was in *The Birds* and
Alien. Jamal said all Angela talked about was her kids.
No mention of a comeback, either. Maybe the celebs in
his limo do that on purpose, talk about ordinary things.
They must be afraid all the time that someone like Jamal
could sell good gossip to *The Enquirer*. Like if Angela ran
down Danny Thomas or said Julie Andrews was mean to
the Von Trapp kids when the director wasn't looking.

Rochester is a very interesting place, and there's lots
to see. Like SNOW! I was pretty surprised, they get lots
of snow, just like us. I guess I thought since Rochester's
so far away in New York they'd be more like New York,
New York. Not like Plattsburgh. Rochester's near the
Finger Lakes Wine Country. Sixty miles from here is where
they invented Jell-O. My room came with an *I Love New
York* book, and there are so many things to do, but no time!
This is where Kodak started, did you know that? Eastman
Kodak employs half the city. Did you know that Paul
McCartney's wife Linda Eastman is of the Eastman-Kodak
family? No wonder she does photography!

I didn't get a chance to go on that tour, but I did go on
one you'd love. Wish you were here. Because the big thing
about being here is that it's very historically significant for
Women! It's Suffragettes Land. The first Votes for Women
was in Seneca Falls. That was too far to get to, but I did
get to a great place in town: Susan B. Anthony's house.
Did you know she was really popular and respected and
always wore that sombre black dress so people would
concentrate on what she said, not her appearance? And
when she was in the audience to see Buffalo Bill and his
Wild West Show, Buffalo Bill rode over and personally
saluted her? She's really famous for making her mother and
friends come with her to the barbershop and vote when it
was against the law. Pretty fascinating. The women who

work there voluntarily are like the Sylvias, only instead of being for Sylvia Plath, they're fans of Susan B. Anthony. And everything they say is Susan this, Susan that. And if the Sylvias were Susans they'd say it was a conspiracy that the Susan B. Anthony silver dollar was almost the size of a quarter. Which caused all kinds of confusion and made it unpopular and the Edsel of small change.

What else? The *Fiona!* people gave me chits for meals, and I used one tonight to go to a restaurant called Mount Etna, yes, after the volcano. I asked someone at the hotel front desk to recommend someplace fun, and she said that this place picks up and delivers and by that she meant guests! You call them and a van picks you up to take you to the restaurant. The driver was very funny but kind of sarcastic as she gave us a City Tour, telling us where to go and not go. She was shocked I went to Susan B.'s part of town by myself, because it's not that safe. When she got us to Mount Etna, it turned out she was also the waitress! At first I thought I should tell Gaëtan about this service for Festin — we could pick up groups at the Queen E. etc. — but I don't think I will. I don't want to pick up, drive, waitress, sing and then deliver guests home, too. (Even though Festin needs something to get things moving again.)

Mount Etna was very Italian, with many frescoes, including one of lava coming down the mountain and people running for their lives. When Anita, Your Driver and Waitress for Tonight, found out I was a serving wench, too, she took me into the kitchen and introduced me. They asked me to send them an 8x10 for their wall, I'm the first customer they had who was a guest on *Fiona!* They warned me I am to watch my back, *Fiona!*'s only six months old, there's lots of competition, she'll do anything to get ratings. I can't let her do the Thumbs Up-Thumbs Down Lions-versus-Christians thing to me. When Fiona does that, the guest is toast. (I kept expecting you to show up as a surprise in the kitchen, it was like you'd briefed them to warn me!) When she drove us all back, Anita told me

Fiona's a real Jekyll and Hyde and goes with her audience, if she thinks they like you, she will, too. So I guess I have to get her to like me, really like me. Ha-Ha.

On my way back to my room, I got to talking to a man while we waited for the elevator. And then we kept talking when it arrived, and he seemed pretty nice. Interesting enough. And then the elevator stopped at his floor first. He held the door. "No thanks. It's not my floor," I told him. "It could be," he said.

Can you believe this? We had talked maybe two minutes! And he was asking me back to his room, and the hand holding the elevator door had a HUGE wedding ring on it. Isn't it terrible how you can't talk to some strangers?

I came back to my lovely room, alone. And it is now midnight. In eight and a half hours, they'll come to get me for the show. But I am too awake to sleep. I think I'm going to rent a movie from the hotel TV. Amity said I could have "up to two." But if I take anything from that little fridge, I have to pay for it. The movies I can pick from are: *The Fisher King; Goodfellas; Truly, Madly Deeply; The Commitments; Barton Fink; Terminator II.*

I remember you and Daniel went to see *The Commitments* when I was doing *The Most Happy Fella.* You went with your Irish Ceili people? And it was loud and fun. I think I'll go for that, I want to have a good time. I will mail this in the morning as I head to my limo. Ha-Ha.

In the Lap of Luxury,
Lenore

PS: It's now three a.m. I watched your Irish movie and now I can't sleep. Because I want to go out dancing wild in a place where I can get up and sing with the band. I won't, of course. But that's what I feel like doing. You know, that little band could have made the big time if they'd stopped fighting every two seconds. Is that what Fighting Irish means? If I can't go out dancing, what am I going to do?

The *Fiona!*s are coming for me in five hours. I have to sleep sometime before that. I read all the magazines I brought for the plane. And the Canadian novel you loaned me takes too much thinking right now, it's too well written. I like that it has a hot air balloon man crashing on the moors and meeting the writer of *Wuthering Heights*, but I never read that book. And so I don't get it, I guess. I can rent another movie (my second of *Up to Two*) or try to put myself to sleep reading the *I Love New York* book. Or all these pamphlets and things I got you from Susan B. Anthony's House.

I have to stop now, I've used up all the hotel stationery!

To: LENORE RUTLAND
        BREWSTER HOTEL
Fax: 1-555-4433
From: HEIDI M. FLYNN

Lenore,

Be great on the Show STOP You'll be the most sincere guest they ever had STOP (I thought you'd like a telegram even if it has to be a FAX STOP) You should know that you are a Cause Célèbre. There's an item about you in the entertainment section of *The Gazette*. And they ran the photo of you as Cleo in *The Most Happy Fella* next to a picture of Reine Ducharme being lead out of her house the day they arrested her. "Too much!" as my tutorial student Devon would say.

Your fan,
Heidi M. Flynn

So here I am backstage at *Fiona!* I am so nervous, even though they keep saying they want us to be comfortable and feel at home.

At home? My home doesn't have a security system like this, TV cameras above surveying us, moving back and forth like in some space movie. And they made us pass through an elaborate booth thing, like they have in the airport, only this one X-rayed us, like we were nuclear power plant workers.

And they took away all our cameras. "Fiona doesn't have time to pose for pictures individually." And this in the town where Kodak is King! And then when they looked through my purse for firearms? "To ensure we'll all have a good time."

Well, the gun search is nuts, but it's also smart, a show like this must attract all kinds. Next week's line-up looks pretty chock-full, too. In addition to *Petticoat Junction*, the Reunion they've got Neo-Nazis in your Hometown. I'd want *them* frisked, I don't want them on the planet, let alone on the show!

Parker, one of the *Fiona!* interns, asked us if we had any suggestions for future themes. The Neighbor of a Neighbor Who Killed by stringing piano wire across her property to decapitate Ski-Dooers suggested they do a sequel to this show. *Fiona!* should look us all up six months or a year from now. And see if our Neighbor is still serving time. Or if they got out and killed again. Or if any of us have turned to crime, following their example.

Parker says they're still interested in Reunion Shows. "Sure thing. Like, Fi's the pioneer in that department!" I noticed her staff call her Fi or Fifi. Such a pink poodle name.

I just had to tell Parker they should get the cast of *Ironside* back together. Parker has never heard of this wonderful TV show, which starred Canada's very own Raymond Burr as the wheelchair-bound detective in San Francisco. But then again Parker is at most twenty-one years old.

Everybody in the guests' waiting lounge is my age or older, and they all agree I have a great suggestion.

"Ironside was a man's man."

"It was inspiring when Mark went from being a felon to a lawyer."

"I loved their big old police van."

"It was weird when they changed policewomen."

"*Ironside* had great ensemble acting."

All us women guests want to be Eve Whitfield, the policewoman from the rich side of the tracks.

"People? Hellooo?" Parker's trying to shut us up. "Like, I hear you. I will do my best to get this *Ironsides* original cast on the show."

Of course, if I have a bad time with *Fiona!* I will feel really bad if they drag the *Ironside* people out of retirement or wherever they are because of my suggestion.

Parker's really surprised I suggested *Ironside* because: "Like, I didn't know you got our shows in Canada." We get ALL their shows. "But, like, they'd have to do them in French, right?" I sometimes watched it in French, too — I was addicted years ago — but we got it in English first. "Wow. Really? Like, now you make sense. I was wondering why your English was so good. It's because you watched American television."

When are they going to take us to the set?

I'm wide awake even though I think I had maybe three hours sleep.

They sure have loads of treats on the courtesy table. That title gives a false impression, because to me it means you leave money for whatever you eat. Like the little fridge at the Brewster Hotel. That's not the case, it's all free, but how much pesto salad and Mrs. Field's cookies are you going to eat when you know you're going on TV in front of millions and millions of people any second now? I can't think about it!

But we're not going on for another forty-five minutes. At least Fiona tapes two shows back to back. The one before us is titled "Sun-Dried Tomatoes, Fact or Fad?" She's got all kinds of tomato advocates and a scene from *Attack of the Killer Tomatoes* and representatives from People Who Are Allergic to Acids in Food. She's out to find badness in anything, I guess.

Parker warned they'll take me for makeup soon. I thought I had enough on. I hope I don't get the same makeup artist who did the people for the first show, they all look very red.

I don't think it's smart to make someone an intern before her time. This Parker girl! She "like" gets far too carried away with her power. She's screamed at the Homemaker from Massachusetts twice already.

"No, you cannot sit in the audience and watch the other taping. Like, that's what the monitor is for! Watch that, okay?" and "Stay here! HERE! Don't wander into the hall. Like, we have a washroom here. We've provided for your every want!"

And when I asked about seeing more than this Green Room, which is pinkish, Parker took it out on everybody. "There will be no studio tours, got that?"

She's called me all kinds of names since I got here. I've been: Laura, Leontyne, Leonara, Lara, Laurel, Lanie, Lee-Ann, Laurette, LeToya, and Lurene.

These *Fiona!* Gift Bags they gave us — a T-shirt, a baseball cap, a coffee mug and a "Talk to Me! I did *Fiona!*" bumper sticker are pretty fun. And I like the I Love Rochester stuff, too: wine from the Finger Lakes in a big yellow thermos bag that looks like a box of Kodak film. They gave us souvenirs instead of money. They said they would cover it if I lost a day's pay, as long as I provide them with a pay slip. After this treatment from Parker, I feel like asking Gaëtan to fiddle the books. Say I make $1000 a day at Festin with tips. I wish.

Amity Smith, who talked me into this, is nowhere around. Parker told me she's in the building, but "she's, like, busy researching," which means calling up people she read about in the paper to trick them into being guests. To think I dared to ask if I could go visit her, I've got time. NO! Parker told me. Amity has work to do.

Maybe Amity doesn't realize I'm here?

"Yes. Of course. She knows you're all here. But there's, like, no time for socializing. We have other shows to do!"

Friendly place, eh?

I can't believe how some of the other guests can eat so much of this courtesy stuff. Piano-Wire Woman, aren't you nervous? She must think it's Thanksgiving. She's really putting it away! I guess she's not afraid she'll bloat like those wild rabbits at her uncle's farm Reine Ducharme told me about — they ate so much lettuce they passed out asleep in the garden. Her uncle had rabbit stew for dinner! But no salad, I guess.

Just sitting here like this makes me anti-social. I would like to talk to someone, but look what happened when the Arizona Rancher tried to talk to the Homemaker from Massachusetts — Parker screamed at him. Because this will destroy the spontaneity.

Even before, when everyone was giving opinions on *Ironside*, Parker looked at us like we were mutineers. Or a jury discussing the case while still in the courtroom.

The Rancher keeps looking over at me and smiling really sadly, I guess because he wants to talk so much and Parker won't let him. It's kind of like being kept after school.

But I guess they want us to go out there and be shocked when we hear the other Neighbors' stories. Or they'll be afraid we'll refer to things we talked about here in the Green Room and it'll be like an In Joke, our audience at home won't know what we're talking about. Parker keeps watching us, little Hitler Youth.

Parker's left! She took Massachusetts Homemaker and Piano-Wire Woman to makeup. I'm gonna try to talk to Arizona Rancher. He sort of looks like Ward Bond, the man who led *Wagon Train*.

From the
Transcripts of *Fiona!*

Taping Jan. 17, 1992
Estimated date of broadcast: Jan. 22, 1992

(THE AUDIENCE GROANS IN HORROR)

FIONA: Stop that moaning, audience. I warned you it would be gruesome. And get over it, it was from a movie!

WYATT: I never seen that movie *In Cold Blood* before.

FIONA: And you still haven't, Wyatt. That was just a clip.

WYATT: But what a clip, golly.

FIONA: "Golly," Wyatt, are you for real? *In Cold Blood* was the closest depiction we could get to what your Arizona

	neighbours did before tossing some of their victims' bodies into the Grand Canyon.
WYATT:	They weren't that mean. By golly, Fifi, what you showed up there was cold-blooded and horrible.
FIONA:	"It was a bloodbath." These are your words from the *Phoenix Record.*
WYATT:	I know, but all they did was shoot them all, once, kind of merciful, fast. And they all had this running feud, it'd been coming for a long time. It wasn't no robbery and random killing by strangers, no bloodbath as bad as that one in Kansas up there on your monitor.
FIONA:	Shame on you, Wyatt Bardo. Big man like you fainting at the sight of blood.
WYATT:	I never did.
FIONA:	Maybe our next guest won't be as willing as you are to eat her words.
WYATT:	Clip of Mrs. René Ducharme being lead to police cruiser.
FIONA:	Until December twenty-third of last year, two days before Christmas, Montreal, Canada was plagued by a serial killer. A specialist in Death by Poisoning, this merciless madwoman killed six people she shared jury duty with because she didn't agree with their verdict. Her name is Mrs. René Ducharme. And here's the neighbour who apprehended her: Lenore Rutland.

(LENORE RUTLAND entry)

FIONA:	Over here, Sweetie.
LENORE:	Someone in the audience had a question.
FIONA:	Later. Park yourself over here for now. Don't talk to them.
LENORE:	Okay.

FIONA: [to audience] Hey, no talking to my guests before I do, got that?

(RUTLAND sits)

FIONA: Ooh, do I detect a little Canadian deer in the headlights?

LENORE: Excuse me?

FIONA: Don't be nervous. I'm not gonna hurt you.

LENORE: Okay.

FIONA: Okay, eh?

(AUDIENCE laughs)

FIONA: You're the first one of my neighbours today who caught their neighbour who killed.

LENORE: I didn't, really. It was a mistake. Madame Ducharme thought I knew everything but I didn't. So she confessed to me. And then police Constable Benoît Archambault —

FIONA: Right, right the cops burst in after you'd done all the "on the grounds" work.

(AUDIENCE responds)

LENORE: No, Benoît had done the ground work.

FIONA: Oooh, it's "BEN-WAAAA," huh? First name basis?

LENORE: Um, well I kind of knew him before this happened.

(AUDIENCE goes "OOOO")

FIONA: How well? Ha-Ha. Calm down, audience, that's for another show. "Women Who Sleep with Cops."

LENORE: I didn't sleep with him.

FIONA: Sure, sure. Right, so BEN-WAAA made the arrest . . .

LENORE: After he'd been doing surveillance. He'd been watching the house.

FIONA: That he sent you into. Were you wired?

LENORE: Was I nervous?

FIONA: No, did he have a wire on you?

LENORE: Were they bugging her using me, you mean?

FIONA: Yes. Yes. You do speak English up there in Montreal, Don't you?

(AUDIENCE laughs)

LENORE: Yes. Benoît didn't wire me. He was there looking for someone else on another case. We both stumbled into her confession.

FIONA: Which was . . . that Mrs. René Ducharme had been systematically poisoning people. Fellow jury members who'd gone along with her on the free-ride, easy-route, quick-fix give-him-a-Not-Guilty verdict for a murderer who was set free to kill again.

LENORE: Madame Ducharme felt awful about that, the not guilty verdict. So, she said, she had to make the jurors and the lawyers all pay for what they did.

FIONA: By killing them? Seems a tad extreme to me!

LENORE: Maybe. Uh . . .

FIONA: Uh, maybe? Has Mrs. René changed her mind?

LENORE: No. Yes. She feels bad.

FIONA: Of course she feels bad. She got caught, she went to prison, she's doing TIME! Thanks to you, the neighbourhood Jessica Fletcher!

LENORE: I wasn't snooping around, it just happened —

FIONA: Don't be so humble. You're the one she spilled the poison beans to. Where was Mr. René Ducharme during all this?

LENORE: There is no Mr. René Ducharme.

FIONA: Did Madame X poison him, too?

(AUDIENCE laughs)

27

LENORE: Uh, no. There's no such person as René Ducharme.

FIONA: Help me here, sweetie. How can there be a Mrs. René Ducharme if there was no Mr.? Or, pardonnez-moi, Monsieur?

LENORE: Because you've made a . . . mistake with her name? Her name is Madame Reine Ducharme. Reine, not René. Reine is her name, it's French for Queen.

FIONA: So she's a Queen, huh? A Queen of Death?

LENORE: She didn't mean to be. She was having a lot of stress.

FIONA: And why was the poor little Madame having that?

LENORE: Everyone was really mad at her and the entire jury about the not guilty verdict.

FIONA: Everyone like who?

LENORE: Everybody in the whole city. All of Montreal.

FIONA: I think they have a right to be pretty mad, don't you, audience?

(AUDIENCE cheers, points thumbs up)

FIONA: Now this Queen got the poisonous stuff from her garden, right?

LENORE: Yes.

FIONA: A garden you watered while she did jury duty?

LENORE: Uh, yes.

FIONA: So you must consider yourself partly responsible?

LENORE: No.

FIONA: Oh, come on now, Lenore. Lucretia Borgia lives next door, she's got this garden filled with Latin-named weirdo herbs, people she was on jury duty with are popping off like shoofly pies, and you don't suspect anything?

LENORE: Yeah, I did. I became afraid Reine would be next. That's why I went over to her house. To warn her that someone might be trying to kill her.

FIONA: Because six jurors had already been killed.

LENORE: Yes.

FIONA: But what you find out is that she's the one who's been doing it all along! With plants you tended for her! A regular Igor to her Dr. Frankenstein.

LENORE: No.

FIONA: Sweetie, you watered her garden.

LENORE: I wasn't the one picking the herbs and making them into poison!

FIONA: If you hadn't watered the herbs all summer while Lucretia was on jury duty in the first place, every poison plant in her garden would have died. Leaving six people alive today! And then, who of all the people in Montreal does the Lady of Charm choose to confess to? You! Maybe it's only me, but I'm getting mighty suspicious here, folks!

LENORE: Well, you're mighty wrong.

FIONA: I don't think so. And you know what else, the theme of this show's changed: "Neighbors Who Are Accomplices," right here, right now on *Fiona!*

WYATT: Hey, hey, you leave that little gal alone!

FIONA: You shut up, you had your turn, Lonesome Cowboy.

WYATT: And you had your turn trying to make her own up to something that weren't her fault.

FIONA: It was her fault. Wasn't it? Audience — is Lenore guilty or what?

(FIONA points thumb down; audience responds 50/50)

WYATT: Hey, Fifi. Looks to me like you got a split decision.

FIONA: They didn't understand the question. Let me help you, audience. The correct answer is, Thumbs Down!

(AUDIENCE Woman in Red shouts)

WOMAN: There's more Thumbs Up for Lenore than Thumbs Down, Fiona!

LENORE: [shouts back to Audience Woman in Red] Anita! Hi!

WOMAN: Hey there, Lenore! We got tickets! Mount Etna's all here for you, baby!

(AUDIENCE Woman in Blue with Woman in Red shouts)

WOMAN 2: Yeah, girl! We're on your side.

WOMAN: THUMBS UP, THUMBS UP, everybody!

WOMAN 2: Thumbs up, we told you!

FIONA: [to them] Okay, enough with the floor show, girls. I get the point, you're on her side. [to Lenore] So, you brought troops.

LENORE: Great, eh, they were able to get tickets.

FIONA: I thought you claimed you were from out of town? Another country, even.

LENORE: I am.

FIONA: So where did they come from?

WYATT: You musta met them at that I-talian place you went last night?

LENORE: Yes.

WOMAN: [shouts again] MOUNT ETNA!

LENORE: A really fun place, everybody!

WOMAN 2: Best Italian food in Rochester.

WOMAN: Anybody wants to go for lunch once this is over, our van's right outside.

FIONA: Hey, hey, hey, I told you, enough! Let's get back to *my* show theme, folks!

WYATT: Yeah, sure. So what if Lenny's neighbour killed six people on her jury that let a killer go free — maybe that Rainey thought she was doing justice a good turn.

LENORE: She did.

WYATT: And the only crime Lenny can be guilty of is a sin of omission. Not knowing what was going on when it was going on.

FIONA: Just because Lenore's neighbour's crime wasn't the Wolverton Mountain one your neighbours committed, Marlboro Man —

LENORE: Reine's *was* different. She felt really badly about it, your neighbours didn't, Wyatt.

WYATT: Jest like I was tellin' ya —

FIONA: When was all this?

WYATT: We was talking back there in that pinky Green Room where you make Parker keep the guests.

FIONA: And you were all talking among yourselves?

WYATT: Hey, if you got us on before them Tomatoes people we never woulda got to talking.

LENORE: And found how different all our experiences with crime were. Are. Um . . .

WYATT: Like Piano-Wire Woman —

LENORE: Oh, yeah.

FIONA: Be quiet! Hush up! She's hasn't been on yet.

WYATT: Wait till you hear her story, folks! Her brush with violent crime's way more different from anything that happened to me or Lenny.

LENORE: And a lot the same, too.

FIONA: People! People!

WYATT: Yeah. But you were lucky, Lenny, you never had to find the bodies.

LENORE: No, thank goodness, eh?

FIONA: Hey, hey, hey —

WYATT: Tell everybody what Piano-Wire Woman told you when they took me away for makeup, about how horrible it was when she found them rogue snowmobilers all decapitated.

LENORE: It was really awful, she said. The Ski-Dooers —

FIONA: Whoaa! Stop right there, sweetheart. She's my next guest, we'll let her tell it, okay? And I better get Piano-Wire Woman on before you two give her entire story away!

WYATT: And get her on fast so we can take questions from the audience.

FIONA: No time for that. You two? Thanks for coming.

LENORE: Do you want us to leave?

FIONA: Yes, I do. Goodbye. I'll be right back after this commercial break as we meet someone they call Piano-Wire Woman.

Fiona!

January 17, 1992

Dear Lenore,

Thanks so much for taking the time to be on my show. I hope it was a worthwhile and enjoyable experience for you. People really responded to you, and I learned that my show can be deeply enhanced when I let the guests take some control over their own stories. Keep us informed how your life goes. Maybe we'll have you back!

Ᏺ

Fiona Phee
FP/as

2

Satisfid? You made a mokery of our
justice systam! Made Canada look bad
all over the USA. HA HA HA theyre
all laghing at us! The Prime Ministar and
the Premiere should kick you out.
You shuld go to jail. You helped her kill
peple. Its all your falt yu merduress.

Conserned Citizen

I thought only the Montreal Canadiens got that sort of reception
at the airport when they won a Stanley Cup away from home, ha-ha,
but there were six people I didn't even know waiting for me! One of
them even presented me with flowers and this helium Suzy balloon.
I guess they really must be People Without Lives, like Heidi says, if
they came out to see me arrive at Dorval Airport just because I was
on *Fiona!* They haven't even seen the show yet! Or how mean and
nasty Fiona was to me. Heidi made me feel better by saying anyone
named Fiona with the nickname Fifi doesn't deserve to be taken
seriously. "She has corrupted a beautiful Celtic name."

I have no idea who wrote the note on my car. I sure hope
Conserned Citizen isn't expressing public sentiment. The ideas sound
like Jemima Farnham, but I know she didn't write it because:

1) she'd sign it
2) it says I was mean to Canada and that's never been a big bother to Jemima, if I ran down the Queen on *Fiona!* I'd know it was her
3) it's not on nice stationery
4) the spelling!

It sounds like someone really angry (deranged? pathetic?) wrote it. Someone who's anglophone and can't spell but has really nice handwriting. "Satisfid" and "mokery" sure sound like Jemima. She always says "Satisfied?" when she tells people off. Or maybe it's a trick from the *Fiona!* people to help her ratings. More controversy? The folks at Mount Etna said she'll stop at nothing for ratings. Maybe she invited me on her show *knowing* this would happen. That it attracts nuts. What if I wind up with a car-stalker pen-pal because I did *Fiona!*, if that's the price of Fame of the Week.

So the note was definitely not from Jemima Farnham, she told me off in person. She wasn't mad that I might have jeopardized our justice system. All she was concerned about was why I went on an American program when Dini Petty would surely have appreciated the boost I could have given her ratings. So I was wrong, Jemima does think Canada First sometimes. I'm sure Jemima's mad that I'm the one from the street who got chosen to go on *Fiona!* Jemima's always hated Reine for being a separatist, and she would have used *Fiona!* to air her opinions on our language problems. As if *Fiona!* would care, they barely know we speak English up here.

It was odd the way it all came up, her "taking me to task." Asking me to come over to her house today, "Around three will do." And it wound up being Afternoon Tea. So good of her to let me use the Andrew and Sarah Engagement tea cup. "Before they became the Duke and Duchess of York." She has quite a collection of monarch tea things. Jemima got the Queen. And I got Fergie, who's been causing Her Majesty so much trouble lately! I was surprised Sarah Ferguson wasn't banished to some cupboard. I wonder if that tea cup was some kind of sign or put-down. Or if it was because my ex-boyfriend was a Fergie. I wonder if Jemina's sons get the Prince William and Prince Harry teacups when they have tea with her.

Jemima must have commemorative plates of everything the Queen ever did: got married, became Queen, visited Calgary. I guess there's no problem knowing what to give her for Christmas! I really liked the cake tray she served scones from: the Royal Yacht *Britannia*. Very classy. I would have been able to enjoy it more if I wasn't thinking the whole time, What is this all for? Heidi suspected two things. One, that Jemima was going to try again to rent my parking space somehow for Blake the Prodigal Son, now that he's in detox. As if I would, and have to kick Heidi's Rabbit out into the streets! Even if she had no car, and I had no car, and Blake got sober (impossible!) I still would not rent out space to a former Drug Fiend. Heidi said it would either be the parking space or, two, that Jemima wants me to speak to one of her groups. The Monarchist League, maybe, because I was a Crown Witness. Anyway, she said I had to go and see what Jemima wanted. So I held Fergie and Andrew and waited for Jemima to make her move. Finally she got to it. "Now that Madame Ducharme's gone, could we try being civil to one another, and possibly be . . . friends?" I felt sad when she said that, she's lonely, I don't think she has many friends. Her house is so very much a little bit of England because she's terribly homesick. Neville, she said, promised her when they came here that "it would be for two years. Five at the outside. We had Alistair already, but then Blake was born here, so we had this . . . bond. We bought this house. Neville's practice is here. He could never leave his patients! So we're all stuck here. Stuck, stuck, stuck. More tea?"

When I showed her the note from my car, she got very quiet. "Oh, yes," she said. I asked her right out, "It's not yours, is it?" "Of course not," she said. "I'll throw it away, shall I?" That was odd, her offering to throw away my note, and stranger yet when I said, No, I want to keep it," and she asked me, "For a souvenir?" What was she thinking, she must know it's evidence if I get any more. And, she cracked, "Judging from all the paraphernalia you have outdoors, you must have more than enough things indoors already without bothering to keep every odd random note left on your car!" I was trying to like her, I really was, but she has to go too far all the time with her snotty Westmount tone. And taking another dig at all my lawn ornaments. Anyway, at least that's when she finally got to THE POINT.

Did I know if Reine Ducharme had any plans for her house while she was "away." I said, like, to sell it? "I don't want to buy it. Well, perhaps I would if it came on the market . . . but no, if Reine has no plans for the immediate future, I thought she might be interested in renting it." But she's not renting an entire house just to get Blake a parking spot, it's for her relatives. A whole bunch of them are coming over in February for the Wedding.

I guess I should have disguised the shock in my voice when I said, "Blake's not getting married, is he?" because then she became either very cross or very sad and said, "No, Alistair." And since he'll be coming home from Drumheller to get ready for the Wedding, there won't be any room for all the English relatives who insist on coming. All eight of them. Two Mums and Dads and their adult children. (Valentine's Day weekend is a romantic time for a wedding . . . in California. Or Italy. Or Australia. But in MONTREAL? Those poor English people coming here to SNOW and ICE and FREEZING COLD?) Jemima says she needs a lot of space, and she suspects Madame's has lots of rooms. So what could I say but Yes, I'll ask her. Jemima says not to tell Reine *who* wants the place, she'll give her a cleaning deposit and everything, not that it will be a problem because her relations are very tidy etc., but she doesn't want Reine to up the price because it's her. So now here's me looking after Reine's chiens méchants and renting out her lodgement!

Heidi thinks maybe I could use the rent money to board Brioche et Montcalm, they were terrible while I was away. Give us all a vacation! They get worse every day, maybe we can get them into detox with Blake! I know I have to get them under control, because they are ruining my life and my carpets and my furniture! And some days they are really, really horrible, and then there's all that yippy-yappy barking! Why doesn't somebody call the cops on me and complain, and then they'd take them away. But the SPCA's going through enough lately, they don't need the trauma of these two even overnight. Because I'd have to rescue them from the gas chamber, no Susan Hayward *I Want to Live!* for these two. Or *Je Veux Vivre!* either.

Lenore,

Your *Gazette* is not here because I took it. I don't want
you to see it. You may be tempted, I know, it's not every
day you get an Aislin editorial cartoon done of you, but
believe me, you don't want to see it. Daniel said you're to
stay away from *La Presse*, too. Forget I mentioned them, go
back to bed. Remember: tomorrow is another day and *The
Gazette* and *La Presse* are in the Blue Box.

Heidi

Not looking at the paper makes me imagine something way, way
worse than reality. Last year Clive said he wasn't going to look at the
review of *The Most Happy Fella* in *The Gazette*. "I know how well I
directed this show. I don't need her validation!" Jamie said that the
year before they thought they had a big hit with *Wildcat*. They really
felt wonderful about the show, and then it got a terrible review, and
even though they knew their *Wildcat* was great, it was ruined. So Clive
doesn't look at all anymore, even if the review's good (like *The Most
Happy Fella*). So maybe I won't look at the paper. But when is Aislin
going to do another cartoon of ME? That's an honour. But then I know
what he's done to some people, even the Pope. So. Maybe I better
not look.

It's not so terrible. He gave me a lot more hair. He went a little nuts
with what a big mouth I have. But what he did to Fiona! is way worse.
If she sees it, she'll sue. Or at least complain to *Entertainment Tonight*.

It was really good of Heidi not to let me see it, to try and protect
me, but everybody was running up to me with copies of it when I got
to Festin. Two customers had me autograph it when I was serving the
meat course. That's okay, they don't know me. But people who do?
How would they not think it would make me feel bad? All they can
say is, "You got an Aislin cartoon of you!"

I still haven't seen the *La Presse* one. People wanted to show "Lulu" (the nickname *La Presse* gave me) but Gaëtan headed them off at the pass three times. One customer was really insistent that I sign it, he agreed with Gaëtan, c'est pas un cadeau, but he really wanted my autograph. They covered it, and I wrote "J'pense que j'aime pas ça! Lenore Rutland." Kind of like "Paid Under Protest" when you get a traffic ticket.

But if this makes the customers happy and brings people to Festin that's good. Heaven knows January is slow, but the theme restaurant business is slower than ever this year. And the GST and the raid because of our illegal wine last Thanksgiving didn't help. Gaëtan isn't saying, but I think we may be in big trouble. So if my notoriety gets people in here, and it sure has so far this week, that's okay. I can take this adoration.

I hope I don't get recognized anymore, I don't want to be notorious anymore! My *Fiona!* Show was on today, and I guess I didn't do too badly. It was odd seeing myself on my own TV. But it was great having people over to watch it. Heidi even cancelled one of her classes so she could see it live with me. "Be in the moment!" she says. And the phone kept ringing. I'm glad they all think I "gave it to Fiona!" because I really thought she gave it to me. I heard from almost everybody, but "Constable Benoît Archambault" never called. He must be away for CSIS. He must be on a secret assignment, I haven't heard from him in weeks. He'll explain what he can when we go to see the Canadiens beat the New Jersey Devils at the Forum. Imagine if I had blabbed about Benoît giving me a hockey ticket as a Christmas present on *Fiona!* — "Women Who Get Bought Off by Cops with Tickets to Major Sporting Events," next on *Fiona!*

Yes, I brought the dogs to Tanguay. I had to, for two reasons. One, because Reine begged me. And two, so she can see what I am dealing with every day! I asked her would her sister in Laval please take them? Reine put her hands to her face, very Piaf-y, and moaned, "Non, non!" Her sister would have them sent to the Big Dog House in the Sky if she got hold of them, "Elle les déteste!" No one Reine knows wants them, and she *needs* to know they'll be waiting for her when she gets out. (When? In 2056?)

So I am stuck with this responsibility; if I don't keep Brioche et Montcalm for her, no one will. And they'll be put to sleep. And she's their maman and cannot see why anyone would want to change them in any way. She knows they are just high-strung, and they missed me when I went away to be on la télévision. She loved me on TV, so did everybody in the lounge! They taped it and have watched it three times already. Someone named Marie-France asked Reine if I'd autograph something for her. Reine shoved it at me, the *La Presse* cartoon! I finally got to see it. It sure wasn't un cadeau! Even though it does kind of look like me, only in *Les Misérables* clothes. It makes me seem so stupid: "Lulu Borgia," the hench-femme, pushing a wheelbarrow while Madame Ducharme fills it with herbs. But Reine likes it so very much that she wrote to the cartoonist to ask for the original. I told her I probably said too much on *Fiona!*, she agreed, but that is épouvantable. People get nervous on TV talk shows seen by millions of people. She's a little wary just talking to that anglo vendu Randall Kingfisher for *Saturday Night*. She's going to be evasive and not tell him everything anyway because she may write a book herself. And she thinks the Lucretia et Lulu *La Presse* cartoon might make a good cover.

Practically all my visiting time was up before I asked her about renting her house to some wedding guests who'll be here for two weeks. She thought two weeks was a long time for a wedding, how many parties are they going to have? And I lied so much and said they wanted to see a lot of Québec, they'd heard so much about how belle a province it is. She liked hearing that. I told her they planned trips to Québec City and probably Hull. (I never mentioned that they also want to go to Ottawa and Toronto.) Reine says she hopes that l'hiver won't scare them off from a trip to the Gaspé, too! She wants to ask a thousand a week in rent, but I got her down to that much for the two. I still think that's obscene. She wants me to keep the money, she insists, and use it to be good to myself, maybe go "à Holt-Renfrew." (Me, at Holt's?)

I told her she must need the money for upkeep of the house, but she says non. Not yet. I am to keep this money. I deserve it for all my "concièrge" work. If she really means I can keep the money, I'm going to see what Jemima's relatives are like. If they're stuffy Brits and fifty-sixth in line to the throne, then they'll pay what Reine asked. (I am prejudiced!) And I'll put the money away till she needs work done on her house. If Jemima's relatives turn out to be regular working people, like the types on *Coronation Street*, then I'll give them a really good, reasonable price and keep it our secret. And use the money for a good cause.

Heidi's smart. She knows what we are going to do with Reine's holiday-makers rent money: get the dogs into training! "These two require serious behaviour modification." She's already looking into good schools, and we'll have to give reasons why we need the dogs trained when we apply. It sounds like we're trying to get them into Loyola or Jean-Brébeuf or Villa Maria, are they going to have to take an entrance exam? I asked her. She's not sure! But Elspeth's friend took Torvald, her hyper Norwegian buhund, for a course, and they need to know you're committed to the program. We came up with these reasons why Brioche et Montcalm need help, we added new ones to last year's list:
1) They are mad because they have to live in English.
2) They miss Reine.
3) I'm not home enough.
4) I don't fuss over them the way she does and when I do they know I'm insincere.
5) I am not a dog person.
6) They are Bad, Bad Dogs.

Heidi also likes the idea of giving any money left after this course to charity. Her New Year's resolution was to be a better person, "to bear witness" and help others. This is all because of her beloved uncle who gets the *Catholic Daily Worker* lending her books by Dorothy Day, who did a lot for the poor. So now Heidi wants to follow her example and help the needy. *The Gazette* has this Help Wanted for People page, where they list organizations that need volunteers, and Heidi's trying to choose from filling food baskets at the NDG Food Bank or working at Father Dowd's Home or reading to people at a seniors' residence every Wednesday afternoon. She figured her other possible choice, helping ex-cult members reintegrate into society, would be too demanding.

I don't know when she's going to find the time to do any of this! She's teaching too many courses at Concordia as it is, at the Loyola campus and downtown at Sir George. And working in their literacy program. I asked her HOW she got such a full work load. She took it on purpose! When it looked like she was marrying Emerson last fall and he was going to make her give up her apartment here and live on his hobby farm just over the border in the middle of nowhere Ontario, she got this weird schedule as a way of having to stay in town!

"It was diabolical, I know." So now she's paying for it. And Emerson's paying for it, too. Heidi's not marrying him led him "into the talons of Tess of the d'Urberblondes." Heidi says Tess is even more blonde than ever, it must take two days to get her "natural highlights" done. Professors Emerson Sawyer and Tess Dudley, what a chilling combo! This match was sure some surprise, I thought Tess's talons were into Harrison Only-A-Borrower-Be. "They were until Emerson was free of me. Tess has just got to have a man. And she calls herself a Feminist."

Dear Lenny,

I sure thought it was strange for *Fiona!* not to give us a professional tape of us being on the show. When we didn't get one that day, I figured they'd send one on the next week. I sure was wrong there. I'll bet you made a copy yourself when it was on TV, but here's as close to a "professional" tape as I could get done. No commercials, great sound, color quality, the works. And it's fixed so you won't never record over it again by mistake.

I sure enjoyed meeting you and having that talk, and I wish to extend an invitation to you to visit. Bring a friend, you say the word and I'll send you the tickets. I want you to see how beautiful Arizona can be any time of the year. How'd you like to see the Grand Canyon right up close?

I mean this very sincerely. It's not often I get to meet people nice as you, and my family would love to meet you, too.

Here's my card so you know how to reach me by letter, jeep phone, fax, the works.

I listen pretty good, as you can see. I remembered where you said you worked — Festin du Bois! You might have thought I wouldn't make sense out of that name, but my family was French way back, how do you think I got a name like Bardo? And I been to Paris a couple of times, I knew your restaurant name meant Feast of the Woods! So I am sending this FedEx package to your place of business. Bon Appétit!

> *Wyatt Bardo*
> Flint Rock Creek, Arizona

Dear Lenore,

I hope you remember me. I was almost related to Heidi? She would be my Aunt now if my Uncle Emerson had married her. My sister and I wish he did. My Mom says his new girlfriend Tess is "much more suitable even if her hair is much too blonde," but we really liked Heidi more because we really liked her apartment, it had so much stuff, and we liked her and all her angry women friends. And Portia (my sister) named her Barbie after her, and if Uncle Emerson marries the new blonde girlfriend, Portia will still call Barbie Heidi. My Mom doesn't know I am writing, she would be mad, so this is a SECRET.

I heard her say to my Dad, there's no love lost between Heidi Flynn and myself. So I guess that means you, too. Sorry.

If you can do me this big favour please send it to my friend Dylan's house, we are in Competitive Jazz Ballet together. She is your fan, too. We saw you on *Fiona!* I was so surprised. I told Dylan we knew you, we were at your house, and you danced with us to all the Supremes songs and "Dancing in the Dark" by Springsteen at the reception for my Uncle's wedding to Heidi that didn't happen. Dylan believes me and thinks it is great we know you. Portia would like a picture, too. That's what we hope you will send to us, pictures of you. I was so mad we didn't tape *Fiona!* when you were on, but we didn't know! Like I said, we were so surprised. So could you send us three pictures for me and Dylan and Portia, but if you can only send one I will make copies of it at my Dad's office the next time he takes me there and he's not looking. He gets me to play with the Xerox machine if he has private calls to make.

I was going to send this to you at Heidi's address, and then I found yours when I looked for hers in my Mom's address book. It was her Christmas Letter list from last year. She crossed you and Heidi off the list for this year. Don't feel bad if you can't send me the pictures. We will wait for the show to be on again, and we'll tape it and Dylan says we can stop the video and take pictures of You on the TV.

Fallon Lyndon
President
Lenore Rutland Fan Club

PS: We are sending you the recipe for After-School Applesauce to make you think of us. Sorry you have to make it yourself, it's too hard to send it in the mail.

Well my Big Date, my first "date" in over a year, sure didn't wind up the way I expected!

When am I going to figure out that something's wrong before it happens? I know Benoît never called me, but I thought it was because of a CSIS assignment or a lot of police work. Or him trying to hunt down Fergie after I gave him all that information for revenge. But I had my ticket, so I went to the Forum and figured I'd meet him there, in the Reds. I was right. And there he was, but he didn't get up or kiss me Allo or anything. NOTHING. He'd only look at the ice.

After a while it hit me: he's mad about me being on *Fiona!* And he's pouting. I wasn't going to let that stop me from enjoying a game at the Forum. I thought, well, I can ignore him, too. Canadiens scored first, three minutes into the game, and I thought it was a sign that things would be okay. But as soon as the first period was over, Benoît left to get a beer and didn't come back till the second period was about to start. By then I'd been recognized. "C'est elle! Lulu! Lulu ça va?" And then it wasn't just a couple of guys from Montreal, there was the row of face-painters from New Jersey, they were some of the millions who saw me on the show in the USA. They were making a big fuss of me when Benoît got back. One of them (Bernie, of Parlin, NJ) shouted over at Benoît, "Hey! Is that the cop that made the big arrest? How ya doin', BEN-WAA?"

This was the first time I got to see Patrick Roy in nets in real life, and it was being ruined by my "date." Benoît was really obnoxious, nasty, yelling at the players, taking it out on the Montreal Canadiens. After the second period, he disappeared, and the guys from New Jersey asked me to sign their Devils pennant. I said I felt like a traitor, so they said I could put "Habs Fan" under my name, which I did. They wanted to buy me beers, I said no. I could see Benoît watching and glaring from standing room. He came and sat down in the middle of the third period. It was really not pleasant. And after all my suffering, we lost! 4-3 for the Devils, and we only got one of the night's Three Stars. But Shayne Corson deserved it — he had a Hat Trick.

As we're leaving Benoît decides he's going to talk to me now, he walks me home. We're yelling in French and English all the way along de Maisonneuve till we get to my house. How I embarrassed him, everyone thinks he's a joke, everybody at the station saw the show, why did I tell the world I never slept with him, he'll never rise in CSIS because of me, why didn't I call him. I told him I did call him, three times, I left messages. He yelled that he was away on a special assignment. Why didn't I make them find him for me? He should have been on the show with me! I didn't make the arrest, he did. He put Reine Ducharme in the police car, he did the paper work. He would have liked a trip to Rochester with me. We could have had a good time, but no, I went on the show alone, I let Fiona! say I was the one who did all the detective work. I owe him some solidarité! What? One ticket to the Forum that he probably got free and he thinks he owns me? I told him that and lots of other things. We were so loud, Jemima came out of her house and spouted, "What's this fracas? Are you all right, Lenore?" And I told her, Yes, thank you, I could handle it. And Benoît said for her to get back into her house, nothing for her to look at here.

I told him we had to talk about this. Maybe inside where my neighbours didn't have to hear everything. That's when he said, "Je reste pas." And I said, Not staying where? And he said, "Avec toi, ce soir. Je suis trop fâché!" And I said, "I meant coffee. Who said you were staying over? I never asked you." He assumed I wanted him to, he figured if tonight had gone better, things would have progressed. We have known each other for a while, we have been through the fire together, who was I kidding? We're not strangers. He likes me. He gave me a plant. And Laura Secords. *And* a ticket to the Forum. And before the last two weeks, we talked on the phone, he'd call me, I'd call him, I gave him all those details about my missing boyfriend, everyone at the station thinks, "Tu es ma blonde, ma main squeeze." And I said "Je suis pas ta main squeeze! NON! Not tonight, not ever after this." So he left. Really, really fâché.

He's nuts. He thought that, after mistreating me all evening, a sleepover was still likely! It's not as if he picked me up before the game and took me to Bens for Smoked Meat or to Bar-B-Barn. Or was attentive to me at the game. I mean, the Canadiens didn't even win! We didn't even have a romantic walk home to my house, we were screaming at one another. Okay, so yes, I have known him since the spring, we've been through a lot, and he didn't say so but I will:

he's really good looking. But he is an IDIOT sometimes. And he has no right to tell me off like that, be such a cop! I don't have to take that abuse. He was a miserable monstre tonight and no fun to be with.

Maybe his feelings are hurt. But I did call him and he was away. I think I gave him as much credit for the arrest as I could on the show. I should have done more, I guess, to make sure he knew I was going on *Fiona!* If he meant anything to me, I would have. Why did I ever go on that show? If I'd listened to Heidi, Aislin would never have done a cartoon of me, I never would have gotten the nickname Lulu. Or penfriends in Arizona and Massachusetts and an admirer named Marie-France in the pen. And tonight might have been really fun and led to something, even if the Canadiens lost.

3

There's trouble at Festin. We need customers. Bad. And Gaëtan must be desperate because he's hired a consultant named Tyler Garrow. (Daniel told me Tyler Garrow approached Gaëtan, not the other way around.) He's done a lot of work in the USA, he's from there, "turned around, saved" scores of theme restaurants. Tyler's first suggestion is that we "go medieval. There isn't an all-out medieval banquet yet in Montreal. And they are BIG in the States. Toronto, too." This would mean a jousting arena and horses and armour and bare feet. We would have to call it Days of Chivalry/Jours des Chevaliers. But Gaëtan said No, he wants to keep it Canadien. And he doesn't care if he's had complaints that it's too happy-habitant, we just have to know how to do it better. Tyler warns that Festin "is losing more market share every night, you gotta get with the program." I'm in on the discussions because Gaëtan wants my opinion. But I'm not used to being around a man in a three-piece suit. He's very business-y, has an MBA and throws me off with jargon. Tyler promised Gaëtan that if he insists on keeping Festin Canadien he'll come up with "something Canuck." He wants to know if any of us can do impressions, and what kind of history do we have to liven things up? "You people have any kind of 1776?" We said we had the signing of Confederation, but that wouldn't be too exciting. Even though Thomas D'Arcy McGee, one of the Fathers, got murdered and there's still talk that they executed the wrong man. "I love the execution angle, and assassination's really hot. What I need is living history, where heroic people could be thrown into prison or hanged for treason? That was ours with 1776. The whole world was watching. You have anything like that here? Man, that would play!" We told him we've had some constitutional crises, some battles, but . . . "Wait, wait, you guys had some war in Quebec?" And I said, "The Battle of the Plains of Abraham?" Tyler got very excited, and Gaëtan said, "On va pas là."

"Huh?" Tyler asked.

"We don't go there," I translated.

"Why *not*? You gotta go there one of these days!" Tyler said.

"C'pas aujourd'hui. Not today. We stay pre-conquest, ça va?" Gaëtan told him.

"Pre-conquest? What's that? If you will pardon my French, your problem, from what I see, is that you're too French. Lemme finish. Yeah, so you had a lot of Montrealers, but they're going to other theme restaurants, mon ami. So what you gotta go for is the tourist dollar. And that is in American currency. And what they like is to have FUN. Be part of the action. Gimme a couple of days and I'll be back to you with the Tyler Garrow blueprint for success."

As soon as he was gone, Gaëtan asked me what I thought of him. And I said, "I think he's scary. He seems kind of a Disneyland TV Evangelist to me." Gaëtan really feels Tyler can help save Festin. My notoriety was the only thing that brought people in during January, and that's sure worn off. So we may have to do what Tyler figures we gotta do.

Another change may be coming, too. Heidi's found a dog school for us. It's so good of her, promising to go through this with me, it was her idea, we can take a dog each. One on One. Every place she looked into involved weeks and weeks of courses, and there weren't enough "windows" for us to be able to manage the scheduling. We needed a course for people who can't let a lot of their time go to the dogs. And Elspeth says this one "specializes in smallish, incorrigible dogs and can determine if the dogs can be modified. Why spend weeks and weeks if it's pointless? And those dogs need help now." So Heidi enrolled Brioche et Montcalm in the Wolfe Weekend Intensive Workshop. This Saturday and Sunday, eight a.m. till six p.m., which still leaves me time to get to Festin and not miss work. No rest for the wicked, eh? And once again, as always with Heidi's "groups," it's in a church basement in NDG.

Boy! Heidi sure had an unpleasant literary experience yesterday. She saw a man roaming around Madame Ducharme's yard in the dark, and then she saw him go into her house. She thought one of Jemima's relatives had arrived early from England, but it was odd that he was alone, no Jemima or me (I was at work) leading the Tour of the Estate. So she went over, Heidi Flynn Investigates.

She knocked on the door, and the stranger opened it and said, "Oui?" He had a perfect accent, but there was an aura about him that said he wasn't French. "He looked so anglo." She still thought he could be one of Reine's lost relatives from Laval, and right away she started to think maybe he'd take the dogs off us. So she began talking to him in French, and he winced and said, very pompously, "Perhaps it would be better if we spoke English."

He is English but not from England: none other than Randall Kingfisher, Madame's biographer for *Saturday Night*. Heidi exclaims, "*You're* Randall Kingfisher?" and he takes it as a compliment, thinking she's read him, when really she just didn't expect him to look like that. "I had such great hopes for a name like Randall Kingfisher. I thought he might be First Nations. But instead he's this white guy who must be the roundest-faced skinny person I've ever seen. He's what Humpty Dumpty would look like if he wrote for *Saturday Night*."

He told her plenty, it seems, and now she's going to do research on him. "I don't trust him!" Heidi Flynn Investigates Some More.

Randall Kingfisher said Reine had given him permission to "faire un tour de sa maison." She'd even given him a key. Heidi said that in the absence of me, the overseer of the house, she would accompany him on his travels.

He let it slip on purpose that he got his masters degree at the Sorbonne. In Paris? "I know where the Sorbonne is," she said. At the end of his house tour (he never took notes), Randall commented that he was surprised, he thought it would be more pronounced. "That she's a murderess?" asked Heidi. "No," he said, "that she's a Péquiste." That's when he went "Ahh," so pleased he'd come across a photo of Reine and her sister at a St-Jean-Baptiste Rally. "Blue and white fleur-de-lys for days," said Heidi, who wouldn't let him have the photo. She said she'd have to get approval from me. "Is this Rutland overseer also her press secretary?" he wanted to know. Heidi said she would check with me, and I would check with Reine on my next visit. He said he would do that, let him have the photo. "How many times do I have to tell you No, Mr. Kingfisher?" "Randall, please," he smiled at her. She didn't smile back. Heidi feels Reine's separatism has nothing to do with her crime. And it's a terrible picture of her, anyway. Heidi has no use for Randall at all and calls him "one of those sanctimonious apologists." He even made cracks about her inability to speak French properly after living here all her life. Then he asked her what she was doing for dinner! What kind of signals are we giving out to guys without knowing it? The Elevator Man Syndrome. Benoît, too!

I wish she had had supper with Randall Kingfisher because she might have found out what he plans to write about Reine. Who knows what he'll tell the rest of Canada she said?

February 9, 1992

Dear Lenore,

Notes on Randall Kingfisher from a number of sources. He was born in Port Perry, Ontario. He's forty-six years old, divorced, no children. Yes, he did go to the Sorbonne. He's written extensively for many magazines, including *GQ* and *Penthouse* (I knew he was VILE) and he's listed as a contributor to *Saturday Night*. He's won a number of writing awards, how he never brought any of those up is beyond me, and he's been involved in two libel suits, both dropped because of Absence of Malice, or, as he would tell us, he was only doing his job, nothing mean intended. Tell Reine to watch what she says! I'm sure she's just using him, too. He's such a pandering opportunist it must shine through. See you tomorrow seven a.m. sharp.

Heidi

"The dog is the only true companion." — Brytton de Tourdenot.

This is what they started our Weekend Workshop off with, and I knew I was stuck in the wrong place for the next two days of my life. Last year, Heidi dragged me to Women Who Love Too Much, these people need a meeting for People Who Love Dogs Too Much. Heidi says she and Daniel are "dog people but not this overboard," and we can be dispassionate about the dogs we brought because they're not ours. We don't love them to bits. All we care about is the final result: Decent Behaviour. We have our eyes on the prize. She warned me not to let on to the others.

The very first woman who talked to me was really odd. She owns Jezebel, a Cavalier King Charles Spaniel, the one that was really Lady in Disney's *Lady and the Tramp*. "People always think it's a cocker spaniel, but if you look at the eyes and the ears, you know." She was almost late for class because of a lost golden retriever that came to her house, hungry, tired and all covered in mud. She knew his owners and called their house, there was no answer. She went over there, rang the bell, nobody came to the door, all the lights were out. She thought it might be a suicide pact, "it happens." The owners were dead! This made sense. That was the reason she could have handled. "I'd rather the owners commit suicide than leave a beautiful dog alone without food." She was about to call the police when a neighbour saw him and called, "Oh, there he is! Brandy! Brandy!"

It turned out the owners, who didn't have a suicide pact, left the dog with these friends, but Brandy dug his way out of their yard and ran away to Jezebel's house. Jezebel's mom was mad that these people were such bad dog sitters and so lackadaisical about the Return of Brandy. They were the type who saw nothing wrong with dogs riding in the back of open pickup trucks! I made the mistake of saying dogs always look pretty happy there, riding in the wind. If I were a dog, I'd like to do that, a dog's idea of true fun. And she said, "Would you like to go through the back windshield or get flung out onto the road when the truck comes to a sudden stop? How much fun would that be?"

This was my first sign that I did not belong in the company of these people. I am not a dog person. I cannot see dogs in this light.

To me, a dog is a dog. But in the case of Brioche et Montcalm, a dog is Satan.

While I was stuck with Mrs. Jezebel, Heidi was talking to the people who run the course, Tatiana and Tamara Wolfe. They are twins but not identical. In fact they so much don't look like one another, you'd think one of them was adopted.

Eight a.m. Time to begin! Tatiana and Tamara walked to the end of the church basement hall, leaving everyone else way on the other end with the dogs. They introduced themselves. "I am Tatiana Wolfe." "I am Tamara Wolfe. No relation." And I said to Heidi, "No relation to each other? They're twins!" "To the famous Wolfe," Tatiana continued. I thought they were reassuring us that they were no relation to General Wolfe who won the Battle of the Plains of Abraham to reassure the francophone dog owners. And us with a dog named Montcalm. Heidi had already joked to me that it would be Wolfe versus Montcalm. But they didn't mean that Wolfe, they meant "Wolfe the Writer." And this made me think they meant Virginia Woolf, who I became "acquainted with" (to use what Heidi calls Sylvia-speak) last year, when Heidi talked me into doing the Dinner Plates Dance we never did because Frayne, our teacher, skipped town because she may or may not be part of some Feminist Underground Network. Or on the run from her husband. Thinking of Virginia Woolf made me sad then, because I remembered the goodbye note Virginia had written to her husband Leonard before she committed suicide, saying what a good husband he'd been and it wasn't his fault. And then she put rocks in her pockets and went and drowned herself in the Thames. Imagine loving someone that much and still doing that to him, dying on him like that. She must have been so unhappy. But then it turned out Virginia was not the Wolf the Writer they were not related to. It was Thomas Wolfe, and Heidi whispered, "*You Can't Go Home Again*," and I said, "Yes, I can. And not soon enough for me!" Heidi said, "No, that's the title of his book. *You Can't* — "and Tatiana and Tamara gave us the Group Glare. They didn't say anything, but in their four eyes were these two things:

1) Do you have something you want to share with the class?

2) I'm going to have to separate you two.

Tatiana snarled that some people must have lots of time to waste. I said if anyone had time to waste, it was her, spending class time telling us who she wasn't related to. She would have kicked me out right there, but the $350 plus tax (per dog!) was non-refundable, so we were stuck with each other. I'll bet that Thomas Wolfe who can't go home again is glad they're not related to him. I kept wishing that the famous British lady who says, "Walkies!" would come to town and help us save these dogs or that Vermont ETV would rerun her series so I could try this at home.

The first thing the Wolfes had us work on was "separation anxiety," it is their belief that all bad dog behaviour starts there. "Every time you go away, your dog pines, dies a little, and thinks he or she will never ever see you again. And even if they don't manifest it by tearing your curtains or barking incessantly, they are fretting inwardly." The twins told us to make all our dogs "Sit." This took thirty-five minutes, they even had to help us. Then they went to the other side of the hall again, and Tatiana said, "Masters, come." And just the people were supposed to go to their end of the hall. Of course that didn't happen. All the dogs followed us over. Over and over again, with a lot of barking and yelping and howling. This took two hours. Geordie the Yorkie bit his master. A Lhasa apso named Tenzing almost made it, staying on the other side till he gave this little whimpering whine and his owner crumbled. "Oh, poor baby, poor baby. Mummy's so sorry she left you." And she ran over to the dog's side. But Tatiana bellowed, "GET BACK TO THIS SIDE OF THE HALL!" And the lady did, but the entire time she had her arms outstretched to the dog, as if one of them was being dragged off to War.

By noon, the impossible had almost happened, all the dogs except for Brioche waited on their side. People were mad at me, of course, my dog was bringing down the class average. We brought all the dogs back for one more try. "We have to move on, we can't let one dog keep us back," Tamara said. Everyone had to agree, even me, I didn't have to admit defeat, they did, they were the professionals at this. Tatiana got down to dog level, and I thought she was talking to Brioche, but it turned out she was giving her a really big biscuit! So Brioche was able to stay behind without me because she was occupied!

"She folded her napkin," Heidi said. This is a family saying of hers and Daniel's. They've seen *The Miracle Worker* too many times, the scene where Helen Keller and her teacher have a drag-'em-out fight in the dining room. By the end the place is a wreck, but Helen has learned, and the teacher says, "She folded her napkin." If only all this training meant I'd end up with someone as amazing as Helen Keller.

All Saturday till six, with twenty-minute breaks "so the dogs can rest," we had these exercises. Then I had to go to work at Festin, which was half full, we're losing more market share all the time.

On Sunday morning the workshop went outdoors. All kinds of snow, but the Wolfes have got us doing manoeuvres in the park. Tamara was putting them through their paces, and that's when I had what I call my heart-to-heartless with Tatiana. She wanted to set me straight.

"You know what your problem is, yours and your friend's there? You're not emotionally attached to your dogs."

I told her that the dogs belonged to another woman.

"Why isn't she here?"

"Because she's in jail."

"Are you two cops?"

"No, we're her neighbours."

"So you're like foster mothers."

"No, we're humanitarians." I got this line from Heidi.

"Have you ever had a dog?"

"No. Never. Heidi and her family did."

"Then you've never known unconditional love. Look at Jezebel and her owner. Mitzi and Zsa Zsa the schnauzer. Or Brindisi and hers. Look at that. You don't get that from people, they always Take. Dogs don't, all they want is you."

"Because they don't know any better. They're dogs."

That's when she gave up on me, and I was stuck watching all these spoiled little dogs running all over the park. It made me think that if I had a dog by choice I'd want a mutt. Maybe Poor Old Hector, the one heck of a seadog from the Walt Disney movie. I liked him. That's the kind of dog I'd like, one that was his own dog, that had been out to sea and had adventures and was willing to settle down. Or go off on visits and come back from time to time. Maybe like *The Littlest Hobo*. Whatever I'd have he'd be a magic dog I could go for great walks with and not have to poop-scoop up after. But these two! They don't even look like dogs, they look like toys.

A man in a Blue Jays hat who looked like an average guy until you saw the chihuahua (Pepe) under his arm came over and confided in me. "You know what they won't tell you, eh? Those two breeds, your friend and you got? They can never get along. They should never be together, those kind. It's like warring signs of astrology."

I told him the dogs got along great together, it was us they didn't get along with.

"Maybe you should get some counselling. My wife made us go. Me and Pepe get along pretty good now. Wish I could say that for me and the wife, har-har. No, eh, but you should talk to somebody about it, you know? If you wanna keep those dogs?"

"But we don't want to keep the dogs!"

"Why not? They're pretty sissy-looking, but they're cute. Not as cute as my Pepe here. Pep-peeee bay-bee."

Don't you think calling a Mexican dog Pepe is racist? "Actually, it's kind of refreshing," Heidi said, "to be so obvious. The names of all these dogs are so affected!" (She would say that, her family dog, the Irish Setter, was named Kelly.)

The reason we had to stay in the park all morning wasn't just because of the training, it was because of the church service, they didn't need to hear these dogs yapping during it. We got the afternoon in the church hall. We did some stuff with leashes and choke collars (on dogs that small? You think I was even going to experiment on Brioche?) and when you can give them "nibbly reinforcements" (treats). And when our two got "out of order" (they were so bored, they were chasing each other all over the hall), Tamara came over and lowered her voice in a weird, almost growling way and stopped them in their tracks. It was pretty impressive. Then the Wolfes said it was time to prepare to show the dogs, some important people were coming. I wondered if this would be some kind of graduation ceremony.

"I think ours will be passed over," Heidi said.

At four o'clock the important people arrived, three women and two men. All really well dressed, one of them on the cell phone all the time. We thought they could be people who: want to buy or franchise the school; make a video of the Wolfe training techniques; have real problem-case dogs that need tutoring; need to adopt a dog; want to give scholarships to promising canines. When the presentation was over, I thought the Wolfe twins' chances for any of the these were out the window. But we were wrong, the strangers were thrilled.

"Perfect! Oh, so many of them are perfect! Especially that one!" the tallest of the women says and points to Montcalm. "He must test first." And that's when it *hits* me: they're looking for dogs to do scientific experiments on — these dogs are so beyond being able to integrate into society that their only reason for living is to become lab animals! I was not going to let that happen no matter how bad my two were.

Tamara brought the tallest woman over to Heidi and me. "They're the foster parents." And the tall stranger says she's with a casting company, and they're looking for dogs for their next project being filmed in Montreal: *Gamon de Pycombe, Dog of the Titanic*. They need to cast all kinds of spoiled, snobby-looking lap dogs because so many people in First Class had them! The tall woman said there was an actual letter from a passenger complaining about "obnoxious American women with tiny dogs." (The poor Americans, always getting blamed for stuff like that. Look at the nutcases in this class with dogs, none of them are Yanks.) And yes, it may be too soon to say, but they think Montcalm is perfect for one of the leads. I told them they can't cast Montcalm without casting Brioche because she'll get jealous. And I have to check with their maman. (And Benoît? Do I have to get police clearance for the dogs of a convicted murderess to be in a major motion picture?)

So that's how our workshop wound up, we didn't get a graduation certificate, we got a business card from a casting agent. Along with an audition appointment. All because (Heidi came up with this, not me) we had Dogs Who Ran With the Wolfes.

The British Are Coming! The British Are Coming! Actually they have arrived! and they're quite a fun bunch from what we can see. They're not stuffy Brits at all. And Heidi's in heaven because they love *Coronation Street*, too, and they're filling her in on the plot. (England's six weeks ahead of us.) I have no idea what they're talking about. I hear Rita this, Curley and Raquel or Mavis and Derek that, and Heidi, a Doctor of English, screams, "No! No! I don't believe it, you're kidding!" Jemima's perplexed, she can't get over how fast Heidi and I "bonded" with her husband's relatives, the Farnhams of "Near Sheffield."

Heidi feels she shouldn't take to Brits, considering what they did to the Irish, but I've seen how she really likes some English people. Especially this bunch, they're fabulous. As soon as the Farnhams of Near Sheffield found out what I did for a living they said they had to go to Festin! "Jemima, we can do that, yeah?" Jemima says they'll be very busy for Alistair's wedding. "It's over by Sunday, isn't it?" She supposes it could be arranged. "Brilliant! Super!" So they're all coming next week. Along with Heidi's parents, who'll be in town, and Daniel. They're all really excited but I am terrified: that's when we'll be trying the NEW CONCEPT.

Tyler Garrow has come up with his "blueprint," and Gaëtan says we have to try it. It's so silly, but I can't begin to say so. And I'm not the one paying this expert, heaven knows how much money it's costing to "redefine" Festin du Bois! When Tyler first came up with his plan, I thought it was a joke. But no, thanks to him I am going to be playing Laura Secord.

"She's kind of like your Fanny Farmer, huh?"

Tyler did research. "Où? À Peel et St. Catherine?" Jocelyne asked me. He was looking for "a quintessential Canadian story that sells." He's designed it all around ME. Finding out I was Lulu as seen on *Fiona!* makes me a "selling commodity." Since I "stood up to Fiona" (for all of ten seconds!) he thinks I am a champion of the people. He tried to find a Québec connection to Joan of Arc, "even if she had any cousins here" but that didn't work. Then he saw this name up in lights ("À Peel et St. Catherine") and he asked somebody who Laura Secord was. And then he asked somebody else, and another person. Three out of three knew she was a heroine with a cow who saved Canada. That's all he needed to get him started.

So what if her story was "in where, Upper Canada? War of 1812? We'll set it here. In New France!" I asked him would we make her French? And he said, "We could. Oh, yeah, no prob. Laura had to tramp through all those woods which are du bois, right? You can be Laura Secord du Bois!" He's even told us the actual story of Laura Secord and how even though she was born in the States, she warned the British that the Americans were coming, "but we aren't married to that." I asked him weren't there going to be a lot of problems with it? Tyler said, "Like, sold out? Like, you have to make your reservations a year in advance?" I said, No, like:

1) The American tourists he promises us. Won't they mind Laura telling on them? Americans don't like to lose. O, he says, because they can turn the tables! "That's the beauty of it, we can change the story every night, get table against table, give it that competitive edge. Give people a chance to subvert history, let the Americans win! Laura Secord had to get past three sentries. Every table will be a sentry post, they'll all have to stop you somehow. They'll have clues! Passwords, they'll love it." But what about

2) Our Francophone customers? There's nobody French in this story. "You said that before! You worry too much. I told you, we'll make her French."

3) French informing to the —

4) Brits? Jocelyne asked. "We'll make them Americans. And she's informing *on* the Brits! We'll see what the makeup of customers is every night and moderate it for them!" I didn't mean to, but I had another worry:

5) What about the Indians who finally took Laura to Lt. Fitz-gibbon? We can have Indians! he says. I told him we can't, that's a sensitive issue. He almost yelled, "Not another on va pas là! What's the problem now? You have those priests in the Festin Show, I read up on them, they were massacred by the Iroquois? Hurons? Some tribe. You got that Madeleine de Verchères, she fooled the Indians into thinking her fort was full of people!" Yes, I said but we never have Native people in what he calls "the show." Tyler says that's what's missing! "Stop being so Politically Correct! Come on. Help me here, my friends. Go with me, here. Otherwise the only New France characters I'm left with are a bunch of good women who started convents." Gaëtan told him we have to try to leave a lot of the Québec stuff in, the coureurs de bois etc. "Yeah, yeah. Especially the prostitutes. "What prostitutes?" "Les filles du Roy. The daughters of

Roy, the hookers, you play one of them." I said we were the daughters of the Roi, the King, not hookers. We came over to New France to get married. "Mail-order brides, huh?" And he loves this idea. Oh, no, he's probably going to give male customers our pictures and we're their wives-to-be for the night.

I can't help it, I feel this is so wrong for Festin, but Gaëtan wants to try it. And Tyler's the master of marketing, and Gaëtan's already given him $4000 up front, Daniel told me. More to come later. Tyler guarantees his work: "No Play, No Pay." I sure hope it takes.

Heidi got to go to Alistair's wedding, and I found a smashed-up Frosty the Snowman. Heidi was the Farnham Family's date. Jemima had a cancellation, and "The Best of Britain" asked Heidi if she'd do them the honour of joining them (without asking Jemima!), and Heidi said Yes.

Alistair's been living with his girlfriend for two years, and she's from Montreal originally, too (isn't everybody in Alberta?), so the wedding was here. They both must really like Bette Midler because the songs at the wedding were "The Rose" and "Wind Beneath My Wings." Heidi didn't like the singer at all, the songs were out of her range, Jemima should have hired me, she said. (Even if the singer was good, she'd probably say that!) She discovered Alistair works at the dinosaur museum in Drumheller, he's a very interesting and sweet man, you'd have no idea from talking to Jemima. Or her other son. Blake, the Best Man, got very blasted (surprise!) and was "completely incoherent when he proposed the toast." And then he tried to pick up Heidi (to Jemima's horror) but realized "I was with his cousin Miles, so he left me alone." Heidi says there's nothing to it, even though she did dance a lot with Miles at the reception. I asked, Why's there nothing to it? Eh? What's wrong with Miles? And she said he's leaving in a week, that's what's wrong. She doesn't want to think about it. "He must have somebody back in England because he's so rugged. Such a man. A real adventurer. Not the type I go for at all. Usually. And not now. He's gone next week, three thousand miles away. It's pointless to start anything! Why did you ask me about him?" Too bad, but it's true. Miles will be in England and she'll be here. And I think he said something about wanting to climb Mount Everest, so he'll be pretty busy.

They were all back from the festivities having drinks at Reine's when I got home from Festin and found Frosty the Snowman. I guess he was from someone's Christmas display, he's big, made of old plastic, and I managed to push his face back out a little, but he's still a mess, it looks like someone punched him. And why was he left on my lawn? Did someone find him and think he was part of my Christmas display? I had a lot of stuff, but I took it all down February first. Gordon, one of the Dad Farnhams, saw me wondering what to do with this abandoned thing and came out and invited me in. He said, "Leave him out there, love. Don't want him melting all over Madame's carpet!" I was there till four a.m. They are lively people, telling us great stories, we'll sure miss them on the street. Why is Near Sheffield so far away?

Tanguay again with the dogs. I am a martyr, Heidi says. But they were pretty good, I must say. I lowered my voice the way Tamara Wolfe did, and it really calms them down. Or terrifies them. I don't care, as long as it works. Of course whenever they started to act up, Reine was a little thrown off, she kept saying, "Qu'as tu dis, chérie? J'ai aucune idée de c'que t'as dit?" because I was talking to them in my Tamara voice, so low she couldn't tell it was growling in English.

Reine is thrilled that the dogs will be in the movies, she thinks this may lead to work for them with Denys Arcand. And their movie earnings can go into a gardener and fabulous plants for her jardin. (As long as none of them are interesting herbs!) At least she realizes that the house is going to need more money. Even so, there is no way I will talk her into renting it to Blake. I know Jemima has her eye on it for him now. I don't mind overseeing terrific renters like the Farnhams, but forget a guy who'd make it one long lost *Wired* weekend.

I can go to the *Dog of the Titanic* audition next week with Reine's blessing. And she agreed that Heidi was right in not letting Randall Kingfisher take that photo of her. It's not very good, and she thinks that she deserves to have a big studio portrait done for the story. Maybe Randall Kingfisher can arrange for one by that famous photographer in Ottawa. Yosuf Karsh? I asked her. Yes, she said, he does famous people. Randall said this was a big, influential magazine with an intellectual readership. They'd expect a good photo of someone they were reading a feature story about. She will ask him about Yosuf Karsh.

I gave her a great report about her tenants, how Heidi hit it off with one of them, sort of. Was Miles going to take Heidi on his trip to Québec? she wanted to know. I said I didn't know. (I think even Ottawa and Toronto are off their list, they're all having too good a time in Montreal.) Reine liked to hear that romance might be in the air for Heidi, what about me? I told her that Benoît, her arresting officer — "Ah, oui. Je me souviens de lui. Oo-là-là, il est beau!" — had asked me out to the hockey game but it was a mess. She said that was too bad, I deserve someone in my life. I said, Not someone like him, and that's when I told her the whole story, why he got mad, she has a face that you'd tell everything to. She's so sympathique, she listened as if she thought it would end happily. She said it still could, we may be meant for one another. *La Belle et la Bête.* There's all kinds of passion, someplace. "Attends, chérie. Attends!" Advice to the Lovelorn from Cellblock A.

Then she had a surprise for the dogs, she'd made them cadeaux! She'd put the wool and needles to use. She pulled out two tiny sweaters, both of them blue and white with fleur-de-lys on them. (And Randall said her being Péquiste wasn't pronounced!) She put them on the dogs, and I had to leave the prison with them wearing these things. And everyone's saying, "Oh c'est tellement mignon!" Or "Look, Ma, the separatists have gone to the dogs!" I got to the car and took off the sweaters. I stuffed them under the seat, and they'll wear them for visits to Reine, that's it. They are not going to their audition in them, either, I don't care if it's Reine's big wish. And the colour matches Brioche's eyes. What was she thinking, that I would go along with this? Parade them all over Westmount in those break-up-the-country-team sweaters? NO WAY. She pushes me sometimes!

�֍ �֍ ✖

Our Farnhams of Near Sheffield leave tonight. Heidi's going to drive some of them to Mirabel. I hope she doesn't get upset, she's really going to miss them. When she was a kid she had a pen-pal in England, a boarding school girl, "sort of a *Bunty* comics type." They stopped writing in their teens, and she always wondered what became of her. Then the Farnhams came here, and she hit it off with Jennie, the daughter. "It's like having my penal again." And she really took to Jennie's brother Miles, even though she won't admit it. Why not? She drives me nuts, she's so evasive/intellectual/sensible sometimes!

There are eight Farnhams at Reine's, and we liked every one of them. Especially yesterday at Festin. They were such terrific customers, really good sports. They got along famously with Heidi's mom and dad, too. Mrs. Flynn says she's been wanting to get to Festin for months, ever since Heidi told her I'd become a singing waitress. Last night was my second night as Laura Secord, and the Farnhams loved the part about telling on the Americans, they thought it was so funny, and they did battle with a table of real Americans trying to stop me from getting to Lt. Fitzgibbon. Daniel Flynn tried to carry me off when I passed their sentry post. His Mom said, "Put Laura down, Danny! Or she won't give us any of her chocolates!" Heidi and Dan's parents were in "great form," as the Farnhams would say. I loved it when Mr. Flynn got up and sang two Irish songs. Then that started the Brits singing pub songs, and Mrs. Flynn loved it. She said it was like TV's *Pig and Whistle*. And Gaëtan was so happy that the people he considers his in-laws were having a grand time. Jemima had come along, but she was appalled. I thought she'd be happy that the British were protected. Even by the Irish Flynns.

It was good that some of the francophone customers participated and tried to stop me from warning the British, but I know they'd prefer more of our original Festin stuff. Or for me to be Laura du Bois and save the French. This second time we did the new concept it worked well because the customers were so crazy and out for fun, they took over and made it their own party. But it won't be like this every night. The first night was deadly, when our customers have been at work or busy all day they don't want to have to work when they're out to dinner!

Last night Daniel said that the owner of the bagel shop next door came into the fire hall and asked could they please help him out? His freezer had developed a huge unmanageable block of ice, and he didn't know how he could get it out. Did they have an axe he could borrow? And Daniel said, "We sure do. And you can borrow me, too." He got one of the fire axes from a truck and went with the bagel man and chopped the ice out of the freezer. But when he was doing this a lady came into the bagel store and got very mad that a fireman, paid by the city, was using city property to clear out a freezer.

So the Bagel Man said to the Angry Lady with Nothing Better to Do, "What did you come in here for?" And she said, "Twelve Vienna." The Bagel man got them for her and said, "On the house. Now shut up about the axe." He bought her silence with a dozen buns. And he gave Daniel three dozen bagels for the firehall.

Everybody danced with Daniel after this story. All the serving wenches and all the Farnham women (except for Jemima) and especially Jennie! Mrs. Flynn was pleased. Daniel keeps putting up these smoke-screens for her.

Giving the winning table every evening a box of Laura Secords is smart. Gaëtan fixed it so the Flynn-Farnham table won, anything for Daniel.

I did a terrible thing. I lied to Heidi's mother. She and Mr. Flynn were going back to Ottawa this morning, but she had to come down to see me because she needed to ask me something important. She wants to talk to Heidi, but she's afraid she'll get mad, maybe I can talk to her? And I thought, I guess Mrs. Flynn doesn't want Heidi to be pining away for a man who wants to climb Everest, not everybody makes it. But it wasn't about Heidi and Miles. It was about Daniel. And Gaëtan.

She knows they're very good friends and that Daniel is his roommate in the beautiful condo Gaëtan owns. But it seems strange to her. She thinks Gaëtan is gay, is she right? I told her Yes, he is. And she had to ask me, Was it dangerous, what with AIDS and all, for Daniel to be living there? Because Gaëtan is gay and could catch AIDS. And isn't that bad for Daniel, living in the same place? And being around other friends of Gaëtan who are probably gay? One of them might have AIDS, Daniel might catch it off the towels or the dishes?

It was very painful, I kept wishing Mr. Flynn would arrive and say, "Flynn Taxi's leaving. Let's go," which he usually has to say at least three times before she leaves Heidi's. But this morning she was at my house, and I had my chance to tell her the TRUTH. But all I could see was that Aislin cartoon of me with my big mouth and then me telling her that her son is gay, his boyfriend is HIV positive, it was me who got Gaëtan and Daniel back together again, and then her face crumbling into tears and her screaming and Heidi and Daniel telling me off, Who was I to tell their mother THE TRUTH, so I said NOTHING. I guess I didn't really lie, I withheld information.

How can his parents still not know? He's thirty-four years old, he's never been married, he's living with a gay guy. Heidi's mother seems so smart, how can she not know? Because she doesn't want to, I guess. But then his smokescreens could let her think Daniel's straight: he's never told her, he was dancing with women all last night, he's a fireman.

I wonder what priests do when they KNOW something that's a big secret. They have to keep it a secret, it's their job, but what do they do when people ask them questions, and they have to pretend they don't know the answers? I'm glad I'm not a priest. Just knowing this one big thing is too much for me.

I have had a very strange experience.

I had to audition for my singing job at Festin. And then to get the role of Cleo in *The Most Happy Fella*. I never had to audition for dogs before. It was truly humiliating.

I had to bring Brioche et Montcalm up to St. Lawrence Street to the casting place. The hallway was full of barking dogs and their owners. I took my place at the end of the line until this lady with Diaspora, an Irish wolfhound (he'd need a entire lifeboat), said I have to register first.

So I go up to the desk to check in. The girl says, "Who told you to come here? To me?" I don't want to blame anyone, so I don't point, I just say, A lady with a dog in line. "Why would she say that?" I tell her, "To be helpful?" That's when I hear this voice in a corner: "Over here, check-in is in here. My office." So I go into this squishy cubicle thing she dreams is her office. She's sitting, but there's no other chair, so I stand while she asks for my papers. Like I'm trying to get into the country. I say, "Papers? You mean for their shots?" And I go to get them out of my purse when she says, "No, their forms? Their agency agreement?" And I said wasn't this an agency? "For casting. Who is their performance agent?" I said, They're not performers yet, I guess their agent is me! That's when she smiled (because she thought she'd get them to work for scale, Jamie told me when I called him for advice). I didn't trust her, so I didn't sign anything, anyway Reine has to do that, I think, as their owner. Then I finally recognized her, and I said, "Weren't you at the Wolfe Weekend Workshop? at the church? with the Two Tall Women and the men?" and she said, Yes, didn't I bring the dogs' 8x10s? "No," I said. "I don't have any. Every picture of them that exists is at Tanguay Prison with their maman."

"Fine, fine! Janis, get me Polaroids on these two!" That's when Janis, the surly girl at the desk, comes in and takes Brioche, who was not happy, out. Meanwhile the woman in the cubicle is getting the dogs' "particulars." She asks me: "Allergies? Problems?" I think she means me. "No," I say. She looks at Montcalm and says, "Oh, really? That breed's known to be prone to sneezing."

Janis comes back in, drops Brioche on the desk and takes out Montcalm, who loves her. Finally she has all our information, Janis hands her the Polaroids, and she attaches them to our file.

"Wait outside till we call you, Lara." Out in the hall, not the end of the line, the Irish wolfhound was gone. And I notice she'd put Lara Rutland instead of Lenore, so I fix it. We wait way over an hour, when finally a Tall Woman makes an appearance and says, "You! Now! Sorry to keep you waiting. Janis, in here!"

Janis and I and the dogs follow her (Heel!) into a big wide white room where the Tallest Woman, the Tall Woman and a bunch of men are seated behind a table. Again there's no place for me to sit. Janis goes and stands behind a video camera in the corner. The Tall Woman looks into our file folder.

"Who scratched the name out?" she yells.

"Not me," says Janis.

"I did," I tell them, they wrote down the wrong name.

"Then you should have had her fill out a new form. This will have to be done again. We can't have messy documentation!"

"Sorry. But they got my name wrong."

"And why was that? So what is it? Laura? What? I can't make this out . . ."

"Your glasses," Janis says.

"I don't want my glasses. She can tell me. What is it? It's not Lara, it's what?"

"Lenore."

"Leeenooore. Interesting. Enfin on commence! This is one of the producers," she says, giving the floor to him.

He says, "Does your dog bite?" And I say, "No." And then I laugh, I couldn't believe he's not kidding. Because "Does your dog bite?" is so famous from *The Pink Panther*. Clouseau asks the desk clerk does his dog bite, the clerk says no, the dog bites Clouseau, he says, "You said your dog does not bite," and the clerk says, "It's not my dog."

The producer says, "What's so funny? Does your dog bite or not?"

And I say, "It's not my dog." And I laugh again. So does another man behind the table.

The producer says, "What am I not getting here?"

"*The Pink Panther*," says the other man. "Right?"

And I nod and say yes.

The producer wants to throw us both out, he thinks this is so not funny, but the Tall Woman insists we stay.

"Janis. Get them on tape."

They tell me to make the dogs sit down and they do. (Sitting, lying down, any sort of lounging is not a problem for these two.)

After, the Tall Woman takes Montcalm in her arms and says, "Janis, get this." And Janis pulls in for a close-up. "Get those big, yummy, doggy eyes," says the Tall Woman, and I think I am going to be sick.

They have to "show the tests to Cotton." She has final approval of which dog will be hers in the movie.

I hear this name and think, Can it be Cotton Brady, who played the best friend and weird neighbour of Valerie Singleton for years on TV's *Salt and Pepper*? Can it be her? I, of course, act like I could care less who the star of *Dog of the Titanic* is, but I'm sure it must be Cotton Brady. I mean, how many people in show business have the name Cotton? Is it even a real name?

I called Jamie to make sure about the contracts, if we get any. He's had some days on films, he belongs to the ACTRA performers guild, and he knows the business. Jamie says I'm to show him the contract and he'll get it checked. He's very excited about all this, he's already getting fantasies: Cotton Brady gets a new TV sitcom, casts the dogs (with me as their handler), and Jamie gets cast as an eccentric pet store owner. And we all move to Hollywood and he wins an Emmy.

To think Jamie's a guy with a terrific normal high-paying job at IBM who lives and works in the Real World most of the time. But he has big Broadway and Hollywood dreams and the looks and talent, I think, to succeed, but he won't make the move to make it happen. I guess this way he has a good life, he can own things, like his condo, his sailboat in Pointe Claire. He can buy every CD of every Broadway show ever done. He goes out to restaurants. A lot.

He must entertain these fantasies because deep down he thinks somehow they could happen. But this latest one? It's funny and silly and *not* what I fantasize! I never want to give up my life and go to Hollywood with these dogs. Jamais! I didn't even like being infamous for a week in January! What if I became a well-known Hollywood dog handler or if I became like that woman who used to go on Johnny Carson with animals from the San Diego Zoo? Or what if Jamie talked Cotton into having me on the sitcom, too, and I won an Emmy and got accepted as a serious actress? And then kept getting cast in the movies, like Sally Field? There'd be no end to my lack of privacy, all the things it would lead to:

1) I'd have to be on a Barbara Walters Special, and I couldn't handle being interviewed by her and crying about my past in front of millions. And I'd have to do it, especially if I got nominated for an Oscar. She always does that to nominees on Oscar night.

2) Fergie would look me up again. And that would mean *The*

Enquirer. "TV STAR Abandoned Boyfriend." "I Was There Before She Became A Somebody." "She Made Me Turn to Gambling." And then there'd be even bigger headlines like: STAR ARRANGED LOVE NEST FOR GAY BOSS (and then Mrs. Flynn would find out THE TRUTH, probably standing in line at the grocery store.)

3) I'd have all kinds of dependants depending on me for their employment: the gardener, the personal assistant, the personal trainer, the performance agent, the ex-husbands, the pool man, my psychic.

No. Hollywood's for Jamie, but not for me.

And why did I even bother calling Benoît about permission for the dogs to be in the movie? I told his machine, "I'm asking you this once, don't say I didn't." And he called me back, What was I bothering him about dogs for? Quels chiens? And I said, "Reine has those two dogs I have to care for, is it going to be a problem, them being in a movie? I mean they were there when she made the poison . . ." And Benoît said, Do I expect him to dust their paws for fingerprints? I said, "Can I take that as a Yes, there's no problem?" And he said, Sure, and was there anything else I wanted to say to him? And I waited, I guess for him to suggest something. And he didn't, so I said, "No. Nothing else. Salut." Reine would want me to read all kinds of suppressed passion into that exchange, but I won't.

March 5, 1992

Dear Lenore,

We sure talked a long time on the phone, I am real glad you didn't mind me calling you up like that out of the blue, but I just wanted to repeat my invitation for you to come on out here and experience the beauty that is Arizona! I will send you the tickets soon as you say the word. Please bring a friend, bring a bunch of them if you want, we got plenty of room here at the ranch. Here's a picture enclosed so you'll believe me. To the left of the main house is the guest bunkhouse if you want your privacy, it can be all yours when you visit. I hope you will. I'm glad you liked getting the *Fiona!* tape and appreciated the difference real professional quality can make! I've watched it a couple of times in my screening room (yes, this place has got it all!) and we look pretty good together. Like I said on the phone, and I'm saying it again, come to Arizona. We'll show you a Grand time and we don't just mean the Canyon.

Wyatt Bardo
Flint Rock Creek, Arizona

Brioche et Montcalm
sont
DOGS OF THE TITANIC

Wouldn't Reine love that? Her chiens with billing like on TV, "Mike Connors is Mannix." Montcalm might have a small chance at this, he got cast in a "speaking" role. He's not only playing Cotton Brady's spoiled little dog Petunia, he's also playing Petunia's great-great-great-whatever-grandmother! (I didn't want to tell them, but Montcalm's a boy dog. Gender blind casting, Heidi says!)

Today they shot Montcalm's first scene. I was there, I have to be, but I don't mind, it's really interesting, and I've always wanted to be on a movie set. But it's not in a sound studio like in MGM movies, where they close huge doors and signs say, "Quiet on the set!" It was outdoors in someone's back yard in St-Lambert.

I may not know anything about the movie business, but I can tell this scene is sinfully CORNY. It made me wonder what kind of major motion picture it's supposed to be, so I asked, and it's for Hallmark Hall of Fame next spring. I like Hallmark Hall of Fame, but not even the commercials that make me cry are this schmaltzy. It may get cut (too bad for Montcalm if it ends up on the cutting room floor, but it would be "a mercy killing," said one of the extras). I'll always remember it, though, it's glued to my mind.

It's the present. This little boy is sitting on his back porch, in the winter, in the freezing cold, at first I thought, poor little child-actor, but I changed my mind pretty quick about that.

He's singing, "Oh, They Built the Ship *Titanic*," the song we always sang in Girl Guides. And his grandfather comes out, played by this Montreal actor who specializes in grandpa parts, "the Geezer Specialist," somebody told me. And the grandpa says, "No, Sonny, no."(A modern-day child called Sonny? And I know it's set today, the kid is wearing Gap and Roots clothes). Gramps repeats himself. "No, Sonny. You should never sing that song!" and Sonny says, "What's wrong with Kerplunk, it sunk, cha-cha-cha, Gramps?" (Do they need any more proof they will have to cut this scene?) And the Grandad goes, "It's really a very sad story." And then he starts to tell him the story, but the camera pans to Sonny's dog, played by Montcalm, who's been outside frolicking in the snow. That's acting for him, he hates the cold. As Gramps-the-grandpa tells the kid the story of the victims, Montcalm starts telling the story of the Dogs of the *Titanic*, one of whom is his great-great-whatever-grandmother, who knew the brave Gamon de Pycombe, Dog of the *Titanic*. And then they're going to do a trick where the snowman Montcalm is sitting next to somehow turns into the iceberg that the *Titanic* hits. They did this corny scene over and over again, and it was so COLD.

The kid was sweet as tarte au sucre while they filmed the scene, and then he'd turn into Damien, the Bad Seed and Rosemary's Baby rolled into one as soon as it was over. Decker Fontaine must be the most horrible child on the planet. Yes, it was cold, but the whining and yelling he did! I wanted to say, "Hey, Decker! You got a day off school and you're making a ton of money! Behave!" The mother had no control, this kid made Montcalm look like an angel. But then the dog didn't have to do the same horrible scene over and over again, he stayed wrapped up in a blanket with one of the PA's cooing over him till right before they had to shoot him.

And how is Montcalm going to narrate this story? They're doing one of those *Look Who's Talking* things. Montcalm looks at the camera and a voice-over speaks for him, or the *her* that *he* is playing! I said, Who will they get? And they said, It might be Kate Nelligan or Margot

Kidder. Or Helena Bonham-Carter. But shouldn't all the dogs Montcalm is playing have American accents?

So that was Day One. We're going to have four more days, but not til next week.

Poor Heidi got fired from the Old Folks' Home! Here she is trying to be charitable, trying to be like Dorothy Day, helping the under-privileged in her free time. Trying to be a good person. And they fire her the first day because they don't like the way she reads? They had the same person reading to them for years and years. But she moved to Oakville, Ontario, and they'd prefer to wait for her to come back. "They have a hard time with change. And your book selection wasn't to their taste, I'm afraid," the Director told Heidi, who said she could read them another book, one they all agreed on. I blame the Director. She left the reading selection to Heidi because the people couldn't decide between the new Danielle Steele or an old Jack Higgins (seven women, three men). So Heidi chose a book they could relate to. A biography. Of Sir Edmund Hilary and Tenzing Norgay. I had to ask her who Norgay was. "His climbing companion, the Sherpa guide who got to the summit with him!" And then I remembered the bébé-là-là Lhasa apso dog at school was called Tenzing, it had been like an omen that Heidi would meet Miles Farnham en route to Everest! I told her she was interested in a book about Everest, but why did she think they'd like it? "It was an amazing achievement, they were all around in 1953,they must remember!" The old folks said it was cold enough already without being reminded of wind chill factors and ice and precipices. They said she was "too solemn," and one lady called her a little smarty-pants to her face. "This after she fell asleep almost as soon as I began reading!"

Heidi's pretty upset, it's pretty embarrassing to be fired from a volunteer job helping the needy. I know she feels blue about being let go because she chose a book that reminds her of someone far, far away. She even almost admitted it: "It's like some schoolgirl crush!" She will look through the Help Wanted (Social Services) pages when she has the heart to try again.

Ides of March! Ides of Tyler Garrow! We had a showdown, but I'm the one getting run out of town. He told us all about the "print ads campaign" he's cooking up. It would be me as Laura Secord in an almost-nothing-left-to-the-imagination bustier. "Wench-y Sizzle!" says Tyler. And the headlines will be "Oo-là-là, c'est Lulu!" and "Lulu's Back! And We've Got Her." Tyler was originally thinking something like, "And you thought her chocolates were tasty!" but he figured the Laura Secord people would get mad. I told him right out I won't let him use me like that, I want to help Festin, but this is too much!

"All that's missing is a whip!" I said.

"A whip? Yeah . . . "

"No whip, no pop-tarty blouse, nothing!" I told him.

Tyler said I've got to be into this, he needs me to be giving a hundred and fifty percent.

Gaëtan told him I always gave two hundred and fifty percent, and he had to agree with me, Tyler should forget all about le rough trade advertising campaign.

Tyler asked Gaëtan, Where does he think he's going to get more customers from, then? Word of mouth?

Gaëtan said, "That has helped, we're up by fifty-six percent."

"That can't last. We only got that figure the week Lenore brought in all those Cockney buskers. And your boyfriend's family."

Gaëtan said for Tyler to rethink the advertising scheme.

"Maybe we should rethink the whole entire thing, Gaëtan. Maybe try recasting for starters. If Lenore's not into it, Jocelyne would make a good Laura."

Gaëtan said, "Jocelyne can't sing." Then he had to leave us for a second, there was a fight in the kitchen. Chef Normand was fâché. Again.

"She can lip sync, can't she?" Tyler yelled over Chef Normand's cursing. "She's a washout right now as Fanny Fitzgibbon."

I had to defend Jocelyne. "That part makes no sense, Fanny Fitzgibbon has nothing to do with the story."

"Oh, little drama queen, you know everything, I guess?"

"No. But I do know that the Laura Secord show isn't working the way you want it to."

"You're right there. That's why we gotta do the sex kitten thing. One month? Let's try it and see."

"Not with me, not like that."

He said, "Then I'm sorry, sweetheart, I don't say I hit one out of the park every time I send one of my players up to bat. Sometimes I gotta make changes in the batting order. Or my game plan. Sometimes both. Do you get what I'm saying?"

That's when Mireille laughed and said his clichés were making her teeth ache. "Ça m'énerve!" And what kind of guy uses baseball jargon in the winter to explain a concept in a city obsessed with hockey?

"What did she say?" Tyler wanted to know.

"That you're losing us."

"You're losing me, huh? Well, you lose me, you lose your jobs. You got that? I am the hired gun here. I'm the one responsible for getting this restaurant back on track. And the only way I can do that is if you co-operate. Why don't you trust me? Huh? What's wrong with me? Come on, be honest. You first, Lenore."

And I was. Will I ever learn?

"Well, you came out of nowhere with these big ideas. You're like somebody Burt Lancaster plays in a movie. Some Elmer Gantry come here to promise us rain."

"Hey, I never promised you rain. Har-har."

"But you promised us more customers."

"And I'll deliver them to you if you give me a chance! I know what's keeping us back, I know what we gotta do!"

Just then Gaëtan returned and Tyler said, "I'm serious, Gaëtan. I say we gotta recast."

Gaëtan said Non, me as Laura Secord wasn't the problem.

"Yes, she is! We have to try some changes. Don't worry, I'll find another role for Lenore."

I was so hurt by all this, I've tried as Laura Secord, I know I have. All right, yes, so I don't believe it, but I have been doing my best. And Tyler was blaming the customers not liking it on me! And that's when it came out, I was sarcastic, I said, "He'd probably like it if I played Laura Secord's cow."

And Tyler said, "Laura Secord's cow . . . "

I was practically hysterical by then, and I yelled, "Yeah, sure, go ahead, put the cow in the show, too. Try all the changes you think will make a difference, but I'm not going to be here!"

"And where are you gonna go?" Tyler wanted to know.

"To Arizona. I am going to Arizona."

And I rushed into the kitchen, where Chef Normand was weeping. Gaëtan ran after me, begging me not to leave Festin. I was c'pas sérieux! Arizona? I couldn't be moving away!

I said of course not. But I had to take some time off. This is too much pressure for me. I need a break, at least a week off, and I have an offer to go to the States, and I'm going as soon as I can make travel plans and filming is complete for *Dog of the Titanic*. Gaëtan was really upset.

What about Festin without me for a whole week?

I said maybe it was me that was holding things back, not being into it. With me gone and somebody else as Laura Secord, they can see. Maybe I've never been open enough to this new approach. It could be all my fault Festin's not doing as well as it should.

"Mais tu reviens? Tu promets, pitoune?"

"Oui. If you want me to."

"Toujours, pitoune. Toujours!"

Heidi says it was too fitting that St. Patrick's Day is one of the days we're shooting the *Titanic* movie. Because so many Irish were in steerage and died. She and Daniel rented *A Night To Remember* for us last week, I had no idea it was that bad a disaster. The two of them are kind of possessed by this story because of what happened to the Irish. And the other immigrants on the ship.

"We have a Third Class mindset," Heidi admitted.

Some people on the set were wearing green, me included of course. And the dogs, too. We caught it from the Flynns. So today was finally the day we met Cotton Brady. The first thing she said was, "What's all the green for?" and I said for St. Patrick's Day. "Oh, is it today? I just got here yesterday. Someone said they painted the streets green?" Her last name is Brady, isn't that Irish? Maybe it's really American now because of The Bunch but I think Brady sounds pretty Irish, how can she not know how important today is? They say Cotton Brady is a space cadet, off in her own little world, probably very mad that Shirley Maclaine got onto the Other Lives bandwagon before she did. And she still lives in her *Salt and Pepper* glory days. I loved the show, but it *was* a sitcom. Cotton carries on like it was *Upstairs Downstairs* or *Roots*. I thought she was kidding at first.

"They keep asking me to revive it. But I said let it go, it was perfect the way it was. Let people remember that. You can't top it. You've got to move on."

I think she's between forty-five and seventy years old.

She loves Montcalm and he loves her. Maybe she'll take him with her! But this could be just one of those show-biz things, when people do a show together, they become like a weird family, but it's over when the show is over. What am I thinking? Reine would never let Montcalm go. But I would!

I am a little awestruck by Cotton, I can't help it, but I can't let on. She was a TV star on a show I never missed! Nobody else seems too impressed, they've seen it all before, washed up former stars who have to do movies-of-the-week here. But it's all new to me. I wonder if she's done *Fiona!* I should warn her if she hasn't been Fiona!ed yet.

Cotton doesn't pay any attention to Brioche, who is playing Frou-Frou, the tiny dog of a passenger named Helen Bishop. "Helen" only has a few lines so she's not played by anybody famous. Her name's Caitlin McGovern, she's done a lot of work around town, and I recognize her from the Pharmaprix commercial where she was the high-powered executive who couldn't find the decongestant. She did a really convincing job of being all stuffed up.

Caitlin saw how green I was and said, "Hey, up the British. Erin Go Bragh!" I told her I guessed her green was under her costume. "I'm not Irish!" she said proudly. (I expect everyone to be as insane about being Irish as the Flynns, but not on this set!) Caitlin McGovern is her latest professional name, she's actually Polish-Italian. Caitlin's done "what research I could" on her character, "but she's an elusive figure." She wasn't too satisfied when they cast Brioche as Frou-Frou because "she's not exactly to scale? Helen's dog was TINY, and Brioche here is not. She's a little butterball if you ask me."

Caitlin McGovern has decided she's not going to get too attached to Brioche. "Only two little dogs managed to escape because their owners carried them into the lifeboats. And Frou-Frou was not one of those survivors."

Show people are very strange. She thinks that because the dog Brioche is playing didn't make it, Brioche won't either. That we won't all go home after this is over. Wait a minute, if Frou-Frou didn't make it, Helen Bishop didn't, either!

"Oh, I did. But not my pooch. But then neither did Cotton Brady's *Dog of the Titanic*. Her character's all made up. Fiction! Nobody cares about accuracy. I've only got two days on this. I really did survive, but I don't get a lifeboat scene. All I do is promenade about the deck a lot carting this dog. I'm going to wind up with tendonitis, I know it, she's so heavy!"

Today was walking-around-the-ship day. They're doing what they call "tight frame shots" so they can use a real boat deck and not have to build one. So filming was down at the Old Port. They set up vans and trailers all over the place, and Cotton kept Montcalm in her trailer with her on St-Paul. I was stuck with Brioche because of Caitlin's not wanting to get too attached. I was with the extras — 3who are treated like steerage, one of them said. We got a box lunch that we had to eat in the parking lot. They finally let us go into a cantina to get warm. That's where I met Marguerite Vichy, the caterer. "You like what I put in the box?" And I told her Yes, it was incredibly fantastic. I wasn't lying, everybody said it was pretty phenomenal for a box lunch, for any kind of lunch on a set, actually. I shared these compliments with the chef and she said, "I know. I am the best!" She told me she's Swiss-Belgian-Greek, and she's a culinary wizard. "Then what's she doing schlepping food to us?" one of the extras said. I didn't ask, but Marguerite gave me her card. "I Am the Best!" The schlepping extra asked me why I wasn't in costume, and I said because I was there as a handler for two of the dogs of the *Titanic*. "You shouldn't be stuck here with us!" She said I deserved better, I was Special Business.

So I left the extras and was roaming around looking for where I was supposed to do my special business when I saw Diaspora and her handler. That huge take-up-a-lifeboat dog got cast. "Because she's so visually interesting," her owner Siobhan said. Then the man who owns an Airedale named Ralph who's playing the Astors' dog Kitty joined us. He said history says there were so many dogs on the *Titanic* that a dog show was planned for April fifteenth. I asked Siobhan were we going to have do that scene today? And Siobhan said, "*No.* The ship *sank* April fifteenth." They were both a little shocked by me not knowing this. It's not like they gave me a script! I'm just there to do their bidding.

Luckily it got more interesting, they did the first all-dogs-on-deck scene. Over and over again. They even had Montcalm run down the deck as Cotton Brady gets a close-up calling: "Petuniaaaaa, come back here! Oh, Petunia. You naughty girl! I don't want anything to happen to you!" Which is what they call foreshadowing and irony at the same time. The next line is by Helen Bishop: "Darling, this is the safest ship on the sea."

Caitlin McGovern had to say this line about thirty times, each time a different way because Cotton didn't like her "tone." It was: too sniffy, too know-it-all, too snide, too put-down-ish, too sarcastic, and too insincere. I think they're going to cut it in the end. Cotton was not happy with the final results, she told me.

"You could see, she was putting me down. Telling me I was stupid to let my dog run off like that. My precious puppy doggie jumped out of my arms, what was I to do? I don't like that Casey girl. And she's too tall."

Cotton is too short is the problem.

And we got to see the other star of the movie today, too, Bruiser Baddeck, a French bulldog from Nova Scotia who portrays champion Gamon de Pycombe.

He's really ugly. I don't think he'll get a lot of close-ups.

My last day of filming. And I got to be in the movie!

Cotton likes me so much she wanted to do something for me. "Name it, name it! I *love* you. You have been so sweet. I could not have gotten through this week without you! What can I get for you?"

I wanted to say, A signed 8x10 of the original cast of *Salt and Pepper* would be great. But all I said was — I have been on a movie set for a week now — "Working with you was enough!"

And she said it again, "You are so sweet. I wish you could work with me forever! I will miss you soooo much! And Monty, oh, I'm going to miss Monty most of all."

Yes, she calls him Monty after Montgomery Clift. As long as it's not Monty for General Montgomery of the British Allies, Reine would never forgive me letting Montcalm get a nickname from him.

"You wanna be in my movie? Of course you do, call Jean-François for me, Lenny. Get him in here."

I told her I didn't want to be in the movie.

"Of course you do. Everybody wants to be in the movies. You're not playing shy with me. I owe you, doll. You won't call him? I'll do it myself."

And then she opened her trailer door and screamed, "Jean-François, get your butt in here, see voo play!"

J-F didn't show up but Jean-Luc, the other assistant director, did. And Cotton told J-L to tell the director they had to talk or she wasn't coming out of her trailer. And today was the Big Scene.

The director came in and fell all over her, even though I don't think he likes her, really likes her. At all, at all. It was so hypocritical and disgusting, I don't think even the Queen or the Pope would get that much fawning from people who can't stand them.

"Is there a problem, Cotton?"

"Yes. A teeny tiny one."

"Not your dog, babe?"

"Oh no, she's perfect. No, Miller, it's just that something's missing in this movie."

"And what's that?" Miller was getting anxious.

"This darling person. This jewel of a girl. My bijou! She has to be in the movie. Look at that face, it belongs on film. Think how sympathetic it'll look gazing back as a survivor in the lifeboat!"

"But babe, the lifeboats are full. Not everybody got to survive, remember?"

"I know. But I want her to. She deserves to live. It's my reward for her being such a magnificent handler. I've never worked with anyone as good as she is."

"All right. Sure. She can be in a lifeboat."

Cotton gave Miller a big kiss. A real smacker.

"Thank you, Miller. So waddaya say, Lenny?"

And that's when I heard myself say, "I want to be a Third Class passenger." I've heard enough from Heidi and Daniel, I knew I had to do my bit to make more of their people survive.

There was a little silence, then the director said:

"Sure, fine. It'll work, you have a working class face. You can play Cotton's maid."

I said, "But the Third Class weren't the servants."

And Cotton said that's for sure. And they never "established" her lady's maid so we can't suddenly do this. And when we're in the lifeboat together Lenny will have to attend to me and won't that draw focus? "We've never seen her before and suddenly I have a maid? I think not!"

They agree they'll put me in another lifeboat. But they'll have to hide all my hair, although the colour will help me pass for an Irish immigrant. But it's not really his concern any more, he'll call in one of the countless assistant directors (J-F, J-L, J-C), they deal with the extras.

I'm bumped from Special Business way down to extra. And they get me into costume, which is a flannel nightgown with a long black coat over it, and they stuff all my hair up and under the ugliest hat I have ever seen. When I'm ready, a day-job actress asks me am I UDA or ACTRA. "Yes," I lie. She was impressed and confused. "You're both? What are they giving you? Day extra? Special Business?" I told her I wasn't sure, I hadn't signed my contract yet.

When we got on set, I saw that Caitlin was there, too. She'd convinced somebody that her character needed more development and deserved to be in the fateful final hours scenes. Luckily I had brought Brioche to the set today, she could use her. She thought it was "hilarious!" that Cotton got me into the movie. She wanted to know about permits and what kind of contract did I get? I told her I was doing this because it was fun.

"No, you don't! 'Don't thank me, pay me.' You don't do this for FREE."

I told her I was being paid pretty well as a handler.

"So, because people think what we do is fun, we don't deserve to be paid?"

I told her I'd get paid for this. Cotton hadn't discussed which category.

Caitlin figured I'd be SOC extra — Silent on Camera. The second I was asked to do anything more than stand there, I would become Special Business Extra. I told her I was getting into a lifeboat. "Special Business." She said her best gig was the time she was on call, got to the set, they ran so late it went into triple overtime and then triple time-and-a-half. She made $4500 for two minutes of work — when she finally got to do it. But poor un-unionized me, she said, even if I get paid by the hour for this extra business, I'll still only make the same rate.

I told her I couldn't go into overtime anyway. I had to be at my real work by six-thirty.

"You can't just leave the set!"

I said I sure could, and I would the minute we hit six p.m. What could they do to me?

"Nothing. You're right. It's not like they can fine you."

The scene took five and half hours, it was so strange. It wasn't even on the ship this time, it was a big fake set in a sound studio near Habitat '67. There was the lifeboat but no water. They were shooting against a blue screen like they used to make E.T. fly.

J-F lined us up on deck and told us what to feel: we were cold and woken from a deep sleep. And we knew there wasn't enough room for all of us. And all the pieces of plexiglass playing ice fell on deck when we hit the iceberg. That's when Miller, the director, took over because some people had lines, and acting was going to be involved.

He grabbed a guy who had been an SOC extra like me and told him, "Kiss her like you're never going to see her again." And the her he meant was me. And before I can say, "Hey, wait a minute!" the guy grabs me and says, "O! Molly, Molly, me darlin'." The director says, "Not that loud. You're only background stuff, little no-name, remember?"

By the time we get to shoot the scene the first time, everyone's been given some "bit of business" to make the scene "live!" The man who will never see Molly, Molly again kisses me goodbye on the cheek.

The director stops the movie, yells, "Plant one on the lips! The lips! What was that supposed to be?" The man says, "A choice. I didn't want to be obvious. And I have a really bad cold, I don't want her to get it."

The director grabs another SOC, a woman, and says to me that she's my best friend, and after he kisses me on the cheek goodbye, I'm to hug her goodbye. Like I'm never going to see her again.

"Neither of them is getting into the lifeboat with me?"

"No!" the director snarls.

"But if he's my boyfriend? And she's my best friend — "

The girl explains: "He's your brother. I've always been in love with him. Being in steerage made me realize that. We won't leave each other."

The director likes this, says he'll go for it. Now, for me to get hugged, hug and get into the lifeboat, next to Helen Bishop and Frou-Frou. (Yes, so Brioche and I share screen time, and Frou-Frou gets to live after all. So much for Caitlin's actual research.)

I feel badly leaving the other SOCs behind, but the girl says, "It's okay. We were never supposed to survive anyway."

And Caitlin McGovern, the Human Cash Register, says, "And you've just upped them to Special Business."

But I don't care if they found love in steerage and won't leave each other, there weren't more than twenty people in our lifeboat, there was lots of room for them. But they had to stay silent on camera, they couldn't say, "There's got to be room for two more!" They just waved goodbye, no questions asked. "Put up and shut up" is what it's called, according to Caitlin McGovern.

I felt like I had to speak up, what would Heidi and Daniel have done in my situation? As they were lifting the lifeboat down, I wanted to yell. "Jump in! Save yourselves! There's lots of room in this lifeboat!"

But I didn't, because Caitlin said the extras didn't mind, and I knew I was there at the demand of Cotton Brady, and I didn't want her to get a reputation for being difficult.

Caitlin told me that Miller, the director, wasn't supposed to give any direction to the extras, that's what he has J-F, J-L and J-C, the

ADs, for. The minute a director gives extras direction, they become actors.

"And then they get paid way more?"

"You said it. And he had no right to be verbally abusive, he could be reported for that."

"But you won't report him, will you?"

"No. I'd never report Miller for that." Her smile made me realize how Helen Bishop's part lasted more than two days.

They'd done my scene by five-thirty, but the expanded role of Helen Bishop meant Brioche had another day's shooting. Helen was going to get a scene on the rescue ship *Carpathia*. Cotton would spy her and say, "Safest ship on the seas, huh?" And after that "Cow gets her come-uppance" scene, Cotton has three more days of principal photography with Montcalm. They sprung this on me, and me heading to Arizona on Monday! Cotton was very upset I was leaving, she'd only been told fifty times. "Oh, but you can't. You can't leave me, Lenny. Oh doll, no, please. Stop that trip. The cancellation insurance is on me. You're the only person on this ship I trust." She thinks everything said in French is a slight against her. And I have to keep translating to reassure her she's never mentioned. I'd be a very wealthy handler if I got Special Business pay every time I calmed her down after one of her, "WHAT? What did they say?" tantrums. She's so insecure for a TV Legend.

Heidi agreed to watch the dogs for me while I was away, with my permission/blessing to put them into a kennel if they went too far. I know this shouldn't mean she's responsible for getting them to the set, too. Lucky for me, she said some bad news might be good news, she was calling in Daniel.

The dozen free Vienna rolls weren't enough to silence that lady in the bagel shop. She'd gone to the mayor's office and complained. She told them that Daniel took equipment her tax dollars paid for without permission, thereby disabling a fire truck, what if it had been called to a fire right then? When he was busy hacking away an ice castle in the freezer? She convinced the people at City Hall that the deed deserved a disciplinary measure, so Daniel's been suspended without pay for a week.

Heidi knows he'd love to visit a movie set and is sure he'll do a great job being a handler. And if Cotton loves him as much as she loves me, maybe more Third Class passengers will survive!

It's kind of weird that someone being so petty has worked out so well for all of us.

WOOF!WOOF!WOOF!WOOF!WOOF!WOOF!WOWOOF!WOOF!WOOF!WOOF!WOOF!

This is to let you know that

Briache and Moncalm

are invited to a
BOW WOW-thday PARTY for
MISS JEZEBEL
on Saturday, March 28th
from 2 paw-m til 5 o'bark.

R.S.V. Paw!
Miss Jezebel

WOOF!WOOF!WOOF!WOOF!WOOF!WOOF!WOWOOF!WOOF!WOOF!WOOF!WOOF!

Here's to the Canine Class of '92! Hope your two can make it. I hope they don't mind being on the same invitation. I sent it to your house because that's the only address the Wolfes had for you. They told me Briache and Moncalm are in the *Titanic* movie? Good for them. Tamara said they loved Jezebel but were afraid she was just "too Disney." Tell me if you saw any dalmatians on that set. And if any animals were harmed during the making of that motion picture.

Faye

4

I leave tomorrow. What was I thinking? Yes, so I've had a few fun and friendly conversations with Wyatt on the phone, and we had a good time backstage in the pinky Green Room and on *Fiona!* And yes, okay, so I've never been there, and Arizona's supposed to be incredibly scenic and beautiful, despite "the glaring omission of *not* recognizing Martin Luther King Day," says Heidi.

And yes, I need to get away, I'll have a week away from Tyler Garrow's schemes and les chiens. And Cotton Brady! That was such a weird phone call last night. She must have been really drunk. Jamie thinks I should consider her offer. "How many people get offered a life in Pasadena? Are you CRAZY saying NO?" I would be crazy to say yes. What kind of life would it be, personal assistant to someone that desperate, full of herself and neurotic? Jamie says he read in *Premiere* magazine that some movie Cotton made almost two years ago is still in the can and not released because the studio's in financial trouble. "She's supposed to be absolutely amazing in it. Another Cloris Leachman in *The Last Picture Show*. She'll probably win an Oscar." I said I hope so because if she doesn't get a really big Ego Boost, she's going to kill herself. Or everyone round her will die of boredom listening to her. We've all heard about *Night of Plenty*. "Yes, that's the title! It's gonna be big! And you'll be there for the ride!" Too bad Jamie wasn't the handler for Montcalm et Brioche, his California Dreamin' could be a reality now. I never even considered it. Despite how miserable I am. And insane enough to escape to Arizona. I could have lied to Tyler, pretended I went to Arizona. And done what?

Stayed home? Hidden out? No, it's good for me to do this, but I must be NUTS. If I hadn't done it at such short notice, in anger or whatever it was, I might have picked a time when Heidi could come, too. Instead of travelling all by my lonesome, as Wyatt would say. I guess it's his *Wagon Train* look-alike-ness that makes me feel safe. And I deserve an adventure, Heidi says. And it is a return open ticket. ONCE I FIND A WAY BACK TO THE AIRPORT! How far away from Phoenix is Flint Rock Creek, anyway? Maybe I'd have to escape across a desert! I think Death Valley is somewhere near there.

I better sleep now. I'm gonna have to deal with a time change when I get there. Or THAR, as Wyatt would say, darlin'.

Five a.m. their time. Seven a.m. mine. I am ahead of them. This is all way too much. The ranch is way bigger than it looks in the picture. And it's not near Phoenix. "Heck, nowheres near, the closest big town to us is Flagstaff," Wyatt told me as we drove and drove past all kinds of cactus trees to get here. And it's so dry, but he's got this huge swimming pool. Outdoors. And horses. And cattle. And Catcher, his friendly ranch dog. (I was afraid I might have a thing against dogs, but we took to each other.) This place has everything I could possibly imagine, everything. Wyatt has trophy animals on every wall, and they're all BIG animals, shot on safari. And a room that's all leopard-and-zebra-upholstered furniture. You almost expect to see Elvis sitting there, shooting out the TV.

My huge room in the bunkhouse with a queen-size bed and a Jacuzzi is pretty amazing. So was the barbecue, held in the banquet hall, where I met "the kids." Ginny twenty-eight, Jack thirty-four, and the twins, Dulcy and Wyatt Jr., both thirty-six years old. Maybe it was me but I thought I saw the kids shooting weird looks at each other, like I wasn't what they expected, I don't know. Three of them are married, Wyatt Jr. isn't. He is going through a bad patch, a real messy divorce, so he ain't lookin', Wyatt Sr. assured me right away. This must be Wyatt's way of letting me off the hook and keep me from thinking Wyatt Jr.'s broken heart is the real reason I've been invited. His thirty-four-year-old son Jack came with not only a wife but a young girl I thought could be their daughter or the nanny. But she sure isn't!

Wyatt wanted to know what I thought of that little gal Jack and the wife had brung. What could I say, I didn't know what to think.

"You ever heard of one of them surrogates?"

"Yes. I watch TV talk shows."

"She's gonna be the mama of Jack's baby. Tomorrow she's being inseminated."

Wyatt's real upset. This little gal isn't even from Arizona! She read about their special need on a computer hotline or somewheres. She's from New York state, for golly sake. They figure it'll take because she's done this same service for another couple. Twice.

"Had two babies for them. Had a baby girl, then a year later gave them a baby boy. She won't take much money for it, either. Says it's God's work, she likes helping people."

We talked till midnight about this.

"And what if that little Frankenstein they come up with is a boy? Wyatt the Third's outta a test tube?"

"If there was gonna be a Wyatt the Third, wouldn't it be Wyatt the Second's son, if he has one?"

"No, that boy is useless. Been married three times. No kids. Yet. He is my heartbreak, I'm tellin' you. I got all these little darlin' granddaughters, thanks to Ginny and Dulcy. And I'm darn content with that. But no, that ain't enough for some people, Jack says someone's got to carry on the Bardo name. His sisters can't, even though they came up with all these progeny!"

"Jack and his wife must really want a baby to be going through this, eh?"

"Course if that sweet-faced Amy he's married to had any spine she'd say No, Jack. No way. But no, it's what Jack wants, don't you see? Nobody asked me what I think. They're living under my hacienda roof, nobody asked me!"

He finally figured I must be getting sleepy. "That darn time change'll do it to ya." Time for us all to turn in. Tomorrow (today) he'll show me around the ranch and local sights, then later this week we'll go explorin'. The Grand Canyon and all that.

But then I had to have a little heart-to-heart with Amber the Mama-to-Be because the walls in this here bunkhouse aren't that thick, her TV was so loud I had to knock on her door to ask her to turn it down. She was surprised to see it was me standing there.

"Oh, hi. I thought it would be Amy."

She figured Amy would have some last-minute instructions. Or maybe she'd be there to ask her to change her mind.

"It happened last time. Then the father found out and he made her see sense. She told me after she was really glad he did because she got her babies. I thought maybe Amy would get cold feet, too. Wanna come in?"

And, instead of saying No thanks, I said Okay. For just a minute.

Amber wanted to show me something because she could tell the grandfather-to-be wasn't too sure about all this. "I'm what you call intuitionative. Mr. Bard's got no idea what beautiful babies I make for people. He won't even look at my photo album."

She had all kinds of pictures of her surrogate baby girl and boy. And Wyatt was right, she's not in it for the money. "I can have babies. It's easy for me. I like helping people."

She works in an Ames Department Store in Champlain, New York.

"You ever been there?"

"Nope."

"It's before Plattsburgh. You said you were from Montreal."

"Yes. But I've never been to your Ames store."

"You should. We have some amazing sales. You and me sure came pretty far to be here, huh? That's so cool how you and Mr. Bardo met. On *Fiona!*. He made us all watch you guys together on the show in the screening room before you got here. You must have been so shocked, a mass murderess is your landlady."

"My next door neighbour."

"Yeah. She poisoned six people and made you help her!"

"I watered her garden."

"She tricked you. Right. You said so on *Fiona!*."

She said she knows how I feel being a celebrity. "They all know me. My customers? About how I like having babies for people. I'm kind of famous for it."

She could never do this for people she knows, "like in Champlain?" because then she'd see her babies. And that might be hard. "You know, passing them on the street? Or knowing what school they're in?"

Anyway, unless Amy made a moonlight visit after me, they're all checking into Phoenix tomorrow. Today. Because it's Amber's "time."

A part of me, my spirit I guess, wants to find Amy, bump into her somehow and find out how SHE feels about this. But they don't have their TV on too loud, so I have no reason to knock on their door to shoot the breeze. And they're in another part of the ranch, anyway. I don't have to share my big bathroom, so there's no chance of bumping into Amy in the line-up for the showers. There's nothing I can do. Que sera sera. And Amy's a big girl, if she doesn't want them to go through with this, she's the one who has to say so. Not me.

I got to see the entire ranch today, and some of the neighbourhood. Local spots. Way more than I wanted to see.

Wyatt had to drive us over to one of the neighbours, twelve miles away! He said he knew I was too polite to ask, but he had a hunch I was hankering to see it: the reason why he got invited to be on *Fiona!*

It was the homestead of that family who were killed. There was nobody home (well no, not anymore), and Wyatt made us walk around the house, all the time telling me the grisly story of the Feud, pointing out where this body was found and the other one. Then he said for me to climb on up here, on this here rock and look inside. And he had me peering in their window at what was once their living room.

"That's where most of it all happened. They cleaned it up some . . . oh, Lenny, sugar, is this too much for you?"

And I told him yes, but it had been very interesting. Thank you for showing me. (Very Canadian, thanking someone for taking me to a murder site against my better judgement.) On our way back to his place I had to ask him WHY he went on *Fiona!*

"When I'm so rich? And I got the world by the tail?"

"Yeah. Why would you need to be on TV?"

"'Course I'm just a businessman, a very good businessman. Yep, I have made a lotta money, but who ever heard of me outside of Flagstaff? I like an adventure. And look how good it ended up, I got to meet you. And now you're here visiting with us! I made the right decision, going on that show! Hey, wanna see it again, on the big screen?"

He wasn't telling a whopper, he does have a big screening room. It's very impressive, he didn't want me to get too tempted because he knew I'd want to spend too much time in there. He's got every episode of *Ironside* there ever was!

"So when you suggested to the *Fiona!* people that they get that cast together again, I was amazed. I sure thought you were some special gal!"

I'd love to see some of *Ironside* again, but not all of it. Especially when there was so much Grand Canyon to see. (Maybe he'll loan me some episodes to take home? Or make me "*Ironside*: The Illegal Copies Collection" as a going away present?)

And all of this was before lunch. (Barbecue again. Bar-B-Barn will never be the same! Then he took us for that "little drive" to the Grand Canyon! It's just too beautiful. Too vast, too big, too grand. One great big wonderful panorama. And I am so happy we stayed for the sunset.

Wyatt says people stay *in* the Grand Canyon, at a hotel in the bottom of it, they get there by riding mules down the cliff.

"Don't that sound like fun to you?"

I told him Yes, it sure did.

"That wouldn't scare you off? 'Cause one side of you's got one heck of a drop."

I figure the mules know their way down.

"You trust animals, do you?"

I said not all animals. But I trust mules because they're like donkeys. And I'd ride one of them into the Grand Canyon.

I had to ask him where they filmed *Thelma and Louise*.

"What's that, darlin'?"

I had to tell him it was a movie.

"Those gals come to the Grand Canyon?"

"They drove their Thunderbird across it. Or into it."

"Be one helluva drop. They'd never survive. What kinda movie was that, anyway?"

Wyatt would pass Heidi's *Thelma and Louise* Acid Test. He wasn't threatened by it at all when I told him the plot. One of these days I'll have to ask him how he feels about Martin Luther King.

And then when we got back to the ranch, dinner was prepared for just us. The "kids" weren't there this time. We didn't mention it, but we know Jack and the Mrs. and Amber-little-mama-to-be are in Phoenix for "the deed."

But someone was there tonight who wasn't yesterday: Darla, the housekeeper. She's been away visiting her sister in New Mexico. She's beautiful, I think she sort of looks like Ann-Margret if she hadn't gone into show business and had black hair. She's about Wyatt's age.

Darla didn't even try to pretend she wasn't looking at me strangely. Wyatt told her off in a friendly way. "Hey, Darla, you seen her before, when I showed you us together on *Fiona!*" Darla nodded solemnly and left the dining room, gliding out like she didn't have any feet.

I was tempted when we finished eating and Wyatt suggested we go to the screening room to catch up on some *Ironside*. But Darla showed up again with another invitation.

"Before *Ironside*, perhaps you would like some tequila shooters in the Sunflower Room?"

We hadn't even said yes or no when Darla opened the huge dining room doors that led into that great big bright flowery womanly room. The only one in the entire place not decorated with antlers.

"You did not see this yet, I think?"

And I knew why! In the centre of it, over a fireplace with the fire going (Darla planned this) was an enormous portrait.

"That is Virginia. Mrs. Bardo."

"It sure as hell is. Wasn't she a knockout?" Wyatt said. "A-course this was done in her younger days. Gawd, I miss her."

I can't say she was a knockout because it would mean I AM ONE, TOO. Now I know why he was looking at me all moon-faced from the moment he saw me. I look like her!

I always thought Wyatt was a Family Man because he seemed so married. And whenever he talked about how they all wanted to meet me, I thought that included a wife. When I got here and never met her, I figured he might be divorced. Or that she was away. Until Dulcy said that her mother had passed away five years ago. And Wyatt told me what Jack was planning would have killed his Mama if she weren't dead already.

And now here she was. In great-big-portrait-over-the-fireplace colour.

"Done when she was about your age, I reckon."

Then he gave me that sad smile. And my plane doesn't leave til Sunday afternoon.

Dearest Heidi,

When you get this you will know what happened! But for now here are —

⟳ *Greetings from the Graceland Wedding Chapel* ⟳

It was Fate! Wyatt and me finally wound up here this morning after a whirlwind of a tour of Death Valley and Oatman, a Ghost Town on Route 66, where he swept me off to a honeymoon suite. You'll know more when I see you before this does. I just had to send it as a reminder of a historic occasion.

Lenore Rutland

I'm keeping my maiden name!

Well, it was sure some adventure! Wyatt took me on quite a road trip after I saw the portrait of the first Mrs. Wyatt Bardo.

I know I did all I could not to look my best. No makeup. Nothing. I let my hair blow to rat-tails. I didn't care if I looked messy in my vacation snapshots, I'd sacrifice standing tangled in front of the scenery just so Wyatt wouldn't think of me as Virginia II, the Reincarnation, but I'd still get to see the sights.

So I sat on a bench at Zabriskie Point overlooking Death Valley. When Wyatt suggested we try walking a little I never thought it could mean I might meet Death in the Valley. Or I would have said no, I'll wait in the Jeep, you go for a little stroll in the desert. But somehow there I was, walking ahead of Wyatt, dodging cactus plants, when out of nowhere he fired his gun. I really thought for one second he had fired at me. But it was for me. Wyatt had spied a rattlesnake lying there in waiting. He's going to get it stuffed or turned into a "pocketbook" for me, he's insisting. At first I thought, Oh, Wyatt saved my life. And then I realized he did it on purpose, put me in danger to show off. What if he'd been too late and I wound up with a rattlesnake bite? And he had to do that St. John's Ambulance rescue thing I saw on *The Rifleman* and every other cowboy show? Where someone cuts a cross into your leg with a pen-knife and sucks the poisoned blood out? That would be some vacation story, eh?

Then he drove us along Route 66 to Oatman, the ghost town named after the Oatman Sisters, captured by Indians. When they got returned to the white people years later, what did one of them do but become famous by writing a book saying the Indians were mean to her. Now their town has souvenir stores and burros that walk around free.

Wyatt said we had to make a visit to the hotel, which isn't really operating, it's a museum. He swept me up all of a sudden. "To visit this room, you gotta be carried to the threshold!" He couldn't carry me over it, there's a cord across the door because the room is historical. It was the honeymoon suite of Carole Lombard and Clark Gable. When it wasn't as rustic and dusty as it is now.

Wyatt says that Clark and Carole ran off to get married in secret, and the tradition is for people to throw coins on the bed, for luck. So we had to. He handed me a Susan B. Anthony dollar. And I thought, How far have I fallen? From Susan's house to being the sidekick of this Macho Macho Man. Throwing money on a bed.

I threw my coin and Wyatt threw his JFK fifty-cent piece. My money bounced off the bed but his stayed. I asked him, "Does that mean anything?"

"If the money don't bounce off, you get your wish!"

He gave me that big sad smile and asked me were there any more stores I wanted to buy out before we went? Just because I'd bought all those earrings made of porcupine quills from a gorgeous native guy dressed like an Indian in the movies or one of the Village People without the headdress. Wyatt took my picture with him. I didn't know Native Americans could be that touristy.

Wyatt said for best visual effect we'd better get to our next major destination *after* dark. The lights of Las Vegas. We had big swanky separate rooms, but what were we gonna do with our evening, he said. Wyatt doesn't gamble: "I never succumbed to that vice."

Wyatt offered to stake me if I wanted to go to the gambling tables or play the slots. He was over the moon when I said even though I was able to make a big down payment on my duplex with Loto Québec winnings, I didn't gamble anymore. He was falling more and more in love with me all the time! I told him I wouldn't mind looking. So that's what we did for an hour, I didn't see very many happy people. Even the people who won didn't smile much.

Wyatt noticed I seemed to have some deep-down resentment of gamblers. And that's when I had a little nervous breakdown, I guess, because I started ranting and telling him all about Fergie. I know I threatened Fergie off, and I'm not in love with him anymore, but I guess I'm not over how badly he hurt me. I should have gone to Partners of Gamblers Anonymous or whatever encounter group there is for people like me who suffered at the hands of the unscrupulous. Wyatt was so sympathetic and hurt for me. And then I got to the last thing Fergie did —

"He put your house on the gambling table as collateral?"

"Yes. When he was in Vegas!"

That was when I finally realized we could run into Fergie here! He might be gambling right now at any one of these palaces. And after over a year I didn't want to see him again! I'm still so mad at him. If we found Fergie here, I knew there'd be a scene, Wyatt had a gun and he'd avenge my honour. There might have been a shoot-out at Caesar's Palace. Boy, the Aislin cartoon I'd get then! So I told Wyatt I was done looking at the gamblers.

"Can we get away from all of them?"

"That's near to impossible, little gal! We're in Vegas. But, hey, who do you like more, Debbie Reynolds or Steve and Edye?"

I said Debbie Reynolds.

So that's whose Vegas show we went to see! I've always loved her, she's so talented and such a fighter. She had those two really bad marriages. First Eddie Fisher running around on her with Elizabeth Taylor, and then marrying that multi-millionaire shoe-salesman gambler who lost all her money. But Debbie's still up there entertaining people, making us forget our problems! We had such a terrific time, and somehow Wyatt had sent a note backstage asking her to sing a special song for the gal from Canada.

I could hardly believe it when she looked out over the audience and said, "It's a French song I got to do in one of my films. Sing along, everybody. You may remember it, from *The Singing Nun*." And Debbie Reynolds sang "Dom-i-nique-nique-nique" especially for me.

Who couldn't like a man who was this kind and considerate? I've never met a man who was so good to me. Except for my dad.

Then the next morning he took me to the Graceland Wedding Chapel. I really thought it was to tour it. And this Elvis impersonator, the same guy who married Bette Midler to her husband, came down the aisle and asked, "Are you two ready to say 'Love Me Tender'? Exchange *I Do, I Do*'s?"

"I'm willin' if she is," Wyatt said. And he gave me that smile and I knew he meant it!

"You want me to marry you? Here?"

"Yes, I do. You would make me the happiest man in all the world."

That was the first time in my life somebody asked me to marry him. And the first time I got to say thanks, but no. Not today.

The King left the room and we left the building.

Wyatt apologized for asking so sudden. But he thought he should carpe diem.

"We was right here, and I thought, Ask her now, you'll be a fool if you don't! It came over me, Lenny. I'm sorry."

Of course I told him I was flattered. But maybe we should just get the hell out of Vegas. As soon as I did some postcards.

"You don't mind missing the Liberace Museum?"

"No. I've had enough glitter for now." The razzmatazz of Liberace after all this would have done me in, I know it.

So Wyatt drove us all the way back to the ranch. And we were able to talk the entire way. If I had tried to surprise someone into marrying me and he said no, I would be speechless, I'd feel so bad. But Wyatt wasn't. He didn't have any resentment at all because he didn't really realize why I said no. He said he couldn't blame me, I deserve a big wedding. With a whole bunch of bridesmaids. In my own hometown, Montreal. At one of them cathedrals or basilicas? (Notre Dame? St. Joseph's Oratory? Our Lady Queen of the World? Saint Patrick's? No way, neither of us is Catholic. Christ Church Cathedral, maybe . . . what was I thinking? No!) If only I would accept his proposal, sorry he sprung it on me like that, he promised he would make me so happy. And we'd have a great big honeymoon in Europe.

"You ever been to Venice? Italy?"

Until this year, I've never been to much of anywhere.

"We'd go away for months and months, like people used to do, go "on the Continent." That should appeal to a gal from a cosmopolitan city! I'd take you to the House of Chanel and you'd get some of their gowns. And when we came back home, you could decorate our ranch any way you like. I know women ain't too fond of how Ernest Hemingway it is, that's who Dulcy's always telling me must have decorated my place. So you could change that. Put pictures up from Canada. Hockey players. The Rockies. Paintings by that Bateman guy who does animals in the snow. Make it a little bit of Canada in the middle of the desert. Chalet Lenore. And you wouldn't need to miss your friends, we'd fly them down whenever they wanted to visit. I'd even get them jobs and green cards if you wanted them around a lot."

What a proposal!

"And we got so much in common. More and more every day. It ain't because I'm way older than you, is it? And I got kids your age? I was real young when I fathered them."

"Wyatt, I'm not in love with you."

"Yet. But you like me, don't you? You like all the things I could give you?"

And who couldn't admit to all that.

"It ain't my grammar, is it? People are always surprised I never did nothing about it when I got so much money. But I wouldn't be me if I talked any other way. I'd never run off and leave you, Lenny. Or put your house on the gambling table, or leave you with stacks of bills like that Fergie did. I'd take care of you so good, you'd never want for nothing ever again."

On and on it went like this, all the way home. And I know I could live the high life if I married Wyatt. I'd have a big ranch, four grown-up kids, grandchildren, at least one of them a surrogate, a screening room full of *Ironside*, I'd get to ride down into the Grand Canyon on a mule, there'd be a honeymoon in Europe, I'd have fabulous wealth to give to charities, I wouldn't have to shovel snow or get the car going in forty below weather ever again. I would never have to worry about Quebec politics or people like Tyler making changes to my place of business, I'd never have to take care of those yappy awful dogs, but — I don't love him. And he's longing to marry me because I look like his dead wife. That's it. And yeah, okay, so maybe he can find a lot of things we have in common. And I'd be the Miss Ellie or Sue-Ellen matriarch of a vast, rich dysfunctional ranch family, but —

"It ain't because Jack's taken on a surrogate to bear his child, is it?"

And I said No.

"What could I do to make you wanna marry me? Name it."

I couldn't say: Be someone I'm madly in love with. Be someone I can't live without. So I told him, Nothing.

It was a long drive; he kept trying to convince me.

"Heck. Just for fun's sake, what could I do with my money that would make you happy?"

And that's when I popped the question.

"Could you use it to make Arizona celebrate Martin Luther King Day?"

He looked at me and then said, "Is that what it would take?" And for a second I imagined what could happen if I said Yes. But I was selfish and instead said, "No. But it sure would make me like you even more."

When we got back to the ranch, Darla stared straight at my left hand. She knew what Wyatt might get up to on his road trip. She wanted to see if I had a new wedding ring. Or an engagement rock. When she saw nothing I thought I heard her gasp in relief.

That night I asked if I could talk to Darla privately. Wyatt must have thought it could mean I was considering his offer, that I was going to see what it would be like to be the mistress of his estate. So he said, "Sure thing, little gal. You two get the Sunflower Room all to yourselves." And that's how we had our Virginia II to Virginia II chat.

We sat under her portrait. Now, if we were in that *Rebecca* movie that Vermont ETV shows over and over, Darla would have used that chance to tell me how I was a nobody and nothing like the first Mrs. Bardo. And then she'd burn the house down and go up in flames with it. But the housekeeper in that movie was in love with Mrs. DeWinter, not Mister.

I told her right out I wasn't going to marry Wyatt.

She got real defensive. "He's not handsome or kind or generous enough for you? He's only fifty-six, don't say you think he's too old for you."

And I said, Wyatt's not in love with me, he's in love with her. The dead wife in the portrait.

"But you look so like her. And you would make him so happy. He's been so lonely. He's a marvellous man!"

I said, Yes but he's looking for a replica of his first wife. He wants Virginia II. Someone who can accept that would be very happy here.

"But not you?" she said, sneering and sad at the same time.

"No. But how about you?"

She didn't say anything. So I did. Right out.

"You're in love with him, Darla. You could make each other very happy."

She tried to lie, say I was all wrong.

I told her she could look like that portrait if she wanted Wyatt badly enough. She could transform herself into a reasonable facsimile. I seemed possessed by some character Joan Collins would play, only I was doing it for a good cause. I advised Darla she could start small, a rinse for her hair, work up to Virginia's colour, then her style, get hair extensions till it grew that long itself. Once she becomes the second Mrs. Bardo, "And you will, believe me" — Alexis Carrington again! — she can start changing back or at least being more what will make her happy.

Luckily I only became a Feminist last year or I would have felt really guilty about doing this.

I could leave there with a good conscience. Wyatt's not getting me for a wife, but he's going to get someone way better — someone who truly loves him if she plays her Virginia II cards right.

Lenny!

Here's my address in Champlain. And there's only one Ames there, so I'm not hard to find. Sometimes I'm in Customer Service or Layaway but I'm mostly on the cash. Come by if you want to see me in my gestation period. I have one of my intuitionative feelings it took. I can't wait! Jack and Amy are going to come to New York when the baby's born. Maybe we can all get together? Before they take whatever it turns out to be back to Arizona.

It would be due in late December, or wait a few days and arrive on New Year's! We'd get the front page in the paper! But I think it'll be way sooner. My other two were both really early. The boy was a "preemie." It was nice meeting you, look me up! If you come see me in the store, I'll let you use my employee's discount. Wish we were going back on the same plane, oh well, Happy Flying. See ya soon, I hope.

Amber

5

Well, I am home. Again. Last year I never left Montreal. Not once. Not even to go to Ottawa. Or Champlain, New York, even. This year's only three months old, and I've been to: Rochester, Phoenix, Flagstaff, Las Vegas, the Grand Canyon, Route 66 and Toronto and Chicago, counting airports.

I wasn't looking forward to walking in the door to be greeted by yapping and fretting and the gnashing of tiny toy teeth. But I wasn't! Hurrah! When Heidi picked me up at Dorval I could tell she had some SECRET. But she managed to wait for us to get home for me to find it out for myself. And it was: DING DONG THE DOGS ARE GONE! THE DOGS ARE GONE! They've gone where the bad dogs go . . . to Tanguay with their maman! I am so happy! Reine Ducharme demanded custody!

And all because of Life Aboard the *Titanic* after I jumped ship.

Daniel had a terrific time on the set, even put out a fire. He kept saying, "It was in one of the staterooms." Actually it was a lit tiparillo Cotton threw into a wastebasket in her trailer. Daniel was there, and because he "saved my life!" the big star said he had to be in her movie, too. He got to be a survivor like me, but not from Third Class.

"He did a lot of row acting. He played the crewman who got to steer Cotton's lifeboat."

This helped him be the handler for "Petunia," who got an extra scene. And that's how we lost Brioche et Montcalm.

"That Gamon de Pycombe dog the picture's named for? Well, it seems in historical fact some man on board released all the dogs from their cages as the ship was sinking, so they would stand some chance. And Gamon de Pycombe was seen swimming valiantly, but alas not successfully, by someone else in the icy yet calm North Atlantic. They decided that, for added effect, Montcalm as Petunia would jump from Cotton's arms and try to join him, save him, whatever."

I asked Heidi, What were they thinking, Montcalm hates the water!

"It was Cotton's idea, she wanted Monty to have more screen time. Daniel says she probably wants them to retitle the picture *Petunia Dog of the Titanic's Owner*.

Montcalm's having to do more special business, which was actually a stunt, meant they needed permission from his owner. So the casting people (that sullen girl Janis, probably) had to call Reine in jail, and that's how Madame found out I'd gone to Arizona without telling her, leaving the dogs with some "inconnu!" she's never heard of (the only men in our lives she wants to hear about are possible love interests). Such a betrayal! While she gave permission for Montcalm to get wet and do the scene displaying his heroic side (and make $300 more), she didn't feel I could be left in charge anymore! So as soon as filming was completed, Daniel was told to have Montcalm et Brioche's things packed and ready, and a guard named Roch Duplessis would pick them all up.

So they're gone and I am DOG FREE! Brioche et Montcalm made Reine a small fortune. And not a bad one for Daniel and me either! Daniel made $1250 the week he was suspended from the fire brigade. Movie-making is not like real life at all, he complained: Where was the iceberg?

It must be an April Fool's trick. Tyler called to ask me out for dinner. But he called me *after* noon, the moratorium on practical jokes. So maybe he was serious. But why? My first night back at Festin, he said they'd missed me, that Festin wasn't the same without me. He said it nicely, like he meant it. And then when he said what a great tan I had, that Arizona sure agreed with me, I kept thinking it was some way to disarm me. After all, I returned to Festin not knowing how they did without me, I didn't know if I had a job, and Gaëtan wasn't there but Tyler was, I thought he was lying in wait to fire me. But he wasn't. All he did was say nice things and now he's asking me out to dinner. At L'Express, on St. Denis. But I said no. "Another time, I hope," Tyler said. "Maybe," said me.

This makes me think: what are the maybes? I would go to dinner with Tyler Garrow:

> 1) to discuss helping Festin
> 2) to go out to a chi-chi restaurant with a man who wears Armani
> 3) if I was attracted to him in any way, but I'm not
> 4) if I wasn't paranoid and thinking it's his way to fire me in a place where I can't make a scene.

Tyler's April Fool's Day invitation really didn't have a chance. I had already had to take one thing seriously today that I thought was a joke. Madame Ducharme called from prison before noon (poisson, poisson), but she wasn't joking.

I could hear it through the phone: she was holding back tears. I thought she was overwhelmed about having her dogs back. (She doesn't really. Roch Duplessis the Turnkey is keeping them at his house and brings them in, this way she can see them more.) Reine was crying because she'd gone through their little suitcase. She was upset that I'd changed their brand of dog biscuits (they were on sale, what can I say), but that wasn't the problème. It was this invitation they received to a birthday party.

I asked her was she upset it was only in English?

"Non, non!" she cried.

It was because they didn't get to go! I had denied them a chance to go. I couldn't lie and say Daniel and Heidi took them because I knew they did not.

"Une fête avec d'autres chiens, Lenore! C'est à leur tour! C'est un peu de joie pour eux! Un peu de joie!"

I asked her, How much more joy can they have? Dogs in party hats is pretty small change after you've been First Class on the *Titanic*.

The film was "travail," this was "un peu de fun! Avec leurs amis!" I think she's been locked up far too long already.

I told her I was sorry, I had no idea it meant that much to her.

"C'pas pour moi! C'est pour mes bébés!"

And their little sweaters were missing. "Où sont les chandails?"

I said I wasn't sure.

Weren't they wearing them to the set every day?

And I lied and said, Yes, but maybe it got warm while I was away? And Daniel didn't think they needed them?

Then why weren't they with their things?

And that's when I told her because . . . they were in the wash. They wore them so much, Heidi had to wash them. They were at her house now. (Pinocchio Girl! A tree trunk was growing out of my face.)

Oh, that made her feel a bit better — to see all their little things and these sweaters missing! She thought they'd been stolen. It was possible, didn't I agree?

"Les chandails sont très jolis," I told her.

I am going to Hell for this. Canada and the Péquistes will put a price on my head. I wonder how Daniel forgot to include the sweaters. He's the one who made the joke about them when he was riding in the back of my car and saw them peeking out from under my seat.

"What are these? Sweaters for separatist leprechauns?"

I told him to shove them back under there. And that's where they are now. Well, one thing I won't be lying about, they do need to be washed.

Tyler certainly underwent some kind of sea change when I was gone. I'm really thrown off, him being nice to me. I think I was more sure of where I stood when he was making life a misery for me and everyone else at Festin.

Maybe it's because things didn't go better without me, the trouble wasn't me after all. He knows he was wrong to make me the scapegoat. And that making Laura sexy was not a good idea! Because it got back to the Laura Secord people, and they are so mad we used the heroine of the War of 1812 they use to sell chocolates without their permission that they're threatening to sue Festin for copyright infringement.

So Tyler had to try a new theme on us. He knew we said we don't go there, but we've gotta try it. The Recreation of the Plains of Abraham. "It all takes place the night before the battle. Guests choose to be French or British. And — " Gaëtan and I both thought it was April Fool's Day again. We could not believe we were hearing this. We didn't even let him finish, we both shouted, "NO. NON."

Tyler promised it would be sensitively handled, in keeping with "this obsession for being so organic."

"Ce plan, c'pas organique," Gaëtan practically screamed at him, "c'est explosif!"

Tyler said, "Yes, that's why Festin's gotta go for it. It's controversial, competitive, it will sell and probably get us on *The National*. Maybe even on *Today* on NBC."

Tyler had no idea that we do not fool around with this emotional issue. How really touchy this is for all of us, how we can be together at a party or anywhere and someone ruins it by saying the wrong thing. On either side.

Jocelyne, Mireille, Micheline, Réal and even Chef Normand joined the debate. Everything poured out because we all have different views and experiences of how complicated it is to be Québécois or Canadian and Québécois. Tyler knows maybe twenty-five words of French, so mostly everything was lost on him except the passion.

But instead of backing down, he was more inspired! Tyler said this was great! Why don't we capitalize on it? "It's been handed to us on a plate. Ha! Make that a buffet table!"

Everybody screamed at him, was he nuts? Maudit fou? Wasn't he listening to us?

Tyler said he sure was listening, and we had convinced him even more that his new plan would work. "Give it a try, mes amis!"

"Non! Va-t'en!" everybody yelled.

Gaëtan said for Tyler to drop this plan and never, ever mention it again. You'd think that would make Tyler quit, after all, he thought it was such a perfect idea. But instead he apologized!

"If it's what you don't want, Gaëtan, I surrender. je m'excuse tout le monde, everybody. Forget I said anything about all that, okay? Look, I'm an American, I don't get your pain."

He says he'll draw us up another game plan. He's got to do it pretty soon, too, the Laura Secord people are only giving us ten more days of grace, as long as Laura covers up. No more Sexy Secord, so I'm playing her again. When Tyler left I asked Gaëtan if we could try going back to what we did before, the old Festin, and make improvements. Gaëtan shook his head and looked very hurt. Maybe because he's the boss and I've questioned his authority but I didn't mean to. Daniel told me he can never discuss business with Gaëtan, and here's me mouthing off. I'm not saying anything again.

There's No Escape from Tanguay! I had to return the petits chandails to Madame Ducharme in person because I can't really leave them to Canada Post, what if they became disparu in the mail? Of course, I thought by now Reine would have made the little darlings an entire new wardrobe of fleur-de-lys-wear. But all her knitting time lately has been spent on a very large sweater.

She was thrilled to get les chandails back and appreciated that they were washed in Woolite and didn't shrink. She apologized for getting so mad at me for leaving her bébés on the *Titanic* while I went to Arizona. She over-reacted to my desertion and hopes I don't miss Brioche et Montcalm too much. But it was "après la pluie, le beau temps" because she now gets to see her ti bébés every day, as well as the someone who watches over them!

"Roch!" she said and smiled a moony smile. I'm pretty sure she has found Love behind bars, or anyway with someone on the other side of the bars. It's happened before, Patty Hearst married her guard.

While I was there Reine gave me her insights on Tyler because he was the reason why I didn't get there for Visiting Day earlier this week. He stopped by because he happened to be in the neighbourhood with a little Franny's Cheesecake. So what could I do but invite him in for coffee? And then he stuck around for hours and talked about how much he wants what's best for Festin. But we're "so darn macramé" he can't give us what he knows will sell. He says maybe his approach seems too gung-ho, too hard sell, we don't think that way "up here." But his approach works great everywhere else, most recently in Iowa for Pete's Buccaneer Cove, where he advised the owner to make the customers dress as pirates or the pirated. And before that, his plan saved the Amish Arbor when he suggested that between courses the guests should get to raise a barn. "Not full-scale, of course." Tyler says he hasn't met this much opposition with other establishments he's presently saving. The theme places in Calgary, Vancouver and Saskatoon are all cool. "Even the ones in Saint John and St. John's." He says Festin doesn't seem open to bold, money-making ideas. Maybe we're afraid of success? But maybe, he admits, it's him. Maybe he misjudged everything from the start. "Trying to make you tart up Laura Secord by threatening to recast the show? I never meant it, you think I wanted Jocelyne to play her, I was bluffing, I knew she can't sing, I thought you'd give in. But you walked out, and there was me stuck with Mireille as Laura Secord the Dominatrix, and yeah, she's sexy, but did she give me attitude! And that approach was all wrong! I may seem pretty sure of myself, but I'm not, my self-esteem's taken quite a beating on this project. But hey I gotta learn. Do you know what will work, Lenore? Tell me. Help me do what's right. You're a Montrealer. You must know what people want!"

I had to tell him I miss the old Festin. "But that was losing you money!" he explained, "That's why Gaëtan hired me." I didn't have any other suggestions for him after that, but he says he's still trying his best to come up with a surefire plan. He thanked me for the tour of my house, he really liked everything he saw, "great place, a lot of character." And right before he left, he said he hadn't given up on having dinner with me on one of my nights off. I don't want to go out with him, but I'm starting to think Tyler's not so bad. I finally noticed he sort of looks like Kurt Russell, only with a ponytail.

Reine asked me if Benoît was out of my love life?

I said he was never in it.

"Dommage. Dommage. Mais je ne suis pas certaine ç'a va finir."

"J'en suis certaine," I told her. It's fini with Benoît, the man makes me crazy. I haven't heard from him in months, anyway.

And she said, Well, am I now considering this Tyler? He's even an anglophone.

"Non, c'pas un anglophone," I told her, "C'est un Américain."

I was shocked when Reine said I probably am secretly attracted to Tyler but fear him because he's a Good Dresser/College Educated/

Authority Figure/Ideas Man/Foreign Imperialist/Ponytailed/Younger Guy.

The problème could be me, she says. Maybe I don't think I deserve a decent boyfriend because I lived with a total rat like Fergie for so long. That could be Why I say No to Happiness when I could say Yes. (Thank goodness I didn't tell her about Wyatt Bardo's proposal, she'd say I deserve to be in St.-Jean-de-Dieu mental asylum!)

Reine's advice is: when he asks me out next time, "dis oui." I should be nice to a man who wants to help my dear friend Gaëtan save Festin. Especially a man who has the good taste to ask me out to L'Express! I never told her that Tyler wanted us to use our political problems to get customers. I just said he keeps coming up with game plans, we've got hardly any time left now with Laura Secord. Never mind Laura Secord, Reine said, she has the solution! It's "Les Vedettes."

She thinks we should get Vedette headliners like Ginette Reno and Diane Dufresne, make it a supper-cabaret club. I love Ginette Reno, but if she's doing all the singing where does that leave me? All I'd get to do is wait on tables. No thank you. But more singing might be a solution, for starters.

On top of that, right as I was about to leave she asked me to find her a tenant, the last people I found her worked out so well. She doesn't mind if they're English again. Roch says it's better for her place to have people in it.

So it's April fourteenth, the day the *Titanic* hit the iceberg. I know this now. And if I didn't before I would after the Wrap Party I was invited to tonight but didn't go to. (I wonder if Reine got Roch Duplessis to take les chiens. I told Janis to call Tanguay when she asked me if my dogs would be coming. The dogs won't want to miss it, un peu de fun avec leurs amis!) I think the only people who will show up will be extras, the Two Tall Women, SOCs, Special Business and handlers with their dog stars. The people stars finished weeks ago. It was good of Cotton to send me a gift through Daniel, though I thought her big feathered hat belonged to Wardrobe. If Cotton was still here, I'd have had to get to the party. I wonder if they're getting it catered by Marguerite Vichy. Why am I thinking of her incredible food when I couldn't go anyway, I have to work. We're in our last days of Laura at Festin. Who knows what we'll have to try next, we'll be down to the wire!

At least Reine Ducharme's not the only person who has given me an opinion on how to improve Festin. Heidi's idea: There are so many women servers, there why not have it be female-driven? Woman heroes. Amazonia. Perhaps even more historical, better costumes, more authentic cuisine — but not too authentic.

"No Caribou, Lenore, please!"

I said, Caribou to eat or to drink?

"To eat. Elspeth went to Labrador once and they served her caribou fondue!"

I calmed her down, it's not very likely, caribou's expensive. We'd have to raise prices, not a good idea right now.

I said, What kills people is all the added tax and gratuities, and Heidi said, Why don't we try having a VAT, like they do in England? (Like Miles must have in Near Sheffield!) We decided that Festin should charge a flat price for everything, in advance, no bill at the end of the evening. As Jocelyne would say, "C'est le vrai deal!"

And then we decided Festin could make it a Bring Your Own Wine establishment. The restaurants on Duluth and Prince Arthur are booming because of this.

Heidi says she'll poll Loyola, the English Department all went to Festin last year. I'm going to ask Jamie, practically everyone from *The Most Happy Fella* was there, too. The question is, What Do You Think Would Make Festin a Better Place?

Maybe I'm doing Tyler's job for him, but if it helps Festin, that's what matters. And Tyler was big enough to admit he needed help. So here goes.

April 16,1992

Hello, gorgeous!

Sorry I wasn't home when you called and talked to my machine. I will ask everybody who's been there about how to improve Festin. And of course, you know what I'm going to suggest: Broadway Show Tunes. All sung by you, my chickepen! I could find you all kinds that have to do with the Bois. *Into The Woods* is chock full of them, as you know. Speaking of that — and I will — I need you to help me lobby Clive into choosing the ONLY show he should even consider for the summer musical. Yes, we are doing a SUMMER SHOW this year. In addition to the Fall one. Anyway, Clive may call around to see what people want to do, and if he asks you, he will, he loves you, you are to say for me, please, that your choice would be *Pacific Overtures*.

So you've never heard of it. And that's what makes it PERFECT for us who specialize in the not-done-very-often, never-been-done, done-once-and-never-again musical. *Pacific Overtures* is about Commander Perry's Invasion of Japan. (WHAAA? I've lost you already, I know, but it's wonderful, believe me.) It's by Sondheim, and you know how much he means to me. And *you*. He wrote "Send in the Clowns." He wrote our duet "It Takes Two." YOU know all this, but I have to say it again, please say *Pacific Overtures* when Clive asks you what you'd go for from this list: *Fiorello!*, *How Now Dow Jones*, *Sail Away!*, *Ballroom*, *Purlie*, *Flower Drum Song*, *Bells Are Ringing*,*Applause*, *Half a Sixpence*, *Pacific Overtures* PACIFIC OVERTURES **PACIFIC OVERTURES**!

Did I tell you how much this means to me? And who would think of doing any of these other shows when there's something by S.S? Anything by S.S! Who has ever even heard of *Sail Away!* I've already done *Applause*. And *Bells Are Ringing* is so passé, along with everything else on this list. FORGETABOUTIT! Except for you-know-what! Thank you! I owe you my firstborn. Make that the second, third and fourth, too. Of course you'd have to have them all for me. . . . And hide this letter! Don't let Clive see it. Of course, if you are home I won't have to give you this note, I'll just say it right to your face. I could have said it if you had a Susanswerphone (the name of the company in *Bells Are Ringing* a show Clive must not do!) Get a machine! I'd rather let my mouth do the talking. Bye. Big hug and kiss to you.

Jamie

April 25, 1992

Dear Lenore,

Heidi asked me for suggestions for your Festin restaurant. We had the best time there that night. I told everyone in my building, and they said when they go to Montreal they want to go. I told them it was $35 a person before the tip and taxes, and they said that wasn't too bad. Heidi said you are going to make it all one price? It will be $35 and that will include everything? That will be good. I thought it was expensive at first, but you get a great meal and we had such a wonderful time that night. That tourtière pie was terrific, especially with spruce beer. I like the real thing, even though La Belle Fermière is delicious. My neighbour Miep, she's Dutch, but she has some old recipes for tourtière, which I copied here for you. She's a terrific cook, so they will be good. In case you want more variety in tourtières. (One of the recipes has veal.) Don't tell Heidi, we know how she feels about VEAL. Thank you for not making us eat caribou. Or any boudin! I tried some in Ireland, they tricked me, they like blood pudding for breakfast. I didn't know what it was till they told me, I thought it was just a thick little sausage. Thank you also for giving us a knife and fork. My friend was at a medieval banquet in Toronto with no cutlery. They made her eat with her hands and she had to tear her food up. Too messy, too much work. Hugh and I loved the meal. And you were wonderful as Laura Secord. Very believable.

To make Festin better, What would I like? I would like you to sing more. I think you should sing all night, maybe they could make the Festin setting like *The Sound of Music* only in Québec, and you had come there, not out of the convent but maybe just off the ship from Ireland? You speak English and most of the people speak French, and they take you in. Like the way the French people adopted those children off the fever ships. That is the most wonderful story. It could be the past or it could be in the fifties. And you are taken in by *The Plouffe Family*. That was a wonderful TV show, we watched it every week. Twice. Do you remember it? Maybe you're too young. They did it in French and then in English, the same show. It doesn't have to be the Plouffes again, but some nice East End family. Maybe you marry one of the sons? And he has all these sisters (the other waitresses) who become your good friends? I think this would be nice.

If you could make it cost less than $35 that would be very good. Maybe have two-for-one nights? We had such a lovely night there, and we loved meeting those people from England. Irene, Miles and Jennie's mother, wrote me when she got back and sent me clippings of *Coronation Street*. She wants us to come visit and maybe we will. Hugh loved getting up to sing. It was all lovely. You made it such a nice evening. But if you want to make it different, I would say you could try to make it like Mother Martin's. Do you remember that restaurant? It was next to *The Gazette*, where it was before it went into *The Montreal* Star building. I loved Mother Martin's. It was very Irish and had wonderful roast beef and lamb chops, and a lady played the organ. Mother Martin's was posh and warm and full of atmosphere. So that's what I would say, make it like Mother Martin's. And you sing all the time. Maybe make it like *Pig and Whistle*. Only with Irish and French Canadian songs, too. You could get many bus trips.

Love,
(Mrs.) Sheila Flynn

PS: Did you talk to Daniel about moving away from Gaëtan's condo yet?

Heidi may have a tenant for Madame's house. He's between forty and forty-five, not married and Ichabod Crane-ish. When she said this, she gave me a look as if I didn't know who Ichabod was but I do. He's the guy who was told not to ride home from the pub through the Covered Bridge after dark, but he did anyway, on a really old horse, and a headless horseman chased him and threw a lit pumpkin at him.

"You read *The Legend of Sleepy Hollow*, by Washington Irving?"

"No, I saw the Walt Disney cartoon of it. Bing Crosby was his voice."

"Oh yes, yes, I saw it, too. With an excerpt of *The Wind in The Willows.*"

"About Mr. Toad and his car."

Being near in age makes you have a lot of the same popular cultural icons, Heidi says. Like Hayley Mills and Patty Duke.

I asked her why she thinks the Possible Lodger looks like Ichabod Crane. "Because he's tall and lanky."

So that's what I'm expecting to knock on my door asking me to show him Reine's house. A tall and lanky Bing Crosby. If he doesn't work out, I can blame Heidi. It was her idea not to put an ad in the paper and open up Madame's house to all of Montreal. "This way we can have some control over who moves in. We'll be the ones stuck with them as neighbours."

Madame Ducharme says it's okay if I show him her place, and she'll give me a rental price once she talks to Roch!

Reine has thought a lot more about how to fix Festin. Other solutions absolu are:

1) Make it a celebration of les Québécois, du Québec, no mention of anywhere else, how distinct we are

2) A dress code, more expensive, exclusive, gourmet food.

She asked if I'd contacted Ginette Reno's agent yet. I said Non, not yet. When I told Heidi about Vedettes, she said, "I'm sure one of the Dionne quints would be happy to guest MC some weekend."

She is so sarcastic, but guest stars is an idea. And why not The Dionne quints? I think one or two of them live in St-Hilaire or the Laurentians. Cécile? Annette? Yvonne? And Festin could pay them well to try and make up for the money Ontario made off them.

Heidi said we should stick with the original coureurs du bois etc. idea, only make each table a different seigneury, and whenever Festiners left the safety of their fort they were in the forest or on Indian lands or in the St. Lawrence River. And I'm thinking maybe we should hire a driver and have a Mount Etna pick-up-the-guests-at-their-hotels bus.

I think we may have something here!

Why did I bother getting all those suggestions? Why did I give Tyler any ideas? This is all my fault. I couldn't believe it when I got to Festin and it's closed for five days for renovations. Because Tyler's turning it into *The Muppet Show*. Or *Country Bears Jamboree*. I'll bet all those talking stuffed animals are rejects from his other theme restaurants.

Tyler told everyone he has me to thank! And Gaëtan's looking so pleased, like this will be the answer. I don't want to ruin anything. Maybe it can work. I can't say it's tacky because, Tyler said, my house and my saying I wanted the Old Festin back inspired him!

"All those taxidermied animals in the cellar, shot by your ex-boyfriend? They made me realize what's been missing. This is the Bois! The Great Outdoors! What started this country off? Hudson's Bay blankets! Hunted-down Animals! The Fur Trade! And how did everybody get from place to place? By canoe!"

That's why he's going to have animal heads popping up from inside a canoe at the entrance.

I saw what was stamped on one of the crates in the lobby: Talking Moose. If we were still doing the Laura Secord Bus and Truck Tour, it would have been: Talking Cow. And yes, yes, so Tyler admits it, it's "Total Kitsch! Go Big or Go Home. Let's Turn It Up. If you got it, flaunt it!"

Mireille says we're going to feel like we're stuck inside Ogilvy's Christmas window. I don't want to know what this will cost Gaëtan. The only people who can be thrilled with this stuff will be Hydro-Québec! But I have to be open to this, not be afraid of success. Have a good attitude.

6

May Day, May Day. Jamie's going to be so upset! Clive did call me to ask about the summer musical he'll direct, but it's been chosen already, and it's not the one Jamie wants about Japan.

"It's going to be *Bells Are Ringing*. It's the only one I'll do for them, I adore that show. And I picked it because of you."

Yes. Clive says *Bells Are Ringing* was his sole intention on the list. "Sure it was a fiddle! I put it on there with a whole lot of ridiculous or totally impossible ones. Like *Purlie*, when we have maybe three black people in the company! And really *Sail Away!* That Noel Coward dinosaur! How could they go for any of the other drivel I gave them?" He rigged it. Of course this is all a secret. Clive wants me to play the role of Ella, the woman who runs the lives of all the people who use Susanswerphone, the telephone answering service.

"You were born to play this role. Since I met you I've dreamed of directing you in this part."

What could I say but Yes, okay, I'll do it. I guess.

"You have to audition first, of course."

I thought he was giving me the part, I didn't think I'd have to audition! And why do directors make people go through that if they know who they want? Why doesn't Clive just cast the whole musical that way and save us all a lot of competitiveness?

I survived last year's show, and yes, I did okay in the end. I think I could get time off from Festin, and it would be fun to do a show again. Clive chose this show for ME. And Jamie, too, Clive said, but I'm not to tell him. (STRANGE MAN!) The audition is next Sunday, which is Mother's Day. I don't get to celebrate it, but still, what kind of people have an audition on Mother's Day? Show people. Nothing is sacred to them, I guess!

Clive came by with the song I have to learn: "The Party's Over." It's a very sad song for a musical comedy. And he gave me these important instructions:

1) Do not rent the movie.
2) Do not borrow the play from a library (if any libraries have it).
3) Do not ask anyone about Judy Holiday.
4) Do not watch any movie with Judy Holiday in it (I never heard of her before!)
5) Do not learn the song from any recording, especially not from the original Broadway show or movie versions, both done by — but of course — Judy Holiday.

It's a bit much, but the song's pretty and short, and as soon as I started to sing it to myself, I knew I'd heard it before. Doris Day sings it. I found that album and gave it to Heidi so I can't be tempted. She can't give it back to me until after I audition. I have to interpret this song all on my own.

Heidi started to tell me about Judy Holiday anyway.

"She won an Oscar."

"Oh no, not for *Bells Are Ringing*?"

"No, for *Born Yesterday*. She specialized in playing blondes who look dumb but are actually pretty sharp."

This was, of course, way more than Clive wants me to know. And what's with him? I am not blonde. I don't think I look dumb. What gives, Clive?

Please come to our
MOONDANCE
in celebration of
OUR MOTHER GODDESS
at this month's FULL MOON.

Bring food, wine, picnic blankets, music.

Shoes optional.
We shall dance in the moonlight with our sisters! Rejoice, it is Wicca!

Lenore:

   I do hope you can be part of the Moondance. Heidi's
attending. She says you may be busy with another play?
Heed the words of Stanislavski: The Actor Prepares.
What better way to do so than by getting more in touch
with your spirit through Our Goddess the Moon? Love
to see you. We'll drink and dance on my lawn by the sea
(Baie d'Urfé!).

Elspeth

   I finally met Reine's paramour. Roch Duplessis came by to see me
this morning for a rendezvous out of nowhere, not even a warning
call from Madame Ducharme. This scary looking man arrived at my
front door, but he had some familiar faces with him, so I guessed who
he was: Brioche et Montcalm under his arms. Neither of them let on
they recognized me, but they ran into my house anyway.

   Now, I guess it's my fault I was so strange with him at first, but
he looks like a prison guard, a really mean one — the kind that would
be sadistic, keep the packages convicts' moms sent and eat their
cookies in front of them. Whenever Reine talks about Roch, I see
Charles Bronson in *The Great Escape*. I didn't expect him to look so
much like a really big Lee Marvin.

   He was very polite and said he hoped I didn't mind, but he needed
some guidance from me. He and les chiens went to the Dogs of the

Titanic Wrap Party and he put "les feelers" out. He thinks that les chiens have a future in le show business. But he has "c'pas le savvy, tu comprends?" I told him that didn't stop me from getting them into a movie, but actually I had it easy, they were discovered at the Wolfe School. He wanted to know what that was. And that's when I realized Madame doesn't know we enrolled her perfect pets in a dog school!

"C'est une école du show business?"

I couldn't keep it a secret anymore, I told him the Truth. But Roch said, It's not possible they completed the course? En tout cas, they don't behave like trained dogs.

I said that they might if I showed him some of what I learned, some shortcuts and extreme measures. He was excellent at the growling Tamara Technique.

Roch said that Reine mentioned that the famous directeur Denys Arcand would love to work with her dogs, did I have his number? I said No, Roch said, Let's look in the phone book. There were ten D. Arcands and two Denis Arcands, but no Denys.

After he put les feelers out, I asked him, did anyone at the Wrap Party give him their card? He said "Ah, oui!" Marguerite Vichy, Caterer.

I asked him if either of the Tall Women had talked to him. He said No, but he saw them. They were always talking to somebody, never for too long, that's because they're producers.

I found the card the Tallest Woman gave me at the Wolfe School and presented it to him. Roch said thanks, but what do I do with it? That's when I phoned Jamie at IBM, and he gave me instructions in that super-straight voice he uses at work.

Roch is to call the Tallest Woman and remind her that she gave him her card at the party when he told them that Montcalm et Brioche Ducharme were under new management. And that they said to come by their agency this month because there was something shooting they might be good for.

Jamie and I have both turned into Alexis Carrington! What if they throw Roch out of the place? That Janis isn't trusting at all. But Roch's pretty imposing, it might work. And Brioche et Montcalm could wind up in The Further Decline of the American Empire.

All right, so I am going to be Ella in *Bells Are Ringing*. But nobody's too pleased. And can you blame them?

Lots of women tried for the role, and they all thought they had a chance. Especially when they sang Ella's songs better than I did, the way they were supposed to be sung.

I should have been thrown out after I sang "The Party's Over" because I did it all wrong. The Party was Over for me. I spent all afternoon watching everyone else audition. That wasn't too bad, most people were very good and sang songs I've never heard before. It was kind of like an amateur Great Performances special on PBS.

Quite a few people were out to make a big statement.

Janet was really mad, they got her hopes up that they would do musicals with Asian leads and give her a chance. She sang "I Enjoy Being a Girl" from *Flower Drum Song*, a pretty sexist song, even though I could tell she didn't believe a word of it.

Jamie, who is still devastated, said he wasn't even going to audition until I convinced him to sing from his beloved Steven Sondheim's *Pacific Overtures*. The song "Someone in a Tree" is for two or three people, but he did it all by himself, he does that a lot, like his "I'm Not Getting Married Today" solo party piece. The song's about a guy watching Commander Perry from a tree when he was a kid. "It's Steve's favourite song," Jamie said," I sang it for Steve. I don't care if they don't give me a part!"

A new girl whose real (not stage) name is Arden Tollhouse sang a depressing song called "Surabaya Johnny," a woman is furious with a sailor named Johnny, who keeps his pipe in his mouth while she calls him a rat. (I thought that could have been me, last year, singing to my Surabaya Johnny Ferguson.) I think Arden's really mad at some guy and took it out on us at her audition.

After all these songs, Gary Halsey said, "Gawd. Doesn't anybody know anything from *Guys and Dolls*?"

And Charlie Greene agreed. "Oy! Even 'Tomorrow' would be a relief."

Then they both got up, one after another, and auditioned for the role of the villain, with the same song, "A Simple Little System" from

Bells Are Ringing. They were followed by Tommy Tzchuck, yes, doing the same song.

Then Kyra Tzchuck did her big number. I never met her until opening night last year, when she and her husband Tommy showed up. The Tzchucks travel a lot and had been to the South Pacific Basin corridor or somewhere, that's why they hadn't been able to "commit" to being in *The Most Happy Fella*. Tommy really thinks he would have had the lead. Anyway, they are both back now and can commit to be in *Bells*, and, as Kyra went up on stage, Jamie whispered, "Attention. La Diva wants to blow us all away."

And she tried her best. She did "Rose's Turn" from *Gypsy*, it's Gypsy Rose Lee's mother going nuts at the end of the play? This song I had heard before, only I didn't know it was about a nervous breakdown. "It is one of the numbers you work up to in a Career," said Jamie. "And she's not quite there yet."

Kyra was also trying to make a statement. Like almost everyone else, she doesn't approve the choice of *Bells Are Ringing*. (So why are they all here? They must have somewhere else to go, something else to do this summer, instead of rehearsing a show they despise in an un-air-conditioned hall in June and July.) Kyra wanted them to choose *Sail Away!*, *Applause* or *Ballroom* because they have older leads and that's her forte. "Old Dames Who Belt," says Jamie. And Kyra intends to play Mama Rose, the one who sings "Rose's Turn," and this was her way to let them know they've got to do *Gypsy* one of these days.

"Isn't *Gypsy* too well known for this company to do?" I asked Jamie.

"And way beyond Kyra. She'd be dead in the water after 'Some People,' her opening number." Jamie's a sweet guy but the theatre brings out his vicious, catty side. He calls it dissing.

Clive decided we'd audition in alphabetical order for Ella, so I had to see a lot of girls go before me. Rian Corbett, star of *The Most Happy Fella* did a really nice job with a song called "Plaza O double-four double-three."

I told Jamie he wasn't allowed to diss anyone trying for Ella even if he thought it would bolster my confidence. Watching them gave me a chance to hear the songs in *Bells Are Ringing*. The only one Clive let me know about was "The Party's Over," and nobody else was allowed to sing it. (STRANGE MAN AGAIN!)

Finally I got to sing. When I finished, there was silence and people were blubbering.

"Man, I never knew how sad that song was," Gary said, wiping his eyes. The song seemed really sad to me, Ella sounds like she's lost everything. The other people at the audition table stared at Clive.

He said, "It was very Piaf-like, Lenore."

I could tell that was wrong! I asked him, "Did you want it more Céline Dion?"

"No," said Philip Henderson, one of the show's umpteen producers, "more like it belongs in a musical."

So that was me, finished. And I wanted to kill Clive for setting me up, making me so embarrassed.

"Could you try something else for us, Lenore?" It was Clive out to torture me some more.

He asked me to learn another song from the show and come back in about thirty or thirty-five minutes when everybody from R to Z had tried for Ella? He handed me the music for "I'm Going Back Where I Can Be Me." Jamie was over by the table by then, pleading my case.

"Aw, please, no, Clive. That's Ella's big Eleventh Hour number, the-end-of-the-show-stopper. Nobody could learn that in half an hour! Give her 'Just in Time.'

Clive said this was Jeffrey's big song. Jamie didn't mind. "Jeffrey can share it with Ella just this once. We'll be back!"

Jamie took me by the hand, and we went off to the foyer. He started to sing "Just in Time" and it turned out I knew this famous song. Jeffrey sings it to Ella, and they dance while she sort of hums/scat sings. Jamie made it a duet, only I would do most of the singing.

I finally asked him, "Who is Jeffrey?"

"The playboy playwright she falls head-over-heels in love with."

"Is his phone number: Plaza O double-four double-three?"

And he said, Yes, Jeffrey Morris, played by Dean Martin in the movie.

We even worked up a dance number. I thought, even if I don't get this part, I don't care. I am having such a wonderful time dancing and singing with Jamie. And isn't this the greatest song, what a feeling it gives me to sing it! We went back in and did the number and Clive turned to the others and said, "See? Hmm? Am I right?"

They said, Yeah, Jamie and Lenore look great together, they're perfect for the parts.

"I knew it. Great, guys!" Clive said.

"Make them read, Clive," Philip said.

So they made me do what they call a Cold Reading because I had never seen it before in my life. It was a speech about a Ticonderoga pencil. It didn't make any sense to me, but they were all falling over themselves laughing.

"We're tired — you're hired!" Philip said.

"You sure are!" Clive could agree now.

So Jamie and I are playing Jeffrey and Ella. That's going to be fun, I think, I hope. Clive must know what he's doing. I sure don't. What have I done to myself again?

Someone came to my door today, and he did he ever *not* look at *all* like Bing Crosby. Or Ichabod Crane! Yes, so he's really tall, a bit like Susan Sarandon's boyfriend. I opened the door and he said, "Hello, there. Would you be Lenore Rutland?" I said Yes out loud, but inside I was singing, "I'm in love With a Man, Plaza O double-four double-three."

There's something about him, I don't know what, but it hit me. I thought I fell in love with Fergie at first sight, but this feeling seemed bigger, somehow. And why was that? So Wilder's good looking. But then I always think guys are better looking than Heidi thinks they are. She could never see how much Fergie looked like Burt Lancaster. Was this going to be another Fatal Attraction? All he said was Hello, there. It was the way he said my name, I guess. And then when he said his name. Wilder Taft.

"My folks named me after Wilder Penfield. What can I say, they wanted me to grow up to be a brain surgeon."

Anyway, love at first sight has to be a passing thing because he's living with someone. He kept mentioning his girlfriend, Katherine this, Katherine that, so I know he's off limits. I asked him if she'll be moving here with him, and he said, "No, Katherine has to stay and teach at Radcliffe. She's an expert on Denise Levertov. The poet?"

I was honest, I said I'd never heard of Denise Levertov.

He smiled and said, "Very few people have."

Wilder's not an English professor (surprise!) he's with the Faculty of Science, teaching Economics here for the summer and fall terms. Then back he goes to Boston.

To his girlfriend, Lenore. The woman he lives with.

I showed him Reine's place. He found it fascinating. He picked up a framed picture and said, "Is this Monsieur Ducharme?" and I said, "No. It's René Lévesque." The rent she wants didn't shock him, and he'd like me to let him know as soon as possible if he can have it because he doesn't like where he is now. He's subletting Tess of the D'Urberblondes's place, and it came with two very mean cats. One of them is even Siamese.

Heidi told me Tess is now trying out Emerson's hobby farm across the border in Nowhereville, Ontario. "She's living in sin with him. In the middle of nowhere at that awful farm! It must be very serious!"

I wondered what kind of person sublets her apartment and leaves her cats behind.

"Someone evil like her. No loyalty at all. And it's not as if Emerson's dog Patch hates cats. He's a very amenable dog."

Heidi says she'll be thrilled if we can wrench the rent money out of Tess's scrawny little hands and make her scramble for a new tenant. Who will feed the cats? I wanted to know.

"Her next victim. Her place is in the Plateau, everyone wants to live there. Till they get her as a landlord!"

Heidi grows less fond of Tess Dudley every day, it's almost pathological, and it's not just because she went after Emerson Sawyer as soon as Heidi told him she didn't want to marry him.

"Don't you remember her scandalous behaviour at Victoria Hall? She made the moves on him then! At what would have been our wedding reception!"

Heidi's not in love with Emerson any more. She never really was, though, so it's not that she's jealous of Tess. "She's welcome to him!" I couldn't tell Heidi what I really thought about Wilder at first sight.

It's embarrassing, at my age. Kaboom! Bells were ringing for me! But I must get over it, get over Wilder, I have to, he's "in a relationship."

My garden's in and am I ever glad, otherwise I would have felt really guilty at the Wicca Moondance.

Elspeth's garden is FANTASTIC. She's going to have a forest of fabulous flowers and herbs! Beth was right, Elspeth's vegetable patch is as big as Saskatchewan.

Elspeth's got a truly beautiful house, even though it looks a lot like the one in *The Amityville Horror*. And so picturesque, right on the water in Baie d'Urfé. I'm glad Heidi made me go with her, the Sylvias and everyone else did want to see me, and Heidi's never been to a Moondance before, so I couldn't make her go to it alone.

The Moondance wasn't what I expected at all, not anything like what I was afraid it would be. I really thought we'd get there and women would be throwing off all their clothes and chanting and dancing on the lawn or in some field in the moonlight.

But we arrived at five o'clock, and the moon wasn't going to be out for a while. Everyone had brought salads and breads and cheeses and desserts, and some had even brought husbands or partners and babies and kids, it wasn't just us moonshine women. All the men there were Feminists, especially Douglas, Elspeth's gristled husband. And so was the sun-bronzed Elijah, the sculptor who was commissioned to do "some very exquisite work" in an area that's not really about flowers, that has lots of rocks and paths and a Zen garden. Then that pond you find when go round a corner, Northrop took us there on our tour to see his mother's special secret-secret place.

Northrop's only eight years old, I wonder if he knows what the "secret" means. The stone wall has Elijah's sculpture carved into it, and when you look at it closely you see what it is!

"Pretty interesting, eh?" Douglas guffawed. He might be a Feminist and married to Elspeth, but don't tell me he thought it was a celebration of the Female Anima. Northrop said his mother likes to do her Mediation here.

"Meditation," Douglas corrected him. Then he turned to challenge us, waiting for our reaction.

"So what do you think?"

Heidi wasn't thrown off by him. She said, "It's a vulva, isn't it?"

If I had a camera I would have taken a picture of it to prove to all mes soeurs at Festin: someone has a sculpture of a Vulva in her garden. Frayne would have loved this place, she'd probably want us to do another Dance Collective here. Judy Chicago's Dinner Party II.

Elspeth's First-born, Frieda, was super busy all week, gathering twigs, old grapevines and twine into a pile so big it looked like we were going to burn Joan of Arc. Elspeth wanted us all to make something from it. "All those assembled here, gather what pieces you will and fashion them into spring crowns." That kept us happy for a while, my head wreath turned out pretty well. Then there was constant food and drink while people "shared." Of course the Sylvias had to do some poetry by Sylvia Plath, they were so depressing, like always: "Lady Lazarus" — some woman who survived suicide, again — and the one about Daddy the Nazi. I asked them what they knew about the poetry of Denise Levertov, and they came up with: "Intensely organic." "Are you reading her now?" "You've got to start with the 'Olga Poems.'"

Heidi and I shared, too.

Heidi's story was inspiring, about a Celtic goddess.

Then they wanted me to sing.

"Oh, yes, sing, Lenore!"

I couldn't be shy. People had brought lots of musical instruments, even an accordion, after being an easy mark for derision, it's making a comeback. And there were guitars and fiddles and flutes and a bodhrun, sort of an Irish drum that looks like a tambourine. So I had no excuse, I would have accompaniment whatever I sang.

"Sing a song from your new show."

I knew I might be in big trouble if I did. Heidi says *Bells Are Ringing*, from what I've told her, is not a Feminist Approved musical. But Heidi saved me, she knew what everyone would like.

"Do 'The Party's Over.'"

And I did, not so sad this time. And Beth demanded an Encore or something else from the show, so I did "Just in Time" and everyone sang along.

Then Elspeth gave a sermon comparing the Life Cycle to Lions:

the Lionesses only really need the Lion for one thing and then they are happy to hang around with their female friends and babies and go hunting occasionally. That's ultimately what we're all about, being Lionesses on our own with other Sister Lionesses.

But then I heard myself saying, "But the Lion is always the Boss."

"He thinks he is," said Elspeth, and she looked over at Douglas. He gave the same weird laugh as at the wall. He's kind of a creep.

I never know when to shut up. "But she hunts for him and has his cubs, she's doing all the work while he sits on a big rock overlooking his Kingdom. And he has lots of other Lionesses, not only her."

Elspeth stared at me, and there was major silence. It's a good thing I never got to college, because I'd have said stuff like this all the time and made the professors wonder, How the Hell did she get in here?

Elspeth got huffy, snarled that perhaps the Lioness is not my ideal, and went into her great big beautiful cottagey house "to see to the couscous."

I thought I'd embarrassed Heidi, asking Elspeth questions in the middle of her lecture, but then she said I was right to do so. It was almost like an Emperor's New Clothes thing. I wonder if Heidi's right to think Elspeth had too much wine because her thought processes weren't that clear. "That's not like her."

But her couscous was good, along with everything else that was served all evening and into the moonlit dance night.

I thought the music for the Moondance would be mystical stuff like Loreena McKennitt and Enya. But it was Bob Dylan, the Supremes, Melissa Etheridge. Even Anne Murray, everyone sang all the words to "Snowbird."

And it was good of Elijah to set up that outdoors pottery workshop and let us create our own Mother Goddesses. I think mine looks like Yoda in *The Empire Strikes Back*, but Heidi said it doesn't. She's so kind sometimes. I thought we'd get our goddesses to take home, like our goodie bag. Too bad we have to wait for them to be fired. I guess my Mother Yoda will go in my garden when she's done.

And if that wasn't enough for one party, Heidi and I discovered we have a Cosmic Connection, and all because Northrop joined us by the campfire with marshmallows and said that it was his birthday last week and did we want to see him do some magic from his set?

Heidi said, "You can be Magic Tom."

And Northrop said, Who's that?

And everybody there over thirty told him how Magic Tom was on TV, and kids got to go on his show.

Heidi asked me if I'd ever been on. I said, Yes, every kid in Montreal was on his show in the sixties.

Beth had been a guest on one of Magic Tom's birthday party shows, she was his assistant for one of the tricks, the tap-tap thing he did with the cone and the candy?

When Heidi was on she read a poem about an elephant and a telephone.

I almost couldn't say it, but I did: "No way, no, you didn't!"

"What would have been better, 'Lady Lazarus'?"

"Once there was an elephant? Who tried to use the telephant?"

Yes, she said, did I learn that little poem by John Godfrey Saxe in school? They had it in their Catholic reader.

No, I said, I heard it on TV. A girl in a plaid dress recited it on *Magic Tom* before I sang a song, "The Champagne Waltz."

"No. Not 'The Champagne Waltz'!"

Yes! We had met before! And not in another life, in this one!

Heidi couldn't believe it right away, after all, it was a popular poem, and a lot of kids could have recited it on *Magic Tom*. Perhaps some other little girl was on who also sang "The Champagne Waltz." But I even remembered her dress.

Heidi says she will ask her mother if she made her wear plaid on *Magic Tom*. When Mrs. Flynn says, Yes, she did, she'll know we really did meet before. We could have been friends long ago, luckily we met up again when we were grownups.

It was quite a fireside chat, there must be something to this Wicca!

And Northrop made a stuffed turtle come out of a hat.

7

Dear Lenny,

    Bet you're surprised to hear from me.

    Saw you on *Fiona!* You're looking really good.

    Hope you got all the money I sent you.

    Won't give you a forwarding address this time. I'm not in Florida anymore. The tourist industry was not for me.

    Wanted you to know I'm thinking of you. No matter what you did to me because you lost it and got angry.

Fergie

After a year and half I hear from that rat? my Surabaya Johnny? He must want money or to move back in. He's insane, writing to me like that out of nowhere. I don't even want to look at the postmark, I don't want to know where he was when he sent it.

I wish I'd never done *Fiona!* and made him finally think about me again. He probably thinks they paid me a fortune.

I'm not going to think about it. I'm not.

Of course I would have gotten his postcard sooner, like two months ago, if he'd put my Postal Code on it. That's him all over the place, letting everybody else finish off what he should do.

I got this piece of garbage from Fergie, and Heidi got a postcard from Everest. She heard from the Top of the World and I heard from the Bottom.

June 1, 1992

Dear Lenore,

Thanks for your big thank-you card and for the swell pictures you sent. I'm happy you had such a darn grand time in Arizona. We sure enjoyed your visit, too.

Here, like I promised, a memento of your brush with death. It was too small to make a pocketbook, so they made it into an evening bag. Pretty elegant, I think. For your next time out on the town. Or ville. Whatever you people call Montreal.

The kids send their best and Darla asked me to say Hi for her, too.

All the very best to you forever. No hard feelings because you turned me down, I mean that. Keep in touch, little gal.

Your pal,
Wyatt

If only I had married Wyatt, he'd make sure Fergie never bothered me again or popped in unannounced. Maybe I should get some therapy to see how I should deal with this. I'm still really angry, I know that. Fergie has some NERVE, but I'm not going to think about it, I have enough to occupy my thoughts without him getting in the way.

This play, for one thing. I have a Really Big Lead Part with a lot of Acting to go with it. Lucky for me I've got Jamie opposite me, and it's not hard to pretend I love him. But the story is so strange! My character Ella has no life of her own, she runs everyone else's lives, but they don't know it. She's just a voice that takes their telephone messages. Jeffrey, that's Jamie, always wants to playboy around, drink and chase women in evening dresses in the middle of the afternoon and not do his work. I go over to his place and make him work, and because of me he gets his play *The Midas Touch* written, and that's one of the reasons why he falls in love with me. I better not invite any of the Moondancers, they will rise up and haul me off the stage, it's so sexist. Even if Beth makes them buy out opening night because she liked what I did with "The Party's Over" at Elspeth's.

And Kyra the Diva got cast, and her husband (big surprise). The Diva plays my boss, Susan, and she takes it to heart that even though I'm her underling she does not have even ONE solo. Even worse, her darling husband Tommy does. He plays Sandor, who tricks Susan into being a bookie, only her employees think the callers are ordering records. From the Titanic Record Company. That ship is following me around, I tell you! I really don't think I'd have agreed to do this if I had known what it was about, in spite of having some fun songs. And the costume designer promises me fifties clothes. "You're very lucky Simon Tratt likes you so much," Jamie says. "Because you should see what he could make you wear on stage in public if he didn't. Barbra Streisand in *Funny Lady* didn't suffer as much as Kyra did in *Wildcat*. What Simon does to anybody he despises! Kyra finally said,' Don't you know who I am?' And Simon said, 'Yes, darling. You're the star of a community theatre musical in Montreal, Québec!"

The Diva and Tommy have a twisted relationship, they do this funny/cute bickering, but they're really one-upping each other. Last week he complimented her, and she said, "He is pleased with me, my Lord and Master." Which Janet told me is from *The King and I*, another show with great roles obviously for me that they'll never do!

There's so much anger and nastiness around the rehearsal hall. And that Arden, who sang "Surabaya Johnny," gets to play the other switchboard operator, and she and Kyra-La-Diva both keep trying to get Clive to give them one of "Ella's many, many songs." It's not fun. And when I ask any questions about my part, Clive groans and says, "Oh, please, Lenny. Don't try and turn Ella into one of those career feminists."

Meanwhile Gary and Charlie play Barnes and Francis, the undercover cops who keep trying to prove Susanswerphone is a front for Communists or Hookers or some other evil fifties thing. Kind of like Benoît's brand of police work last year trying to get into CSIS. So whenever Gary does his part as Barnes of Vice, I'm haunted by Benoît!

And I'm sorry, but the Diva's husband, Tommy, is even more full of himself than she is. Hard to believe. He owns a plumbing company, Plomberie Tzchuck, but "my true love, my real métier is the Arts. As soon as I retire I'll fully commit to it." He goes on and on about how he studied at the Old Vic. Years ago. And yes, even I know that it's some hoity-toity theatrical school in England, and now I also know where he got his phony British accent. But every time he says Old Vic all I can imagine is him acting out plays in the basement at the Royal Victoria Hospital. And my fantasy turns into those brainwashing experiments they did on people against their will for the CIA at the Allan, on the grounds near the Royal Vic. I can't help myself!

Heidi made me watch *The Country Girl* last week on PBS. She thought I'd appreciate it because it's about someone suffering because of show business. Grace Kelly marries Bing Crosby, a fall-down drunk, liar and actor, and they live in a dingy apartment like *The Honeymooners*, only it's a tragedy. Grace had a line about how she's a stranger — the people of the theatre mean nothing to me, I'm just a girl from the country. Okay, so I'm not from the country, and some of these people do mean something to me, but I am a stranger in the theatre world. Grace Kelly married Prince Rainier after this to become Princess Grace. Hollywood *tried* to drab her up as *The Country Girl*. She got an Oscar for it. Heidi says this adds to the findings she and Daniel came up with during this year's Academy Awards.

FLYNN FINDINGS: HOW TO WIN AN OSCAR

1) If you're beautiful, don't be. No makeup, ugly clothes. Play poor. Sure thing.
2) If you're always good, be BAD.
3) If you're always bad, be good and have some handicap.
4) Be a comedy or TV star or sexpot and prove you can ACT.
5) Be around forever, make a comeback and win in Best Supporting category.
6) Return to the screen after an illness. What does not kill you may get you an Oscar.
7) Be a big male movie star who turns to directing.

Still here's me, no chance for an Oscar in sight, some sort of tourist in the theatre world. I should have known better, I should have stayed away. And done what, sat around waiting for Fergie to show up on my doorstep? Come up with even more ways to try and save Festin's bacon? I mean, the raccoon-and-bear-paw show Tyler has us doing, serving the meat course in snowshoes. And he hasn't once tried to ask me out to L'Express since Gaëtan went for this master plan. I am in Hell there. So this is my break, my little holiday from REAL LIFE. I better try to enjoy it.

Yur house is a eye sour. All it neds is one match.
No one wud miss it.

Conserned Citizen

I know Wilder is taken. And I am enjoying his presence as a person, that's all. I wonder when his Katherine will come up to visit him. I hope that it's soon, that she's really sociable and can be a friend, and then I can stop thinking of him as a possibility. Because he's terrific. Really friendly and considerate. Not like Fergie at all. Not like anyone I ever went with.

There I was gardening, and Wilder said he had a few hours to kill, would I let him do some digging, hoeing, whatever — do my bidding? And then when we got done we sat on my garden bench that Reine gave me with the iced tea Wilder made and talked till it was time for me to get ready for work. It was so pleasant. I think we may turn out to be good friends.

Another thing that makes Wilder special: he was really understanding about the donkey and cart I found. I've always wanted one of those lawn ornaments, but I never bought one, and then this morning there was one on my steps. But it was crusty with mud and three of the wheels were off it.

Wilder came out of Reine's right at that moment. He wants to fix it for me! He even said he'll find it some wheels because the little donkey seemed to have found its way to my house.

Of course Heidi doesn't approve. When I asked her if maybe it was a sign, Wyatt asking me if I liked mules/donkeys and then this one shows up on my doorstep, yes, so it's plastic, and right then this man I like (the way Wyatt liked me) comes out. Is heaven trying to give me a message?

Heidi says someone is. What about the smashed up Frosty the Snowman I found in February? Two of them, both in bad shape, it's not a coincidence.

"Maybe people regard you as some sort of Lawn Ornaments Rescue Service. We can probably expect flocks of broken-winged pink flamingos next."

I had forgotten about Frosty. But it is odd. And it's the same week I got another one of those Conserned Citizen notes. I don't know if I should show it to Benoît. It says my home is an eyesore, maybe it's only me, but it sounds like a threat, like Conserned Citizen wants to burn down my house, maybe with me in it. I'm going to make copies of Les Belles Lettres and drop them off at the police station for Benoît. Just in case.

Wilder went to the mountain today. And took me with him. Well, actually I took him, he needed a guide, he said.

We walked all around Beaver Lake, and now Wilder's looking forward to winter because he can skate there. (I guess I went on and on about how much fun that is, when's the last time I did it, twenty-five years ago?)

We walked up to the Chalet with the lookout, Terrasse du Mont-Royal as it's properly called. I think the last time I was there was with Dad. Probably the same day I went skating. The Chalet is so picturesque, I had forgotten, with that historical panorama of Montreal painted all around the top inside. When we gazed out over my city I couldn't understand why it took me so long to get back here. It's good that new people come to town and make you rediscover where you live.

But Heidi took an ungrateful somebody on a tour of Montreal once. At the end of it he complained, "You have a lot of big churches, don't you?" And that's when she realized she'd dragged him to Notre

Dame, Bonsecours and St. Joseph's Oratory. "I think he was overwhelmed." He didn't appreciate any of it, not even "the cheap thrill-seeker aspects" like Brother André's Heart preserved under glass and how it got kidnapped. And he didn't even love Notre Dame Basilica. Anyone who doesn't must be seriously flawed, Heidi said, and I agree, it's got to be the most beautiful church in the world. Wilder will think so if he ever says he needs a guide again.

We were out on the Terrasse when Wilder asked, "What's up there?" I said, "More Mountain."

Wilder thought he was original saying Mount Royal is not a mountain, it's a hill. But I told him Maisonneuve declared it a Mont, a Mount Royal no less, and that's what it's always been and always will be.

So we "climbed" some more of the mountain. I really didn't know what we'd find at the top, but then there it was: the Cross, the great big steel one that shines down across the city.

I've been here all my life, it was there, but I'd never seen it up close. That big, right in our faces. I told him, "De Maisonneuve planted the cross there, to thank God for us not being wiped out by the floods."

Wilder said, "It's held up well for three hundred and fifty years, huh?"

We were the only ones around. I couldn't help thinking that this day was wasted on the two of us. It would have been romantic for a couple to have it. I never saw any of these sites with Fergie, but he wouldn't have liked them anyway. He'd never walk all the way up here. If he did, he'd swear and complain and ask why didn't we bring any beer.

My romantic thoughts came out my mouth. "I guess you wish Katherine was here with you, eh?"

"Instead of you? Because this is a spot for Lovers?"

I babbled, Yes, the Terrasse lookout and the Mountain and the Cross, even though it's steel and covered with lights and full of religiousness for some people, was a Lovers' setting, and maybe it would have been great for him to be here with her.

"I'm here with you. And that's pretty great."

I know it's NOTHING, why am I making such a big deal of this? Get over it, Lenore.

All he said was he was happy to be there with me. Okay, so it was great to be there with me. Instead of the woman he lives with. Katherine. He was being polite. Or maybe that's all he could say. Because if he'd said, "Yeah, it is wasted on you and me. I sure wish Katherine was here. God, I miss her so much," that would be kind of thoughtless to me, but honest. And loyal. But when I think of it, what kind of man goes sightseeing to a lookout with a woman not his girlfriend? A man who's certain of his relationship, that's who. And he didn't know the lookout was there, I did.

FOR WOMYN ONLY

Dear Sister,

First, let me tell you this is a different kind of chain letter. You can say *I never do chain letters*, but this one is different. It's for WOMYN ONLY. You have received it because you are a woman another woman deeply respects. She knows *you make life happen*. And she hopes YOU will succeed in becoming rich, influential and powerful. This is why SHE chose you to receive this and why you must be selective in who YOU send this important message to.

If you do what you must do, you will receive $6000 in the next nine days. *This letter will make it happen for you* if you make it happen for yourself and other women *you* feel *deserve to profit*.

Send one $2 bill, inconspicuously wrapped, to the first name on this Top Six list. Then remove her name from your list. Add your name to the bottom and make TWELVE copies. Send this letter and the list to TWELVE women you know-WOMYN ONLY.

DON'T BREAK THE CHAIN*DON'T BREAK THE
CHAIN*DON'T BREAK THE CHAIN*DON'T BREAK
THE CHAIN*DON'T BREAK THE CHAIN*DON'T

Mail the letters within *the next twenty-four hours*. When
your name reaches first place, you'll begin to receive the
gifts you deserve. If everyone joins together to make this
happen, you will have $6000 in time for the Solstice.

This is LEGAL. It was started by Ruth Elizabeth Farrow
in Dallas as a way to acquire investment money fast. It
worked for her. She now *owns* a shopping mall, a chain of
health clubs and a riding school.

Send this letter today to women you love, honour,
cherish, respect, want to know better. Your mother, your
sister, your relative, your friend, your lover, your fellow
worker. If you don't want to be part of this *greater good* for
the sisterhood, return this to the sender within eighteen
hours.

> *Elspeth Torrington*
> *Beth Manion*
> *Charlotte King*
> *Viola Turcotte*
> *Tess Dudley*
> *Heidi Flynn*

I was going to kill Heidi for sending me that chain letter, but it
wasn't her idea! She threw her letter away, she didn't even return to
sender Elspeth within eighteen hours. Heidi's even madder than me.
"What is she doing? And listing Tess Dudley as a woman she respects?
What's wrong with her? How insincere can you get? And HOW did
my name get there at all? You have to send the initial twelve letters to
be able to make the bottom of the Top Six list. I never did. Not even
one!"

I told Heidi, sure, it's swell that Elspeth wants me to prosper and
considers me important, but where was I supposed to find the time
to write a dozen letters?

"And make all kinds of enemies!"

Heidi has only ever given in to two chain letters, one was a recipe club her cousin Sandra got her into and said it would be a family shame not to participate. The other letter was "somewhat whimsical" so she did it.

"You had to send people a dishtowel. A new one, of course. I didn't get even one in return, though. Someone broke my chain."

That's a lucky thing, she could have ended up with six thousand dishtowels. The worst kind of chain letters are the ones with threats. Heidi's gotten a couple that said they would invoke saints' blessings if you obeyed and death in a fire or a bridge collapse if you didn't.

Heidi called Elspeth to try to tell her we were flattered and all that, but we couldn't commit to the chain. We are sending the letters back, all right? But Elspeth says No, it is NOT all right. She didn't choose just anyone for these letters. She chose us, and now this is a slap in the face. She's truly, deeply, very disappointed in both of us, what about all the positive energy we emitted at her Moondance, was that some fabrication? Was our Wicca manufactured? What about our Mother Goddesses that have been fired once and await our glaze before they can get a final firing?

So now we're being victimized and learning the newest chain letter curse: If you won't do it, you betray the sisterhood.

The summer solstice, the day we would have been $6000 richer. That would have been a nice birthday present for Heidi, whose day is today, Father's Day. So of course they are making us rehearse.

At least when I get back from *Bells Are Ringing* we're going to have Heidi's birthday dinner party at my place because it's bigger. We could have had it in the garden if it wasn't so cold and rainy, like WINTER. Heidi's running her own festivities for the big Thirty-Eighth. Elspeth won't attend. "You both know about declining. And desertion. I do, too." But Beth is coming and the Judys, Charlotte and Viola. The Judys must be upset, Peter Allen, whom Judy Garland introduced to Liza and who wound up being her first husband, died of AIDS this week. I hope Charlotte and Viola don't mention it or go on and on the way they do sometimes about all things Judy Garland. But poor Peter Allen, he was only forty-eight, now he's somewhere between the moon and New York City. I love that song he wrote for *Arthur*. I never knew all that much about Judy Garland before I met Charlotte and Viola. Isn't it strange how your friends' interests become your interests, even if you're not interested? I guess it's catching. It's a sad year for Liza Minelli, divorcing her latest (Third? Fourth?) husband and losing her first one to AIDS. Just hearing about it makes me worry about Gaëtan. He won't be at the party tonight with Daniel, he says it's because he has to run Festin, not everybody can have the night off. But I know it's really because the "charade" for Daniel's parents upsets him. Mr. and Mrs. Flynn are coming in from Ottawa. I wonder if Mrs. Flynn will figure out what's what about the Judys. Probably not. Wilder seemed really pleased to be invited, Heidi said I could. It would look more obvious I'm interested in him if I avoided him, and I am not being disloyal to women just because I happen to like someone who's taken. It's not as if I've done anything about it, and Heidi knows I won't because it's stupid and wrong. He can be a friend.

Like her and Miles of Everest? He sent her a birthday card and a little Buddha he got in Tibet. Or Nepal. Wherever Everest is, that he didn't get to the top of. "There's always 1998,"he wrote. He has to start raising funds and sponsorships so he can try again. WHY? WHO WOULD WANT TO GO THERE? It's so high and so cold! Miles got to 27,600 feet but had to turn back. I was shocked, I thought if you got that high you were more than there! Heidi says no, it's 29,028 feet. Yes, now I have another new interest: Mount Everest, thanks to Heidi and Miles. "We are long distance friends," is all she'll admit to. Because that's all it is or can be for now until one of them takes some action.

Wilder kissed me. What did he do that for?

It was much more than friendly, it was a major kiss.

But it only happened because it was late, the party was over, everyone had left, he was saying goodnight. He had a great time.

Another great time, like our day on Mont-Royal.

I wish he had said he missed Katherine that day on the mountain, that he wished she was here. What am I saying? I am all mixed up now. He made the move on me, why did he do that? It changes everything. No, it doesn't. But it could. But it was nothing, Lenore. It had nothing to do with Lust. HA! — maybe it had only to do with Lust. No. I can't think that way. It was just a simple goodnight that got too personal, and I didn't mind one bit. I do now, though, because I am so confused. I am not myself.

I'm turning into Elspeth! I shouldn't make fun. But Beth says something's really wrong with her, she's acting very erratically. "That Lioness diatribe at the Moondance? And now this Get-rich-Sisters chain letter?"

Beth did the chain letter "to placate her." She's received $22 of her $6000 fortune so far.

She feels it could be much worse, Elspeth might have tried it on at the Moondance, got us all together and then sprung some pyramid jewellery-selling scheme on us.

"Don't scoff, it happened to me. A dean at McGill invited us to his home, and then he and his wife brought out a jewellery case and launched into a demonstration! We'd all become rich, rich, rich standing at the top of our pyramid of others selling these bagatelles! We'd be covered in riding stables and shopping malls! I told him no thank you!"

Heidi asked her if he'd retaliated.

"Denied me tenure? He wasn't Chair of the English Department. But he never talked to me again."

Just like Elspeth, who's giving us the silent treatment. Heidi says we could just ignore her, but she's afraid it's some deep, dark problem.

It's probably Douglas, as Beth suspects. He's a dreamer and a schemer, always trying to invent things. He's still upset someone beat him to Trivial Pursuit, it was always his idea but he never had enough capital. Beth's afraid Douglas is up to another disaster that Elspeth has to finance.

"And they've got that great big house!" I said.

"And it's got a great big mortgage," Beth told us.

"And what do you think all those renovations in her kitchen just cost?" Heidi added.

I said now I felt bad I didn't do the chain letter.

"Don't give in to tyranny, Lenore," said Heidi.

"Beth did, and she's already made $22!" I whined, but I didn't mean it.

We all agree we have to help Elspeth if we can. If we were in trouble, she'd help out. "She'd have Douglas killed, or at the very least driven out of our life, if one of us was married to him. Maybe she'd even make him shave! That three-day growth he always has, horrible. But she believes in him, totally. A fatal attraction, like Sylvia and Ted."

Uh-oh. I'm trying to think of Elspeth but I'm back to ME. I can't sleep or think straight because the man next door kissed me goodnight. Thanks a lot. Whatever it was. Nothing really. It can't be anything. Because that's not fair to Katherine or to me.

I should go over, knock on his door and confront him. Say, What was that all about, anyway? Don't you have a girlfriend? Aren't you in a steady relationship? Why are you taking advantage of me in my vulnerable state, eh? I haven't had a boyfriend in eighteen months! Was that kiss supposed to lead to something else? Will it? Well, it can't, okay, so leave me alone. Don't try it again. Got that?

Maybe I should do that, but I won't. *Waterloo Bridge* is on Channel 6. I'll watch that. My mind can be on Vivien Leigh's problems. I think she jumps off a bridge or gets hit by a train in that one.

8

Wilder's not around that much anymore. That's probably good. He's mostly at Concordia. At the Sir George campus downtown. Heidi sees more of him, I think, with her weird schedule that takes her there as often as to the Loyola campus. Yes, so I don't see much of Wilder. And I'm glad, why look at what I can't have? What would Tess Dudley do in this situation though, eh? The girlfriend not here and him kissing her goodnight at two a.m.? She'd pounce. But I am not Tess of the D'Urberblondes, I am Lenore of the Don't Two-Time With Me. And I would not want another woman to go after my boyfriend just because I wasn't around. No matter how tempting he might be. It's DISLOYAL and we have to stick together, women. We do. I'm trying my best, heaven knows. The few times I have seen him, he acted like nothing ever happened, which is true. I over-reacted, lucky for me I kept it to myself. Wilder's remained his friendly, easy-going self. My pal. But why do I feel like I'm chasing him even if all I can say is good morning?

Anyway I still have the SHOW to worry about.

And I am so unhappy.

Clive knew I can't really act. I told Jamie that, and all he said was, "That's what Audrey Hepburn thought when she got her first major role, in *Roman Holiday* — 'Now all I have to do is learn how to act.'"

I am not Audrey Hepburn.

And I'm not Judy Holiday, either!

Clive was so upset with me the other night when he handed me a video and said, "Watch this. Over and over again if you have to!

Till you get what I am looking for. What I see in you that you cannot seem to find! Steal all her inflections, come through for me!"

Of course it was *Bells Are Ringing*, and if he had let me see it in the first place none of this would have happened.

Clive says he cast me because I am the role. All I have to do is play myself. "You are Ella."

I told him, "I'm not Ella. I don't even have an answering machine!"

Clive feels I am letting the entire production down, it's costing them $65,000, in case I care.

How is it costing $65,000 when none of us are getting paid? And it's an amateur show?

"Royalties, darling. The orchestra. The costumes. Renting the Centaur. Advertising? $65,000 is a conservative estimate."

I was doing the scene where I go to talk to Dr. Kitchell, the dentist who really wants to be a songwriter and plays tunes on his air hose, when Clive yelled at me.

"She hasn't a clue. Do you get what I am saying?"

I don't agree, Ella's running everyone's lives, and by the end of the show they're all a success. She must have lots of clues.

"The script says Ella's got a 'quick mind,'" I told him.

"You see Comden and Green in this rehearsal hall?"

"Who?"

"You don't even know who wrote this and you're spouting off. I don't care what they think, I want you to play dumb," Clive yelled.

"She's not Dumb!"

"Dumb is funny. Smart isn't!"

Clive feels I am giving him grief. "But hey," he said, "I deserve it because I didn't hire an actor." That's when I told Clive that the word "hire" means "pay" (Caitlin McGovern taught me a thing or two on the *Titanic*), and he had not hired me. Clive said, "Well, we're even, because you're not an actor, either."

This was my chance to walk out of the entire $65,000 mess. Why didn't I? Instead I looked at Clive and said, "Well, you get what you pay for, Clive."

That did Clive in for the moment. He left, told Paul and me to run our lines. We didn't know and I didn't care where he went.

Paul says he's dealt with idiots like Clive all his acting life. "When you're part of an Acting Family, you see it all." I was almost in denial when I found out Paul is Kyra's brother! So we have three Divas in the Cast. Paul never once spoke up for me when I was "discussing" the scene with Clive, he just stayed silent. "A real worm," Janet calls him.

The Divas only talk about their own roles and their past roles. THEM,THEM,THEM. No, I'm wrong, Paul has another subject: stage blood. His special recipe: corn syrup and raspberry juice. It's been used successfully in two murder mystery weekends. He wants to patent it someday, get it on the market. "It's superior to anything anyone else has ever used. Even the blood bags you buy at Johnny Brown's. And it's washable."

"Their shallowness knows no depths," says Janet. She's my defender again, along with Jamie. Janet promised they will lead a revolt if Clive tries to fire me.

I'm not leaving this show. I said I would do it and I will. People are depending on me, and many people I know bought tickets for Opening Night. Only six days from now!

I love singing these songs and dancing, it makes me feel great. No one is going to ruin this for me. Even if I wind up ruining it for Clive, too bad if I'm not as clueless or as Ella-ish as he thought!

Wilder and I went to the Botanical Garden today, another incredible place I haven't been to in years and years. The flowers there, wow. And the quirky greenhouses, one's got my dream: the Garden of Weedlessness.

In the Chinese garden, standing there in the silence among the pagodas with the Olympic Stadium rising up practically in front of us, it was all so Montreal. We were having such a tranquil time, not saying anything, but then Wilder had to speak and threw me off again. Why does that always happen amid major landmarks?

"You're terrific, you know that?"

I didn't answer. I was pleased and surprised and wondered what he really meant, all at the same time. And I was worrying, is he making a move on me at the Botanical Garden?

"You are so terrific. Going around here with me when you're so busy. A full-time waitress job at Festin du Bois. The starring role in a community theatre musical. Giving up your free time for me, I really appreciate it."

And what did I say but, "Oh, good."

Because it's all I could say. Or should say. He should have said, "You're terrific. None of the flowers in this entire botanical garden can surpass you! And thank heavens I've finally realized I was happier being there on the mountain that is Mont-Royal with you than I ever would be with Katherine. And to think, here we are again, sharing a Montreal moment. The Big O, the Chinese Garden and us. You're the woman for me. No, don't apologize, Lenore, it's not your fault, you've never once been disloyal to womankind. Yet you made me realize that what I have with Katherine, it's not . . . right. So I'm leaving her because we haven't been happy for months now, maybe years. And you make me happy. You do." Etc. etc. etc.

But no. All he says is thanks for being my tour guide, you are such a busy lady.

The ice creams from the cantina that's lost in the thirties or forties weren't bad. Wilder's future Montreal taste sensations list includes: Schwartz's for Smoke Meat, Bens for Smoke Meat, Orange Julep, Hot Dogs at the Forum. And of course: "Katherine says I have to try poutine for both of us. Save her the trouble."

And I wanted to ask, "Why doesn't Katherine come up and here and try it for herself and save me the trouble? Get you out of my thoughts?"

Wilder's still with Katherine, even though she's down there in Boston and he's here. She's always in his thoughts. And he'll be dining out on Québec's ode to gravy, french fries and cheese curds just for her. It must be love.

I don't think I can play tour guide for him anymore.

July 6, 1992

Dear Lenore,

   I thought I'd pop this into your letterbox so you could drop it off at the Centaur box office today for me. My friends and I want to see the production of Noel Coward's *Private Lives* the Young Vic is bringing to the Centaur for one week. And since it's on at the very same time as your show, at the smaller space, I knew you could bring this in for me. They wanted the payment this week, it's cash and cheques as you can see, twenty-six of us are going from our group. Thank you so much.

Jemima Farnham

PS: Please be sure to bring me a receipt.

I am going to do this show
I am going to do this show
I am going to do this show
I won't be a Diva
I won't be a Diva
I won't be a Diva

This has been one really unhappy experience, let me tell you. Never again. No more show business for me. This has been HELL. I am doing my best to keep my spirits up and all that, but Clive hates me and the Divas are fighting all the time. Good thing I have Jamie and Janet and Gary and Charlie, we're all in this together. But we open tomorrow and Bells should not be Ringing, the show's not ready! Everybody's blaming everybody else. Jamie says it's not us, it's THEM, they are trying to pull this show off without enough time or people power. The fall musical has a bigger production staff, everyone's at their cottages in the summer. It's not selling, hardly anybody's left in the city in July, and nobody feels like coming back to see *Bells Are Ringing*.

"If we were doing *Cats* they'd make it back in, oh yes!" Kyra sneered.

The advertising campaign is "really cheesey!" When I saw the ad in *The Gazette* last Saturday I had a fit, it looked like they'd hired Tyler Garrow to come up with it. When we posed for all those publicity shots, we started fooling around a bit. I never thought they'd use the silly ones! They're so corny no one could think they'd sell tickets. Jamie says maybe we did it subliminally to sabotage sales, and if we did, that's a blessing, the fewer people who see us, the better.

"This production has no vision! All Clive has done is block it! It's not even a send-up. When you think what Hal Prince could do to revive a chestnut like this!"

Jamie was crushed, I didn't know who Hal Prince was. Is. "Has your time with me been a total waste? Have I taught you nothing, Lenore?"

"I don't care, Jamie."

"But you should. These names and details are important!"

"To you, maybe."

He apologized, this show has not exactly been a Mickey and Judy experience for us. I gave him a look.

"Oh, please don't tell me you don't get the *Babes on Broadway* reference?"

"With friends like Charlotte and Viola? I get it, Jamie. But I never once expected this to be a Mickey and Judy experience."

"Because there's no uncle with a barn?"

"Because all those *Babes* things were movies, Jamie. This is reality."

"This is not reality, it is theatre. What am I saying, it's not even that. What is it? What are we doing? What is it that we're living for? Not this, not this!" He takes show biz so seriously. I guess I should, too, but I know it will be over in a few weeks. Sooner, if we close because no one buys tickets. In spite of that story in *The Gazette* on the production (all $65,000 of it!) and the headline about the woman known as "Lulu Borgia" starring in it.

"You've turned us into a Peep Show," Kyra Diva accused.

"Hey, if it's selling tickets, shut up," Janet told her.

The women's dressing room is such a warm, friendly place!

At least Opening Night is sold out, probably because Beth's selling *Bells Are Ringing* to everyone she knows. I have to do this show. I am doing it for Heidi, Daniel and Gaëtan, and all my friends. Because they believe in me. But if it wasn't for them and Jamie and some people in this cast, I would have been like the song. "I'll fly away, O Lordie, In the great by and by, I'll fly away." And then Arden Tollhouse could have her dream: the understudy must go on! Take my part, please!

Bastille Day, and no one is storming the box office to see us.

Clive truly hates me now. All because I survived *The Gazette* better than he did. And he said he won't read his notices! He told Jamie we'd betrayed him by not listening to his direction. "What there was of it," Jamie said. Anyway, I am finished with show business forever, once this is over. I don't care if Clive somehow forgets this fiasco and comes to my house in the fall or next spring and hands me sheet music to some future tacky mess he says he's picked especially for me, I will say NO. Even if it's *Calamity Jane* or *The Pajama Game*. Or any of the shows I've never heard of that people say I have to do one of these days. They all said I was nothing like Judy Holliday. (Now I can watch her in the movie. And maybe some of her other movies, too. There weren't that many. I feel so badly now, I didn't know she died young.) They said our *Bells* was nothing like the film. And Jamie wasn't Dean Martin-ish at all, either. They never expected the Golddiggers to dance out and light his cigarette. What a surprise. They didn't recognize it. Did we make a lot of changes?

The *Gazette* critic even asked could she dare to suspect we'd "put a little edge into it?" She thought my Ella was "too together"(!) and would have been CEO of the Bonjour Tristesse Brassiere Company and Susanswerphone rather than simply toiling as a wage slave. But the critic had to admit that even if we were good, which we never were, not even for one number, she couldn't possibly like this show because it was against her religion. Why did *The Gazette* send a critic who hates fifties musicals? She despised everything, especially "I'm Going Back Where I Can Be Me." She says it's truly obnoxious. It's my favourite song in the show. The audience, what there is of it, really likes it. Maybe because they know the show's about to end, who knows? It's lucky for me I don't need the smell of the greasepaint and roar of the crowd to be a happy person. I am not going to grow up to be a DIVA. I am going back where I can be me.

My loyal friends were all here for Opening Night. And — surprise, surprise — Wilder showed up, too, and almost overdid it, but did I mind? He sent flowers to the dressing room, brought bottles of champagne when he came to see me backstage after the show, kissed me congratulations, said he loved *Bells Are Ringing*, and then gushed some more. "You are so unbelievably talented. What a dynamo! I am in awe!" The way he kept looking at me . . . I feel so guilty, and I haven't done anything. He sat in the row behind Heidi, Gaëtan and Daniel, the Judys and Beth the lone Sylvia. Elspeth was not in attendance. Yes, so they all feel "the plot leaves a LOT to be desired," but they overlooked that because we were all trying so hard to do a good job. "You and Jamie were superb. You transcended your material. But you would do that, Lenore, even if it was Handel's *Messiah*," Heidi told me because she'd had too much of Wilder's champagne. Beth had to say she was offended by the sick plot device of Ella letting Jeffrey, her love interest, not know who she was and call her "Ma" as his phone service. "Acting as a Shadow Mother Figure. Didn't they detect something Freudian in all that?" Then she was enraged when Wilder said that, as a man, he could appreciate seeing a character like Ella on the stage. "It was so refreshing, someone in control yet still incredibly feminine, such an uncomplicated girl." I really think Beth would have thrown champagne in his face, but there was none left in her Dixie cup.

We're stuck in this show for two more weeks. TWO! But then it's over, this party's over, and I will never again have to spend a major holiday in a rehearsal hall being screamed at by a sadistic director who says I'm not giving him what he wants. Ever!

※ ※ ※

Benoît was at the show last night. He stormed into the dressing room at intermission, looking all confused. He doesn't think it's proper. "C'pas bon ça! C'est dégueulasse!" He found out when he read about me in *La Presse*. "Regarde ce que Lulu fait!" Why didn't I tell him I was going to be in a show? Do I know how this looks? It's not bad enough that he found out I make visite to Tanguay to see La Dame we both put behind the bars? (If he only knew that La Dame thinks I should choose him for mon boyfriend, that he could be the one for moi.)

Jamie saw Benoît badgering me and did his awful Queenie act. "Bees to honey. Aren't you popular? Street-walker!" and he sashayed out.

Benoît said, There, there! See? This was what he meant. What kind of atmosphere was this for a material witness? And he didn't like the way the undercover police were being played, either, in this spectacle, not realistic at all. Vice squads looking for hookers who run a Lonely Hearts Club — "Stupide!"

The stage manager called, "Places," and I wanted to exit, but I had to ask him, "Did you find out who left those notes on my car?"

He's had long enough to know something, it's been over a month. Benoît stared and stared at me, then said, "I think you know who sent them."

I told him No. He made his suspicious I-don't-believe-you face. "Aucune idée, hein? Personne?"

I couldn't name anybody, even though I know it could be Blake Farnham mad about the parking space. But he's never been around, so I can't really give Benoît a name.

Benoît said it's not much use to him if I don't know nothing. I told him he's the cop, he's supposed to find this out, isn't he? Get fingerprints?

The orchestra was almost done playing the second act overture, Janet rushed in and yelled, "Lenore! Arden's going to go on as Ella if you don't move it!"

I told Benoît he's got the nasty notes, but if he can't help me, just say so! He didn't say a thing, and I ran out and made it on stage two seconds before Arden did.

149

Benoît's so gorgeous but so useless.

And I'll bet he got a comp. Two comps, and he brought along some sweet, unsuspecting woman he met on duty.

A big surprise last night: Elspeth and her family came to the show. She's speaking to us now. Beth convinced her she had to see it. And Heidi has conducted such a successful phone and Hallmark card campaign that she's come round to forgiving us. I hadn't done my bit to help her until last night. When I saw Elspeth's Mr. Trouble husband Douglas and Paul, our Dr. Kitchell and creator of stage blood, in the same place at the same time, I figured maybe it was Fate. Two inventors, two creeps. Paul has investment money to throw around or away, and Douglas might help him refine his stage blood, patent it, market it. If Paul does have a superior product, let him prove it. All the movies now are blood and guts. If this is the right stuff, theatres and movies everywhere will use it. I think I've played Ella too long, I'm trying to get people together so they can succeed. Anyway they've had their first meeting, and I hope it leads to happiness for Elspeth. Peace of mind, anyway, and no more chain letters.

Of course Elspeth hated the show. She gave her entire opinion when I took her, Northrop and Frieda on a backstage tour. She did manage to say one nice thing. "You were marvellous as long as you sang and danced. And I mean that, Lenore. I'm not over-compensating." But she would advise me and her children never to be part of anything so heinous again. "I want to be a Actress," Frieda told me. Elspeth was shocked, then Northrop said, "I want to be a stage hand." "No, you don't, you want to be doctors," Elspeth declared. Frieda replied, "A Actress can be a doctor. Like Dr. Quinn, Medicine Woman." Elspeth got very upset. "Did Daddy let you watch *Dr. Quinn* again?" Northrop doesn't know any better, he added that Daddy lets them watch everything when she's out at courses. (On Saturday nights?)

Last night Emerson Sawyer came to *Bells Are Ringing*. Without Tess. Or if she was there I didn't see her, and she's hard to miss. He was falling all over me in the Centaur lounge, how much he loved the show, he even sounded sincere. It was so strange, the last time I saw him, last December, he was marrying Heidi and I was going to sing at their wedding. Now he's living with Heidi's arch-enemy and I'm pen-pals with his nieces.

Last evening was odd, but this afternoon was even ODDER. Emerson came to my house, to my garden. He'd been ringing my doorbell with no luck, and he was "perturbed and puzzled." Then he remembered my back yard. And its gate. He should know the place, he was here upstairs at Heidi's enough last year. I was out basking on this gorgeous HOT and SUNNY day, and then I looked up and it was ruined — there was Emerson.

"You didn't hear me come in," he said in a tone that meant, Lucky for you I'm not an escaped convict killer loose in your neighbourhood.

Then he told me, "I really like what you've done with the yard." (Nothing more than last summer . . . except for the donkey and cart with its great new wheels and the pelican with the broken beak that I found on my porch last week.)

I knew Emerson had some secret purpose, he was lying to beat the band. He hates how tacky he thinks my lifestyle is. He's called me the Queen of Kitsch to my face. I am so glad Heidi didn't marry him!

He asked if he could sit down and he did, on my Reine bench. And there I lay on my chaise-longue. Caesar and Cleopatra. Ha-ha.

Then he complimented me again on my performance last night, said it was even better than last year in *The Most Happy Fella*. But then this part was much closer to me, I was playing myself, he thought, so well done! I was thinking, Get to the point, mister. What do you really want?

Then he did. He said I might be startled by what he was about to say, but last night made him realize more than ever that he wants me, needs me, must have me . . . SING AT HIS WEDDING. His wedding? Yes. He is marrying that TESS!

The wedding's going to be in August at his parents' estate, the one Heidi went to that's been in *Country Living* magazine, the one known as "The Cottage."

I have a voice from heaven, he says, the voice he wants to hear singing in the church and perhaps also at the reception in the gardens under the marquee at The Cottage. Tess has specific requests, too.

"Not any of the same songs you wanted when you and Heidi were going to get married?"

Oh no, no, of course not.

"No Sondheim, Cy Coleman, Lorenz Hart, Comden and Green, Frank Loesser, Kander and Ebb. Or Rodgers and Hammerstein." (Who's left?)

Well, Emerson was right, I was startled. I was more startled when he said they'd pay all my travel expenses and my fee would be $1500 US.

But Heidi was the most startled when I told her I'd said NO. NO WAY.

"Are you insane? $1500?"

She didn't understand: I can't do this to her, sing at Emerson's wedding to someone else.

"Better to someone else than to me!"

"To Tess Dudley?"

"They deserve each other! Lenore, it's $1500.US!"

"It's disloyal to you."

She thinks this is so sweet and kind of me and she appreciates it, but she wants me to do it.

Even though it's a one-upwomanship tactic by Tess?

"It's gonna cost them $1500. No, demand more."

I said $1500 is obscene.

"They're loaded! That's cheap, it's nothing for them. Double your fee! Tell him you want $3000."

"No. Tess might be trying to buy me to get back at you."

"Then let her in-laws pay through their snobby noses!"

She doesn't care that it seems like Wyatt Bardo trying to buy me, I said No to him and he had a lot more to offer. And I really like him, he's a friend, but these people!

Heidi says she will one-up Tess if I do it. Believe her. When did Emerson say the wedding is?

"Next week! August first."

That's when Heidi said I absolutely had to do it, oh yes, for sure. "We can go together."

This was disturbing, I thought, She wants to go to Emerson's wedding? But no, she's speaking at a conference in Massachusetts that week. In Fall River.

"It'll be marvellous. I didn't want to go there by myself. We can go on holiday together. And Emerson will pay for your vacation! Call him, say you'll do it!"

And all I could think was, Am I being shanghaied? I didn't know how I could call Emerson up and maybe get Tess and have to tell them I'd changed my mind, there was a way I could do it. But he called me! And I'd barely said Hello when he said,"$2750.US. Please. You must do it."

And what could I say but, Sure, yes. Okay.

Well, *Bells Are Ringing* no more for us, the show's done, and now I have my next performance to worry about: Tess and Emerson's Wedding.

I wonder why Emerson waited till the last minute to hire the singer? And what kind of people want this many Andrew Lloyd Webber songs at their wedding? I mean, "Memory" for the vows? One of them has a secret side, "Close to You" and "We've Only Just Begun." Closet Carpenters lovers, says Jamie. They've got me singing quite a bit. Oh well, let them get their $2750 US worth, eh?

I have to arrive there on the Thursday to practice with the accompanist. Boy, I'm going to be BUSY! It will be interesting, too, after everything Heidi told me about how strange the Sawyers are. At least I know what The Cottage looks like and I won't gawk when I get there. Mrs. Flynn found the *Country Living* magazine featuring The Cottage at a garage sale.

I still think I'm doing the wrong thing, taking this much money for one singing engagement is obscene. And I have to get more time off from Festin, after Gaëtan did without me for twelve performances and the dress rehearsal. He's been really understanding, especially when he must suspect my heart's not in it at all. I am like some Stepford Wife waitress, serving and singing without meaning it. And you never know what's going to happen there anymore, like the other night, those muskrats exploding out of nowhere, bits of synthetic fur and microchips all over Festin. And if it's not muskrats, it's some other puppety critter shorting out or blowing all the fuses in the kitchen, making Chef Normand start ranting. One of these days they'll probably set off the fire sprinklers, and when they do, Tyler will probably switch us to a Rain Forest Theme.

Anyway, I must desert my post again, oh well, it's for Heidi. She sure is overjoyed that the bride is Tess and not her when she thinks of the summer she'd be having now if she'd married Emerson last year.

"Stuck out on that farm. Six months pregnant. At least. Hot as Hell. Emerson out back counting the pigeons in that rickety barn. Maybe he'd shoot one, or some poor starving rabbit, then bring it in and say he was going to whip it into a cassoulet."

Heidi's quite happy with the way things are now, with this romance with Miles on hold or in fantasy or whatever. She refers to Miles as her long-distance dalliance and feels it's the best thing going not to have to do anything about it yet.

"It's not what you'd call unrequited. What is it?"

"Unattempted?"

Like mine with Wilder. I think Heidi and me are involved in parallel love lives. Lost in the Galaxy of the Celibates.

Wilder wanted me to go for a picnic with him tomorrow to Man and His World, the reincarnation of Expo 67. I had to tell him I was going away, I had a singing gig near Boston.

"Boston? Hey, my town!"

"Yes. You watch mine while I'm away."

"We'll go to Expo 67 as soon as you get back, how's that?"

So of course I said he could go to Expo 67 before that and told him about Lenore's Folk Art World.

"You have your own museum?"

"I sure do. In my cellar."

He says it's another of the Seven Wonders of Lenore. He's impressed that I made it into a guidebook, even though the notice only got me two visitors so far.

"Three now. But I'm here on your recommendation, not the book's."

He had no idea I had so much interesting stuff. Of all kinds. He loves the Expo 67 memorabilia. That was such a great summer, an amazing year. The world came to us, we're always meeting people who said they were here then. Not him.

"A lot of my friends got to it, not my folks. Neither of them ever learned to drive, and Expo 67 was a driving holiday."

Maybe it's good that he never got to Expo 67. If I discovered he'd been at Expo at the same pavilion the same day as me it would have been another *Magic Tom* thing, finding out we had a cosmic connection. It would have been too Fateful. But it got fateful just the same.

"This is all pretty amazing . . . like you. I've never met anyone like you before."

It might have stopped there, leaving me reading a lot into nothing again, but I'm almost positive that Wilder was about to make a major move on me. I was saved, though, because that's when we heard, "Hi? You home?"

It was Heidi. Wilder gave me this look, and for a second I thought, I won't say anything and she'll leave. But I came to my senses pretty quick and yelled up, "We're downstairs."

And Heidi found me. Us.

"Who's we? Oh . . . hi, Wilder."

"Hi, Heidi," he said right back, like he had no plans for anything, like he meant just to sign my museum visitors' guest book and leave.

And that's what didn't happen with my third official visitor to Musée d'art folklorique à Lenore/Lenore's Folk Art World.

9

Heidi and I had a great drive down here. I loved the trip through Vermont, New Hampshire and into Massachusetts, and so did Heidi, even though it brings back memories of her relationship with Emerson.

I kept thinking that this is the way Wilder drives to get back to Boston. He kindly offered to watch our places and water the garden. And nothing happened in my museum.

But what if Heidi hadn't walked in? It's lucky that she did. I don't want to be the Other Woman. What kind of person would I be? And Wilder, too, cheating on his girlfriend?

I mean this, I hope I do. Nothing is going to happen. We can be friends. Good pals. Only. And I will be happy with that. I lie, I lie, but oh well.

Heidi said we could go somewhere special in Concord before she dropped me off for the wedding gig. She'd always wanted to go there:

Orchard House, the home of Louisa May Alcott and her family, where she wrote *Little Women*. Heidi knows everything about Louisa May, she's read all the books*, Little Men, Jo's Boys*, little this, little that. I think I only read *Little Women*. Heidi was a big hit with the tour guide. She asked questions and we'd both ooh and ahh and be interested, everybody else just listened.

It was enlightening to learn that Louisa May really wanted to write horror books, but the sweet books were big hits, and this is how she supported her family. Like when actors say, But what I really want to do is direct, Louisa May said, But what I really want to do is write Gothic thrillers.

I liked their museum gift shoppe (that's what Lenore's Folk Art World is missing) where Heidi bought a Louisa May Alcott saying done in calligraphy. She wants to frame it, but I think it will scare men off. It proclaims: "I'd rather be a spinster and paddle my own canoe."

Heidi thinks it's so self-sufficient, so empowering. But have you ever tried to paddle a canoe by yourself? How do you get it down to the water alone? They're so awkward. And even if it's already in the water, doesn't it need two people to make it glide straight? I've never paddled my own canoe. Not even at Girl Guide camp.

"I didn't either. I had to go out in one with this abusive British girl. She knew everything, she thought. And she kept saying how useless I was."

I can see why Heidi thinks going solo in a canoe is better. Of course the saying means much more than what it says. Heidi claims it's about many of us.

"We are the New Spinsters. We are defining what it is to be on our own, unwed. Unshackled. Unfettered. Free!"

Spinster is usually a nasty word, like you're a pathetic loser, an old maid who never met the right guy, never got married, and you live in a little room with a bunch of cats. How did it come to mean all that, anyway? All spinster means is an unmarried woman. And hey, that's been me all my life. Even when I was living with Fergie. No one would have called me a spinster then.

Spinsters led to one of Heidi's discussions when we got back in the car. About how well off we are, being free, paddling our own canoes. I am better off without Fergie, anyway. I don't mind being free most of the time now that I'm used to it. I should know when I'm well off. So why do I keep looking at Men, including ones that are taken. And here's Heidi acting so independent but longing for Phantom Miles in England. She must wish he'd paddle his canoe over the Atlantic and say, "Hop in, love!"

It took us another hour on secondary route this and exit that to get to where I have to be. Now Heidi's taken off to Fall River and left me here.

All right, so I won't be staying at The Cottage for the wedding. After all, that's for family, and I am the entertainment, the hired help. But Fairhurst Acres Inn is some gorgeous place. It's got a pool. And room service. Wow, my second time in a hotel in a year. Lenore and the High Life. The accompanist is coming for me in an hour. I hope Heidi has a good time at her Lizzie Borden Conference. I thought I got myself into some strange things, look at her, she's giving a paper at the Centennial of a Famous Double-Axe-Murderess. Because some of Heidi's people think what Lizzie Borden did or didn't do (yeah, right) was a Feminist Act.

What a scare! All I did was put the TV on to relax and there's me, on *Fiona!*

I sure earned my $2750!

I sang every song Andrew Lloyd Webber ever wrote! No, it just seemed that way. Some of them aren't so bad. My favourite was "This Is Not Like Me at All," which is about love hitting you when you don't expect it to and how it changes you (Emerson's choice). It was super-strange when Tess and Emerson spoke/sang the Love Theme from *The Phantom of The Opera*, but that made one less song for me to do. They saved practically every single thing the Carpenters ever recorded for me to do at the reception. (I didn't mind. But who would have expected that from Tess? There's hope for her, maybe.)

Bryant Dewsbury, the accompanist, was loads of fun to work with, but he's very gossipy for a straight man. He has played at dozens of society weddings and gave me filthy dirt on everybody. Of course I'm never going to see any of them again, well, hardly any of them, so why do I want to know all this? What a nasty wealthy Peyton Place.

Bryant trashed one woman who cha-chaed by us, he knew so many really intimate details about an affair she had that I asked him, "How can you know all this?"

"Who do you think she had that sleazy affair with? ME!"

He also told me WHY I got booked to sing at the very last minute. Hilary Rutledge had been hired, she's great, "Sounds like Dinah Washington only she's white." And even though Miss Hilary was not happy about all the Andrew Lloyd Webbers, she would do it anyway. But the Duchess, Emerson's mother, fired her when her daughter-in-law told her Miss Hilary was having an extra-marital affair with her darling son, Grantham the Second. The Duchess told Emerson there would be no singing at his wedding. He said, Oh yes there would be. "And there is, look who's here. Miss Lenore."

I don't know how someone can play piano so well all night after drinking that much. Bryant can sure put it away.

It's so seedy, but it looks so beautiful. The church was exquisite, great big bows on all the pews, the whole place dripping with tulle. It was the first wedding I was ever at where I didn't cry. And that's not because I had to be able to sing every ten seconds. Bryant said they were the first couple to attempt "a Sung Wedding." I guess I never cried because I didn't believe they meant it, and I don't like either the bride or the groom. I'm totally insincere, only in it for the money.

But being there meant I met up with my Fan Club! Those girls are really cute. Fallon introduced me to her best friend Dylan, who is the vice-president. Fallon's sister Portia is the secretary-treasurer. This is all secret, though, Fallon said. Her mom, the lovely Amherst Sawyer Lyndon, who never spoke to me, not once, doesn't know they wrote to me or are my fans. That's why they never sent anything to thank me for the pictures I sent them. I said they thanked me often enough with that After-School Applesauce recipe they sent me. Fallon was so happy. "You made it?" I said, Sure I did, lots of times, and the girls cheered. They made such a big fuss of me, they loved my singing, my dress, my hair, my evening bag. They were thrilled to bits that it was a gift from Wyatt Bardo, my fellow guest on *Fiona!* "It was a real rattlesnake? And he shot it for you?" Portia asked. Fallon was amazed there were no bullet holes. Amherst glared over our way. "My mom's not happy you're here, but we are!" Fallon said. "We were so happy when Miss Hilary couldn't sing because she's fooling around so much with our Uncle Grantham," said Portia. They were over the moon that there was a rerun of my *Fiona!* show on Thursday. They got it on tape this time. But their mom was mad, she heard somehow I was on again. And she was afraid I'd "cast a pall" on the wedding. Amherst has no worries, nobody here wants to talk to me, nobody except the girls. They wanted to know where I was going next, was I going to Boston? When? How long would I be there? Where was I staying? What was I going to go to? Real little groupies, very sweet. Of course if I really was famous and they became my fans for life and knew everything about me and never got over this pre-teen thing, it would be really sad.

Emerson and Tess didn't say a word to me about my singing. Nothing. I said congratulations to them outside the church, but maybe they knew I didn't mean it.

If Tess had said anything, it would have been, "Don't lie to us. We bought you off for $2750 US."

August Fourth, 1992. One hundred years ago today Lizzie Borden might have killed her parents: her stepmother (forty whacks) and her father (forty-one). And here's a college filled with scholars and aficionados discussing Did She or Didn't She? They're even going to re-enact her trial, where she'll get away with it again. Everyone here's hoping for Lizzie Borden House Tours: the one where she murdered her folks and then up to Maplecroft, the big place on the hill in Fall River bought with all the money she inherited once she got her Not Guilty verdict for killing them. From what I've heard — and it's been way too much — she did it. They never found the murder weapon, and she burned the dress they thought she did the murders in, so they didn't have much hard evidence. Of course she got off, her lawyer told the ALL-MEN JURY that if they could believe a woman like this could kill her family, then they'd better watch out the next time they heard their own daughter's footsteps approaching.

I get to be here in Fall River because I have a Friend Who Knows Too Much about this subject. It's strange for Heidi to be this way when she has such great parents. "I have always had a strange fascination with this case. I should have known better, but I couldn't help myself." Heidi did really well presenting her paper, "The Oppression of Lizzie Borden's Irish Maid." There are all kinds of theories about her, too. Some people, *not* Heidi, say she did it. Or at least was an accomplice.

One of the professors gave a paper titled "How Many Pears Did Lizzie Eat?" (Lizzie Borden said she was getting fishhooks and eating pears in the yard at the time her father was being murdered by some unknown assailant who'd arrived in a black coach.) An entire paper on pears. I now have lots of them as friends, but I don't understand academics! I am kind of ashamed of myself, bumping into that pears speaker on purpose in the hallway just because she was from Radcliffe and asking her if she knew of Katherine Melbourne? She teaches poetry? "Dr. K.M. Melbourne? Of course. Her paper, "Levertov's Vendetta Against Edith Sitwell," was in the August *Tri-Quarterly*. Have you read it?"

No, I had to say. (And who is Edith Sitwell? I'm never going to catch up!)

"Would you like to peruse it?"

I perused it, and I have no idea what it said. Why did I even do that? What does this make me, a voyeur? I am not like me at all, as the song says, I've become obsessed by a poet I don't understand. I read some of her Olga Poems and another one about Gertrude Stein's dog going slurp slurp in his dish in Paris. I am so lost!

I was spoiled by Bryant Dewsbury. I expected the Radcliffe Woman of the Pears to give me some good gossip about Katherine Melbourne, not this thing she wrote that made no sense to me. Katherine must be so smart.

Heidi's paper was nicely done and well received. A lot of people like the Irish connection to the Crime of That Century. Heidi admits she'd love to see the murder house, but it's closed to the public. (We live next door to a murderess, and Reine killed three times as many people. Isn't this enough?) Heidi heard that the kids who live in Maplecroft gave tours the other day when their parents were out. "They sold rusty nails from a barn out back!" The Lizzie Borden barn nails. Heidi thinks going to Lizzie's gravesite, where she's buried next to the people she murdered, "should suffice this sensationalistic need of mine."

I am so glad I don't have to go to the entire conference and can just peek in at talks that sound intriguing. The one on Forty Whacks wasn't at all what I expected. Lucky for me I can spend time at all Fall River's outlet stores. Heidi can't go to any of them, but she did get to the *Titanic* Museum behind a jewellery store in Indian Springs before I got here. (She thought I might be *Titanic*-ed out, I AM!) She says it has real stuff from the ship under glass. She bought *Titanic* fridge magnets and gifts for Daniel and me, which were supposed to be for whenever *Dog of the Titanic* opens. But she can't wait till next year, so she gave me mine, a pen with a clear top with a lifeboat, the *Titanic* sinking and an iceberg inside. When you move the pen, the lifeboat floats and the iceberg bobs a bit. I never expected anything so tasteless from Heidi. Till now! — she's not pure anymore because of being a delegate at a conference on Lizzie Borden! Soon as she's done with this, we're off to Boston.

Boston's one terrific city, that's for sure. We wanted to see every sight going, we did the Freedom Trail, Fanueil Hall, I had my picture taken in front of Old Ironsides. I did that for me and Wyatt, he will like a picture of that. Anywhere Paul Revere did his midnight ride, we went there, too. We tried to do the entire city, but you can't, of course, there's just too much of it that's interesting. And we only had two days.

On Friday, our second and last day, Heidi said there was some place Daniel had read about on Newberry Street that has gargoyles statues you can buy. It has Gregorian monks chanting from speakers and dead leaves all over the floor and clerks dressed like Friar Tuck. I was thinking, Maybe this is a store we should visit with a car, what if we buy a lot of them and have to lug them back to Nessa's place in South End? when Heidi said, "Oh, the Mapparium is somewhere near here." I thought she meant a street guide on a pole. But no, the Mapparium is a stained-glass walk-in globe at the Christian Science Publishing Building, right next to their church. "Mary Baker Eddy

Land," Heidi calls it all. Anyway, the Mapparium may turn out to be the place I met my destiny.

I was surprised that Heidi wanted to see anything run by Christian Scientists. I thought Catholics weren't allowed, but I was wrong. The Mapparium turned out to be amazing, you get to stand on a glass suspension bridge, very Superman's Fortress of Solitude, you're inside a globe done in stained glass showing all the countries of the world in the 1930s. And if that's not awesome enough, the way it's built makes sound travel up and down and around the bridge. Someone way at the back can whisper, and you can hear them like they're speaking right into your ear. And what I heard was, "Hello, Lenore."

I thought I was hallucinating, and then I heard it again.

"Hello, Lenore. I'm six feet behind you. Look back."

I did, and there was Wilder! And he spoke/sang, "I'm in love with a girl, Plaza O double-four double-three —"

What could I say, especially when I didn't know who would hear me? The sound doesn't always work directly, the person you're aiming at doesn't always receive it, it could bounce to someone else's ears. But Wilder sure knew how it works, his words got to me. Words from my own musical echoed back to haunt me, in 3-D. We didn't even stay for the tour guide's speech, we all rushed out to the street.

Heidi spoke first. "What are you doing in Boston?"

"Looking for you!"

Wilder looked right at me. I was struck speechless.

"I thought, How come they get to go to Boston and I'm stuck here?"

"Because you have classes to teach," Heidi said in her officious voice.

"I gave them some reading days. I missed Beantown."

"But you didn't really come looking for . . . us?"

Yes, he certainly did! He thought he would try, and he succeeded. He was watching our places, remember? I gave him all the details, where we'd be, every single location. He'd been to Nessa Stewart's townhouse that morning, she told him she believed we were starting with this area, so he'd looked in all the likely places.

He smiled at me. My mind went nuts. Why had he sung that song to me? Which girl did he mean? Could it be me? Or was he just being flirty? I mean, why did he come to Boston all of a sudden? Maybe he missed me? He came here to break up with Katherine because of me, because my museum tour made him realize he's too attracted to me and thinks he's got to make a decision? If this is true, why doesn't he say so? Then what we have doesn't have to be unrequited anymore, and we could go into a big romantic clinch in front of Mary Baker Eddy's church.

But all he said was he'd love to show us more sights of Boston. Heidi said really coldly that she wanted to see the Museum of Fine Arts or the JFK Library, and he said, "Be indoors on a beautiful day like today? Nahhhh."

Heidi didn't even argue with that, she agreed to go where he would lead us, and Wilder became our tour guide. He took us on the T subway and on a walking tour of Beacon Hill, then for lunch at the Bull and Finch, the *Cheers* Tavern. Heidi was "perplexed by its popularity," she's only seen *Cheers* once or twice. So it was wasted on both of us, I was in a daze. I was there but I wasn't, I was still in shock.

We were crossing the street to the Public Garden when Wilder said, "Make Way for Ducklings!"

We didn't know what this meant because we're not from Boston, but it's a famous kids' story about a family of ducks who end up living near the famous Swan Boats in the Public Garden. "The Swan Boats. The girls told me at the wedding we had to try them," I mumbled. Wilder insisted they were a must.

So he bought us tickets, we got into a boat shaped like a huge swan, and it paddled out on the lagoon. And there we were, gliding along in a Swan Boat in Boston on a beautiful, hot, sunny day and not inside some museum looking at pewter objects. Even though I didn't know what Wilder was up to, it was still kind of perfect, like bliss. And that's when I heard it: "HI, LENORE! LENORE!" It was coming from the Swan Boat behind us. I thought for a second I'd been spotted from the *Fiona!* rerun. But it was way more complicated than that.

That Swan call was joined by two others.

"Lenore! Here we are!"

"Lenore, LENORE!"

"Heidi! Heidi! Remember me? I named my Barbie Heidi after you."

"Yeah, and she's still called Heidi! We wish you were our aunt and not that Tess. She is the worst!"

It was Fallon, Portia and Dylan. They had tracked me down, too!

Heidi said, "It's Emerson's nieces!"

"And their best friend. Dylan."

"You know those little girls?" Wilder asked, charmed to discover another of the Seven Wonders of Lenore: I'm Mary Poppins.

"They're my fans," I explained.

The whole way round the big lagoon the girls waved and called, and I called and waved back. As we passed under a bridge, an adult voice from above called out, "What do you think you're doing, Lenore Rutland?" It was Amherst, the Mother, yelling at me and no place to hide.

"Lenore, don't you DARE try and steal my girls!"

"Your girls awn't in this boat, lady!" a passenger called back.

"Portia, Fallon! Get out of that Swan Boat! Now!"

If they'd listened to their mother, they could have drowned, both boats were in the middle of the lagoon. We paddled around a little island where the Ducklings in the book lived, the guide was telling us this, and Amherst was screaming at us from the shore.

"Kidnapper! Child stealer! They're my girls, not yours! Don't you dare corrupt them!"

Heidi was right later when she said it could have been much worse, Amherst might have jumped into the third boat and said, Follow that Swan, and we'd have started a regatta. We were also very lucky she didn't dive in and swim over. "She's a self-proclaimed excellent swimmer, always boasting that if she'd trained she'd have made the 1976 Olympics."

When we got to shore, Amherst tried to go for me, but Heidi and Wilder stopped her. As soon as the girls' Swan Boat docked she rushed over and dragged them out. Once she'd gathered her ducklings and their friend, she began yelling at Heidi. It's scary to think Amherst was almost her sister-in-law.

"Dr. Heidi Flynn! Of course you'd be in on this with her."

"In on WHAT, Amherst? We never saw your girls till they chased us with their Swan Boat."

Amherst turned on her girls. "A sleepover, Fallon? Portia? A pajama party at Dylan's?"

Some Swan Boat operators asked could we make a scene somewhere else, we were preventing potential sailors from casting off. The girls tried to defend themselves.

"We did have a pajama party at Dylan's."

"But where did you tell Dylan's mom you were during the day yesterday and today?"

"At the library. Working on a project. For school."

"In August?"

"Yes."

"And what did you tell her Portia was doing?"

"Cutting things out for us."

"This is the lie you told?"

"Yes. Dylan's mom believed us."

"Of course she did. Dylan's mom is a fool."

"No. She just sleeps a lot."

Amherst had found the pictures I sent when she discovered their Fan Club Headquarters (under Fallon's bed), along with notes on bus schedules to Boston. She shoved a paper in my face.

"Is this your itinerary?"

I had to say Yes, it was. How did they find out all that?

"You told us. At the wedding."

Come to think of it, too late, Dylan was the one who told me "to do the Swan Boats" when I said we'd be in Boston Thursday and Friday. They had staked out the Public Garden for two days. They missed us arriving because they'd gone to McDonald's to get Happy Meals.

"We were only away ten minutes."

Wilder was so good, he suggested we all go somewhere and discuss this calmly, he was sure none of it was ill-intentioned. Heidi had to agree. Amherst didn't.

"Oh, you shut your trap! You're her accomplice! Don't tell me you're not!"

Wilder suggested we find another part of the garden, quiet and out of the public domain, and not leave till this was settled. And when it was, as our Mediator he'd treat us all to Steve's Ice Cream cones.

"Steve's!" the girls cheered. Amherst was not in agreement.

"You don't deserve Steve's Ice Creams! Ever again in your entire lifetimes!"

For almost two hours we tried to convince Amherst it was a little girls' prank.

"How do you know? You don't have girls of your own, you never had children!"

Heidi reminded her that except for Wilder, we'd all been little girls, and we'd been "highly capable of this kind of subterfuge."

But no, not Amherst.

"I never was. I never did anything like this. Ever."

Heidi said she mustn't have had any fun.

"Oh, I had fun. I had plenty of fun. But hopping on a bus to Boston? What kind of bus driver lets two ten-year-olds and an eight-year-old ride into the city alone?"

"A driver with a really full bus," Wilder said.

She didn't think this was at all funny. Heidi and I didn't, either, but we didn't say so. He was trying to help. But what terrible things could happen to little children on their own like that! I don't want to think about the danger they were in from being my fans because I was on one *Fiona!*

We were about to try and go for ice cream when Harmon Lyndon found us. He'd run all the way across the Common from somewhere. He hugged Fallon and Portia.

"Oh my girls. My girls! You made Daddy so worried!"

Amherst glared at him. "Mommie was pretty worried, too."

"Oh, of course you were, pumpkin!"

"Where have you been?"

"With a client."

"I told your office the girls were in peril! Didn't they call you?"

"They couldn't reach me."

"You have that private cell phone number so the office can always reach you."

"Not here, Amherst. This is not the place nor the time."

"Oh yes it is! WHERE WERE YOU?"

And that's when Harmon was saved by Etiquette.

"Oh, hello, Heidi. How have you been?"

And then he introduced himself to Wilder. He said they'd all better get home, traffic would be terrible getting out of Boston.

"But Wilder's taking us for ice cream, Daddy."

"I told you, no ice cream, ever ever again!"

Then Amherst ordered them to say goodbye to me forever, and they did, and we all cried. I had to promise never to be in touch with them again or there'd "be litigation" and extreme punishment: even if accepted, neither Portia nor Fallon would be allowed to go to the college of her choice. The Lyndons and Dylan walked off across the Common.

"That sure made for an interesting afternoon!" Wilder said. I was grateful it was over and hoped I wasn't so famous from *Fiona!* that our child custody fight in the Public Garden would make headlines in *The Boston Globe*.

"I cannot abide the woman," said Heidi, "but I feel so sorry for her. Poor Amherst."

"Me, too. She must have gone crazy, worrying about her little girls and then not reaching Harmon," I said.

"Do you think Harmon's taken up with that Miss Hilary, the singer?"

"She'd be pretty busy! Not her, but somebody, eh?"

"With a client?"

"They couldn't reach him?"

We were on the verge of a really good discussion/gossip-fest when Wilder spoke up. But not about the dysfunctioning of the Lyndon Family. He changed the subject completely, he started to say said he'd love to take us both for dinner, but Heidi jumped in.

"Sorry. We have to decline. Nessa is having a small dinner party for us."

"Oh, that's terrific. I didn't want you to have nothing to do tonight, but actually there are things I have to see to."

Oh, we know, Heidi and I both said.

"What are you doing tomorrow?"

"We're leaving." Heidi took care of all the answering.

"Too bad. I thought you might like to get to the ocean."

Wilder figured I'd love to see Martha's Vineyard. Carly Simon and James Taylor have places there, and that's where the famous Black Dog Restaurant is. He has connections, he could even get us on the ferry. But too bad, we were leaving. He walked us back to Nessa's, said, "See you in Montreal." Then he went home to his place with Katherine in Back Bay.

Nessa's dinner party was all very elegant. She had Sistine Chapel paper napkins, guests got to wipe their face and hands on Michelangelo's Masterpiece. I'm sure they cost at least $6 US. Heidi's Lizzie Borden anecdotes were a big hit, and I should have made a better effort as a party guest, but all I could think of was how weird it all was. And what does it all really mean? When Wilder said he had Martha's Vineyard connections, did he mean he was going to go on the ferry with us? Did he hope Heidi would stay behind in Beantown? Did he want it to be a romantic rendezvous?

We made one stop before leaving town the next morning: the gargoyles store. We almost had three accidents getting out of Boston, I thought I should have bought one of those "I Survived Boston Traffic" T-shirts. Heidi said there was one last Massachusetts site she had to see.

It was in Salem.

We drove past all the kiosks of T-shirts and bumper stickers and by the House of Seven Gables and the Salem Witch Museum, which I thought sounded neat. "Salem's rife with them, it has a Witch Dungeon, too, with re-enactments on the hour. The Witch Hunt is a tourist industry." And she knew because when she was a kid and her family went to Hampton Beach she talked them into a Day in Salem and dragged them though every witch house. "Of course, then I didn't know how terrible a devastation witch hunting was." Then I got one of her mini-lectures about how for centuries millions of women were executed for being witches. Whenever a woman was feared for being too smart or having too much land or displaying any kind of curing abilities, like a doctor, she was put to death as a witch. I always thought of witches as stars of *Bewitched* or *The Wizard of Oz*. Now I'll never look at them that way again. Especially because the place in Salem Heidi wanted us to see was the Witch Trials Memorial, erected for the Tercentennial of the Witch Trials in 1692 when many women and men, too, were killed for being witches. We found it behind a tacky haunted house where a recording on a loudspeaker announced the next tour.

"That's certainly unfortunate," Heidi said when she saw the site. But it was chosen because they believe this was the very place where people were hanged or pressed to death. Heidi can find the most cheerful spots to take me on summer holidays.

The Memorial walls have flat, round stones jutting out for seats. Sort of like little sideways tombstones. Each one is named for a Salem Witch Trial victim, and each one had a fresh rose on it. There was a sentence carved into the ground floor: the truth about her innocence would be found out one day. These were the last words of Goody Nurse before they killed her. She was eighty years old. Salem did all this for the Three-Hundredth Anniversary to make people think about human rights and intolerance. It sure worked for me. It's a very sad place. I'm glad I saw it and everything, but it was an odd ending for my vacation, and to speak my mind to Heidi.

"Are you doing your best to keep Wilder away from me?"

"If I was, he wouldn't have spent the entire day with us yesterday. Do you know how much I wanted to see the JFK Library?"

"You could have gone on your own and wasted a sunny day inside."

"Did you want that? Was I in the way?"

"I don't know. Maybe he's in Boston to break up with Katherine."

"Then why didn't he say so?"

"Because it's too painful? Too recent? It's about to happen?"

"I don't think so."

"It's possible."

She sighed, "Everything is possible with you, Lenore."

And then she hugged me and said she was sorry if she was being overprotective. "I turn into my mother sometimes."

The rest of the drive home was pretty good. We never mentioned him again, and whenever I thought about Wilder, I tried to do it without Heidi noticing. Why didn't we have a couple more days in Boston, why did I have to get back to Festin, I could have been at Martha's Vineyard. What if Wilder did go to Boston to finish with Katherine, what if I'm right — and he comes back to Montreal to

ME? — he's only there till December. And in the months before I have to think about him leaving, what will we talk about? If I get involved with him? We don't really have anything in common. He's a professor of economics. What is economics anyway? How do you talk about that?

10

Why did this heap have to sit here all week?
It's leaking oil in case you care. It's a hazerd.
Muve it!

Conserned Citizen

What a waste of time going to see Jemima about my third Conserned Citizen note. When she opened the door she said, "Oh, good, Lenore. I wanted to talk to you." She didn't care that I wanted to talk to her FIRST. I showed her the note and asked her if this was Blake's. She said, "Of course not. Look at the spelling. And it couldn't be Blake's, he's been away."

"Away where?"

She said he was getting cured, if that was any of my business. I told her it sure was because I was getting threatening notes, and I thought they could be from him.

"No. I can assure you. I'll give you the number of the centre. You can call his counsellor. His doctor, even."

And she said there was no need for me to take such an offensive tone with her in any case, her nerves are somewhat shot.

"Because of Blake?"

"Why do you always blame Blake? He is trying his best to get better, and it doesn't help when people are so disparaging."

I could have left then, but she had to insist on telling me what had shot her nerves.

"The troubles Her Majesty the Queen has seen this year. It's been terrible. I don't know how she's coping."

I feel badly that the Queen is having so much trouble with Fergie and Diana and Charles and Camilla, but I have enough other worries, and Jemima seemed about to launch into a big long list of royal woes. I told her I had to go.

"No, not yet. That isn't what I wanted to talk to you about."

She needed to tell me about *Private Lives*, the British comedy she went to with all her friends instead of seeing my show.

"Who do you know at the Centaur?"

I said I knew everyone in Centaur Two when we did our show, I don't know anybody there now.

"Could you find out who I should talk to? About our seating?"

Because she wants to complain! She's mad because Centaur doesn't have numbers on the tickets, it's grab the best seat you can get as soon as you get in.

"No numbered seating! Atrocious! We had to wait in a line-up snaking through the lobby and up that see-through staircase. There were twenty-six of us, but such a crush of people ahead of us we weren't able to sit together when we got into the theatre. We were flabbergasted! We had to scour and fend for our seats! Do you know how difficult that is? Well, no, you wouldn't. You were on the Centaur stage, not watching it. Oh, I saw your review. Tsk Tsk."

This is what I had to go through to find out Blake didn't leave this note. Or maybe he did, and she's lying about his spelling. If only Jemima had to leave the house for a minute when I was there, and I was able to go though his old school papers, I'm sure she kept all his copybooks. I'll bet I'd find a heep of leeks and hazerds there. Conserned Citizen sure can't spell, and if I find out Blake can't either, BINGO! I've got someone Benoît can say "j'accuse" to. I don't care if Blake's drying out or getting sober, but if he is away, like Jemima says, who else can be putting this stuff on my car?

❧ ❧ ❧

Well, Wilder returned, and he called over to me from Madame's garden, "Hey, Lenore, I'm back!"

And here was me waiting for him to say, "I've left Katherine. I'm yours, if you'll have me!"

But he didn't. Heidi knew he wouldn't, she is so much smarter than me, it must be all that college education. Instead he said, "Katherine came back with me. She's looking forward to meeting you!"

Katherine wasn't there right then, she was out on the town.

"She's doing her own Westmount walkabout. Exploring 'The Village.' Getting acquainted with where she'll be staying for the next couple of weeks."

Wilder wanted to know what night's good for Heidi and me? Katherine's a gourmet cook, they want us to come over for dinner.

I told him I work every night except Mondays.

Monday's a ways off, but fine, he said, he knows I'll get to talk to Katherine before that. He was so right because just then she got back. She had little bags and bags of every gourmet item "The Village" sells. He grabbed them all from her and introduced us.

"Katherine, this is Lenore."

"It is? Oh, hello, Lenore."

"Hi, Katherine," I said. And then there was SILENCE. I thought: She's heard all about me and way too much, or She's heard nothing about me.

"Lenore's the singing waitress, Kath."

"Yes. I know. We'll have to go to your restaurant while I'm here."

And that's when I really felt it: shame. The Old Festin, the Laura Secord Show Festin, even, but no, please don't come to what we've got going on now. Festin on the Midway.

"They just underwent extensive renovations, isn't that right, Lenore?"

Yes, I told him, but there are still some kinks. (Some!)

"Not that many, I'm sure." Katherine said. "And your tenant, Dr. Heidi Flynn, she lives upstairs?"

"Yes. She's my friend, too. Heidi's at Concordia, like Wilder. She's a Doctor of English."

"Like me. I know. Wilder told me. I want to have a dinner party —"

"We thought Monday would be good, honey," Wilder said.

"Monday? I was thinking more Friday or Saturday."

"Yes, but Lenore works. At Festin? Her only night off is Monday."

"Oh. Well. Fine. Is Monday good for Dr. Flynn as well, do you think?"

Yes, I told her, but don't change everything for me. Really. Have it Friday or Saturday.

"Oh, no. We want you there, too. Is there anyone else I could invite?"

Wilder had some suggestions. "Heidi's brother Daniel's a really nice guy. And his partner Gaëtan? He's Lenore's boss."

"I was thinking more of women, Wilder."

"Academics, Kath?"

"*Yes.*"

That's when I came up with the Sylvias.

"The Sylvias?"

"Uh, Heidi's friends and mine, Elspeth and Beth. Doctors Torrington and Manion. They're both English professors, too. Very Feminist ones."

"Why did you call them the Sylvias?"

"Because they know a lot about Sylvia Plath. They avenge her whenever they can. They're out to get her ex-husband, that Ted Hughes."

"Do they call themselves the Sylvias?"

"No, Heidi does. They don't know."

"Oh, very clever. Yes, I'd like to meet them."

"They'd like to meet you, too. They told me to read the Olga Poems, by Denise Levertov."

"They did? Why?"

"Because they're . . . so good? And like Sylvia Plath poems?"

"Not really. But I'd still like to meet them. Anyone else?"

Wilder looked at Katherine like he was going to be tortured. "Is it going to be just me and all women?"

"That won't be a problem for you, will it?"

"No."

"Would you invite them all for me, Lenore?"

"Sure."

"That's very good of you," said Katherine, real cool.

"I told you she'd make you welcome in her city," Wilder said.

What stars am I living under? What kind of carpet am I standing on that keeps being pulled out from under me? I'm stuck inviting people to a dinner party given by the woman I hoped Wilder was leaving for me. I was feeling sorry for her, even! And what kind of party is it going to be? Wilder, me and Women Doctors of English! I am going to have to do more than read those Denise Levertov poems again to keep up with the likes of them! Here I go again, going round and round in Academic Circles.

I could get out of that poetry party with a real reason.

I didn't know what to expect when Gaëtan asked me if I could come in this morning. He looked so sad when I walked in, I dreaded one of two things: he was going to fire me, or Festin had to close.

The first thing he said was that he didn't know what he was going to do, he's tried his best, but Festin's lost a fortune already. That was no big surprise. The only new customers this dog and pony show is bringing in are kids, and they eat for half price and get pouty and mad because they're not allowed to touch the muppet thingamies, no feeding, petting or riding the animals. Then they're so noisy and bored after twenty minutes that they drive everyone else away. It's been going badly all summer but Gaëtan would always be optimistic — "C'est juin . . . c'est juillet . . . Ah, mais c'est aôut" — But every month it got worse!

Gaëtan's not the same person at all. He's what they call a broken, crestfallen man, it's taken so much out of him, it's like he doesn't want to try anymore. The man I talked to this morning is practically destroyed. And after all the dirt he took from Chef Normand, all those temper tantrums and hissy fits, Norm's leaving us to exercise his culinary genius on a cruise ship! That's when I mouthed off, "Good riddance to Chef Normand. Don't try to talk him out of it, let him walk their gangplank. I'm glad he's going, he has a bad attitude!"

Who is going to cook for us then, Gaëtan asked.

And I told him I may know of somebody.

"Toi?"

"Non. Marguerite Vichy."

He didn't remember that I told him about the Swiss-Greek-Belgian caterer who fed everybody so fabulously on *Dog of the Titanic*. But it would be no pique-nique with her, she's really full of herself, she's difficult and eccentric.

"Van Gogh, quand même," Gaëtan said and told me to try and hire her. He trusts my judgement, especially after I got him to take on Marie-France when she got out on parole, look what an asset she's proved to be as a sous-chef-in-training and dishwasher. (Marie-France showed up at my house and presented the Lulu Borgia cartoon I'd autographed for her at Tanguay as her identification. She had a letter of recommendation from Reine Ducharme.)

Gaëtan saying he trusts me with attempted hiring made me brave enough to tell him I've been doing a poll of what would make Festin better. And some of the ideas are pretty good. He wanted to know why I never spoke up.

"Because you're the Boss. And I didn't think you'd appreciate me telling you what I thought was best."

Instead he listened to Tyler, he said. "Tyler. Maudit fou, maudit —"

I apologized to Gaëtan for letting Tyler trick me into not challenging the electric circus theme. It's my fault it got through. And I started to cry.

"Non, Lenore. Non. C'est de ma faute!"

And then he hugged me and started crying. But a cry was very good for both of us. When we finished, Gaëtan said, "We will rebuild. We're going to go back to the old Festin and fix it from there." And he not only wants all my input, he wants me to run it! He said I have no idea how much he missed me when I was in Arizona and then off doing *Bells Are Ringing*. And it would mean the world — or part of the world anyway — to him if I could devote as much time as I can now to Festin. Because he really needs a break. If I say yes, he and Daniel are going to take a vacation. Hit the scenic road for a while.

"Can you be the Boss for me, Lenore? J'en ai besoin maintenant."

And what could I say but Yes, of course, I'll be the Boss. (Because I'd do anything for you, Gaëtan.) AM I OUT OF MY MIND? NUTS,

NUTS, NUTS? I KNOW NOTHING ABOUT RUNNING A BUSINESS. I still don't know the difference between being in the red or in the black. I guess I'll have to learn, and fast.

Maybe it's wrong and an invasion of privacy, but I'm glad I called Benoît this afternoon and asked him to see what he could find out about a Tyler Garrow who fixes restaurants. Why didn't I think of asking him to use his CSIS connections before?

And maybe I'll ask Wilder to help me with the economics of all this. Look at the books, whatever. I'm going to call in everybody I can. But no matter what, I can't use being Festin's Florence Nightingale and Patron as my excuse not to go to Katherine's Dinner Party. Dommage.

I went to the Dinner Party with ammunition on Denise Levertov. I remembered hearing how Dr. Joyce Brothers won *The $64,000 Question* by becoming an expert on a subject she knew nothing about. Boxing. She said that cramming makes everything go into your mind all at once and stay there long enough to win the jackpot. So, I thought, I would try to do what Dr. Joyce did and my subject would be "The Life of Denise Levertov." Not the poet. The person. I knew I could talk about that. How she was a nurse, born in England, came to the States, her father was Jewish, her husband was in the army. And she was outspoken about the Vietnam War and Nazi war criminals. Conversation starters like that.

I was surprised when Elspeth arrived early and told Heidi and me she had a surprise for us in her new Dodge Caravan.

"New?" Heidi said.

"Yes, I've christened her For Womyn Only. Isn't she beautiful?"

She gave a smug smile, and I looked at my wreck of a Dodge and Heidi's rusting-away red Volkswagen Rabbit in my driveway.

"For Womyn Only? Like the name of your chain letter?"

"Exactly! They work if you commit! Look what For Womyn Only and I brought you. You may have abandoned them, but I didn't!"

Our Moon Goddesses.

"Elijah and I did your second glaze so they could receive their final firing."

Elspeth made me choose a prominent place in my yard for Yoda (who she thinks I will call Thalia because she suggested it). Heidi put her Mother Goddess Thera (for the Earth) in her bathroom, for now. Elspeth didn't approve of the name.

"But Heidi, she looks more like a pagan goddess co-opted by Christianity. Like your Saint Brigid. Or Mary Magdalene. You could call her Magdalena."

"St. Bridget is an Irish saint! And Mary Magdalene — well, I am not having that discussion with you ever again, Elspeth. I am calling her Thera. If you do not approve, you can take her back."

"She's your goddess, hon," Elspeth conceded.

Then Beth arrived and agreed with Elspeth that they couldn't wait to meet Katherine Melbourne. She is such an authority, world expert, blah blah blah.

Heidi was in no big rush, she said she's only read two Denise Levertov poems in her entire career. "And I may have read 'A Tree Telling of Orpheus,' but I'm not all that sure." She hadn't done any research for tonight even though she was the one who got me all those books on her. I was in shock to think I knew more about Denise Levertov than Heidi does.

I still had no idea WHAT they were saying through most of the gourmet courses. Wilder would flash me a secret smile every so often, I think it said, "I have no idea what they're talking about either!" With all their critical thinking I was afraid if I said anything uncritical Elspeth would make the face she made at me at the Moondance, when I asked too much about Lionesses.

Then he said, If we didn't mind, he was going to see *Batman Returns*. And I wanted to say, Take me with you. But then I always want to say that! And that's why being at the party was so tough! I was such a hypocrite, sitting out there on Reine's back deck, eating this woman's fancy food, all the time thinking, What does he see in her? Yes, so she's really intelligent, but kind of scary-smart. And every so often I'd see her looking at me, probably thinking, How did this woman get into my party? Why's she sitting here with us when she could be up clearing the table, doing the dishes?

Wilder still wasn't back when everybody was leaving, the party ended way earlier than Katherine expected. But I did tell her why

Elspeth and Beth were called the Sylvias. So Katherine was asking for it when she said Sylvia Plath didn't deserve a posthumous Pulitzer Prize for her *Collected Poetry*. Heidi did her best as a mediator, but trying to get people to be reasonable only goes so far when they're hysterical. And Elspeth was screeching.

Katherine was what they call perturbed. "Please, keep your voices down. The neighbours!"

"The neighbours are all here! And they agree with us!" Elspeth shouted. "Didn't SP deserve the Pulitzer? For Poetry?"

And Heidi and I said she sure did. We had all turned on our hostess. Heidi took it even further.

"And she should have won the Pulitzer posthumously for *The Bell Jar*."

"Yes! Yes!" Beth and Elspeth both cheered and pounded the table.

Katherine retaliated. "Oh please. For *The Bell Jar*? But of course you'd think that, your critical senses are so dulled you said Plath's poems were similar to Levertov's!"

Elspeth and Beth said they never did.

Katherine looked at me. "No? Lenore said you Sylvias did."

SILENCE. That's when Elspeth saved my face. "So what if we did? It was only to say Levertov's works are inferior to Plath's!"

Heidi rose from the table and thanked Katherine for this evening, but we all had to go home, and as soon as possible. The impasse was getting bigger by the second. As we left, Katherine screamed after us, still mud-slinging,

"Did Plath ever achieve anything close to Levertov's 'During the Eichmann Trial'? All she was capable of was self-indulgence! A poem about the Tulips in her hospital room? Tulips?"

"Better than some Nazi war criminal. Or Gertrude Stein's dog drinking in Paris!" Elspeth screamed back.

Heidi and I made it out to the street as Beth headed to her Honda and Elspeth to For Womyn Only. But they were all still mad and discussing like crazy. Beth was horrified that Katherine's vilification of Plath had made them resort to attacking Levertov. She liked her poems, they were intense yet lyrical. Elspeth wanted to know, was Radcliffe aware that they had a professor who was a Plath-basher? They were so loud that Jemima came out of her house and said if we didn't lower our voices or take this skirmish inside she'd have to take measures.

"They're just leaving," I told Jemima.

"Make it quick. Or I'm calling the police." And she slammed the door.

"Who the hell is she? The street House Mother?" Elspeth wanted to know.

"She's Jemima Farnham —"

"Farnham? Her name's not Farnham?"

And we said Yes. Heidi said not everyone in Jemima's family was like her. Her nephew Miles-by-marriage is very —

"Is her husband a Brit, too?"

And we said, Oh yes. His name is Neville.

"Not Dr. Neville Farnham?"

Yes, we said.

"Oh, God. He's my gynecologist!"

This made the entire evening just too much for Elspeth, and she drove off in her chain letter van.

Heidi invited Beth and me back to her house, but I knew they were going to go through the entire evening again and rehash it to death. All evening Katherine had been making digs, before she attacked Sylvia Plath, she had called Margaret Atwood overrated and said a bunch of other nasty stuff, too. Anything they respected, she'd dumped on. Every time one of them tried to challenge her calmly, she'd changed the subject and brought out another magnificent course.

I left Heidi and Beth to talk and talk some more, but I felt sorry that the night ended so terribly. Here was Katherine trying to get to know some Montreal women and making this gourmet dinner with specially selected expensive wines (she never used any of the bottles we brought), and we all walked out in huffs.

I will never learn, I guess, because instead of going back to my house, I went to hers. Well, hers with him. Madame Ducharme's.

She was still sitting on the deck at the messy table, drinking wine and tearing grapes from their stems off the cheese and fruit platter.

"Forget something?" was her warm greeting.

"Just to say I'm sorry it turned out like this. But you can't attack Sylvia Plath —"

"I wasn't attacking her. And she's not even worth arguing about. Or defending so vehemently! My God —"

"I don't think we should talk about her anymore. Because we don't agree," I said.

"As if you know anything about Plath. But there is at least one subject we agree on, isn't there?" And I knew what subject she was talking about, it chilled my soul the way she said it.

"You mean Wilder?"

"Of course Wilder."

"We're just friends."

"Oh, I know." And she looked at me like Sigourney Weaver facing down Alien.

"You don't look like Judy Holiday. That's who I was expecting. He told me you were in *Bells Are Ringing*. He told me so much about you. What did he tell you about me?"

What was I going to say? That from Day One he made sure I knew he had a girlfriend, that he was in a serious relationship, that she was a bigwig professor at Radcliffe, that she wanted him to try poutine for her. But never once did he say he loved her. Or anything about her as a person. Like that she was a good dancer, or was kind, or was someone's devoted aunt or godmother. The first real thing he ever told me was that she was a gourmet cook, and tonight proved that was true.

"Did he tell you that he told me that if I didn't come back with him from Boston, he wouldn't be responsible for what happened with the woman next door?"

"He didn't tell you that?"

"He implied it loudly enough. I can always tell what he really means even when he doesn't say so."

She was really mean drunk, so much for the theory that you can't get drunk on good wine. She was so smashed by now it seemed as if she'd had a whole bottle right after we left her to have our street fight. I knew the situation was just going to get worse, so I tried to leave.

"I'm going to say goodnight now."

"You do that, little snowbird songbird."

I didn't get to make my exit on that because Wilder made his entrance. Katherine snarled at him.

"Oh, look, Lenore. Batman Returns!"

He could tell the night had not gone well, but he tried to pretend everything was okey dokey.

"Hi. The Party's Over?"

"It was over," Katherine said, all slurry, "before it began. They hate me, they really hate me."

I said, No, we didn't. There had been some literary disagreements after he left. He looked up at Katherine.

"Ah, Kath. I asked you not to give your opinions on Canadian literature or to start in on Susanna Plath!"

"Sylvia, Wilder, Saint Sylvia to them!"

"They were your guests, Katherine."

"They're all idiots! And Lenore's the biggest idiot of all. A waitress for Godsake! Go HOME!"

And she stumbled off into Madame Ducharme's house.

"Katherine! Don't talk to her like that! I'm so sorry, Lenore —"

And I said, "She's the one who should say sorry, Wilder."

"She has difficulty with that, saying sorry, ah —"

"Wilder!" she screamed at him.

"We'll talk, Lenore, I have to go." He disappeared into the house as she turned off the deck lights.

August 18, 1992

Dear Lenore,

I'm so sorry. I'd like to talk to you about it, but circumstances make it impossible until Katherine returns to Boston. I have some idea what she may have said to you, and I regret putting you in such an awkward position. I really hope I can explain. Sometimes I play a sober George to her Martha. It doesn't happen very often, but when it does there are innocent victims. This time it was you. I am so sorry.

Wilder

✻ ✻ ✻

I thought by George and Martha he meant the Washingtons, George the Father of his Country, but I never heard that he and Martha didn't get along. Patty Duke played her in a made-for-TV movie, but I didn't remember any marital problems or drunken brawls.

Lucky for me I have a Heidi and a Jamie, and they both knew which George and Martha Wilder was talking about.

"He must be making reference to the Albee play."

"Albee play?"

"Who's Afraid of Virginia Woolf."

Heidi gave me her college professor version of it, and later Jamie gave me his movie version. "Elizabeth Taylor and Richard Burton! She was Martha, this vicious drunk, and he was George, her pathetic loser professor husband. And she insulted their guests. Oh, you gotta rent it!"

I told him I saw enough in real life, thanks a lot. Anyway this leaves me thinking lots of things:

1) Does Wilder think they're Taylor and Burton?
2) Can their relationship be saved? And if not, what happens then?
3) When is she leaving?
4) How much did he say about me for her to get that nasty drunk?
5) Did she really come up here for two weeks because she's afraid of me? Who's Afraid of Lenore Rutland? Maybe Katherine is.

I can't think this! So I won't. Well, not anymore today if I can help it.

Reine had to see me, we could not do this over the phone. C'pas aujourd'hui! I wanted to say. My life is too full, trop trop plein right now. I'm the Other Woman when all I've done is think about it. Festin needs me every second God sends, and you want me to drive all the way up to Tanguay? But I went anyway. My trip turned out to be good and bad.

Reine had an advance copy of *Saturday Night*, Canada's Magazine. Randall Kingfisher's so conceited he'd autographed it.

He hadn't gotten her Yosuf Karsh like she'd requested, instead some hot shot Québécois photographer took these really weird pictures. (She likes them!) They don't really look like photographs, more like a reflection in a bathroom mirror after a shower. Very strange. And there's this soft-focus (out of focus) one of Brioche et Montcalm.

Reine needed me to explain what Kingfisher's really saying. She got most of it but realized that there were nuances that escaped her. Are there ever! She got me to read a line to myself, then translate it for her. She'd gasp at least once a paragraph.

"Mais j'ai pas dit ça! Non!" She's still pretty happy with the essay. Heidi won't be, she's going to do more than gasp when she reads it. Because Kingfisher did a number on her!

In a week or so, this magazine is going to arrive free with our *Gazette*s. What'll I do then? Hide it on her the way she hid my Aislin cartoon? She'll still hear about it. Tess of the d'Urberblondes Sawyer (I'm still in shock she took his name) will probably shove a copy in her face the first chance she gets.

"OOOH! If it isn't 'the hyper-critical, publicity-seeking, overly sensitive neighbour!' Would you also be 'one of those dyed-in-the-wool anglo Montrealers who never took the time to master the one official language of the ever emerging Québec?'"

Poor Heidi, he's really snide about her. And what a big liar he is, too. He wrote that Heidi kept pointing out items in Madame's Maison that "pronounced: Look, see, she's a murderess."

I wish I could hide them all from her, make sure that no one in Montreal gets *Saturday Night* free or pays for it, either. But what about the rest of Canada? What could Daniel and Gaëtan, me, the Sylvias and the Judys do to stop this? Maybe I could call in Miles Farnham, the Man Who Almost Climbed Everest, to lead us to the barricades as we stop all the magazine delivery trucks. It's too late to stop the presses. I wish advance copy meant it could be stopped from advancing.

Didn't Randall Kingfisher realize he could really hurt her feelings? Very little of this is true, okay, so her French isn't that great (but he's got no idea how guilt-ridden she is about that), and so he has one sort-of fact, but the rest is all his opinion. And Freedom of the Press shouldn't count when you use it to get back at someone because she was so unimpressed you went to the Sorbonne that she refused to have dinner with you!

Once Reine knew what *Saturday Night* had said about her, "a pure-laine Péquiste," she wanted to know about another one of her favourite subjects: La Monde de l'Amour. Mine. She asked me if anything had happened with Tyler, and I said Oh, yes, he's done his best to bring Festin to its knees. We're almost bankrupt because of him.

"Mais, L'Express? Ça va pas?"

No, I told her, I never dated him. He never asked again and am I ever glad about that! I've got Benoît investigating him. "Oh, c'est bon ça!" she said because Benoît caught her, maybe he'll catch Tyler, and by doing so he'll catch me! I told her I wasn't interested in Benoît catching me. "Non? Dommage. Mais peut-être c'est lui, après tout!" No, I told her, he won't be the one after all, we can't get along. She said there had to be someone I wanted, there must always be someone or Pourquoi Vivre? Madame Reine Ducharme, My Love Connection in the Lock-Up. "Mais si c'pas Benoît, c'est qui?" She had a strong feeling there was someone special. Anybody from my play? No, I said, everyone worthwhile is gay or married. À Festin? Gay or married, I told her again.

"Franchement, Lenore! Il te faut quelqu'un!" I didn't want her to be disappointed in love (my lack of it), and she was right, there is quelqu'un, so I told her all about the mess I'm in with Katherine and her tenant, Wilder.

"Willard? C'est un nom étrange, hein? C'est comme l'homme avec le rat? Dans la chanson de Michael Jackson?"

No, I told her, not Willard with Ben the rat, his name is Wilder.

"Comme Docteur Penfield?"

"Oui!"

"C'pas pire, hein?"

And then I gave it away just by saying, "Non! C'pas pire." But she took it to mean much more, she asked me if I'd taken him as my Lover.

"Non."

"Vraiment?"

"Vraiment. Non."

Then why is his girlfriend so fâchée? And I said that's what I want to know. Reine said I must bide my time, that's what she did with Roch, let one expresso lead to another, she can't thank me enough for bringing her that machine, Roch makes sure she never runs out of Van Houtte's. I had wondered if she was grinding beans from the prison cafeteria, she never asked me to bring her more coffee.

To be polite, I asked her how the dogs' movie careers were progressing.

"Les Chiens de *Titanic*? Ils ont fait la Première?"

And I said No, les chiens' latest motion picture career, run by Roch, who's put out les feelers.

"Comment? Roch? Il a rien dit! Avec mes bébés? Non."

I said, Maybe he's keeping it as a big surprise, he doesn't want her to know until they get hired. He wants to spare her knowing about all the humiliation involved in getting work in le show business.

Humiliation was the wrong word, it set her off. She started ranting and screaming. How could her dogs be put through this without her being told? Is Denys Arcand involved? Are they being made to do dangerous stunts again involving ice floes? Her bébés treated like one of the Gish sisters in *Birth of a Nation*?

Visiting time was up, I asked them to give me a few more minutes to try and calm her down, but they said I'd upset her enough already. Now I get to upset Heidi. Live from Toronto, it's *Saturday Night*!

I want to tell Heidi but I don't have the magazine, the physical evidence. Too bad I upset Reine, she might have let me borrow the advance copy. Or she could have used Roch's influence to get the prison people to make a photocopy of it for me. And she'd have made me an espresso while I waited. But with no proof, it's just Shoot Me, I'm the Messenger with the bad news. Besides I might make it sound way worse than it is. Or I might not make it sound as bad as it is.

I'm going to call Daniel, he'll help me break this to Heidi and talk her down.

She's not taking it very well. And all she has is my version of it. Wait till it's a reality. Right now she's a madwoman planning desperate measures.

"Can you get me into Tanguay?"

Madame's in a bad, betrayed way, but I can try.

Heidi almost had one of the *Saturday Night* editorial people sending her an advance copy till she lost it on the phone. I heard her yelling at someone in Toronto, "Has the sky fallen? *Saturday Night*'s usually a highly respected and researched publication. Or have you changed your mandate because sloppy journalism and sleaze sells? Are you now *The Saturday Night Enquirer*? Hello? Hello!"

It's like we've angered some god we don't know about and we're being punished. (Maybe our Mother Goddesses don't like our statues of them.) This morning I found my planter chicken with its head cut off. Well, sawed off, her chicken head stuffed inside the plant container. Heidi declared that this time it's personal, it's not like the beak-impaired pelican or the busted donkey cart or the punched-in-the-face Frosty, it's one of my own. And it's been mutilated. "This was a deliberate act of butchery." "Butcher knifery," I added. Cutting through plastic can't be easy.

Wilder came out of his kitchen when he saw Heidi and me in the back yard. All the time he was talking to us he kept glancing to his bedroom window, like he was afraid Katherine was watching us from up there. But she wasn't, I suppose, because he took the chicken and said he's going to try and glue the head back on for me. That's so thoughtful of him, Fergie would never have done that. He might say he would if I promised to make him steak for dinner. And then my chicken would have sat down in the basement forever waiting to be re-headed. I've got to stop this, I keep comparing Wilder to Fergie, but there's no comparison and no point. And if I don't stay away from Wilder, it'll be my fault if Katherine turns into a full time smashed-out-of-her-mind alcoholic. Heidi suspects Katherine did this. I told her that's insane. "Yes, it certainly is. And why do you think Wilder was so quick to offer to repair it?" I said he likes fixing things for me. "Especially things his girlfriend destroyed in a jealous fit. Don't forget, Madame Ducharme has that fine collection of Henckel knives." She figures Wilder came down to the kitchen this morning and saw a gaping vacancy in the Henckel rack. Then all the little red and white plastic shardy bits on the floor. Maybe he knows Katherine's not only a Martha, she's a Martha Glenn Close would play in a movie.

Today, August twenty-fourth, an engineering professor went crazy and started shooting people at Concordia, just walked down the hall and started firing. This was at Sir George. Downtown. Where Wilder is and Heidi is some days. Like Mondays. Like today.

I heard about it on the radio, I drove my car down there and triple-parked it, I didn't care. There were cars and police and fire trucks and Urgences Santé all over. And I ran all around trying to find Heidi, I even tried to get into the Hall building where it happened, but they wouldn't let me in. I was demanding, Did they know who'd been shot? and no one could give me names, and that's when Heidi found me. I couldn't stop crying. I was so happy she was safe. She told me she'd seen Wilder a few minutes before, he'd just gone to phone me to assure me they were both okay.

I was so frightened. When I heard the news there'd been shootings at Concordia, I thought, He's shot Heidi, I've lost her, some maniac has taken my friend away from me. I thought for sure the gunman would go after women professors because of the Polytechnique Massacre. But no, it was professors of engineering he went after. Some of them are dead. Some other people are in the hospital. They said a secretary ran down the halls warning people that he had a gun. Many people at Concordia knew this man was mad at the world. He'd threatened his colleagues often. I am so sorry he killed all those people and so grateful he didn't kill Heidi or Wilder. I'd go out of my mind, I think. What a terrible, terrible thing this is.

❧ ❧ ❧

Four engineering professors are dead. All men. He killed four people and injured three others because, he said, he was oppressed. It makes me want to scream, and I don't even work there. Heidi says they brought trauma specialists in to help them get over it. I asked her to give me tips. I'll take whatever she can pass on.

Now that she's gone back to Boston, Wilder came over and tried to explain about Katherine. It's a very complicated relationship, he says.

They've been together six and a half years and most of them have been good. Her drinking problem is a come-and-go thing. It's always brought on by other people in her territory.

"Oh, the Lioness Theory," I said, talking to myself.

"Whose is that?"

"Elspeth's. Is it other women that make her react like that?"

"Not always. Last year it was a lower-ranked networking male professor threatening her authority at Radcliffe. You've never seen a cocktail party get so ugly."

(I guess not, because I've never been to a cocktail party!)

I asked him right out if he used a threat to get her to Montreal.

"It was an entreaty, not a threat. I needed her to be with me for a while. To keep me honest."

And then he smiled at me, as if I knew what he really meant. But if he rushed down to Boston like that to make her come back with him, why did he go looking for me at the tourist spots?

"Katherine had to be at Radcliffe that day, I'd come all the way home to her, but there I was sitting all alone in our co-op. I knew you were in town. And I thought, Wouldn't it be fun if I could play tour guide for Lenore? And Heidi, too, as I found out."

"Well, you showed us a good time. Because of you we got to *Cheers* and the Swan Boats."

"Hey, and a meeting with your fans, don't forget! You got to see an American dysfunctional family on full alert! But it was a great day, huh? Here's to as many more as possible before I leave. Thanks for letting me explain about Katherine."

He had to go to work, so that's how we left it, even though he hadn't really explained at all. The conversation left me wondering all kinds of things. Why did I thank him for stalking me in Boston? Why didn't I tell him off for turning his girlfriend into a jealous monster? Why did he tell her a bunch of stories and insinuate things when nothing's going on? I never ask the right questions when I should. Like, when he gave me a brand new plastic chicken because he wasn't able to repair my other one, all I said was, "Oh, you didn't have to do that," when maybe I should have asked, "Why did you think you had to do that? Hmm? Is it because your girlfriend's insane?" Some people would be flattered that someone like Katherine went to so much trouble to show how jealous she is. I'm not, but maybe Wilder is. I don't want to know!

11

That Benoît. He shows up in the middle of a heatwave, in his uniform, and he doesn't even look hot. How does he do that, look so cool when he's such a hothead most of the time?

He handed me a printout.

"Pour toi, Lenny."

He was on duty and couldn't stick around for coffee or anything. He hopes this helps me somehow, he had to take time out from searching for Conserned Citizen to do this latest assignment of mine. He wants me to call him one of these days. Maybe we could go see Les Expos.

I said Sure, that would be great.

"Quand? Samedi? What's good for you?"

I said, I can't say yet, I'm crazy busy with Festin. But I'll call him, I will.

"Right. Okay. You call me. Soon, hein?" he said and marched out.

Thanks to his visit, I was armed and dangerous when Tyler finally showed up to supervise the exportation of his Sideshow, all packed up in back waiting for him to take it away.

"Hey. Too bad it didn't work out, Lenore."

"The same way it didn't work out for Days of King Tut. Jungle Nights. Seventh Heaven —"

I held up Benoît's printout.

"How'd you get this?" He acted like he was charmed that I went to the trouble.

"What's it called in the States? Freedom of Access to Information? No, that's not it. Wouldn't an American know what it's called?"

"I don't care," Tyler said.

"Because you don't know. Because you're not even American."

I think I saw him blink at that, but he couldn't deny it.

"I have an American license plate."

"No. Someone named John Biddiscombe does."

"That's me," he said.

"I know. John Biddiscombe, born in British Columbia."

"So what?"

"So what was all that for?"

"The big 1776 act? Come on, Lenore. Who's gonna listen to some Canadian guy from Abbotsford, BC, no matter how much he knows?"

"Or how little. All the names on this printout are big failures. How many would Festin make it?"

"I told you I'm sorry about that. Look, Festin doesn't have to stay on the losing end. I've got a way out of this tunnel. And it's beautiful. Let me light the way."

Tyler wasn't at Festin today with all his clichés only to pick up his stuffed animals, he was there representing some people. The ones who are bringing North America a concept called Prom Night. Theme restaurants devoted to reliving your Prom. Or Grad night, as Tyler admits he knows we Canadians call it.

"Customers arrive, you outfit them in the prom dress, the tux, the corsages, the works. People who are too shy for that can go for the Chaperone, the Punch Bowl Supervisor, the High School Coach, the Principal, the Dweeb. In October you can switch it to a Friday the 13th at the Prom Night theme. And there's room for a High School Reunion spin-off, too."

Calgary and St. John's have already signed.

"Did you sabotage their restaurants first, too?"

"I didn't sabotage anybody's restaurant. I admit it, I gave them ideas that didn't fly."

"So they'd go bankrupt, and then these people you represent could buy them for a song? Isn't that like insider trading, against the law?"

"Oh, Lenore, you've got some conspiracy-theory mind! I only found out about the Prom Night franchise recently. And what a godsend. I didn't know how I could help my clients who wouldn't listen when I said change is necessary, is written on the wall. Now I do. I can dig them out of this mess, let them save face. So, where's Gaëtan, anyway?"

"He's away on holiday. I'm in charge."

"You? You're not the Boss?"

"Yes."

"So he left Laura Secord holding the fort, eh?"

He had this tone in his voice that said, Well, Gaëtan's sealed Festin's fate now, baby. It's going down for sure.

"So, Lenore. What's Festin got going for it now?"

"Pay $34.95 and find out."

"I know you've got some Swiss chef. And she's very difficult."

"So was Van Gogh. Okay, so she's very temperamental. But Marguerite Vichy makes the finest Québécois fare Festin's ever had."

"Boudin-blood pudding? Turnip soup? Snails! What are you trying to do, turn this into Festin de Shudders? Montreal already has a Haunted House theme restaurant! But, hey, if she's as good as you say, there'd still be a place for her with Prom Night. You, too."

"Who do you want me to come as? Carrie?"

"Not unless you want to."

"I don't want to do anything with you. Or for you. You're not welcome here. So take your Toys R Us and get out of here."

But he didn't want to give up that easy. "So now you've got earthy Québécois food, you've also got everybody up doing Québécois dancing —"

"We've got all kinds of dancing."

"But you've gone big-time Québécois since you got rid of me. That was always my suggestion, but you'd all whine, 'No, no, we don't go there.' Not till the Ideas Man was out of the picture."

"You didn't want to celebrate being Québécois and Canadien. You wanted us to exploit our problems."

"Wait till you see the problems — like bankruptcy — that Fantaisie Québec is gonna get you into down the road. And that printout of yours? I wouldn't keep it for too long. Those names, they're history. Dépassé. Didn't think I knew that much French, huh? They're dépassé. Fini. Like Festin. The only kind of Retro people want in a Theme Restaurant anymore has to be from the sixties, seventies or eighties. Disco's even stayin' alive. But you're stuck in the 1600s. When you want out — and you will — have Gaëtan gimme a call."

He slapped down his new business card on the bar and walked to the back. I picked up his card and tore it up.

"We don't need your card," I shouted at his ponytail. "If we ever want you — and we won't — you're in the book under Con-Man-Piece-of-Garbage!"

I wish I'd thought of a more clever or worse name to look him up under, but that was the best I could come up with on short notice. I'm not even going to tell Gaëtan he offered us Prom Night. It will just make him madder to think Tyler came in here trying to franchise the place up when we're desperate. When he's the one who made us desperate.

Heidi's terribly upset with her sudden notoriety. *Saturday Night* is out. On the stands or free with your *Gazette*. Now she knows how glaring fame can be when you're a Neighbour of a Neighbour Who Killed. Especially if you're the neighbour who speaks bad French.

She's been invited to be on two radio talk shows and refused both of them. Even though she wouldn't go on the English one, she was the subject of an anglo call-in anyway, Anglo Apologists saying, What's wrong with not speaking French perfectly as long as you try? followed by Anglo Activists who said, Why speak French at all? or Why isn't there any English on our signs? and If we ever get English back on them it should be for us, not because we're losing tourists. Then some francophones got on, and their English was crummy, good or marvellous.

Heidi tortured us both by making us listen to it, all three hours. She almost called in herself a few times, she felt so personally attacked. "No mention, ever, of the man who lied and defamed me in print!"

It was a good thing I was able to stop her, but I won't always be there for her. Like, the next time someone says, "Saw your name in *Saturday Night!*" She almost went berserk when Elspeth said she'd bought a copy of the magazine this month because she knew I'd want to keep mine. Heidi screamed at her, "My friends don't keep a copy of this month's issue. It's a rag. If you care about me, follow in Lenore's footsteps. Throw it where it belongs. In your Blue Box!"

Yes, so what, Katherine is gone, they're still together in his heart. And that's fine by me because I don't have time for romance. Not even with Wilder, even if he was free, which he's not. And it's just as well, he'd probably be all wrong for me.

For starters, I told Heidi, Wilder's completely not like me, he hardly has any stuff.

"He's Spartan?" she said.

I told her if that meant he had no things, yes, he's Spartan.

Anyway, she agreed it's odd. I said maybe it's because he's an economist. He's economical with stuff. She didn't accept this excuse. "He can't be that minimalist. He must have some things."

"Did you see any when we were there for the party?"

Heidi figures that Katherine made him put them all away. Or we missed them, or they're all in the bedroom.

"He must have brought some mementos? Football trophies? A picture of his parents? A pet?"

I said he mentioned a dog once, but he couldn't remember its name.

"He forgot his dog's name?"

"Yeah. And his parents never learned to drive."

"Did they have some disability?"

"No, I don't think so."

"Neither of them? But they're American. Lenore, one of them must have known how to drive. Does he have any brothers and sisters?"

"Not that he talks about."

"And he's chained to that Medusa. Hmm."

She didn't say a thing after that. But I know she thinks it's odd.

She must, because I sure do. I guess I am happy to learn weird things about him, it makes him easier to resist.

Elspeth wanted to thank me so much for introducing Douglas to Paul and making them Stage Blood Brothers (their company name), she's insisting on taking Heidi and me to a play that's going to be done in the original Welsh. The ad in *The Gazette* showed barefooted women walking on newspapers spread on the floor in some loft and climbing big stepladders. I had to tell Heidi I just couldn't face it. Not after last year's *Force Majeure*. I can only take so much feminist drama, you know? But will I be insulting Elspeth when I say no?

"I don't know, I certainly hope it won't be another chain letter betrayal fiasco."

We tried to make up a really good excuse — reason — why I can't go. I said I could lie that I am going to an Expos game with Benoît. Yes, we'll tell her I finally have a date.

"Are you insane?" Heidi said. "Tell Elspeth you're not going to see *Glamna rhr Chllywellyn* because of a man?"

I said Elspeth was no one to act high and mighty when she was a slave to Douglas.

"She's not such a slave that she'd miss *Glamna rhr Chllywellyn*! Lenore, it's been proclaimed the best play of the nineties!"

"In Welsh. And the nineties are two years old. I can't go, Heidi, please don't make me go."

She said, We can't say I'm working because the tickets are for Monday, and I'm not working.

"Tell her I'm putting my tomatoes up. I'm doing my Tomatoes con Lenny. And it's got to be Monday night or they'll all rot."

Not good enough, she said. I could do that during the day. Ah, but wait! She has a good one!

I am going to tell Elspeth that I have to go over a new seating arrangement with Gaëtan. Elspeth will accept this.

"What sort of seating plan?"

"I don't know. You're the restaurant expert. No, say you've got to discuss yet another new theme."

"But Gaëtan and Daniel are still away on holiday. She might find out. You might let it slip tonight."

Heidi says I am making it very hard for us to tell untruths. We will never be able to get on *Fiona!* next year as experts on The Pinocchio Factor: Women Who Lie Well.

We can't come up with anything better, so Elspeth will have to accept that I can't go to the Welsh play because I am meeting with Gaëtan. And to appease her, Heidi's going to say that the first edition Sylvia Plath book she bought for Elspeth in Boston is from her and me.

Lucky Heidi got to see the feminist Welsh play of the century. I am so envious. She told me I missed an amazing piece of theatre, doesn't she know me by now? I will never like anything like that. Unless they translate it into English and it's a send-up and stars the original women cast members of *Saturday Night Live*. I miss Gilda Radner. And I will never like a play where women in overalls do "such interpretative things with oranges."

Elspeth came and picked Heidi up, they gave the other ticket to Charlotte, who was thrilled to go. I went out to wave goodbye, have a good time (so glad it's you and not me!) as Heidi left with them. Elspeth got out of her still brand-new For Womyn Only Caravan. She was wearing one of those African tuques, I'm always suspicious of white women who wear those things. I can't help myself. (That and men with ponytails. Why didn't I listen to myself way back on that one?)

"Tell Gaëtan next time to be considerate of Female Bonding, girlfriend."

"I'll do that, have a good time," I told her.

"If Gaëtan cancels on you, there are still a few tickets left, if you can believe it. Join us. If you can get that heap of yours out of the driveway! Bye now."

They were off, and all I could think of was, Did she mean heap or heep? Could she be Conserned Citizen?

I asked Heidi where Elspeth got that African hat. And she said, "Elijah the sculptor gave it to her."

"But Elijah's not black."

"Never mind that, Lenore. He gave her a hat. They glazed and fired all our goddesses for us in the heat of the summer. What do we make of that?"

Elspeth wished so much that Elijah had seen the play. "He can relate so much to Womyn's Works." This pronouncement makes Heidi and I pretty sure Elspeth and Elijah are an item or are about to be, and this is why she's so grateful we've got Douglas obsessed with a new invention. We're helping her have an affair! Now I know what course she's taking Saturday nights when her children get to see *Dr. Quinn, Medicine Woman!*

But Elspeth's wasn't the only surprising pronouncement of the evening. Heidi was let in on a bombshell she wishes she didn't know. She thought she shouldn't tell me, I'd get too upset. I promised I wouldn't. So she said, "Charlotte is leaving Viola."

I broke my promise, I got upset.

"Oh, no. Oh, no. But they've been together for so long. Like, twenty years?"

"Sixteen."

"They never fight. They're so happy together."

"Charlotte isn't."

"Has she met somebody else?"

"She says no. Viola wants them to go for counselling, but Charlotte says it's no use. They're over. There's nothing worth reconciling."

I said this was awful, the world must be falling apart. They were a perfect couple, they have that beautiful house! Viola and Charlotte breaking up, can you count on nothing in this world?

Sixteen years together, I said. But Viola was talking about them having a baby.

"Charlotte said Viola was pressing for it, but a baby won't fix things. They have nothing left in common."

"They've got Judy Garland."

"Judy Garland is not enough. I brought her up, Charlotte said Viola was always more into the whole Judy thing than she was."

✾ ✾ ✾

Yes, I love to cry at weddings. Especially forty-five year-old ones! Hugh and Sheila, Mr. and Mrs. Flynn were married forty-five years ago on Saturday, and what a celebration their kids threw for them in Ottawa. Some year this is, I can add Ottawa to Arizona and Rochester and Boston! And Ottawa's now on the list of my Concert Dates. Daniel and Heidi asked me if I'd sing at the wedding? I was thrilled and honoured. It meant I couldn't run Festin on a Saturday night, but Gaëtan said I'm working too hard and Mireille and Jocelyne can co-boss for one night. He's back from a month's holiday, but he says he's still not ready to go back to work yet, he can't compete with me as La Patronne (yes, you can, I want to say, please come back!), but I can leave Festin for one night. Après tout, it's for Daniel's parents. Anything for them, anything for Daniel. Even though he's Daniel's significant other and he can't be there. Just as well. Gaëtan would have had to face Daniel's brothers again and meet dozens of aunts and uncles, and he feels nobody's ready for that. Especially not Mr. and Mrs. Flynn or Daniel. You don't come out at your parents Forty-Fifth Wedding Anniversary. And if you haven't by then, forget it!

I thought I'd get to sing from above in the choir loft in this magnificent basilica, but the priest had me sit up on the side by the altar. So I got a real close-up view of Mass. I have never been to one before.

The entrance procession was sure impressive. The Knights of Columbus, marching in fabulous outfits with different coloured sashes and Three Musketeers hats, all the Flynns grandchildren: Patrick, Siobhan, Sheila Mary, Hugh Joseph, Meaghan, Sean and Tatum. And then the Bride and Groom, Mr. and Mrs. Flynn. People cheered and whooped and hollered, I like that, it wasn't solemn at all. (I started to cry, but I didn't allow myself to give in to that, I had a song to sing.)

Father Sullivan, who celebrated the Mass, was the original priest who married them. But he's kind of caught in 1947. Or even way before that, because he picked things for readings and gospels that were not Mrs. Flynn at all, and definitely not Heidi Approved.

That one from Genesis about Adam and Eve, how she was made from his rib and was on earth to be his helpmate and do what he wanted, and how she would always be second best. And all women after her. The priest didn't read this one, Heidi's brother Patrick did. Then there was a Song of Solomon passage, not too bad, read by her cousin, Don't-call-me-Kathy Kathleen. For the Gospel Father Sullivan read from the New Testament. I've heard this story before in Sunday School, and I always wondered about it.

I could see everybody in the church from where I sat, including Heidi and Daniel making faces. I had to keep a straight face, and it was hard because of what it was doing to Heidi. Even I, who wasn't brought up with this much Church, knew it was the wrong reading to pick to celebrate forty-five wonderful years.

It was the story of Martha and Mary. Not Mary, the Mother of Jesus, another Mary. Jesus is coming to visit, so Martha cleans the house and bakes and works like a fiend while Mary goes off to the hills and sings and picks flowers. When Jesus arrives with all the apostles, He tells Martha to stop working and join them, be like Mary. Take your shoes off, relax, chill. This would show him respect. Mary is the one who gets all the credit for being peaceful, and Martha gets told off. After Father Sullivan read it, I figured, well, he's going to say that this was the first time Jesus missed the point. I mean, how did all those men think the food got to the table? Why didn't Martha say, Jesus, if Mary had helped me I'd have had more time to relax! She's a lazy slob. We'd all like to go off singing and picking flowers, but someone had to do all the work!

But no, Father Sullivan said this story was a parable explaining the success of the Flynns' marriage. It exemplified the value of dedication by wives to their husbands, that Sheila Flynn was a true helpmate to Hugh, she was both Martha and Mary. If she was them, who did Father Sullivan think Mr. Flynn was?

It was funny later when Heidi made a crack about the sermon and how amazed she was her mother didn't laugh. Or walk up to the pulpit and say to Father Sullivan, "You sit down now. I have a few things to say about this!"

And Mrs. Flynn said, "The sermon?"

"Yes, Mommy. Martha and Mary?"

She didn't remember the sermon or the Gospel reading. She was so nervous over having to say their vows again.

"To love and honour, yes, but that vow to obey? Not unless he promises to obey me! I told Father Sullivan to take obey out, I was afraid he'd sneak it back in."

This time after the service the bride and groom thanked me for my singing. Their absolute favourite was "our song," "True Love," from the 1956 Princess Grace and Bing Crosby movie *High Society*. Mr. and Mrs. Flynn were married nine years before they finally knew what their song was! One of the church ladies told me Father Sullivan really likes the Flynns, that's why I got away with singing so many songs that were unliturgical.

I told Mrs. Flynn how much I liked their church, especially all the old-fashioned holy statues.

"We kept them despite Vatican II. I love them, they're pretty, eh?" she said.

I didn't know who most of them were. I recognized St. Patrick though. And St. Joseph and Mary.

Mrs. Flynn asked me if anybody had left a Blessed Virgin Mary statue on my steps or in my back yard? She'd heard about my orphaned lawn ornaments. Heidi lost her patience. "I told you no already, Mommy. That would be too obvious. Like leaving lawn jockeys."

"They have Marys. But people don't have lawn jockeys so much in Québec."

"Thank goodness."

"And Lenore doesn't have any, eh?"

"Of course not. Lawn jockeys are in bad taste and racist."

"Heidi, people don't have them because they're racist. If Lenore tried to have one, you'd probably kidnap it."

"No. Because if I kidnapped it, I would have to keep it in my home."

"You could bring it to Ontario. We could drive it to some rural place where it would be welcome."

Heidi and her mother have this sort of discussion all the time.

Mrs. Flynn said someone stealing a Mary statue from a home-made shrine (turned up bathtubs with lights in them) was asking for big trouble. It was also bad luck to play Mary or Jesus in the movies. Those actors always died in fires or by falling off balconies. I sure missed a lot by not being a Catholic.

Heidi put on a brave face when her Aunt Kit came over and presented her with a *Saturday Night*.

"We thought you'd like another copy. I showed it to everybody, I was so proud. I said, That dyed-in-the wool anglo is my niece!"

Other than that, we had a grand time at the anniversary party, with a live Irish band and all that food and the singing. But Daniel wasn't as much fun as usual. He was blue, I'm sure, because Gaëtan couldn't be there, too. And never would be if they don't tell anyone in the family except Heidi. All Daniel said about their trip was that it was great fun and they saw a lot of places they've always wanted to see. And that they were so grateful I was able to take over at Festin and make it possible. Daniel says he hopes it hasn't been too much for me and I can keep up the good work. Gaëtan was really burned out by the summer and needs more time before coming back.

Daniel and I had long talks because we danced together a lot. This didn't go unnoticed by his relatives. Mrs. Flynn was very happy. There I go again, handing her false hope, giving her new ideas, leading her astray.

Late breaking bulletin, after less than eight weeks of marriage, Tess has walked out on Emerson. She's left the Farm and moved back into her Plateau home. With the sublet tenant still in it. As well as the mean cats. (If the tenant's smart he'll pull a midnight move and flee in the night.) This was the big news in the English Department today, and Heidi phoned me right away. Was it something I sang?

Viola warned Heidi she was about to burst in on her in less than an hour. She had to give us some terrible news about Charlotte. When I got there, Heidi was madly trying to clear things up. I love Heidi, but she is a really messy person.

"Why are you cleaning up?"

"Viola has enough chaos in her world as it is. And she's a freak about tidiness!"

"When's she getting here? Next Wednesday?"

Heidi says I have developed "an occasional sarcastic streak" since we became friends. She hopes she's not responsible. She thinks I caught it from her mother. I was helping her shove stuff under stuff in the living room when her doorbell rang.

"Throw all this in my room!"

Which is terrible, a bulldozer couldn't save it, Emerson's Nazi neatness was the only good thing he would have brought to their marriage.

Viola was a wreck. "There is someone else! There always was someone else!" she announced as she stormed in. Apparently Charlotte was not all that truthful with Heidi at the Welsh play. "She's been seeing this home-wrecker since the spring."

That's why Charlotte thought counselling would do no good, why Judy had lost her allure. Not for Viola, though. Could Heidi put this *Best of Judy Garland* tape on? She was playing it in the car on the way over. She finds it oddly soothing. So Heidi did, and Judy started singing about what Love can be.

"You won't believe who it is," Viola began.

And I thought please don't say it's Tess of the D'Urberblondes. I can't take this, especially when we can't have anything stronger than Earl Grey tea because I have to go to work in a few hours.

She made us guess. But it wasn't Tess. And it wasn't a man. She had to tell us, it was "One of what they once called the Beautiful People. And she's twenty-two years old!"

"A younger woman?"

By now Judy had sung that Love can be insane, a life of sadness and pain, an evil-doer dirty shame, and could put you in a fog that made you feel like a dog. How did Viola find this comforting?

"Yes. A beautiful younger one. You know, I see beautiful people every day, too! All right, perhaps not every day, I work in a lab. But there have been temptations. Lots of younger ones. Technicians. Students," said Charlotte.

"Oh, yes," said Heidi.

"You must remember Amanda?"

"Yes. Not that I thought of her —"

"No. Well, you wouldn't."

"No, but I know there *are* temptations," agreed Heidi.

"Like who?" I asked Heidi. She never told me about anybody except Miles of Everest, and he's her age.

"Devon."

"Devon? Your tutorial student?"

"Yes. I've thought about it, but I wouldn't do anything, no matter how incredibly alluring he is. I'm not some pathetic sexual predator Older Woman! Even if I sometimes wish I were. He's twenty-one years old, for heaven's sake. He's my student, and it's forbidden to betray student-teacher trust. It would be stupid and wrong. But some people don't see it that way."

"Like Charlotte! Her new girlfriend's not only younger and beautiful, she's a model! An eighty-six-pound model."

They met on a photo shoot Charlotte did for Eaton's Christmas catalogue. It's so sordid, and it's going to be a real mess. This model from the New Breed of Beautiful Young Lesbians (Viola's words) is on her way up in the modelling world, claims Charlotte. By twenty-two, don't you have to be there already? Don't they know by then if you're a Cindy Crawford or Naomi Campbell? Charlotte kept mentioning that Eaton's photo shoot at Heidi's birthday party, the theme was Bored and Beautiful Youth in Hush Puppies. Her super model was modelling frumpy shoes. But Charlotte plans to follow her career. She believes in the new Twiggy so much she's moving to Toronto, her model has a fashion spread for *Chatelaine*. And if Viola wants to keep their beautiful house, she has to buy Charlotte out.

"I wanted us to have a baby, she's taken up with one!"

Before I felt badly for both of them, now all my sympathy's with Viola. She's the Wronged Woman in this break-up. I know when both people are your friends you're not supposed to take sides, but I can't help it this time. I am so mad at Charlotte I'm glad I didn't try to recommend her to do Reine's portrait for *Saturday Night*.

I didn't know how Viola and Heidi could be so deep in conversation that they never noticed what Judy was singing. A comfort to Viola, I don't know HOW, but a torture to me. Because one of the songs was all about how she couldn't ignore the boy next door, she loved him more than she could say. Judy was singing to me. And I had to face it: I'm still not over him. I'm still wild over Wilder.

So you're heep's still here.
If yo can get it started, going to
drive it into the Lachine Cannale?
If you dont somone else will!

Conserned Citizen

Now I've met somebody else from Wilder's Life. The doorbell rang and Wilder asked me to get it because he couldn't leave his stir-frying. A young man stood at the door.

"Hello, there. Would Wilder Taft live here now?" he asked.

"Yes."

"Great! Got the right place. Can I see him, please?"

"Now? Are you one of his students?"

"No," he said, "I'm his son."

"His son?"

"Yeah."

"Does he know about you?"

The young man said, "Of course he does. I'm Trey."

"Très what?"

"No, that's my nickname. It means 'the Third.'"

"You're his third son?"

"No, I'm Wilder the Third."

By now, Wilder the Second had left his stir-frying. He was thrilled to see his surprise guest.

"Trey! Buddy!" Wilder put his arm around the son I didn't know he had, and they walked into the living room.

"Hey, great place you got, Dad. It's pretty French, huh? Kind of foreign. Oh, I forgot my stuff on the porch."

His stuff was a big suitcase and a knapsack. I brought them in.

"Thanks," Wilder II said. "Trey, this is a woman I want you to meet, a great lady."

"Hi, Katherine," Trey said.

Wilder said I wasn't Katherine.

"No? Oh, sorry. Hi, there."

"This is Lenore, she lives next door."

206

"Wow. Hey. All right! Next door. Glad to meet you, Lenore."

Wilder told Trey I was a friend and tonight was my night off from work at Festin du Bois.

"What's that? I don't speak French."

"It's a theme restaurant, very French Canadian."

"Awesome."

"She's the hostess there now."

"Like a maître d'?"

I spoke up. "Like the manager. I sing, too."

"Wow. All right! That's great."

Trey wandered into the dining room.

"Hey Dad, you expecting a power blackout? What's this all for? Dinner by candlelight?"

Wilder had lit quite a lot of candles all over the place. It looked pretty romantic. Trey suddenly realized that, too.

"Oh, Dad. It's for you two. Bad timing, wow, sorry."

And we said No, it was great timing, the food was ready even. Wilder blew out almost all the candles. "Hey, we don't need all these!" And he was sure right, all through dinner they caught up on father-son stuff and news about Trey's mom. And his sister Bonnie, too. Wilder's other offspring.

And now it's eight-thirty p.m. and I am home. I don't want to have any suspicious thoughts, but I can't help it. I think I have some new things for my Weird Things About Wilder list. Because, if Trey is Wilder III, there had to be a Wilder I before there was the Wilder II who said he was named after Dr. Wilder Penfield. How old was Doctor Penfield? Wilder's father would have to be born in the 1920s or so. Was Dr. Penfield doing brain surgery then? Was it even invented? Why doesn't my Folk Art World have the *The Canadian Encyclopedia* in its collection! And Heidi's not home. She's gone with Viola to see *Death Becomes Her* with Meryl Streep and Goldie Hawn. I'm going crazy wondering about this. I wish there was some 1-800 hotline I could call for help about Canadian Heroes. And the Westmount Library's closed. There should be a way to get vital statistics like birthdates in emergency situations. Like when you think someone you'd like to think is a friend told you a BIG LIE.

And finding out he has not one but two kids he never mentioned, a son and a daughter he doesn't even have pictures of on Reine's photo gallery table. And why did Trey think I was Katherine? Has he never met her? Wilder's been with her six and a half years! He's an odd man, this boy next door. A Man of Mystery.

I am fixating on this, "it is a puzzlement," as the King of Siam would say. Heidi will help me figure it out.

Heidi had Dr. Wilder Penfield's dates — of course, she has everything up there — 1891-1976. Which means that Wilder Penfield would have to be really famous as a neurosurgeon by the 1920s to have a baby named after him, Wilder I, father to my friend Wilder II. Which really meant, to me, that Wilder had to be fibbing big time (lying) about being named after Wilder Penfield because his parents wanted him to grow up to be a brain surgeon. That's what I thought he told me when we first met. But I was wrong! He really told me, he said, that he was named Wilder II *after* Dr. Penfield had made the name Wilder famous.

I feel so guilty, how could I ever think he lied to impress me that he was an American named after a famous Canadian (born in Spokane, Washington). It's a good thing I got it cleared up by asking him right out how there could be that many people named after Wilder Penfield in his family. But it was me who got it mixed up, my comprehension skills need work, I guess.

I'm just so glad to find out Wilder didn't lie about his name. I asked him if it was Wilder like in the *Little House on The Prairie* books. "No relation to Laura Ingalls Wilder, sorry. Or Thornton Wilder. Or Billy or Gene Wilder."

He apologized for Trey's arriving out of the blue when we were having dinner together. Nosy me, I had to ask him how come he never mentioned him.

"I don't get to have him around much."

Had his wife got custody?

"She's not my wife."

"Sorry. Your ex-wife."

"We never got married."

But they had two kids?

"No. We had one."

So where did Bonnie come from?

"Another woman. A girlfriend in college. Jesse didn't want to get married, but she wanted to keep our baby. Yes, so I have not one, but two grown children. It's complicated. I guess that's why I never mentioned them, they take some explaining. I'm embarrassed. I'm not exactly Father of the Year."

He admits it's strange that he doesn't have any photos of his kids up here.

"But Madame Ducharme's got enough family portraits for me!"

He didn't want to dislocate any of her stuff. He's got a picture of Bonnie and Trey in his office, but he feels hypocritical, like it suggests he's a family man. "And I am a total failure at that."

I told him Trey doesn't seem to have any complaints.

Trey's going to be here for a while, Wilder doesn't know how long. This may be good for both of them, Wilder can get back in touch with his Father side.

Heidi still thinks Wilder lied to me, and never once mentioning he had kids is really strange. But she admits she can't trust any man whose girlfriend is psychotic and a psychopath.

12

Heidi and I got invited to be on *The Dini Petty Show*. The Dini people said the *Saturday Night* article is creating "a buzz in TO and across the country." Randall Kingfisher's already agreed to be a guest. They wanted me to be on because of being on *Fiona!* and the person Reine confessed to. I told them sorry, no. I have no free time, I have no life. I am too busy keeping Festin afloat. They said, Did I think Heidi Flynn would make a good guest? And I said, Not unless they were planning a televised killing. Because there will be if Heidi gets near Randall ever again.

They said that while civilized debate and banter is good, mud-slinging that leads to violence is not their style. Maybe they'll just stick to Kingfisher, but did I know how I could get hold of Madame's little dogs? The article said they've already been in a movie? If they're trained, they could maybe do a trick or something on the program.

"They are not trained. They went for training but it didn't take."

"Do you know how we could get them?"

"To do what?"

"To be on *Dini*."

"To be what on *Dini*? Well behaved?"

"No. Just on the show. Look, where are Briand and Fontaine? Where can we find them? They can't be in prison with her. They're not staying with you, are they?"

"Why ask me? Just because I looked after them for a while?"

"I thought I heard dogs before. Little barks."

"Next door."

"They sounded really close, like they were right under the phone."

"No. Sorry. Got to go. Thanks for calling."

I can't believe the dogs are back and I'm stuck with them! Just because Reine's romance is no longer a fine one.

I'll never forgive Roch Duplessis for bringing the dogs to Festin. On our first truly busy night, when *Gourmet* magazine decided to review us for the Dining in Canada issue.

But my goddess Yoda must have changed her mind and decided she likes the statue I did of her, because Festin was pulled back from the brink not once but three times. In the same night. Who could have hoped the *Gourmet* reviewer had the same breed of obnoxious toy dog as Brioche? And that her favourite vacation spot in the world has always been Berne, Switzerland, Marguerite Vichy's hometown!

Then those hyper-allergenic dogs running around the kitchen and barking so much, the only way to shut them up was to sing to them? They were in every single musical number, and the Festin diners loved it. That doesn't mean there will be a Return Engagement, even though there's one for them here. Chez moi!

Trey's still around and he likes les chiens. They've bonded. A Boy and His Dogs. I am so happy! He takes them to the park for me. He plays with them, he's even having success with some of the Wolfe Techniques Heidi and I could remember. I am so lucky he has nothing better to do with his life right now. Trey's a great twenty-year-old. A tribute to his dad. I can put Trey on the Good Things about Wilder List, even if he never would have mentioned a son if one hadn't shown up.

I should never have just dropped over to see him, but all I've done since is talk to him on the phone. The last time I saw Gaëtan was the day he asked me to take over Festin. That was over two months ago, and today it hit me how long I've gone without seeing him. And how much better Festin will be run when he comes back. So I went over without warning to their place, my camouflage being that I needed to talk about business in person. That's why I went over there without telling him, why I showed up in the middle of the afternoon when Daniel was at work. I rang their bell, and Gaëtan's voice on the intercom sounded very stressed.

"Lorraine?"

Lorraine? And I said, No, it was me. Surprise. Coming to visit.

"Lenore? Pitoune?"

"Yeah! I miss you! Can I come up?"

He said No, it was a bad time. Standing there, I had two terrible thoughts. One: he's had a nervous breakdown, is really depressed and can't see anybody, he's done one of those crawl-into-the-hole-and-hide-from-the-world things. Two: he's having an affair. Gaëtan's got someone with him. Or maybe he's expecting someone, and it's a her, Lorraine! This made sense, why he was so upset I was there. I was getting mad at him for being unfaithful to Daniel and about to tell him off through the intercom when he changed his mind and told me I could come up.

And that's when I found out why he had to go on holiday to see things he's never seen before, why he hasn't been back to work, why he's probably never coming back.

Gaëtan is sick. Really, really ill. And they didn't want anyone to know because it would upset us. Us. They were going to go through this by themselves. Daniel's been taking care of him at home with help from visiting CLSC nurses, Lorraine has the afternoon shift.

Gaëtan always sounded like himself on the phone, he sounded great. Funny and charming like always. I knew he was HIV positive. I knew the real reason he wasn't coming back to work was because he was sick. I knew it, I must have, deep down. He doesn't look the same at all, he's lost so much weight. I know he can't get better now. Nothing can stop this, it's only going to get worse.

Heidi and I will be part of the Palliative Care Team for Gaëtan. Who ever knew there was a community health service like Project Access to help provide care for AIDS patients? The CLSC nurses are angels helping Daniel take care of Gaëtan. We're going to work out shifts. Caregivers round-the-clock. This way maybe he won't ever have to go to a hospice, he'll have friends around, and maybe some of his family, too. Gaëtan says Daniel can tell his sisters and brother he's sick, even though he never wanted any of us to see him like this.

Heidi and I walked a lot this month. We did Ça Marche to raise funds for AIDS/LE SIDA and the Breast Cancer Awareness Climb to the Mountain. We raised a lot of money for both of them, I am so proud of that. Heidi said it was her way of trying to make good on her Dorothy Day Resolution. As if she's not doing it now, helping with Gaëtan.

We asked everyone to pledge for both walks, half and half. And they did. People were very generous. Wilder pledged $250. We didn't even ask Viola because she's got too many money worries now. She has to get a mortgage on their place. She and Charlotte were together so long they owned it, now she has to start with a mortgage again.

Heidi was right, though, it wasn't fair, when we were doing a good deed, that we got tormented by people we marched with. I was recognized a few times: "Lulu!" and "Hey, that Aislin cartoon, eh?" and the ever-popular "You really think she did it?"

Heidi said, "She's guilty as sin."

"Je ne suis pas certaine," one woman said. A lot of experts don't think so. There was a Letter to the Editor in *Le Devoir* the other day that maybe she was set up. Another lady said that when she called into a radio call-in show, the host agreed with her, maybe Madame Ducharme's neighbours framed her.

"We're her neighbours!" Heidi yelled at her. "She poisoned six jurors."

"Hey, you must be the other anglo neighbour! The one who can't talk French. I saw that pompous, witty guy on *Dini*!"

"Someone said the evidence was all circumstantial."

Then more people started in on it.

"Sa confession n'est pas bien faite."

"Elle est pas coupable, vraiment."

"She didn't mean to confess, eh? You and your cop boyfriend tricked her, eh, Lulu! You said so on *Fiona*! I recognized you when they reran it!" a voice yelled over. And it belonged to our fellow Wolfe School student, Blue Jays Cap Man with Pepe. And Pepe was wearing a child's Ça Marche T-shirt that was way too big for a chihuahua.

"Hey, what happened to your little pooches?"

"This is almost surreal," was all Heidi could say, and we ça marched faster, away.

The Bardo & Delargo families
are pleased to announce
the upcoming wedding of

Darla Delores Delargo
and
Wyatt Ulysses Bardo

on Saturday, October the seventeenth
at 3 p.m.
at the future hacienda Bardo-Delargo.

Hope you can make our day!

Dear Lenny,

I am going to be one truly happy man! The girl of my dreams was right here all along, and I found her because you told her to make chase! Sure am glad she caught me! Hope you can make it. We'll have a grand old time! You gotta be here! Call me if you can share in our special day, and we'll get you fixed up with plane tickets pronto. Bring some friends, bring a date, someone like you must have a special somebody in your life by now, gal! Bring him along. You are some matchmaker. And thanks for the photos of you and Old Ironsides from Boston. I really appreciated them.

Your pal,
Wyatt

God Bless You! *Darla*

Arizona would be such a great break for all of us. If I had my wish we'd all go, and Wyatt would know of some AIDS cure that works in New Mexico, and he'd be so grateful he found Darla because of me he'd pay the entire shot, no matter how much it costs in the American medical system. We'd get Gaëtan down there and everything would be fine. I am reading about possible cures and therapies and diets all the time and hoping, hoping, hoping, even though I know it's impossible. Rock Hudson went to that special hospital in Paris, and it didn't help him. When it's gotten this bad, there's no stopping it, no matter what you do or how much money you throw after it. We don't want to lose Gaëtan, but I just want it to be over for him. Daniel says we're not talking months anymore.

❧ ❧ ❧

Trey sure enjoyed his visit to Tanguay. I'm glad I prepared the prison path by phoning Reine to explain that her chiens were coming to visit her, accompanied by a nice young American guy.

"'Ton amour?"

Non, I told her, the son of the man I would like to be mon amour.

"Le fils de Wilder?"

"Oui. Son nom est Trey."

"Très quoi?"

I told her Trey looks très much like his father so she'll have some idea what I've had my eye on since May.

"La Katherine? Elle reste?"

I said she rests in his heart and that's for the best, my life right now is Festin and Gaëtan. And that's why someone else has to bring the dogs for visiting day. Is there any chance Trey could leave them with her?

"Non! Non! Pas de place! C'est fini, fini avec Roch!"

Trey said he was hoping they'd show him around the prison, but that didn't happen. (Just what you'd need if you're a woman behind bars, a good looking young guy strolling through on a tour.) He said he had a great time anyway.

"Her English is pretty good, huh? She's a really classy lady. She didn't know the word for it in English but she says you are so chalheureuse, that must mean you're pretty special."

I guess Reine hopes he'll pass that opinion on to his father.

Benoît came over to put me in my place. He said, Well, now Les Expos are no more. We never got to a game, but hey, Lenny's been too busy, Lenny's always too busy, she can't call to say, Let's Go, Expos. Nothing! He's given up waiting for me to call, tu comprends? Because I always have something else that's more important. Like now. If he was stupid enough to ask me out again, what would I say? I'm too busy?

"Yes," I told him.

"Pourquoi? You are so busy, why, hein? Tell me. Say it. I am so busy because . . ."

"My friend is dying."

This time he didn't give me his I don't believe you, you're lying face. He looked at me, he didn't know what to say. He'd been treating me like some hostile witness, and I wound up being a devastated friend. And then I did what I said I can't do, because I can't be a baby about this, I can't be weak, I have to be strong. But I couldn't help it, I started sobbing.

"C'pas . . . Heidi?" he asked, and I said Non, but thinking that made me cry even more.

Benoît put his arms around me and said, "I am so sorry. Pauvre bébé, cry all you need to, pauvre fille."

Benoît said he could stay for a while, he wasn't on duty yet. After a long time, and once I'd calmed down from telling him everything about Gaëtan, I finally asked him why he was here today. I didn't think it was just to tell me off for not going to see the Expos with him. He said it was, but he also had some insights into who Conserned Citizen might be. He'd even had the handwriting analyzed. The last note I'd sent him about throwing my heep in the Lachine Canal helped find his findings. I told him I could handle this news now. Benoît says Conserned Citizen is:

1) mad at my house or my car
2) pretending he can't spell
3) quite strange but not dangerous
4) possibly on some kind of medication
5) not a stalker
6) a man
7) always uses a Bic pen but not the same one.

He'd gone to all that trouble, so I finally told him I think it's Blake Farnham, a neighbour's son. Benoît wants to interrogate him, but I said that would make his mother very mad if my suspicions are wrong. I haven't even seen him around for months, the last sighting of him was at a Valentine's wedding when he tried to pick up Heidi.

Benoît said we must catch Conserned Citizen in the act. He could put surveillance cameras on my house if I want, it's not standard procedure because it's not life-threatening, but someone in the department owes him. I thanked him, but I want him to save that debt for a woman who needs it for a real stalker. So then he said if I need help I am to call him.

"If you don't call me this time and you need help, I will get very mad. I mean it, là. I am your friend, okay. I am here for you anytime. Don't forget, Lenny."

Benoît's list might be useful, but Conserned Citizen is Blake. I really think it's got to be him. Even if it's too obvious and I can't prove it yet. But how are the lawn ornaments getting here? Heidi and I are almost convinced that the decapitated chicken was Katherine's doing, but all the others?

LIST OF SUSPECTS SO FAR
1) Jemima. She started the petition against my lawn ornaments last year. But I don't think she could stand to buy them/steal them/have to carry them for any length of time.
2) Blake. Him again.
3) Some kids from another street.
4) Cheechio, Fergie's best friend. First the postcard from Fergie saying he should be mad at me for getting mad at him. Maybe he is really mad, and he's got Cheechio sending me lawn warnings that he's coming back. He did write me that second postcard about how good I looked on the *Fiona!* rerun. Was that to torment me?
5) Tyler. Revenge for Festin. But they started way back with Frosty, before Tyler came to try and conquer us. Cross off Tyler.
6) I am some sort of Lawn Ornaments Rescue and people are leaving them, like the Kingdom of Lost Toys in the *Rudolph The Red Nosed Reindeer* special with Burl Ives as a Snowman. Like Frosty! Coincidence? Maybe I'm a secret sleepwalker. At night I go out and find ones I like and pretend to leave them for myself.
7) Okay, if I can accuse myself, how about Wilder? It's ridiculous, I know, and I am only thinking it because I've seen so many bad movies lately, renting them for Gaëtan.

Still. How could I ever think it was Wilder? Well, maybe Frosty the Snowman was a lone incident, with nothing to do with the rest, which all arrived *after* Wilder got here. And who was Johnny on the Spot the minute I found the donkey and cart with missing wheels? Wilder. He came out of his house right that second and said he'd fix it for me. And then when I found the chicken with its head cut off, he offered to fix it right away, too. Because Katherine had destroyed it, since she knew he was leaving me lawn mêmentos as a gesture — of what? What, Lenore? It's not him. It's not me. Then who is doing this? It's another puzzlement! And another lawn ornament: a large frog with one eye out this morning.

So the *Gourmet* review's going to be a rave, Marguerite Vichy says. The critic called her to ask about some of the ingredients in her recipes, her handwriting's really bad, épouvantable, and Marguerite asked the critic what her review would be. "If I am to be executed, I should be told!" I don't think you're supposed to ask a critic right out, but that's Marguerite. That should really make reservations pick up even more. I wonder if we could get an advance copy so I could read it to Gaëtan. I don't think I'm doing enough for him. He was pleased when I brought Brioche et Montcalm over, and they love it when he speaks to them in fabulous French. They had a good time sitting on the bed with him until the nurse arrived, now they're banished.

It's fortunate that I have Trey to amuse les chiens because I'm hardly home anymore. Heidi says maybe Trey regards me as some sort of benevolent and cool stepmother figure. How could I have a stepson that old? How old was I when Wilder had him? I keep wondering, What if Katherine leaves him and Wilder and I get together? I'd be the stepmother to two kids I'd never see. But maybe I'd wind up being a mother myself, too. But that's not going to happen. Nothing will. Even though we're getting a rave in *Gourmet*, I don't feel like things will get better.

※ ※ ※

Two calls from the *Fiona!* show this morning. The first from Parker, the Hitler backstage Youth. She got Amity's job. They want to do a Where Is She Now? of me. Even if it's only been nine months. Nothing's changed. Reine's still in prison. Parker said they got a lot of response from my segment, the audience wants me back. She can't understand I don't have the time. Even trying to tempt me, "Like, how about we do you with a reunion of your favourite show. *Kojak*."

"*Ironside*," I said.

"Oh right. Ironsides."

I wouldn't do the show, I said, even if they brought Doris Day out of retirement to co-host with *Fiona!* I lied, maybe I would. But no, I wouldn't, I don't want anyone I care about to ever go on that show. Maybe I should tell them Tess or Jemima will go on in my place. Anyway I told Parker, Never, no way, and twenty minutes later they phoned again. But this time it was Fiona! herself. And really sweet, like she was my best, best friend.

"Lenore. Fi. You gotta do my show again, sweetie."

"Why?"

"The Made-for-TV Movie, babe."

"What Made-for-TV Movie?"

"The one they're doing loosely based on your real life drama."

"No one asked me."

"That's the thing, they're making them all without permission. They take basic details and do a quickie. Yours is gonna be called, what is it? Yeah, here it is. *Garden of Secrets: The Louise Durham Story.*"

"Who's Louise Durham?"

"The character based on you. Only they're setting it in Wisconsin, Indiana, some heartlandish place. And it's gonna be over two nights, with a big sensational trial."

"There was no trial."

"*Garden of Secrets* has a Trial."

"How? When Reine confessed?"

"She goes back on her confession. Never confesses, something like that. She and her lawyers trick you, frame you. They're prosecuting her but they pull a switcheroo and you look guilty! Which state has the chair? Not Wisconsin, Jeffrey Dahmer didn't get it. They killed him with a broom. Anyway you're in some heartlandish state with the electric chair. Lethal injection, whatever they do. I should remember, we did a week on it. Anyway you, Louise Durham, are looking at capital punishment! You save yourself by making a big scene in court. 'How could you betray me? I was your friend!' Pandemonium, the whole nine yards. If they get Valerie Bertinelli, it'll be big."

"Valerie Bertinelli is going to play me?

"Or Melissa Gilbert. Or Jaclyn Smith. They've already signed someone for the Madame. And guess who it is? Cotton Brady!"

"No. Not Cotton Brady."

"She went after the role big time. Because she's just done a film in Montreal and loves the city."

"Cotton is going to play Madame Ducharme?"

"Mrs. Charmin for TV."

"I worked with Cotton."

"Yeah. We heard! She only found out after she got the part, she was so amazed that her personal assistant was the original Louise Durham."

"I'm not Louise Durham! And I was her dog handler, not her personal assistant. But we got along really well. How can she be this disloyal? Be in a movie based on me?"

"Loosely based, honeychild. You must feel pretty surprised, invaded, what would you say?"

"I say it's not right."

"Want to say that on my show?"

"No!"

"Oh do my show, pleeease, sweetheart. I want to kick off the week with you."

"A week of what?"

"Women Whose Lives Have Been Turned into Made for TV Movies Against Their Will."

"There are lots of us?"

"More and more every single day! And some are women whose real life stories the movies discovered because of *Fiona!* We had them first."

"You did, eh? Well, maybe we can get a class action suit against you for invasion of privacy."

"I don't think so. You don't want to mess with my litigation team."

"Don't you feel any GUILT about this?"

"Don't you feel any anger about being used like this? Co-opted?!"

"Yes."

"Then do my show, come on, tell the television viewing world, what do you say?"

"No. If I knew how, I'd sue you. And so would Madame Ducharme."

"Aw, honey . . . aw, lamby-pie . . ."

It wasn't working. Then she turned into the real Fiona! "Is it money? Do you want money? Is that it?"

"No."

"Then what do you want?"

"I want to never have to talk about it ever again. And I don't want to know what network is broadcasting *Garden of Secrets*. Or how many Emmys it wins. Goodbye."

And I hung up on her! Then I took the phone off the hook. I didn't want to be tempted, I can only be so pure. For all I knew Parker was on the phone to Doris Day to ask her to guest host *Fiona!* for my episode, promising her I'll bring Brioche et Montcalm, and we all know how much Dodo loves dogs.

Gaëtan died this morning.

The doctor told him in August that he might last till Christmas. I don't think Gaëtan wanted to last one more month like this to prove him right.

Daniel thinks we should hold the Memorial Service for Gaëtan on his birthday. I don't know how Daniel can think of anything at all right now. I don't know how he's not dead from heartbreak. I am.

Yur final notis: this heeps got to go.

Conserned Citizen

What I did this morning! I guess I am in "over-reaction mode," like Wilder said, because of Gaëtan. It's all tied up with the mourning process, I'm all over the place. It's like I'm in this intense universe of my own.

If I could sleep, it never would have happened, I'd still be in the dark. But there was me, sleep-deprived all night again, trying to stop being awake. No luck. And then it was five-thirty, and I thought I heard *The Gazette* being delivered. When I opened the door to look, I saw a shadow over my heep, putting a note on my windshield. It was Jemima.

I ran out at her like some madwoman. I pushed her up against the car, the way you see cops do to criminals on TV.

"YOU! You're Conserned Citizen!"

And she said, "No. I was just removing the note for you."

Why? I asked her. Why would you do that for me at five-thirty in the morning?

She said because she knew these hasty notes upset me. I wasn't very nice, I called her a liar. I was pulling out all the stops. My face was in her face.

"Yes, I am," she admitted. "You're perfectly right. I am a liar."

"The notes are yours?"

"No," she said. "They're Blake's."

That's what I said, way back in February! And she's been lying to me all these months to protect him?

"I had to, I'm his mother."

Is he really Away?

Yes, but he comes back occasionally. And that's when he leaves the notes.

"And busted up lawn ornaments?"

"No!"

"No? Frosty the Snowman? A donkey cart with one wheel, a beak-less pelican, a frog —"

"Blake left the notes, that's all. He's not the one leaving you the lawn ornaments." She said it like she knew who was.

"Do you know who is?"

"Yes. Of course. You have an admirer."

"An admirer? And you've seen him?"

"Oh, yes," she said, all scoffy. "I informed him once that I didn't approve. I told him you have more than enough already. If anything, he should be taking some away, not bringing you more."

"You've talked to him?"

"Yes. But I was afraid reprimanding him any more would only encourage him."

"Who?"

I was afraid she'd say, "That Wilder," or "That Cheechio," or, worst of all, "That Fergie," but she didn't. It was nobody I ever suspected.

"It's the Bin Man."

"The Bin Man?"

"The sanitation engineer. Trash collector. The garbage man."

Jemima has been in Canada for over twenty years, how come she still says things like "the Bin Man"? And how come she knows he's been leaving me these things? She's even told him not to.

"The garbage man has been leaving me broken lawn ornaments?"

"Instead of crushing them out of recognition in his truck, in lieu of using waste disposal to dispel of offensive objects, he carts them back to you."

"Which Bin Man is it?"

"The burly one with the kerchief on his head."

"The one who looks like Springsteen?"

"Hardly."

"I think he does."

"Well, he'll be pleased to know you think so highly of him. Maybe he knows that already. A wink or a nod can lead them on to these acts!"

How did she explain Blake's Acts of Consern?

"Blake's acting out, you see."

"Acting out what?"

"His anger. His guidance people, they say he should. Because you're the Straw."

"The Straw?"

"That broke the Camel's Back. It may seem a small thing to you, but denying him parking in your extra space —"

"Heidi needs it."

"But before Heidi bought that rusting red Rabbit, it was left empty by the desertion of that Fergie man you lived with. And Blake had a chance for it, a parking space of one's own, an opportunity to be accepted on this street. And it would have been your little way of showing your approval, you see. But instead it was a big No, persona non grata, because you didn't believe he could change. Where was the trust? Nowhere to be found! And who were you to pass judgement on Blake? When you lived with that horrible freeloader Fergie for so long? The counsellors told Blake that if he was going to get better, he had to focus and channel his raging anger by acting out."

"I don't think the counsellors wanted him to act out by sending hate notes to a neighbour! And threaten to burn down her house and push her car into the Lachine Canal."

"No. But it worked. Blake's been much better. He's almost off drugs and alcohol. He's practically cured. You were inconvenienced, I'm sorry, but Blake's improving because of you. And it is much better he took it out on you, Lenore. A stranger."

"Than who?"

"Than me. Imagine all that channelled anger directed at his mother. I mean, really. There's no telling . . ."

Jemima promised there would be no more notes and no cause for future skirmishes. I told her I'd already turned the notes over to the police, and now that the case has been solved (and the perp is the most obvious suspect!) Constable Benoît Archambault must be informed.

"Oh please, don't resort to that. No police intervention, please."

"Then you just make sure Blake doesn't leave me any more notes, eh? And maybe you should buy him a dictionary for Christmas."

"He was being inventive, his spelling's not that bad. You should see what convolutions he came up with on some of the notes I managed to take off your car before you got them! Again, I am so sorry. Her Majesty is so right. It's certainly been an annus horribilis."

Off she went. And that's when Wilder spoke, he was standing in his doorway, he'd seen most of it. He said in a pretty good English accent, "Taking notes, was she, love?"

"Yes, but not fast enough, I'm afraid, mate."

He could tell I didn't want to be alone, so he invited me in for breakfast, me in my pyjamas and him in an old bathrobe over a T-shirt and jogging pants. It was very comfortable, like we were a couple who'd been together a long time. He was so understanding, all I did was talk about everything that's happened to me and Heidi lately. And of course, all about Gaëtan.

Heidi said Jemima should get Blake into a drama class if he needs to "act out" anything ever again. "And that's supposed to be done under supervision. They get in a drama therapist. Or a psychologist, at the very least."

Then what?

"They do improvisations. In a controlled environment. Blake would play himself. They'd make up scenarios."

Of what?

"Of whatever Blake needed to deal with. They might say the objective was acceptance. So Blake would act out asking you for a parking space."

"But his mother was the one who asked me, not him."

"And who told Blake you gave him a big No? Who set you up to be the villainess? To be the Straw, as Jemima called you? Well, you were just the last straw in an entire House of Straws she built with him in it! Jemima let you take all the blame. That woman is pathetic. Anyway, Blake himself would have to learn how to make it all come out his way."

"But it can't ever come out his way, I can't rent to him. Even if someday neither us has cars. Maybe I'm not forgiving enough and I'm being mean —"

"He's not your son, Lenore. He's not your responsibility, he's hers. And she's got him in the wrong program with a bunch of flakes. Or at a rehab that's seriously underfunded."

She's going to ask Jemima just exactly who and where is treating Blake. They obviously need some help and guidance.

That's Heidi, using Education to find a solution. I never thought of that, I was just hoping it was over and I was done with it.

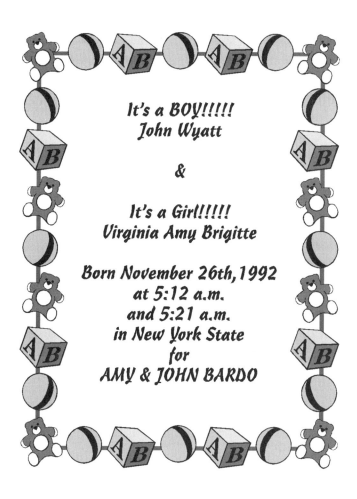

It's a BOY!!!!!
John Wyatt

&

It's a Girl!!!!!
Virginia Amy Brigitte

Born November 26th, 1992
at 5:12 a.m.
and 5:21 a.m.
in New York State
for
AMY & JOHN BARDO

Hi, Lenny!

I kept meaning to send you this announcement. Like, right when my Baby Boom happened, but I was kind of busy having the little guys! They were both so beautiful. But way earlier than I intuitioned they'd be! We all had some Thanksgiving, you bet! Jack and Amy were real sorry they missed the birth, but who guessed I'd be almost six weeks early like that? Thank goodness they got medical proof the kids are Jack's or they'd think I was pregnant

before I got to Arizona! But you only had to look at them
in the incubators to know they were Jack's, John Wyatt
and Virginia Amy Brigitte Bardo were teensy tiny preemies.
But we were never afraid they wouldn't make it, so that
was lucky. Jack and Amy were so thankful they got two
for the price of one they gave me double the money. It sure
will come in handy for Christmas shopping, I'm going to
buy out Ames! Too bad you couldn't see those new Bardo
babies before they got big enough to leave. (I've got
pictures in my album, don't worry.) I thought I'd send
out this announcement with my Christmas cards. Hope
to see you in Champlain one of these days. Maybe when
I start to have some kids of my own.

Amber

I'm not the only one losing control and turning into a warrior
because I'm so depressed. Heidi got involved in a Food Fight today
at Loyola. With Tess.

The English department collects stuff for Christmas baskets. They
were up to six full boxes of food until Heidi walked by and saw Tess
taking cans out. "I was trying not to be judgemental, it is the holiday
season." So Heidi just watched.

"Spied!" Tess accused after.

Heidi tried her best to think Tess of the d'Urberblondes had a
humanitarian reason for taking the cans of fruit cocktail and cream
of mushroom soup, the package of pasta bows, pesto salad dressing,
the Marks and Spenser shortbreads, the great big box of Kellogg's
Corn Flakes, the Turtles . . .

"I tried to tell myself, Perhaps she plans to organize the cans,
cookies, chocolates and corn flakes and put them in alphabetical
order."

But no, Tess loaded all the cans and stuff into her gigantic L.L.
Bean bag. And that's when she heard the voice of Heidi say, "Where
do you think you're taking all that?"

Tess didn't even try to lie. No Pinocchio Factor for her. "To my home in le Plateau, where do you think?"

"You're stealing food from the poor?"

Tess said she's given enough donations to Christmas funds to take a few groceries. She has guests, she hasn't got time to shop. And none of those poor people are that poor, lots of them are welfare opportunists and scam artists who get on all kinds of Christmas basket lists and wind up with ten or twelve baskets. They weren't going to miss a can of Campbell's mushroom soup.

"Or pesto salad dressing. Or a box of Turtles —"

"Who would put Turtles in a Christmas food basket? Who thinks such rich food would ever get anywhere near the poor? What idiot would do that?"

"I did," Heidi said. "They should have some nice things besides tuna and macaroni."

"And tri-coloured pasta bows?" Tess snarled.

"Yes, the 300-gram size."

"Keeping account, were you, Heidi? Of course you'd never borrow anything from a poor basket. You're so perfect."

Elspeth warned Heidi that Emerson made a few too many comparisons to Tess "in deference to me." Meaning that Emerson got his digs in at Tess by hinting that Heidi would have been a better wife and life partner. And being stuck out on the farm really made Tess resent Heidi for not being there instead of her.

"You and your little do-gooder marches. Pledge for this, pledge for that. Reading to old ladies. Taking care of a sick friend. I won't eat Veal, the poor little baby animals. You wear leather shoes, don't you? Emerson says you've eaten the occasional Harvey's hamburger. Even Bens Smoke Meat! What a hypocrite! Keep the damn Turtles!"

She shoved them back at Heidi and started to walk out.

"Put back the rest, too."

"Make me."

And that's when Heidi grabbed Tess and her L.L. Bean bag and created what she called "such a ballyhoo" that two cans flew out of the bag and smashed into a computer that was on and had everybody's marks in it. The fruit cocktail went through the screen, there was so much velocity, the computer "went down" and all the marks have to be put in again. On a computer that's working.

Heidi says this showdown with Tess has been coming for a long time, but she never thought it would be a feud over a food basket. The English department secretary says he's glad they smashed up his computer, it was a dinosaur and Concordia's been promising him an upgrade for two years now. So fa-la-la-la-la.

Heidi and I: The Loose Cannon Sisters! We're Lethal. Luckily we were right when we've gone in for the kill. But what if I'd been wrong and Jemima was taking the Conserned Citizen note off as a neighbourly gesture? And what if Tess was taking food from the rich basket to give to the poor in the Plateau? Egg on our faces! But we were right. Not that I think we should make a habit of this, but a girl's gotta do what a girl's gotta do sometimes. We don't know what we're doing lately, we're both taking Gaëtan's death so badly. Heidi seems even more distant, too, she clams up whenever I want to talk about Gaëtan. Maybe it's because he was more family to her because of Daniel and it's too personal how she feels.

13

Heidi and I are back on Amherst Sawyer Lyndon's Christmas Letter List! Maybe because Heidi's no longer a threat as a possible sister-in-law and Amherst's completely forgotten she thought I was out to kidnap her daughters. Maybe Portia and Fallon sent these to us without her knowing. Or maybe it's a cry for HELP!

Happy Holidays, Family and Friends!
Merry Christmas and a Happy New Year.

This isn't going to be full of the usual Holiday Cheer, an endless List of what we did all year. Because everyone had the same hobbies and pastimes, and I don't feel like being cheerful. Surprised? No, you're not. Nobody is. Everyone knows by now so why pretend, right? Harmon and I separated two months ago. Harmon tells everyone it's temporary, but I say it's over. How could he take so many years from me and then throw them away for a cheap tryst with a woman he always referred to as "A Client." It's so tawdry, it's almost laughable. But I'm not laughing. It's

Christmas — but there's no HO HO HO in it for any of us. I could have stayed in college and gotten my MA or PhD, or taken two years off and bummed around Europe like Grantham did, or run off as a Draft Dodger to Canada, like Emerson. Maybe I would have trained for the 1976 Olympics. But instead I married a promising young man, Harmon Lyndon. I know I did everything to make a successful, happy life for everyone else. Don't worry, Portia and Fallon and I are going to be just fine, despite them giving me the scare of my life in August. Their father and I will share custody of the girls because I need some time to myself. To travel and explore. I may be going back to school. Maybe study poetry. There's a course at Radcliffe I might take. Maybe I'll go to Italy, learn Italian and paint again. Perhaps I'll go at it full throttle, finally, and become a lawyer or an art-restorer. I've found some comfort in getting back to my cello, the winter afternoons don't seem so long now. That's Schumann for you.

So that's our newsletter *this* Christmas, thank you very much, Harmon Lyndon, Adulterer. Maybe this was not what you expected to read in a Christmas Letter, so sue me. But it needed to be spelled out to all 120 of you still on my mailing list.

Best wishes for your holidays and I hope next year is a brighter, better one for all of us. God Bless America, God Bless Us, everyone. We need it.

Amherst Sawyer, Fallon & Portia Lyndon

Heidi thinks it's the first she's seen someone use a Christmas Letter for therapy. Not very much in the Spirit of the Season, more naked pain. Heidi hopes it doesn't mean Amherst's fishing for an invitation for her and her cello to stay with one of us so she can travel and explore. The Radcliffe poetry course she wants to take better not be with Katherine Melbourne! What a happy little class that would be, especially if Katherine ever mentions Montreal.

❀ ❀ ❀

Today's Gaëtan's birthday. He would have been forty-two. I hope
he enjoyed his memorial service. Of course, he'd be embarrassed to
see that many pictures of him all over and that poster-sized one of him
on his last holiday with Daniel. Right before he started looking sick.

Jocelyne sure has a flair for decorating. She went a little nuts with
the candles, but it was pretty beautiful.

Daniel was right, having the memorial in a church wouldn't be
very Gaëtan. So we're lucky we found a setting that was: Festin du
Bois. Festin Gaëtan today.

Réal started off our celebration of Gaëtan's life so meaningfully by
saying some people are so special you only get to have their light for
so long. I never expected that much sentiment from a coureur de
bois. If Gaëtan hadn't been so special maybe he'd still be with us.

His sisters and brother read his poems, his letter from camp, the
story he wrote when he was eight for Mother's Day. We were all
laughing and crying so much, Micheline said we'd do ourselves in
with "Trop de feelings."

Then I got up to try and say what Gaëtan meant to me, and all I
could manage was, I can't believe he's gone, I miss him so much. Then
I became a total wreck. I'm so lucky Jamie ran up and held me and said
I could talk more later if I felt like it. Let's have some songs now.

I remember Gaëtan humming the song his sisters and brother
sang. I really didn't think I'd make it through the memorial when his
high school girlfriend sang what she called "notre chanson."

Jamie said we didn't have to sing. And I said we did. I could. I had
to. Somehow I was able to do Gaëtan's special requests, and then Jamie
and I got through that medley of Sondheim songs he put together.

Daniel spoke so beautifully. Good for Heidi, keeping Mrs. Flynn
from coming to the Memorial Service because, she said, "Gaëtan was
such a nice man."

"I talked her out of it. Can you imagine the scene we'd have?"

I said Well, yes, her mom would have figured it all out.

"Then again, maybe not. Mothers don't want to know what they
don't want to know. But her being here might have prevented Daniel
from saying how he really feels."

233

Daniel doesn't want his mother to know. And what purpose would it serve now? Gaëtan died of AIDS, she'll worry herself sick thinking she'll lose her son that way, too. But what's Mrs. Flynn going to think, Gaëtan left the condo to Daniel.

Daniel was able to say how he felt in English and French, how much he loved Gaëtan and how much Gaëtan loved us. By the time he was done, Festin was one great big emotional wreck. We were all sobbing and hugging one another.

Thank God Marguerite Vichy put an end to that for a while. "Assez! Enough! No more crying. C'est Fini. Mangez!"

She'd made all Gaëtan's favourite foods, and never in our lifetimes would we taste them made this well.

Daniel had something else he had to say, but privately. He seemed anxious and didn't want to wait for later, he asked me and Heidi to join him in the alcove.

"It's about Festin, Lenore." Daniel said.

And I thought, Here it comes, the family wants to sell.

"Gaëtan left the condo to me but he left Festin to —"

"His family. To his sisters and brother?"

"No. He's provided really well for them, but he didn't leave Festin to them. Not even a share in it."

"Then who got Festin?"

I thought Daniel was going to say, Have you heard of an enterprise called Prom Night? My nightmare didn't happen, but I still can't believe what did. Daniel said, "Gaëtan left Festin to me and you."

"Me and you?"

"Yes. We own it, Lenore. Festin is ours."

"Ours? It's mine, too? To me? Why me?"

"Because Gaëtan loves you. He said you are L'Espirit de Festin. Without you, it would have fallen to ruin. And without you, he never would have gotten me."

And that's when Marguerite Vichy walked in on us, bawling again, and said, "Sacre Bleu! Enough! You're making me feel bad. Didn't I make enough food?"

❅ ❅ ❅

John Biddiscombe a.k.a. Tyler Garrow sure didn't waste any time at all. He's so crass, asking me out again for dinner at L'Express.

"You said you'd go with me sometime."

"No, you said you hoped I'd say I'd go with you sometime."

"Oh, Fun with Semantics!" He laughed and tried his Charlie Charm act again. "It doesn't have to be L'Express. What do you want? Gibby's? Chez Pauze? Bar-B-Barn? What?"

"I want you to leave. I told you already, you're not welcome here."

"Aw, please don't be like that. I was way out of line. I got the wrong idea before. Look, I am so sorry. I didn't know you were appointed to watch over the place because Gaëtan was sick. I am in shock, too. He didn't look sick. Such a sweet guy. He sure went fast, but that's what I'd want."

"No, it isn't. No one would want to go fast that way."

"Well, no, I'm sure it was pretty terrible. So he left the whole place to you."

"And Daniel Flynn."

"His long-time companion. But it wasn't even that long-time, was it? He sure lucked into it. Is Danny around?"

"No. He's working. He has a full-time job already."

"So he's left everything up to you? In Lenore We Trust?"

"Yes. I'm the one with the restaurant experience."

"The waitress-turned-manager, now co-owner. Impressive. Lot of learning on the job. Pretty heady, but pretty terrifying."

"What do you want?"

"To make it up to you, that's all. Look, I want us to be friends again."

"We were never friends, John."

"We almost were. Why'd you keep saying no? Did Gaëtan say anything to you?"

"Not till later. When he was sick. And I told him you'd tried to ask me out. And he was surprised, he didn't know you were bi-sexual."

"I'm not," he said, "but I occasionally make exceptions. I would have been for you."

"To get me on your side. To influence Gaëtan."

"No. Give yourself some credit, Lenore. You're pretty hot some-times, especially now that you're a Business Vixen."

"You're sickening. Stop wasting my time, Tyler John." I gave him the cold, hard silent treatment till he had to give up.

"Okay, I'm here to make you an offer," he finally admitted. "And not for a franchise. We want to buy Festin."

"It's not for sale."

"Lenore. You've had long enough now to see Festin can't turn any profit the way you're running it. Every stupid mistake you make costs more money. And that endangers the livelihood of everybody who works here, including you. If you and Dan sell it to us, you're free of responsibilities, no more hassles. You can stay on here, if you want. Think of it: a steady paycheque and tips, no worries and a hefty little nest egg in the bank. Or use it to pay off your mortgage on that quaint place of yours. You don't want to run this restaurant completely into the ground and wind up with nothing to — hey, where are you going? I have a deal here for you. A good one. Hey, hey!"

I'm not going listen to him anymore. We've listened to him too much already. I don't owe any kind of politeness to someone who is VILE and tries to make me feel as if I'm nothing and he's doing me a giant favour. I am so proud of myself for walking out on him like that. So what if it's not a management technique, I marched into the kitchen and asked Réal to sort him out and show him the door. And tell him he's barred, too. For life.

I would burn Festin du Bois down before I'd sell out to Tyler. No, I wouldn't. I love Festin. And how bad would it look, a big fire in a place co-owned by a fireman? And all the fingers would point at poor Marie-France first. They'd say we let her serve her parole at Festin and she thanked us for giving her a chance by burning it down. We couldn't let her take the rap, I'd have to confess. I'd commit it as as a Crime of Passion, but the arson investigators would think I did it for the insurance money. And I'd wind up at Tanguay with Madame Ducharme. So I would not burn down Festin to the ground to keep Tyler John from getting it, but I'd sell it to somebody else, almost anybody else, first. But Festin's not for sale.

Whenever anyone would ask how Festin was going I'd say "Fine" or "Okay," but I can admit it now: it's been doing way better than fine. I'm not doing a bad job. We're getting more customers, people are happy, they tell their friends. When Gaëtan asked me to be the Boss I never thought it would be forever, I always thought he'd be coming back soon. Or that I could call him for advice, and if I did really badly, I could say, Gaëtan, please get somebody else. And quick. Because I don't know anything about financing and how you keep books, about making sure people get their salaries. Or when to advertise, how much food to order, or how to keep the peace when I make up the work roster. I have to learn all these things! What do I know? I'm a singing waitress! But I did learn somehow, I'm learning all the time, every single second. And now I'm not only the Boss for good. I'm the owner, too. Well, co-owner. And that can be for good, too, if I can believe in myself more. I have to believe I am L'Espirit de Festin the way Gaëtan said. I can't worry about what if I mess this up and everyone winds up out of work, including me?

What did I do to deserve this? Cotton Brady's found me again. She came to my house, Montcalm went crazy when he saw her.

"Monty! Monty! Monty!" she whooped and gave him a squeeze that almost had him in the death throes. Brioche wanted all her attention, too.

"Oh, yes, and his friend, little Balderdash."

"Brioche."

"Oh, right, like the croy-sant. Did you miss me, too? Little Brisket? It's not a bad time, is it, doll? I can visit for a bit? I can let the taxi go?"

Her visit-for-a-bit was hours and hours, but Jamie helped me get through it. I knew he should be aware she still wanted me to be her personal assistant.

"You are too much. I love you. I'm coming over. I'm taking a half-day off. As of now!" he said when I called him at IBM and told him to make up an excuse. Of course if he decides to take a whole lot more days off from IBM — like the rest of his career — to be "her houseboy in Hollywood," I'll be helping him fulfill his fantasy. And why shouldn't I do what I can? Did I ever think I'd be an owner of a restaurant?

Cotton's here for a two-day stopover "to do research for *Garden of Secrets*." Ha-ha. She's here because she has to see a colourist she discovered when she did *Dog of the Titanic*.

"No one can touch him, I want him to relocate to LA. I can't keep coming back here, well, I could, I suppose. Because, I mean, what Thor can do with roots, he's a magician."

She shared her insights on show business with me. I never asked her to, she just went on and on, and I kept thinking, When is Jamie going to get here?

"You know, Lenny, when I started out, I was with the Actors' Studio. But not for long, because I got the series and had to leave New York. But I'll never ever forget how the Method stressed the importance of research, 'engaging,' learning the craft and all that. I didn't use much of it with *Salt and Pepper* because, I mean, what research was there to a sitcom? Say this, be funny, say that, be wacky, fall down. But I never forgot that you should know a lot about your character. There's always a whole lot more going on between the lines. And then, well, it was Fateful, I wanted *Garden of Secrets* because I had this connection to Montreal. Of *Titanic* proportions. Like that joke? It's mine. Can I smoke in here, sweetie? Not even one? Why not, honey? You allergic or what? Got any little mints? Nicorettes? M&Ms? Anything. Yeah those are good. Anyway, what do I find out when I do *Fiona!* but —"

"You did *Fiona!*?"

"Well, yes. Last week. It's on for the Christmas Sweeps."

"You took my place?"

"It was my place. I'm the one who's going to be in the movie. And that's when I found out you're Louise Durham, the gal who helped Mrs. Charmin poison all those jurists."

And I could have argued or clammed up about it, but my brain started storming: maybe this is les chiens' ticket out of my house at last! I laid it on. "I may be Lulu Borgia, but that's nothing. Monty here? And Brioche? They're Madame Ducharme's dogs."

"No! That is just too over-the-top fatalistic!"

She always felt Monty should be cast as her dog in *Garden of Secrets* because they worked so well together before. But now, now she's going to push casting "Monty and Brideshead."

"That's up to Madame Ducharme."

"I need a meeting. How soon can I see her?"

"Visiting Day."

"Hospital?"

"Prison."

"Oh, right, she really is in prison."

Where do they have her in the movie script?

"At her house. Because she didn't confess. You're the only one who says she did it. She never goes to jail. Till the end. And what an end, the electric chair! With Louise as a witness. Because you've forgiven me, ya see. Big, big tearjerker scene! And no reprieve from the governor, either. They thought Susan Hayward wanted to live. Wait till they see what I do with it!"

The more I hear about this movie, the more it doesn't sound like my version of events at all. Cotton wanted to know how loosely based it all was, she got bored pretty quick.

"Oh, babe. You were never her unwilling accomplice? Ohhh. The real Mrs. Charmin confessed just like that, they took her away, she's in jail? That's it? Not very dramatic, huh? But I still need you to do this for me. Take a few minutes and look at these lines, then rush over to me like we're in court and scream them like I've broken your heart."

She pointed to a page in a script where Louise says, "How could you betray me? I thought we were friends!"

"Yes, but say it like you mean it, babe. Take a few minutes. Think about it, doll. Let it sink in. Between the lines, remember? It's very powerful stuff. To think it's only for TV. I could spit."

That's when Jamie arrived, and they hit it off so well she never made me ask again, "How could you betray me? I thought we were friends!" When Cotton finally left, she said she'd had a great day with me even though I made her smoke on the porch. "In what is it, three thousand below zero?"

She loves me, the dogs, Jamie, the world. Jamie's going with her to Thor the colourist tomorrow, and he'll bring Brioche et Montcalm to her in Hollywood, if her movie people say Yes and Madame says Oui, too. It'll also be a great help, Cotton said, if we could ask her these few questions she scribbled out that will enhance her understanding of Mrs. Charmin. Ducharme.

14

I recognized him. Before he even said who he was, I knew. Gaëtan showed me his picture once when he told me he'd been deserted, too. So this was Edward Benning, the man who left Gaëtan HIV positive. Edward said he just heard, he's been away, studying in Europe.

"You missed the memorial service," was the first thing I could say to him.

"Yes. I should have been there. Someone could have notified me. I was with him for seven years."

I wanted to scream at him, Yes, and then you were promiscuous, and Gaëtan wound up HIV positive, too. And now he's dead and you're alive and back from studying in Europe. And how old are you anyway and still a student? I don't even want to look at you. But, I thought, I can't judge him. He must care, he must be grieving even though he's holding up well. He hasn't cried even once yet.

"Seven years should count for something, yes? Certainly more than, what did he have with Daniel Flynn? A year and a half?"

"A little more than that."

"But Daniel gets the condo. Daniel gets all his money. Daniel gets half of his business interest, you get the other. And he gave me nothing."

"After you gave him AIDS."

"Nature gave him AIDS! And maybe he's responsible for me being HIV-positive. We were going through a bad time, why do you think I left him?"

"Because you met somebody clsc?"

"And so did he. Daniel Flynn, the Fireman. And when did he meet you? You're pretty new to the mix, too."

The mix? What did he think we were, a radio station?

"I've worked for him at Festin for years."

"And now you own it. With Daniel. How did you two manage that? When you were doing all your care-giving? The will can't possibly be legal, it was drawn up when he couldn't know what he was doing, September of this year."

"Who told you that?"

"There's a network, dear."

"If your network knows all about the will, it must have known that Gaëtan was sick. How come it never told you that?"

"There was nothing I could do for him," Edward said, all hurt.

"You had seven years together, they should count for something, right? Like coming back to help take care of him."

"So I could then be entitled to a lot more than nothing? It's not just about who was with him at the end, it's also about who he was with for the longest time. I called Daniel but he hung up on me. Not wise. Does everyone down at the fire station know he's gay?"

"Is that a threat that you'll out him?"

"I will. I can do a lot of things to get some of what I deserve, you know? Like appeal the will. Tie up Festin in litigation. And then how will it look if it gets out Festin is temporarily closed because of an AIDS dispute? I'll even get Act Up involved if I have to. And Gaëtan's family could have some serious disputes with the will if I talk to them. His sister Violaine was always broke when I knew her, she might want more than she got. I could talk to lots of people. But I don't have to, if we can reach an agreement ourselves. Let's be reasonable, shall we? I'm sorry I have to be like this, so nasty. It's not like me. But I have to look out for myself, I may need expensive treatments myself someday. I have to think of that. So let's you, me and Daniel set up a friendly meeting and be done with this."

I was in such shock I asked him if he could start by being reasonable enough to wait till after Christmas. "Oh, sure, of course, if we have to, yes," Edward said. He took out his Day Book. The nasty hardliner was melting. He became the man Gaëtan had been in love with, and he was acting kind like he was my best friend. As if he wasn't setting a date to try and take everything away from us. As if he hadn't threatened us with blackmail. "Does Monday, December twenty-eighth, suit? Here at Festin? Say two p.m.? We can head into the New Year on friendly terms."

From the Desk of Mrs. Wyatt Bardo

Dear Lenore,

So sorry it took us this long to write but we just got back from our honeymoon in Europe! Thank you so much for the beautiful wedding present. Now we have our very own signed Bateman print. Wyatt and I were so happy to get it, especially him. He said, "That Lenore, she remembered me talking about this artist!" It was really good of you and so thoughtful at such a difficult time for you, how is your friend Gaëtan doing? Our prayers are with you and him.

I'm sure you remember the Sunflower Room? Where you and I had tea that last evening? Well, the next time you come to visit us, and soon, we hope, you'll see that your Bateman deer has a place of honour, next to the portrait of me Wyatt's having done to hang over the fireplace!

Tons of love,
Darla Bardo

Trey has finally left us to be with his mom for the holidays, then he's going back to school, his dog days are over. So it's me taking les chiens for le Visiting Day. But then it's me who's supposed to ask Reine all those not-Cottony-soft questions. Like: Did you plan to kill that many jurors? Or did you just get carried away? Did you practice your poison recipe before you used it? Did you put it out in the bird feeder to test it? How do you feel knowing there's no way out for you? That this is the end of the line?

The hardest question of all was going to be mine: Can my friend Jamie take your dogs to Hollywood and then right to Victoria, BC? That's where they'll be filming *Garden of Secrets*, as Butchart Gardens stands in for Mrs. Charmin's garden. And they've found a Victorian mansion there to be her house. So much for attention to realistic detail.

The first thing Madame said to me after she hugged and kissed "mes chien-chiens" was, "Chérie? C'est quoi ça, un 'callback'?"

She got a message this morning from Janis at that Tall Women Agency saying Montcalm et Brioche had a callback for Bibites.

"C'est quoi ça, Bibites?" I wanted to know.

She says it's a new dog food for small dogs. It's called Lil' Bites in English.

"L'audition pour les Bibites était le tour final de Roch."

It was the last audition Roch Duplessis put the dogs through before she pulled the leash from him. Roch had told her they had to be patient, you didn't always hear right away, il faut attendre, he was right.

But she'll be forever mad at Roch, she knows it was the dogs and not her he was after.

But I said, It's not like he could ever have her? Right?

She said Roch's a by-the-book corrections officer. He would never break the rules.

I said, But he must have bent some quite a bit, taking in her dogs, all those expressos?

"Mais pour une visite conjugale? Jamais."

(Don't you have to be married for conjugal visits? I wonder where they have them? Do they let you have a little house or a camper trailer on the prison grounds for the weekend? For someone who never intends to land in prison — except as a visitor — I am a little too curious.)

Reine's come to reflect that she's in here forever, all those consecutive life sentences, and it's not fair to les chiens, they have a futur, if not avec Bibites, avec something else.

Now if I didn't know about *Garden of Secrets* and Jamie frothing to get out of the gate, I'd have had a fit when she blessed me with, "Mes chiens? Leur avenir? C'est entre vos mains." Any other time, if she'd said the dogs' future was in my hands I'd have been practically hysterical, but not today.

I told the whole story of Cotton and *Garden of Secrets* and how Jamie is taking a leave of absence from IBM, he's so committed to being their handler and manager. And we hope, somehow, someday soon, their co-star.

Reine's not offended at all that they're making a movie loosely based on us against our will. She thinks it's fantastique! Maybe they could get a special screening? Here, of course. I told her that will be a condition of casting her chiens. What else would she like?

She said, Just that the dogs would be happy and have a good life. And that Jamie or I take the dogs to le callback. This way, if they get the Bibites ad, she can see them on TV in the prison lounge.

Wilder is jealous of the garbage man! He was on his way to work this morning when I was thanking Thierry Racine for all the treasures he's left me.

Thierry confessed he's always admired what I've done to my house because it is so "c'pas Westmount!" He's found lots of bébelles de jardin, but the only ones he brought to my place were ones he felt would fit in. It was fun to be anonymous, and he was thrilled when he saw that I had repaired them and given them places to stay.

"Mais, la Dame sans Merci, là?" Thierry said, pointing over to Jemima's house. She tried to warn him off, and that made him find even more for me, just to annoy her. He was very pleased that I appreciated "les objets d'art en plastique," I thanked him, and off he went.

"It's not every day you see someone kiss the garbage collector on both cheeks. You are so Montreal," Wilder said.

I thought it was a compliment, but maybe not. Maybe Wilder doesn't like it when I kiss burly, piratey, sexy guys who look like Springsteen who bring me lawn ornaments their girlfriend didn't carve up.

"If I only knew that's all it takes to get a kiss from you," Wilder said.

"Hey, I'm not always that easy," I laughed.

"Don't I know it! But what would you do for a broken lawn chair?" Wilder laughed back, and off he went to work.

I don't want to think about it too much, but what did he really mean by that lawn chair crack? Was Wilder trying to be funny? It seems more naughty/rude to me. Men's sense of humour is so different from ours sometimes.

Madame Ducharme's très heureuse, Montcalm et Brioche got the Bibites commercial. They shoot on Wednesday, and then they're off to Pasadena, the day after Visiting Day. I can't go through that emotional farewell, they're all Jamie's once they bid au revoir at Tanguay, he has to endure it. I know I'd break down myself if I saw Reine have to say goodbye to those two. Even though I am thrilled to bibites they'll be out of my life! Reine loves them so much, but it's going to be bye-bye-là! UNLESS she changes her mind. "Non! Abandonnez-moi pas! Ne me quittez pas! Restez! Restez!" Jamie's very persuasive, I'm sure he can convince her even when she pulls a last minute I-can't-let-them-leave-me act. Jamie's got his eyes on the prize, nothing can stop him. If it was me, all she'd see is the fear in my eyes that they were coming back to my house.

I'll still be visiting Reine, of course. She needs me as sa confidante and to give reports on her maison.

"Mais, chérie, en janvier Wilder ne sera pas là? Non?"

She has to remind me? Yes. Wilder's leaving.

Reine wants her house to be waiting there for her when she gets out exactly the way she left it, so she won't put it up for sale. She'll need a new tenant soon. I'll have to tell Heidi to start her search again, but not yet. Maybe Wilder will get an extension. Maybe he's going to get the winter term at Concordia. Maybe that's the surprise he says he has for me.

❀ ❀ ❀

Wilder's surprise was the Montreal Jubilation Gospel Choir and way more.

I always heard the Jubilation Choir were terrific and found out for myself when Wilder took me to their Christmas Concert at St. James United Church downtown. I was in total awe, they are so fantastic! I kept thinking how wonderful it all was, so joyous, so Christmas-Kwanza-Hannukah-y, and I felt so happy to be alive. I did. And how lucky to be there with this terrific, thoughtful guy. I didn't want to think that he was leaving soon. I was feeling so fine when the choir started singing "Glory Train."

When they invited people in the audience to come up and join them I didn't think twice! I ran right up there on that altar stage, everyone sang with the choir, it was heaven. And if that wasn't enough, the director would give people the microphone so they'd get to sing "Glory Train" with the choir backing them up and Professor Trevor Baynes chose me. So there I was, soloing with the Jubilation Gospel Choir. And it all happened because that man sitting there, smiling at me, knew enough to get me a ticket, and I was smart enough to run up and join the singing. Halleluiah!

When we got out onto to the street after the Concert ended, I thanked Wilder over and over again.

"You're welcome. You were having such a great time up there."

Yes I was, I told him. I never wanted to leave.

"I love how much you love to sing. Up there tonight with the Jubilation Choir, at Festin, in that corny musical this summer. When you're out in your backyard. It makes me very happy to see how much singing frees you."

"Uh, thank you," I said, what else do you say to that?

Then there was a long pause. We started walking home along St. Catherine Street. Wilder finally talked first and almost stopped me in my tracks.

"I love so many things about you, Lenore. You're so real, so different. And uncomplicated. I realized that tonight, seeing you up there. I'm hopelessly, absolutely crazy about you, Lenore. You're the woman I should be with. You're the woman I want."

I've been waiting MONTHS to hear this. It's practically word for word what I imagined he'd say! But he only realized this now? When he's about to leave? And what about Katherine?

"I'm leaving Katherine. We're all wrong for each other."

"Have you told her that already?"

"Not yet. No. I just decided tonight, just now. I'm going to break up with her."

"But, Wilder, Christmas is almost here."

"Yes. And?"

"You're not going to break up with Katherine at Christmas?"

"No. But right after. Before New Year's."

"Fergie did that to me."

"Fergie left you a goodbye note on the fridge, Lenore. I'll tell Katherine in person. We'll sit down and discuss it amicably. She can't say it's a surprise, she must suspect how I feel about you. I can tell her before Christmas if you insist. I could call her as soon as we get home tonight. You can watch me."

He's been here since May and he finally decides this now? Just because I was up there singing my heart out? It was all too sudden. He must be overcome by the spirit of the season. Now he wants to break up with Katherine over the phone? And he wants me to watch? And how's she going to take this? Not amicably, not one bit.

"Of course, she'll be very upset."

"Well, yeah!" I said, way too emphatically.

Wilder was all mixed up.

"What do you want me to do, Lenore? Break off with her now or later?"

I said he had to be very careful how he did this. And when. "Because Katherine's really . . ."

"Volatile?" I was keeping myself from saying crazy, dangerous, cuckoo, crack-a-loony, nutbar!

I was polite, all I answered was, "Yes."

"It's all down to me," Wilder admitted. "I bring out ugly aspects in Katherine's personality, her love for me occasionally gets overtly expressed —"

"Like what she did to my chicken?" I said. I couldn't help myself.

He looked shocked, grief-stricken.

"You knew?"

"Yes."

"You're very astute."

"No. Heidi guessed. She was astute first."

"How did Heidi know?"

"Well, we both think Katherine's kind of psychotic."

"Katherine is complex and high strung but not insane. She's a highly intelligent, beautiful woman."

"Sure she is." I didn't want to argue with him. I wanted this whole discussion to be over, but he continued.

"You want to talk about psychotic? What about your recent high octane antics? Some people could think attacking your neighbour for removing notes from your car is insane. Or how about the destruction of university property because you think people are stealing from the Christmas food basket?"

"You think Heidi and me are insane?"

"No, but some people could. Some people do. Heidi's certainly been disruptive. This ongoing feud Heidi has with Tess Dudley?"

"Tess started it."

"But launching cans of food at her? It got way out of hand, Lenore."

"You don't know, you weren't there!"

"Neither were you. And why are we arguing about Heidi and Tess when we should be talking about us?"

"But there is no us, Wilder."

"Not until there's no Katherine and I?"

"Yes, uh, no. I'm not so sure anymore, Wilder."

"And why is that, huh? Do you have to discuss it with Heidi?"

"I'd like to discuss it with you first."

"And then you'll want Heidi's opinion?"

"Probably. Sure."

"Have you talked about me with her a lot?"

"Of course." Why would I lie, I mean, are we not Women?

"You discuss everything, I guess?"

"Well, yes pretty much. We are best friends. She's like a sister to me."

"I guess Heidi told you to stay away from me because I was in a relationship?"

And I told him I came to that decision myself.

"Even though you knew I was really interested in you."

This was getting so strange. It was like some game of He Loves Me, He Loves Me Not, He's Not So Sure.

"Yes, I knew you were interested, and that really threw me off. Because you seemed devoted to Katherine."

"But Katherine was in Boston. And I was here. And you were, too. So why didn't anything happen? For months! I gave you enough hints. I started to wonder, has she no clue? How can Lenore not know? Is she misreading my messages on purpose? I kept thinking you'd take the initiative."

"Why?"

"Why not?"

"Why was it up to me to make the move? Would that make it okay for you to cheat on your girlfriend if I was the one who went after you?"

"You didn't owe Katherine any loyalty. She hates you."

"And why's that, eh? I'd hate me, too, if I were her. Why were you still with her if you're both unhappy?"

"She loves me too much. And I — it's too complicated."

"Did she threaten to kill herself?"

"No."

"Did she threaten to kill you?"

"No . . ."

He was hiding something, I wasn't going to let him off.

"Did she ever take the scissors to all your clothes?"

"Once. But it was only my ties."

"All your ties?"

"Only ones she thought were too alluring. We have a complicated relationship. You can't understand."

"Why not? I was in a big complicated mess myself for eight years. But I never sent out signals so somebody would try and cheat with me."

"All right, so I did. I sent out signals every time I saw you. I know you want me, too. We'd be great together, you know that. I don't have to leave so soon. I can stay for Christmas."

"And ruin Katherine's? And then what after that? Can you get Concordia to keep you on?"

"No. I have to go back to Boston. And you could come with me."

"I can't do that."

"Not right away, I know. But soon. Are you worried about papers? Work visas? If there was a problem we could get married."

"You want me to leave everything, just like that?"

"Not right away. You'd need time to settle up here. I'm sorry. It's all happening really fast, isn't it?"

"And it's all really impossible."

"Why?"

"Because I own a duplex here. I have a home."

"In Lower Westmount. You can rent it in a second."

"I don't want to."

"You don't have that many ties, Lenore. You've got no family here."

"Heidi and Daniel are like family now. And I have all my friends."

"They can visit us. Hey, we'll take them to Martha's Vineyard." It wasn't insane enough that he had offered to marry me, now he was making travel plans for Heidi, Daniel and everyone else in my life who'd love to get to see James Taylor's house.

"I have a great job, Wilder. I have Festin."

"There are restaurants in New England, Lenore."

"Not a Festin."

"America invented theme restaurants. We'll find you one. Sell your half in Festin while you can, when it's still something of a going concern, maybe you can get a partnership in a place down there. Or just have the easy life and go back to waitressing. And if it's the singing you'll miss, we've got community theatres that do musicals."

We were at Peel and St. Catherine, right next to the Laura Secord that inspired Tyler Garrow. And here was Wilder, a man I thought I was in love with, sounding just like him! And that's where I made my stand.

"Keep your Boston community theatres that do musicals. I don't want to be in show business ever again. And keep your theme restaurants, too. I love running my own restaurant here."

"But you don't love me, is that what you're saying? You could never love me?"

"I don't know. Maybe I could have. Yes, so I've been really attracted to you ever since you arrived. And I enjoy being with you a lot. I kept hoping something could happen."

"It can."

"You have a girlfriend, Wilder."

"I won't have her if you say the word."

"Why can't you say the word, Wilder? Why didn't you leave Katherine a long time ago? Why is it all up to me?"

"Because I have to be sure."

"Me too. And right now the only thing I'm sure of is I don't want to leave."

"Not ever?"

"Not now. Not soon. Who knows, maybe not ever."

"You must want to leave someday. I mean, are you crazy? You're an anglo. And I think I love you. This is your invitation out. How can you stay?"

"Because I love it here."

"How can you love it here? Your political situation is a mess."

"Everybody's is, one way or another. If everybody leaves, how are we ever going to fix things?"

"In your fantasies, my darling. You are never going to fix this Québec mess the way you want. They are never going to give in to your idealism about Québec and Canada."

We stopped at the Ogilvy's Christmas window. People were oohing and ahhing at the Old Mill and the Steiff barnyard animals doing things. We were arguing about Québec. How to ruin an evening.

"I'm not listening to you talk about the future of Québec! You're not from here, you have no idea —"

"I can still see that there are issues that will only be resolved with separation."

"That is not going to happen. Don't you dare say that. Don't you dare side with the PQ!"

"I'm not siding with anybody. But you can't continue to be so naive. The entire country gave that Charlottetown Accord a great big NO two months ago. What do you think that means?"

"That Mulroney's leaving! There is hope for us! I am not talking about this at Christmas."

I didn't want him to see he was making me cry about politics, so I turned away and looked into the Ogilvy's window, and there was the hedgehog pushing a cart up a hill, never getting to the top but never letting it fall back to the bottom either. Year after after year he did that, and I thought, Maybe that's me. But at least I'm trying to do something, I'm not giving up. I'm not giving in. This is where I should be. I have my friends, my home, I have my life, I have Festin. I love this town. I faced him again. Wilder tried to apologize.

"I'm sorry. You're right. Politics are off limits forever. It's just that I want to offer you something more, something better. An adventure. Love! And you could have a much better future. Heidi knows that."

"Knows what?"

"That your futures don't have to be here. She's leaving."

"What?"

"She's got an offer from York."

"In Ontario?"

"No. In England."

I said Heidi would have told me.

"You don't discuss everything, I guess."

How did Wilder know and not me?

"I do have other friends in that English department. How do you think I got stuck with Tess's place in the Plateau?"

I wanted to think it was all Tess again, planting some lie.

"Heidi's food fight temporarily overshadowed all the speculation about her York offer."

Speculation doesn't mean it's true.

"It's very true, Lenore. Ask her."

I was pretty devastated, but I didn't want him to see that either.

"And if Heidi's leaving, why stay? Why are you thinking so much? For a wonderful, simple girl, you're getting very complicated."

And I thought I'm with some Jekyll and Hyde. If Heidi is keeping this secret from me there must be a good reason, why did he tell me for spite? He's said Festin has no future, Québec in Canada has no future, I have no future except with him. He's not thoughtful, he's cruel. And all the time I thought he was being too flirty for a guy with a girlfriend, he did mean more. He was giving me signals that I had to do all the acting on. So if anything happened, it would be my doing.

I would be the temptress, seductress, sinner. And if I got hurt when he left me, it would be my fault, I'd deserve it.

"Wilder. The night you invited me over for dinner by candlelight?"

"And Trey showed up unexpectedly?"

"If he hadn't, were you expecting me to 'take the initiative'?"

"Yes. That wasn't the only time," he admitted and smiled.

"What you really want is for me to take some sort of initiative?"

"Yes. Please."

"Because you can't."

"I'm so mixed up."

"Well, my initiative is to tell you that I am not interested in going through with this relationship-romance-adventure."

"What do you mean?"

"Oh, but I forgot, I'm a simple girl, I should tell you in my simple way: I don't want to be your girlfriend."

"I meant 'simple girl' as a compliment, Lenore."

"It isn't. I am crossing over to the other side of St. Catherine Street now. Do not dare try and join me. If it's too cold for you to walk any more, take the Guy metro."

"Did somebody knock the Jubilation out of your concert, chile?" Heidi said when I showed up at her place. I had to talk, about Wilder and about her great big secret about leaving to go to England. I didn't know which subject to tackle first. She started it with Wilder.

"I never took to him, you know."

"Never?"

"Not really. I couldn't. Parizeau was an economics professor."

"But you got Wilder to rent here."

"Only to get back at Tess. And then once he got here I couldn't help noticing everything."

"Like what else?"

"That he's a control freak, Lenore."

"You think so?"

"Oh, yes, everything has to be his way. He is such a man. He took over from the second he met us in Boston."

I thought he was being gallant, being our tour guide, taking us to lunch, being the mediator for people who were fighting with us, paying for everything all the time.

"He doesn't think women should go Dutch. He's generous."

"Because it gives him control. He's charming and he paid you a lot of attention, but he's such a weakling. And know what I think? When he tormented Crazy Kate so much she had to come to Montréal for two weeks, it wasn't just because he needed her to keep him honest. It also served the purpose of you getting to see what he had to live with. Poor Wilder, with this madwoman for a girlfriend, won't someone rescue me? The old Mr.-Rochester-with-the-Mad-Wife-in-the-Attic syndrome. And then he expected you to do all the chasing, but who gets blamed when all goes bad in Eden? You. Poor Eve. They don't call it the Sin of Adam."

"I was tempted . . ."

"Of course you were."

"And not just because he's not at all like Fergie."

"But he is like Fergie, Lenore. Wilder is a deceiver, too."

"Because he wanted to fool around on his girlfriend?"

"Way before that. Remember how he got you all mixed up, saying he never said he was named after Wilder Penfield?"

"Yeah."

"He said exactly what you thought he said. He told the same story to somebody else."

"To who?"

"Tess of the d'Urberblondes."

"She told you?"

"It came up in conversation."

"You're talking to Tess now?"

Time for Heidi to confess her embarrassing secret. "I have to if I want to stay on. The English department brought in a crisis intervention specialist because Tess and I required joint counselling to reconcile our differences. We have to talk it all out. That's how I heard from her own collagen lips that Emerson made her nuts, always saying how even I would have made a better wife than she did. Yesterday's session was all about how I had stolen her sublet tenant from her for spite."

"Which is true."

"Which is how I found out Wilder tried the same pick-up line on her."

"'My parents named me after Wilder Penfield . . .'"

"'. . . because they wanted me to grow up to be a brain surgeon.'"

"He did lie about that? But, Heidi, that's . . ."

"Diabolical? Pathetic? Somewhat pathological? I didn't want to ruin your Jubilation Choir date by telling you."

"But you were going to tell me?"

"I was biding my time. It was such an I-told-you-so thing, and I thought you'd feel rotten that Wilder was duping you after all."

Why would anybody say he was named after a famous neurosurgeon?

"Because it gave him instant endearment. Someone from another country says he's named after one of our heroes and we go all aflutter."

I said she was going overboard there.

"Really? Let's say you meet some guy from Louisiana. Or Rhode Island, say. And he tells you his name is Maurice. Because his parents admired Rocket Richard?"

I'd be impressed.

I would be, too, she told me.

I had to ask, "Say it was some guy named Miles."

"Yes?"

"And he said, 'Heidi, love. Why don't you get a job here, yeah? Near Sheffield. York, say?'"

"Miles never asked that."

"Somebody did. Are you going to York?"

"Who told you that?"

"Wilder. He said you had an offer. Is it true?"

"Yes. For a year. Starting in January."

"Oh."

It was the truth! What a terrible evening I was having!

"But I turned it down."

"You turned it down? Why?"

"Because of Gaëtan. I couldn't leave you and Daniel now."

I should have said, sure you could. You should go for this, Heidi. It's an adventure, you need a change, things could happen. You'd be able to see if there was anything for you and Miles Farnham besides long distance. But I didn't. I was so selfish. All I said was, "Thank you."

Wilder's gone. He left. He didn't even come over and say goodbye. Or try to win me back. It wouldn't have worked anyway, but I think he could have made some effort.

Why Was I Ever Wild About Wilder?

1) He was good looking. I never thought he looked like Ichabod Crane.
2) He was the first man I've really liked and been attracted to since Fergie who turned out to be straight.
3) He said he was named after a beloved Canadian.
4) He didn't make fun of all my things or my lawn ornaments, he even fixed them for me.
5) He wasn't like Fergie! He didn't gamble, as far as I know. He had a job. He could cook. He was sensitive. He wore ties well (the ones Katherine didn't cut up).
6) He helped in my garden.
7) He made me feel special and desired.

Why Was Wilder Wrong for Me?

1) He lied about being named after a beloved Canadian.
2) He had two kids he never told me about till I met one.
3) He had no things (Spartan).
4) He had a live-in psychopath girlfriend.
5) He thinks there's no future for Quebec in Canada.
6) His parents never learned to drive.
7) He had a dog with no name.
8) He called me a simple girl.
9) He wanted me to be the Seductress and take the Blame.
10) He is resentful of Women's Friendships (Heidi).
11) He was jealous of Thierry, my garbage man.

12) He suggested that Heidi and I are insane because of our recent high-octane antics.

13) He drove women wild. First Katherine and then me. How many months did I waste fantasizing about him, and all that research on Denise Levertov? For what?

So yes, Wilder's gone. And he's so flawed I can't even keep him as a friend. I should know better, but I'm still going to miss him.

15

Hey, Lenny.
I won't be home for Christmas.
You can't count on me.
Have a Merry one anyway.
Cheers, babe!

Fergie

The gang I had for Christmas dinner could be called the Lonely Hearts Club: me, Heidi, Daniel and Viola.

Everybody loved everything I gave them, and Viola and Heidi really went nuts over the porcupine quill earrings I've kept for them since Oatman! I got some pretty great cadeaux, stuff I'd never buy myself. Viola gave me the "Lions and Tigers and Bears, Oh My!" Plate from her collection. "I'm down-sizing my Oz things," she said. Daniel gave me tons of gifts and Heidi gave me one great big amazing present, but when can I use it?

"I haven't booked us the London Show Tour yet. These are just brochures as an IOU until we know when we want to go. We'll get to see Musicals and Big Ben and visit the Farnhams of Near Sheffield." All that in one week?

"Well, a week is all either of us can manage till the summer."

I don't know where I'll even find a week. Daniel says I have to. It's an order.

"You can give yourself a week off, you're the Boss!"

Heidi says maybe we can try for the same time the Farnhams came here, like last February.

"Not around Valentine's Day?" I said, thinking England in the midwinter must be as miserable and cold as it is here, only bleaker, with rain all the time. I think they even have a hymn about it.

We could try for Valentine's, Heidi said. And she'll see Miles again and find out if there's anything more to this pen-pal flirtation, which, she admits "has gotten to the point of being ridiculous. I'm thirty-eight years old, for heaven's sake!"

I can't tell her Valentine's Day week is no good, it'll be a big one at Festin. If we're still open despite that Edward Benning. (I've gotta stay positive about this meeting, have a good attitude.)

Mrs. Flynn gave me something fabulous. Heidi and Daniel tried to stop her, but she insisted, "Lenore likes them, she said so." So now I have my own Mary statue, with a blue veil and dress and with her hands folded, she looks very kind and wise. She'll go out in the spring in the garden next to my Notre Dame de Paris Boston gargoyle.

"You don't have to, Lenore. You could just put her out when you know my mother is coming."

"But she doesn't always give us warning, Heidi Mavourneen," Daniel said. "And it weighs a small ton. Can you see us lugging it back and forth?"

"I like it!" I told them.

"If you insist, but we will draw the line at anything else, anything too shrine-like," Heidi warned me.

"Like if Thierry, your garbage man, decides Our Lady needs accessories," Daniel added.

"Such as an errant bathtub or fairylights," Heidi went.

The phone rang all day with everybody wishing me Merry Christmas. Elspeth, Beth, Reine, Benoît, and even a long distance call from California!

"It is so weird!" Jamie said, "No White Christmas, very surreal, but I love it! We are having Christmas with Charles Nelson Reilly and Julie Harris, can you believe it? Anyway, we have even bigger news, but Cotton wants to tell you."

Bigger news? Jamie has gone from houseboy to toy boy to fiancé. Or Cotton got Jamie cast as the cop loosely based on Benoît in *Garden of Secrets*. But it was neither.

"Lenny, sweetie? Merry Christmas, honey! Monty, not up there, get down! Give him another cookie, Jay. One for Bagel, too. Len, I have NEWS! Remember *Night of Plenty*? That's been in the can for, what is it?"

"Twenty-eight months," I heard Jamie tell her.

"Forever! Well, they got it out for Christmas release. And everyone is talking Oscar! For me! The studio's planning a big campaign. They want to take out "For Your Consideration" ads in the trades, but we can't agree on the category. I want it to be for Best Actress."

"Best Supporting Actress," I heard Jamie advise her.

She yelled at him. "No. For Best Actress! I deserve that much, Jay!"

"You won't win there. In Best Supporting, it's yours."

"Why do you say that? You think I'm a landslide as a sympathy vote? I'm not some eighty-year-old making a comeback! And I was more than supporting, Jay, I carried that picture —"

They had called all the way from California so I could hear them arguing. It made me miss him, Jamie was bossing her the way he wanted to boss me when he tried to give me career advice.

"Anyway, doll, when the Oscar nomination happens —"

"We'll save you a seat at the Dorothy Chandler Pavilion, Lenore," I heard Jamie yell.

"They only let us have two seats, Jay," she told him.

"There are places in the cheering section. For dear friends and fans."

"I always thought that was for industry people who wanted to get nominated but weren't. Oh well, plan a trip to LA in March. I miss you. Love you! Bye. Here's Jay again."

"Isn't that the best news? Didn't I tell you, Lenore? She'll win an Oscar and then an Emmy in the same year. Her work in *Garden of Secrets*! She'll blow you away."

"Oh, Jay, you are so sweet!" Cotton said, "You really think so? I don't know, can they give an Emmy to someone who killed that many jurists?"

"Jurors, Cotton, Jurors! Jurists are judges!"

"How am I supposed to know everything? Where did you hide my smokes? Jay? Jay! It's Christmas Day, lemme have one!"

"Here! Smoke your face off now. No cigarettes in the limo. No, light it yourself," I heard Jay/Jamie tell her. It was like they'd been together forever, not less than six weeks! He was George to her Martha. But Jamie didn't mind one bit.

"Oh, Lenore, I am in paradise! I am so happy I'm practically delirious. I did the right thing. And it's all because of you. Did my postcards get there?"

"Yes. And Madame Ducharme really appreciated the ones from Brioche et Montcalm. Even though she said they're losing their French. But keep sending them, eh, please."

"Will do, ma capitaine. Gotta go, the limo's here. Joyeux Noël, Love ya. Big kiss, bye."

But now Christmas is almost over til next year. And there's no putting IT off or making Christmas excuses. December twenty-eighth, two p.m., will be here pretty soon. Daniel dreads it, it's the first time he'll meet Edward Benning, there could be a fight. There could be all kinds of things. I have some really weird ideas I want to ask Daniel about, but I hope he knows how strategy works because I sure don't. And if we lose this round, we're finished.

Beth wanted us to accompany her as she spent all the money she got from the For Womyn Only chain letter at the Boxing Day sales, but I declined. Beth made $424 off that thing. Who could have known? It depressed me losing an opportunity like that. So I stayed home, and instead I got a big surprise from Jemima. She came over with an Ogilvy's bag.

I thought, She's been to the Boxing Day sales and that's all she came back with, one big plaid bag that wasn't very full! And she wanted to show it off.

"Oh, it's not from Ogilvy's, Lenore. I came across this bag and it fit so well in here. Oh, what an intriguing house you have. I've never been in it before."

She's right, all this time we've both lived on this street. I asked her to come in for tea or something stronger. "No, no. Just tea, thanks."

She admired the music I had on. My Jessye Norman and Kathleen Battle in Concert tape. One of the many Gifts of the Daniel.

"Ah, spirituals of the season? But wasn't that only available through a generous contribution to Vermont ETV?"

"I guess so. My partner gave it to me."

"Your partner? You've found someone to take that Fergie man's place?"

"Not yet. Daniel's my business partner. We co-own Festin du Bois."

"That restaurant we all went to last Valentine's? You own it now? Aren't you the cagey one. I had no idea. Well, well done."

When I brought all the tea and things out, she made a wincey face, "Oh, no, not more mince tarts."

This woman sometimes! Anyway, she said she had this mêmento I'd probably put to use. She never used it. Go ahead, look in the Ogilvy's bag. It's yours now.

A really sweet birdhouse.

"Neville bought it when we first came here. Twenty-four years in Westmount and we never got around to putting it up. Pity, yes. I imagine if the birds had made their nest in it, I might have, too. I found it in the cellar, and it seemed somewhat symbolic? I thought you might want it. For the spring. So I am giving it to you."

As a goodwill gesture?

As a goodbye present. She was going away.

"To a sanatorium?"

"Why do people always think that? No, I am moving. I'm going home to England."

"Not for good?"

"For as long as it takes."

"To do what?"

"You must have heard the Queen's Christmas Day address?"

Who would miss this year's? We all wanted to see what she'd say! Jemima was right, how much could one Queen take? All in the same annus horribilis? Fergie, Di, Charles, the Rottweiller, Windsor Castle burning down, finally paying taxes, far, far too many Royal Antics.

"At least Her Majesty has had some joy this year."

"When?"

"Princess Anne and Royal Navy Commander Timothy Laurence."

"Oh, yeah, Anne got remarried."

"But her Majesty's address had such a personal message in it for me. It *is* time for us all to try and put these difficult days behind us."

Yes, I went for that, I told her.

"And then when she said how her family was like so many other families this year with troubles of their own."

I hear you, I thought.

"And that it was the prayers and understanding and sympathy that we had given her that had supported her through this dark year."

She was giving me a full recount of the speech.

"That message touched my heart, she was speaking directly to me. Giving me a purpose. I'm doing no good here. Heidi Flynn was right to berate me, a year of Blake's life in the wrong drug rehab program! A neighbour, a stranger had to point him in the right direction! I have been such a complete failure here. I've never taken to Canada. That's why I've written to Her Majesty. And other people connected with the Royal Family."

"To express your support and sympathy?"

"Yes, and my pledge to help her in any way I can. I don't care which castle or palace she wishes me to work from. Perhaps she'd like a new companion, a lady-in-waiting. I would even walk the corgis for her. Whatever. I shall do what she requests. She needs a true friend."

"You're really going to England to Save the Queen?"

"As soon as I can. Her Majesty needs me."

I tried to talk her out of it but it's no good, she's going. Of course, Heidi doesn't approve.

"Does Jemima have any idea how many letters the Queen gets?"

"She's written to other people in Royal Circles."

"How well placed are they? Why doesn't she go through the Monarchist League? Or call up the British Embassy? To make sure!"

I wanted to know, Why did Heidi care so much?

"Because if Jemima gets over there without any kind of royal appointment to walk the dogs of the House of Windsor or whatever, she'll come back here!" she said and laughed.

"Oh, whatever will poor Neville do without her?" I said in my bad British accent.

"Rejoice, probably! Oh, Beth and I met one of Neville's patients downtown." Heidi sounded a bit scandalized.

"Somebody's running around with Neville?"

"No, with Elijah! Elspeth has no shame!"

Beth and Heidi met them at Le Commensal, measuring out their lunch. I tried it once with Heidi, it's so odd, paying for your lunch by its weight.

I was shocked, too. I mean, Elspeth was in from Baie d'Urfé and out with her lover Elijah the Sculptor on Boxing Day, what about Douglas and the kids?

"They're at Universal Studios. In Florida."

"And Elspeth stayed here?"

"That Paul he's a Stage Blood Brother with has a time-share. And Paul has a cousin who may know someone, and they might have a meeting with some studio exec. And it all started with you, Lenore!"

So I am to blame for Elspeth and Elijah being obnoxiously in love.

"They were sharing a plate! And she's wearing these hideous huge turquoise Kokopelli earrings and bracelet Elijah designed!"

"But Elijah's not an Indian."

"He's not her husband either. Does she care? Flaunting her Lover all over downtown Montreal! I don't know why I expect better things from a feminist, but I do."

So today was it, there was no turning back, our Hour of Reckoning: our meeting with Edward Benning. And Jonas Weller, his latest new partner, we found out.

"Don't worry, he's not a lawyer," Edward said jovially.

"No, he's just the man you want to share everything you get today with," Daniel said really coldly, hiding his I-could-kill-you how-dare-you-sit-there how-dare-you-show-your-face feelings.

"So you admit I'm entitled? That's a good start." Edward beamed.

"No, it's not. I never said you were entitled to anything."

"Then why are we meeting informally? You're already being unreasonable," Edward whined.

Jonas took his hand in a supportive-partner show.

"Are you prepared to offer anything? Or do I bring in lawyers?"

"Before you do that, let us bring in someone else. Lenore?"

"Constable Benoît Archambault," I called, like we were in court, and Benoît came out of the kitchen. He has never looked better in his uniform, I couldn't take my eyes off him. He had me mesmerized. He had Edward Benning terrified.

"The police? You called in the cops?" Edward was so betrayed.

Benoît stared at him for at least thirty seconds before he spoke.

"It better be a criminal lawyer you got, Edward Benning, because you will need one."

"What can you charge me with?"

"Murder. You were not careful, you gave the HIV knowingly to Gaëtan. He died of le SIDA."

"I did not. You can't prove that."

Benoît had another printout.

"You think Non? I know Yes. You had it first, Edward Benning, three months before you leave him. You knew you were carrying the virus."

"That doesn't make me a criminal."

"In my book, it does," Benoît said.

"Not in the Criminal Code. Not yet."

"In the human being code. You didn't tell Gaëtan he was at risk."

"Yes, I did. He knew! I told him," Edward said so big we could tell he was lying.

"Hey, Gaëtan's not here no more to say if you did and you didn't, hein?"

"Those medical records are confidential."

"Not to everybody, not to . . . CSIS," Benoît said.

"What the hell is CSIS?" Edward wanted to know.

"It's like a Canadian CIA," Jonas informed him.

"And it knows more than the RCMP." Benoît smiled.

"It can't know this, those records are private! And it's not even true. None of it will hold up. You can't threaten me with a murder charge, and you know it!"

"I know you come here and threaten Lenore that you can close Festin and give it a bad name. You think Festin's the only thing that can get a bad name? What kind of guy will the world think you are, hein? When they know you give HIV to your partner, you go off to Europe, he gets sick, he's dying, you never visit, you never call, you are never once a caregiver to him? And then you show up and say, I want money, where is my money?"

"I am entitled. I was with him for many years."

"You were not married to him," Benoît said.

"We're gay. We can't get married."

"Nobody gets nothing if they're not married in Quebec. Men and women. Nobody. The only thing you get is what you bring in. And all you bring in was sickness."

Jonas started to speak.

"Edward brought a great deal more than that —"

"You shut up, little boy, I am talking to him. And why are you with a man like this? You know what can happen to you, being with him, if you're not careful, hein? Do you know how terrible it was for Gaëtan? And he comes here and wants money?"

"You can't accuse him of murder, that's ridiculous."

"Oh, murder, it's not the only thing. How do you like extortion? That's what we call blackmail."

"Blackmail?" Edward was more upset with this than murder.

"You say you'll go to Gaëtan's family and get them to say they don't like the will."

"I said I might. I can."

"We save you some time. Lenore?"

I knocked on the kitchen door, it swung open, and Gaëtan's sisters and brother came out.

"I don't believe this!" Edward said.

"Oh, but wait," Daniel said, "there's more."

"There can't be," said Jonas.

"Way more," I said.

Edward tried his je-suis-ton-ami technique on Gaëtan's siblings. "Violaine! Ça va? Jacinte, Jacques!"

"Tais-toi, maudit cochon!" Jacques snarled.

"Va à l'enfer!" Jacinte added.

"I guess they're not going to show you much support in your suit, Eddie Boy," Daniel said.

"They will when I talk to them in private. What have you promised them? Violaine! Violaine! Combien t'a-t-il donné?" Edward yelled.

"Gaëtan m'a donné assez, serpent!" she yelled back.

Benoît said, "The only one who wants more is you. Now voyons, calling in ses soeurs et son frère won't work for you. What other blackmail did you say you will try? Oh, yeah, you say that Lenore and Daniel tricked Gaëtan to make his will good for them? And you said you would OUT Daniel? Tell everyone he was un homosexuel? Maybe tell his mother?"

Edward was stammering, "I never mentioned his mother —"

"That would be no good for you. His mother knows en tout cas," Benoît said and called over to a dark corner table. "Madame Flynn?"

"Oui, officer?"

"You know your son is gay?"

"Oh yes. I think I knew before he did. Daniel is my joy. He's so brave being a fireman. Of all my three sons, he's the most accomplished. His father and I are so proud of him," Kyra the Diva doing her Mama Flynn Act pronounced. It was a role she was born to play, so over-the-top, but it worked. Heidi also did very well, playing herself. "Daniel's always been Mama's favourite," she said, sitting next to her mother. Kyra/Mama Flynn began to launch into her Eleventh Hour number, crying and heaping on more praise, but Benoît stopped her.

"Merci, Madame Flynn. Hey, Edward Benning you must think quick now, hein? Who else can I tell on him? Yeah, his mother knows, his family knows, but maybe it would be bad if everyone at the station des pompiers knows, hein? What do you think? Me, I'm not so sure. Pompiers!"

Seven off-duty friends from the fire station poured out of the kitchen, in their helmets and long firefighters' coats. It was magnificent.

It really looked for a second or two like Edward Benning had stopped breathing. But we weren't finished. Benoît shouted, "Les gentils hommes!" and we brought out two more men from the kitchen for the kill: Réal in his coureur de bois outfit and Thierry in his garbage man pirate ensemble.

"Who the hell are they?" Jonas wanted to know.

"Part of Daniel's network in the gay community," I told him.

"It's all a little too Village People for me," Edward said. "Come on, Jonas." And off they slinked, I'd say into the night but it wasn't even three o'clock in the afternoon yet.

Heidi and Kyra came out of the dark corner.

"What a touching, ultimate gay fantasy portrayal of my mother. Thank you." Daniel said as he hugged Kyra.

"I was convincing?"

"You convinced me. You were magnificent."

Kyra wasn't overwhelmed with such praise. "Well, anytime, Daniel, I was just so fortunate to be part of this performance. Heidi was very supportive playing my daughter, wasn't she great?"

Heidi accepted this faint praise. "Well, I did play Beatrice in *Much Ado About Nothing.*"

"At the convent, Mavourneen, when you were in high school! You've gone a lot of years between shows," Daniel said.

"But you couldn't tell? Edward did believe I was me?"

"You were brilliant," Daniel said.

"Kyra was fabulous, but if there's ever a next time you need defending, Mommy should play herself."

"But then she'd have to know," Daniel said.

It was difficult for her, but Heidi said it, "She does have to know one of these days, Daniel. Think about it, would you?"

"Okay, all right, I'll try. But can I have Kyra as our Mother again, if necessary, in the very near future, what if this isn't over with Edward Benning?" Daniel said.

"Oh, I think it's over. He won't come back around here no more, we played pretty dirty with him, he knows it will be worse the next time," Benoît assured Daniel in that police way of his.

Thierry said they were so happy to be able to watch it all unfold on the monitor in the kitchen.

"Tu as fait un bon show, Lenore!" Thierry said and made everybody applaud me. I thought I was finished with show business. But this was more of an opera.

"It was pretty big, Lenore. But nothing succeeds like excess, and excess sure worked!" Daniel said and hugged me again.

Les girls started showing up, Thierry's wife had been waiting out in the car, Micheline, Jocelyne, Mireille and Marie-France arrived with Marguerite Vichy, Festin was turning into a celebration.

I thanked Benoît, I hope he won't get in trouble for this, if Edward Benning files any kind of complaint. Or calls in the dogs. Benoît shrugged in a way that made me realize it was very possible, he could get in big trouble for this.

"For you, I don't mind. Anytime you need help with the bad guys, Lenny," he said.

Daniel got so upset when I told him that part of my plan included asking Benoît to investigate and help find as much dirty laundry on Edward Benning as he could.

"He could get fired or suspended, he's not allowed!" Daniel warned me.

"He didn't say so."

"Of course not. Because you're the one who keeps asking him to exploit any CSIS connections he may have! Anybody else, he'd say, Es-tu folle? You wanna get me fired? You make that man crazy for you, you know that?"

I knew I had to make sure Benoît knew how much I appreciated what he'd done for Festin.

"You saved the day!" I told him.

"I just do my job."

"You went way above and beyond the call of duty for me, merci."

"Why do you think I do that, Lenny? I don't do that for everybody."

"Non?"

"Only for you."

Daniel was so right, I do make the man crazy. I had to make amends.

"I'm sorry for what I said about you on *Fiona!*"

"I watch the tape a few more times, she tricked you."

"Too bad you weren't there on the show with me."

"Maybe that's not so good, I always say the wrong thing around you, Lenny. I am always going the wrong way."

"Not today."

"But other times? Les Canadiens au Forum? I was so mad because you hurt me very badly, ma fierté. But I was wrong to be so mad at you and so mean, Lenny. And so stupide because then you never want to see me again. Unless you need me to find out things for you. Hey, I don't mind, I see you that way. And I go to watch you in the *Bells* spectacle where you're singing every two minutes. Me, I never go to plays, but I sit there alone because I want to see you so much. But what do I say when I can find you in the dressing room? I tell you I don't like the play. Do I say you sing so good, Lenny, you look incroyable in those dresses, I wish you were ma blonde, I would be so proud. Non, I say all the wrong things. I make you mad at me. You don't say, Hey, Benoît you came to my show! What a guy. You must like me. Stay for a drink after. Maybe we can do something. No, all you say is, What about my notes on my car? The Conserned Citizen notes, voyons, that's all I'm good for!"

"No. But why did you act so suspicious of them? Like I was guilty?"

"Because you act like you have a big secret with them," he said.

"I told you —"

"Only after, not right away!"

"I'm sorry, so I knew who was sending them —"

"Why didn't you tell me, hein? And save me thinking strange things?"

"Like what?"

"Like . . . that you were the one sending them to yourself."

"Me? Why would I do that?"

"To have raison to see me."

"What?"

"There I go encore. I say the wrong thing to you. But it was what I am thinking. I am hoping Conserned Citizen is a way for you to say, Let's be friends, Benoît, save me. Voyons! Some things on the notes, Lenny, they were true. Your car is a safety hazard. It is leaking oil all over the place. If it went missing, it would be a good thing! Give it to the scrap man. But no, it's nothing you make up, it's for real, you have a crazy neighbour, you do need me to help you. And I do what I can. Like today. And we can be friends maybe that way. Because we don't get along too good, us, when it's not police business. Why is that, Lenny?"

Because there's something more to all this, with you and me,

Madame Ducharme says, I almost told him. But I didn't think Benoît would welcome advice from a woman behind bars. Benoît kept talking.

"I do what I did today for you, Lenny, because Edward Benning is a very evil man and because I like you a lot. I have liked you for a very long time now. Eh bien, my work today, it's done. You don't need me here no more, you need me again, call me." Benoît left the banquet hall.

Music was playing, people were whirling and dancing all around Festin. We were the only ones who hadn't joined in.

I had my chance to let Benoît get away, to walk out of my life, to paddle my own canoe, but what did I do? I took the initiative, I followed him to the entrance of Festin and called him.

"Benoît. Reste, s'il te plait, stay?"

And then Benoît made an all new face, one I never saw him make before, smiling at me as if this is what he's been waiting for all along. Maybe it's what I've been waiting for, too. Who knows? Perhaps c'est lui. Madame Ducharme may be right. Or she may be really, really wrong. Whatever, I've got to find out.

When we returned to the banquet hall, everyone had their eyes on the doorway, on us. Heidi and Daniel were smiling, like they just knew all along. Benoît and I stood there, frozen, we didn't know what to do. Heidi had the answer. She called across to us.

"Vas-y, Benoît. Ask the girl to dance!"

And he did.